ALSO BY ELIN HILDERBRAND

The Beach Club
Nantucket Nights
Summer People
The Blue Bistro
The Love Season
Barefoot
A Summer Affair
The Castaways
The Island
Silver Girl
Summerland
Beautiful Day
The Matchmaker
Winter Street
The Rumor
Winter Stroll
Here's to Us
Winter Storms
The Identicals
Winter Solstice
The Perfect Couple
Winter in Paradise
Summer of '69
What Happens in Paradise
28 Summers
Troubles in Paradise
Golden Girl
The Hotel Nantucket

Endless Summer

Stories

Elin Hilderbrand

LITTLE, BROWN AND COMPANY

LARGE PRINT EDITION

Little, Brown and Company
Hachette Book Group
1290 Avenue of the Americas, New York, NY 10104
littlebrown.com

First Edition: October 2022

Little, Brown and Company is a division of Hachette Book Group, Inc. The Little, Brown name and logo are trademarks of Hachette Book Group, Inc.

The publisher is not responsible for websites (or their content) that are not owned by the publisher.

The Hachette Speakers Bureau provides a wide range of authors for speaking events. To find out more, go to hachettespeakersbureau.com or call (866) 376-6591.

"The Surfing Lesson," "The Tailgate," "The Sixth Wedding," and "Summer of '79" were previously published by Little, Brown, in slightly different form, as ebook originals. "Barbie's Wedding" and "The Country Club" previously appeared, in slightly different form, as bonus content in special editions of *The Rumor* and *The Identicals,* respectively.

ISBN 9780316460910 (hardcover) / 9780316474528 (large print) / 9780316504157 (Canadian)
LCCN 2022933911

Printing 1, 2022

LSC-C

Printed in the United States of America

*With love and gratitude to my "work husband,"
Tim Ehrenberg, @timtalksbooks.
He makes signing books in a scary basement fun.*

Contents

Endless Summer

Introduction

I'll think of summer days again...and
dream of you.
         —Chad and Jeremy,
          "A Summer Song"

I started my writing career as a short-story writer. In 1990, my senior year at Johns Hopkins, I submitted a story called "Misdirection" to *Seventeen* magazine. It was accepted for publication and I was paid eight hundred dollars—and my belief in myself as a published writer was born. I continued to attend creative writing workshops—at the Ninety-Second Street Y in New York City, at Bread Loaf in Middlebury, Vermont, and finally at the University of Iowa graduate creative writing program—and I would persistently mail my stories to literary magazines across the country. I found success at places like the *Mid-American Review* and the *Massachusetts Review*—and I garnered at least half a dozen encouraging rejection letters from the mothership of important contemporary fiction, *The New Yorker.*

While I was at the University of Iowa, I was abjectly miserable. I felt like a literal fish out of water—the program was competitive, nearly cutthroat; I missed being near the ocean; I longed for my family and friends back east. The university offered free therapy and I would go every week and cry for the entire fifty minutes. At one point, my therapist said, "I think it's clear what you should do." I thought she was going to tell me to give up and go home. I have to admit, I was surprised; I didn't think therapists were supposed to suggest quitting (but if she was about to give me permission, I would take it and run!).

"What?" I said.

"You should start writing about Nantucket."

The next day, I started my first novel, *The Beach Club.*

What follows in these pages fuses my love of Nantucket with my longtime affection for short fiction. Included here are novellas, short stories, and extra chapters that are related to but not part of my summer novels. Three works here have never been published and the rest have been published only in exclusive editions by certain retailers or only in electronic form. It's a great joy to give you all of the pieces in one volume. I do ask that you read the introduction to each story first—the pieces will feel much more textured and nuanced (and make far more sense!) if you've read the original novels.

And for those of you literary detectives out there looking for my first published work, "Misdirection," you can check out the January 1993 edition of *Seventeen* magazine!

Thank you for reading. I love and appreciate you all.

—*XO, Elin*

The Surfing Lesson

(Read with *Beautiful Day*)

Here is my first-ever e-short, a short story that is of a novel but not part of it. "The Surfing Lesson" is a prequel—it occurs a few years before the action in *Beautiful Day,* and in it, we get to experience some of the history between my main character, Margot, and her husband, Drum. The opening scene takes place at the Juice Bar, a Nantucket institution. Margot and Drum bump into one of Drum's ex-girlfriends and instead of feeling jealous, Margot realizes she needs to ask Drum for a divorce. The second part of the story is set at Cisco Beach, which is the best beach on Nantucket for surfing. I loved being able to describe the history of Margot and Drum's relationship here, because there was no room to do so in the novel. This story also reminds me of the happy years when my two sons were in middle and high school and they used to spend all day long surfing at Cisco.

If anything was going to change Margot's mind about divorcing her husband, Drum, it was the presence of Hadley Axelram ahead of them in line at the Juice Bar on the third night of their Nantucket vacation. The day had been hot and sunny, with a high of 89 degrees, the second-hottest August 18 on record. There were forty-five or fifty people packed into the front of the shop and in a line snaking down Broad Street, creating a traffic hazard for the Jeeps and SUVs streaming off the late ferry. Margot's attention was consumed with making sure her three children didn't get hit by an overly excited driver, so it was surprising that she even noticed Hadley Axelram, although for the past ten years, Margot had experienced a personal barometric drop whenever the woman was nearby.

Storm approaching.

Hadley Axelram had dated Drum off and on for the three years before Margot met him. Hadley Axelram had a certain kind of look—to Margot, she looked like a twelve-year-old boy—that Drum and various other men found themselves powerless to resist. Hadley was five foot two and weighed ninety pounds. She had no chest and no ass; back in the days when Margot used to see her in a bikini, she had been startled by the sharp protruding bones of Hadley's hips and rib cage. Hadley wore her dark hair in a pixie cut, which made her brown eyes look enormous and sad, like the eyes of an extraterrestrial stranded billions of miles from home. Hadley always wore a choker. Years ago, it had been a black suede cord wrapped around a jade-green stone that nestled in the hollow of Hadley's throat. But now, the choker was caramel-colored leather embellished with recognizable gold hardware—Hermès. When Hadley reached up to idly finger her choker, Margot noticed that her nails—longer than anyone would expect on a person so obviously striving for androgyny—were painted the purplish blue of Concord grapes.

Drum had spent much of those three on-again, off-again years competing with his best friend, Colin O'Mara, for Hadley's affections. Colin had been the second-finest surfer on Nantucket, after Drum. Drum was as graceful and elegant as a person could be on a board. "Like watching fucking Baryshnikov," Margot had once heard a spectator on the beach say. Colin's surfing, on the other hand, was all about brute strength and the relentless desire to outdo Drum.

The same dynamic had been true in their pursuit of Hadley Axelram.

"Look," Margot said now, nudging Drum and pointing ahead in the line with her chin. "There's Hadley."

Drum nodded once but said nothing, which meant he had already seen her.

Over the past ten years, Margot had pieced together the following facts: Hadley, who was Indonesian — her grandparents were some kind of royalty in Jakarta — had spent the summer of 1999 drinking nightly at the Lobster Trap, where Drum worked as a bartender, until Drum finally asked her out. They fell in love — Hadley first, but Drum harder. That September, Hadley left Nantucket for graduate art-history studies in Florence. Her departure had stunned Drum and everyone else who'd assumed that Hadley was little more than a Lobster Trap brat and a surfing groupie. Drum felt like he had been shot in the chest (his words), but he put up an unaffected front. *"Ciao,"* he'd said to Hadley when he dropped her at the airport with her steamer trunk. *"Arrivederci."* When Hadley returned to Nantucket the following summer and appeared at Drum's cottage unannounced, Drum administered what he called a "hate fuck" and then showed her the door. And this was when Colin O'Mara stepped in. Supposedly with Drum's "blessing," Colin dated Hadley all summer, going so far as to let Hadley drive his beloved CJ5 all over the island and letting her live with him rent-free in his parents' enormous summer home on Shawkemo Hills Lane.

The line for the Juice Bar moved forward a bit. Margot and Drum and the kids crossed the threshold into the actual ice cream shop, which smelled powerfully of vanilla and just-pressed waffle cones. The kids knew the rules: Once they were in, they were allowed to talk about what flavors, what sauces, what toppings, what kind of cone. Drum Jr. and Carson became absorbed by this, as did Drum Sr., who read the names of the flavors out loud to Ellie. Margot was free to scrutinize Hadley Axelram, who was four people over and two people ahead, one spot away from ordering.

Hadley had her two children with her. One was a boy Drum Jr.'s age, ten, who had inherited Colin O'Mara's Irish coloring—the strawberry hair, the freckles. The other child was twoish, younger than Ellie, young enough to be carried, and this child, also a boy, had dark hair and olive skin like Hadley. Margot wondered how Hadley could stand having the child straddling her hip in the close, crowded heat of the shop. She was a good mother, Margot supposed.

The first son was Colin's, born only five months after Drum Jr., as though getting accidentally pregnant outside of wedlock had been a fad that year. Unlike Drum and Margot, Hadley and Colin had never married; they stayed together for a couple of years and then split. Colin lived in Kauai now; he sent Drum and Margot cards at Christmas, pictures of himself on far-flung beaches or on the lips of volcanoes. In the last picture, there had been a Polynesian woman in a grass skirt at his side; it looked like he had snagged her from the luau at the Hilton.

These cards made Margot sad.

The second son, Margot knew, had been sired by an up-and-coming painter named Jan Jaap. In a victory of biology over history, his pale Dutch coloring had been overpowered by Hadley's Indonesian genes. Margot and Drum had unwittingly walked into one of Jan Jaap's art openings in SoHo, and, finding Hadley there, they were treated to the love story. At that time, Hadley had been pregnant. She looked as though she had tucked a cantaloupe into her camisole.

That night had ended in a vile fight between Margot and Drum, as so often happened on nights that involved Hadley. Drum had climbed into a cab and screeched back to the apartment alone, and Margot stumbled into a Burmese restaurant and cried over her momos.

That painter, Jan Jaap, had never quite lived up to his potential, Margot thought. She wondered about the Hermès choker.

Drum Jr. declared that he wanted vanilla ice cream in a cake cone; he was overly cautious with his taste buds, afraid to try anything new no matter how alluring his father made other choices sound.

"How about chocolate fudge caramel ripple, buddy?"

No. Drum Jr. would not be budged. Margot sighed. A twenty-two-minute wait for vanilla in a cake cone?

Carson went the opposite route. He asked for a

waffle cup with a scoop of raspberry sherbet and a scoop of maple walnut doused with hot fudge and topped with gummy worms. Margot admired his creativity even as she knew this would end in a stomachache and possibly a cavity.

Ellie wanted a cup of mint chip with chocolate sauce and a squiggle of whipped cream. She would eat three bites, and Margot would be left with the rest, which meant Margot shouldn't order.

Drum Sr. turned to Margot. "I'm going to have the pistachio."

He was as predictable as their eldest child. Margot said, "Note the look of surprise on my face."

That decided, there was nothing to do but wait. Margot eyed Hadley Axelram. The woman had inspired jealousy more insidious than Margot could have imagined. How many times had Margot told Drum that she knew he was still in love with Hadley? How many times had Margot ransacked Drum's underwear drawer, where he kept photos from the summers of 1999 and 2000? These photos were mostly of Drum and Colin and Dred Richardson and the other guys who had surfed Cisco back then, but some of the group photos featured Hadley. Margot would stare at Hadley's waifish, sexless figure and wonder what it was that had been so attractive. Then Margot admitted that there were certain women who possessed magic powers, who bewitched and captivated, who got into a man's bloodstream like a virus that never died—and Hadley Axelram was one of them. Every time they had happened across Hadley in the past ten years, Drum got a look on his face like a kid who wanted a puppy.

But now that Margot's reservoir of romantic feelings for Drum had run dry—and when she said dry, she meant *dry*—she found herself excited, happy even, to have an unexpected encounter with Hadley Axelram. This might be just what Margot needed. Hadley Axelram's presence at the Juice Bar might be seen as a miracle, a last lifeline. Jealousy as defibrillator.

From her spot a chess move away, Margot listened to Hadley Axelram order. Double scoop of butter pecan in a waffle cup with caramel sauce and crushed Heath bars for the older son, a kiddie cup of cookie dough ice cream for the younger son, and . . . pistachio in a waffle cone for Hadley.

Margot almost couldn't believe it. But then she recalled that during the periods when Hadley and Drum were dating—not only the summer of 1999 on Nantucket, but also part of the summer of 2001 on Nantucket and briefly in the winter of 2002 in Aspen—Hadley exerted enormous influence over Drum. She was the reason he'd gotten the tattoo of the god Ganesh on his hip, she was the reason he listened to Better Than Ezra, and apparently she was the reason he always ordered pistachio ice cream. For all Margot knew, Drum and Hadley had come to the Juice Bar too many times to count and ordered pistachio ice cream together.

Margot wanted to care. She yearned to care.

Once Hadley had received her cone and cups, Margot beamed in her direction, her smile as bright as a searchlight.

Hadley turned, saw Margot and Drum, and her expression appeared to be one of genuine delight. Not at seeing Margot, of course, but at seeing Drum.

"Hey!" Hadley said. She had her hands full with her ice cream and the child's ice cream and the child, and she had to twist and maneuver through the crowd to Margot and Drum, which was not a path anyone waiting in line wanted to clear for her.

Margot heard Drum mutter, "Oh, Jesus."

Normally, it was Margot who would have said this. Years before they had bumped into Hadley at the art gallery, they had seen her at the Matterhorn, in Stowe, Vermont. Wearing a white cashmere sweater and jeans and long feather earrings, she had been drinking a beer at the bar, surrounded by men ten years her junior. Margot had spotted her first and said, "Oh, shit." She and Drum had had both boys in tow; Carson was pitching a fit after having spent all day in the Kinderhut, and all Margot had wanted was a glass of wine. She was the one who had insisted they stop at the Matterhorn, but once Drum saw Hadley, Margot's dream of a fun, relaxing après-ski was ruined. Hadley had shrieked with joy upon seeing Drum, causing her other suitors to scatter. Margot was left to deal with her recalcitrant and exhausted children while Hadley and Drum "caught up," Drum with that insipid look on his face. Margot had been bitterly jealous then, her stomach roiling with concealed rage.

She wanted rage now. She wanted to feel *something*.

"Hey, Hadley!" Margot said. She bent in and kissed the woman's tanned cheek. Soft as suede.

"Hey, guys!" Hadley said. "Hey, Drum!"

"Hey," Drum said. He gave her half a wave.

Suddenly, it was their turn to order. No time for a reunion. Margot said to Hadley, "Why don't you wait for us outside? We'd love to catch up!"

Hadley said, "Yes, of course!"

She scooted past Margot and Drum and the kids, and Margot caught the scent of Hadley's intoxicating perfume, a scent that had nearly caused her to vomit at the Matterhorn and again at the art gallery. Did Drum smell it? She looked at him. His mouth was a grim line.

"What's wrong?" Margot said.

Drum didn't answer her. He was placing their order with the adorable fifteen-year-old server who wore her hair in two Alpine braids like Heidi. When he was done, he said, "I don't feel like dealing with Hadley Axelram tonight."

"We aren't 'dealing' with her," Margot said. "We're just going to say hello."

"It always ends in disaster," Drum said. He looked at her. He had gotten some nice sun on his face the past three days, and his eyes seemed very blue; he was getting the golden streak back in his hair that Margot had so loved when she first met him. He was such a great-looking guy. He was kind and sweet and a fabulous father and a doting husband. He was the best surfer she had ever seen and maybe an even better skier. But she didn't love him; that knowledge pierced her like a Chinese throwing star in her gut. "You have to admit, it always ends in disaster when we see her."

"Well, guess what?" Margot said. "It won't tonight. I promise."

Margot met Drum in the summer of 2001, eight days after his second breakup with Hadley. Hadley and Colin O'Mara had been "taking a break" that summer, and one late night at the Chicken Box, Hadley and Drum found themselves on the dance floor, stuck together like magnets. But by the end of July, Hadley had become frustrated with Drum, saying he didn't make enough time for her, and she returned to Colin. That summer, Margot had been on Nantucket for just one week — the first week of August — although in the previous twenty-five years of her life, she had spent the entire summer on the island, at her family's home on Orange Street. But that year, Margot had an internship at the executive search firm of Miller, Sawtooth, and a week was all she could finagle. She was lucky to get a week.

Margot had been lying on her towel at Cisco Beach, intent on finally getting some sun on her office-worker-white body, and whiled away the hot hours by watching Drum surf. Margot's brother, Nick, said he knew Drum casually from "around"—which meant, Margot assumed, that Nick and Drum drank at the same bars and hit on the same women—and Nick introduced them when Drum came in off the water. Margot had been surprised at how tall and solid Drum was; on his board, he crouched and bent and twisted like a jockey riding a temperamental horse. Up close, Margot could see his eyes were silvery blue, the color of water, and he had sun-bleached streaks in his hair. He was as handsome as Apollo the sun god, but Margot refused to let herself worship him. She was twenty-five years old, halfway through her MBA at Columbia. She was a serious person, beyond gushing over a surfer.

Who wanted to be treated to their love story? Drum had asked Margot out pretty much on the spot. "Do you have plans tonight?" And because Margot did *not* have plans and because the other girls on the beach were looking at Drum covetously, Margot said no. She had always had a competitive streak.

Margot and Drum had gone out every remaining night of her vacation—drives up the beach in his Jeep to see the sunset, dinners at the Blue Bistro and the Galley and Le Languedoc (where Drum always paid with a wad of tens and fives, his tips from bartending). They went to one movie (*Ocean's Eleven*) and had lots of very exciting sex in the down-at-the-heels cottage Drum rented on Hooper Farm Road. When Margot left at the end of the week, although Drum had her number and her address in the city, she thought, *I will never see this guy again.*

A part of her had also thought — admit it! — *I won't go back to New York. I'll quit my internship. I'll stay here the rest of the month and watch Drum surf.* She had taken this a step further, thinking, *I won't go back to business school. I'll go to Aspen with Drum. I'll get a ski pass. I'll work as a barista.*

But she had gone back to New York. Drum stopped to see her on his way to Aspen. He had shown up wearing jeans and a wrinkled white linen shirt and flip-flops; when they made love, Margot noted he still had sand in the whorls of his ears. But during that twenty-four-hour visit, Margot learned other things about him: Drum's father was an executive with Sony, and Drum had grown up jetting back and forth between New York and Tokyo. He had attended the American International School in Japan until tenth grade and finished high school at Dalton. He could negotiate the subway better than Margot could. He took her to a sushi place in the East Village where the chef came out from the back and conversed with Drum in Japanese. Margot was stunned. Drum had instantly become a different person; he had become a wonder. But no sooner did Margot have this revelation than he was gone to the mountains.

There had been phone calls that winter, drunk, late-night phone calls, most often initiated by Margot, who would sometimes cry. Sometimes she called and Drum didn't answer. He was asleep. Or he wasn't home.

The following summer, Margot had a bona fide job offer from Miller, Sawtooth, but in a brilliant bit of negotiating, she didn't start working until September 15. She would have all summer free to spend on Nantucket. She would have all summer with Drum.

By Labor Day weekend, she was pregnant.

Hadley was standing right outside the door when they exited. Her younger child's face was smeared with ice cream, and the older son grimaced at his mother and rolled his eyes. He looked so much like Colin O'Mara at that moment that Margot wanted to hug him.

There were repeat greetings. Margot kissed Hadley again; Drum kissed Hadley; the children were introduced.

Hadley said, "Wow, I can't believe I bumped into you. I've been thinking about you all day."

This was obviously a statement directed at Drum. Hadley would never be thinking of Margot all day, or even for a second.

"We always come the last two weeks of August," Margot said. "We like to save it for the very end."

"I've been here all summer," Hadley said. She set the child down, which caused him to whimper, but she ignored this. "I left Jan eighteen months ago. I was dating a private-equity guy, and that has sort of ended as well, although he's letting us use his house all summer. It's on the water in Monomoy."

Margot nodded. It wasn't surprising that Hadley had left Jan Jaap, nor was it surprising that she had traded up from Starving Artist to Private-Equity Guy. What set Margot's mind reeling was that Private-Equity Guy would allow Hadley and her children to stay in his waterfront house despite the fact that their relationship had "sort of ended." This was the kind of thing that only happened to Hadley Axelram.

"Nice!" Margot said. She took quick stock of her children—all consumed with the business of eating ice cream. "So, you were thinking about Drum today?"

Drum made a noise of exasperation, which Margot ignored.

Hadley raised her big brown eyes to Drum. Here it was, Margot thought, the kill. Drum had never been able to resist that look from Hadley. It turned him to vapor. He could deny it, but Margot knew better.

But not today. Today, Drum was staring at Hadley like she was a skunked beer or an invoice for back taxes from the IRS.

"Curtis really wants to take surfing lessons," Hadley said. She nudged her older son, Curtis, who was staring at his untied Osiris sneakers. "And I found myself wishing that you were around, because who better to learn from than Drummond Bain?"

"No," Drum said.

And at the same time, Margot said, "Of course!"

There was a look of confusion from Hadley, then an awkward silence, which was broken when the little guy started to really wail and Hadley bent to pick him up.

"I don't give surfing lessons," Drum said.

"Sure you do!" Margot said. For the past three days, Drum Sr. had tried to coax Drum Jr. out to the waves. Drum Jr. had no interest in surfing. He would fool around in the water with his brother, and when he tired of that, he would get his lacrosse stick and go in search of other kids to play catch with.

"I really don't," Drum said.

"All right," Hadley said. "Okay."

"You could, though," Margot said. "You could give Curtis a surfing lesson. We don't have anything going on the rest of the week. You could meet him anytime. You could meet him tomorrow morning."

Drum hadn't touched his pistachio ice cream. It was starting to drip. He smiled at Curtis. "There's a guy who hangs out down at Cisco Beach named Elvis. He gives lessons."

Hadley shook her head. "No," she said. "That's not going to work."

"Oh," Drum said. "Right."

Margot looked from Hadley to Drum and back. She had never heard of anyone on Nantucket named Elvis, although he was clearly a holdover from their surfing days. Maybe he was one of the people in the group photos in Drum's underwear drawer. Maybe Hadley had slept with Elvis. Margot would have to ask Drum later.

Curtis kicked a pebble and it ricocheted off the side of the building. "That's okay," he said. "My dad said he'd teach me when I go to Hawaii in February."

Drum smiled at the kid. "Your dad is a great surfer."

Hadley made a face. She said, "February is fine, but it's six months away. I thought it would be nice if Curtis could learn the basics now. He's ready."

"I can wait," Curtis said.

Drum coughed and stared at the melting ice cream in his hand as though he couldn't figure out what it was doing there. To Margot he said, "We have nothing tomorrow morning?"

"My dad is taking the kids out for breakfast," Margot said. "And I'm going running. But you are as free as a bird."

"I'll meet you at seven o'clock," Drum said to Curtis. "At the antenna. Do you have a board, or should I bring you one of mine?"

"I have a board," Curtis said.

"Oh, thank you!" Hadley said. "This is so great!"

"Great!" Margot said.

When she told Drum about the pregnancy, Margot had been certain he would insist on her terminating it. Despite their luminous summer together, their lives were about to go in different directions. Drum was heading back to Aspen to ski, and then in late March he was flying to Sri Lanka to surf. Margot had her job waiting for her in the city. She was going to wear a suit every day and get an expense account. The managing partner of Miller, Sawtooth, Harry Fry, *loved* Margot. He saw something in her—a tenaciousness, a natural instinct—that made him believe she would succeed. His faith in her would be shattered if he knew she had allowed herself to become pregnant at the age of twenty-five. *Go home,* he would say. *Spend your days drinking wine out of sippy cups with the other mommies at the Bleecker Street playground. Or hire a nanny and do charity work.* Harry Fry would never have hired Margot if he'd known this was going to happen.

But instead of giving Margot the money for an abortion, Drum had taken Margot to dinner at the Blue Bistro, where the waiter served her a diamond ring embedded in an Island Creek oyster. When Margot saw the ring, she ran to the ladies' room to vomit. Once she returned to the table, Drum had cleaned off the ring; it was perched in its velvet box, where it belonged.

He said, "I want you to marry me."

She said, "Aren't you supposed to ask?"

He said, "Margot Carmichael, will you marry me?"

Margot knew the sane answer was no. It would never work. Neither a baby nor a husband figured into her plans—not now, possibly not ever. But there was the specter of those drunken, late-night phone calls, a loneliness so profound that Margot had cried, despite living in a city of eight million people. She thought,

Drummond Bain, king of the South Shore, wants to marry me. As it turned out, her heart was steel-plated on only three sides. As it turned out, her body was holding on to the cluster of cells growing inside her.

"Okay," she said.

"Okay?" Drum said. "Aren't you supposed to say yes or no?"

"Yes," Margot said.

When Margot was a junior in college, she had "fallen in love" with a graduate teaching assistant in her philosophy course, a Canadian named Reese.

Reese had not returned Margot's love. Reese had also, thankfully, not seen fit to use Margot for sex and walk away. Reese had been a good guy. When Margot made her feelings known to him one night in the reserve reading room over a confusing passage of Hume, Reese had held her chin and told her the following words about love.

"Nobody knows where it comes from," he said. "And nobody knows where it goes."

Where does it go? Margot wondered.

That night, after the kids were in bed and Margot and Drum were sharing the bathroom, washing the stickiness from their hands, Margot said, "Who's Elvis?"

Drum said, "This guy."

Margot waited him out. He knew that answer wasn't close to sufficient.

Drum said, "He was always cool with me. He developed a little bit of an obsession with Hadley, I guess. Called her all the time, sometimes didn't say anything, just breathed into the phone. Drove his pickup back and forth in front of her rental house, showed up at the gallery where she worked, that kind of thing."

"And this was...before you? After you? During Colin?"

"Oh God," Drum said. "Who can remember?"

The winter of the drunken late-night phone calls — which was the winter after the summer that Margot and Drum had first dated, which was also the summer that Hadley had taken a break from Colin, reunited with Drum, then left Drum and returned to Colin — Hadley traveled out to Aspen on the sly. She showed up at the Aspen Club Lodge, where Drum was working the night desk in exchange for a season's ski pass, and they shacked up together for a week, until Colin appeared, banging on the door, claiming to have a gun. Drum said he knew Colin didn't have a gun, he knew Colin was just sad and desperate at the thought of losing Hadley, so Drum opened the door and let Colin in. Margot imagined some kind of hairy scene where Drum and Colin battled over Hadley, but Drum said it was low drama. Drum explained to Colin that he

and Hadley had had some unfinished emotional business but that it had been brought to a close. Hadley
was free to go with Colin if that was what she wanted.
Drum was going to pursue this other girl he'd met, a
girl who lived in New York.

Drum and Hadley, Hadley and Colin, Drum and
Margot, Drum and Hadley, Hadley and Colin, Hadley and Jan Jaap, Colin in Hawaii hiking the ridges of
active volcanoes and drinking mai tais with the descen-
dants of Princess Kaiulani, Hadley and the Private-
Equity Guy who shopped for her at Hermès, Margot
who had spent the past eighteen months wondering
where love went when it left, where could she find it,
how could she get it back?

In bed, she said, "I'm glad you're giving Curtis a
surfing lesson tomorrow."

Drum said, "I'm not."

Their life in New York had been enviable from the outside, she supposed. Drum's parents had bought them
an apartment on East Seventy-Third Street, a spacious
three-bedroom in a prewar building with good water
pressure and crown molding and a responsive superintendent. Margot worked at Miller, Sawtooth, and
Drum cared for the kids starting practically the same
day she popped them out. Margot expressed milk in
her office between meetings, and Drum would wait in
the lobby of her building for Margot's assistant to run
the bottles down to him. Drum changed the diapers,

he hand-pureed baby food, he took the boys to the playground and to their baby classes in Spanish and classical music. He did the shopping and all of the cooking and the laundry. In his downtime, he smoked weed and watched Warren Miller films. Once the kids were in school, he took up running; he dropped fifteen pounds. He spent time on the Internet planning their vacations to Costa Rica and Park City to surf and ski. On these vacations, Margot cared for the kids while Drum did his thing—eight to ten hours a day on the water or the slopes. Margot wanted to complain, but she knew that, for Drum, this was working. It was professional fulfillment.

Meanwhile, Margot toiled and strove and accomplished at Miller, Sawtooth. She appreciated the foot rubs and the glasses of chardonnay when she got home and the hot mushroom strudel with arugula salad at her place at the dinner table, but sometimes she looked at Drum and thought, *Why are you slaving over me this way? Why don't you get something for yourself?*

They became friends with a couple named Teresa and Avery Benedict, the parents of Maurice, who was Drum Jr.'s best buddy at preschool. Teresa and Drum Sr. had forged the friendship; they started going for coffee after dropping off the kids. Sometimes they hung out together all morning—shopping, going for lunch. Teresa bought Drum Sr. a subscription to *Bon Appétit;* the two of them shared recipes. The two of them— Margot was sure—complained about their spouses and the obscene hours they worked and how grouchy they were when they came home. Margot wondered if Teresa and Drum Sr. were having an affair. And then one day she realized she *wanted* them to have an affair—she wanted them to drop the kids off at school and go back to one apartment or the other and fuck until they were sweaty and seeing stars.

Margot once said, "So, what do you think of Teresa?"

Drum said, "What do you mean, what do I think of her?"

"You like her, right?"

"Yes, I like her. Of course I like her. She's cool."

"Do you ever..."

"Do I ever *what*, Margot?"

"Do you ever..."

"No," Drum said. "I don't."

There were other tense conversations, whispered late at night after the boys were asleep.

Margot said: "It's exhausting, you know, being the only one who brings home a paycheck."

Drum said: "You don't have to work as hard as you do, Margot. The apartment is paid for. You could make half of what you do and we'd be fine."

This infuriated Margot, mostly because he was correct.

Margot said: "I like working hard. I love my job. I want to make partner."

Drum said: "Okay, so why are you complaining?"

Why *was* she complaining? Drum was taking care of the home front so she didn't have to. He was a classic 1950s housewife but better because he was handsome and sexy and everyone loved him. He wore flip-flops and Ron Jon T-shirts even in December. Margot wasn't sure what the problem was. If pressed, she might say it was Drum's lack of ambition. He seemed to expect nothing from his days but smiles on his kids' faces and dinner with his family. Wasn't a grown man, a man of thirty-five, then forty, supposed to want more?

She said to him one night, "It's like you don't have dreams."

"Dreams?" he said.

Then Margot's mother, Beth Carmichael, was diagnosed with terminal ovarian cancer, and Margot's world was thrown into a tailspin.

In one of the last conversations Margot had with her mother, Beth had grasped her daughter's hand and said, "All a mother wants, Margot, is for her children to be happy. And that may take different forms at different times."

"I am happy, Mom," Margot said.

Beth had seemed unconvinced. But that could have been the morphine at work. Margot said, "You don't have to worry about me."

Beth said, "Ever since you were a little girl, you've been too hard on yourself. It's the curse of the first-born. You need to cut yourself some slack, allow for your imperfect moments. You need to be your own best friend."

Margot had squeezed her mother's hand. "I have a best friend," she said. "It's you."

"Oh, honey, I know," Beth said, and her eyes fluttered closed. "Just listen to me."

When her mother died, Margot cleaved to Drum. She couldn't get him close enough; she wanted to inhabit his body. She wanted him to absorb her pain, to sop it up like a spill on the counter.

During this period of grief and renewed closeness, Margot got pregnant again — with Ellie. To have a daughter and not have her mother to share the experience with? God, the pain! When the doctor placed Ellie in Margot's arms, Margot gazed up at Drum and burst into tears. And he had wept right along with her and said, "I know, babe. I know. She should be here."

A week after Ellie's first birthday, Margot made partner at Miller, Sawtooth. There was a party and, of course, a large raise. This was when things drastically slid downhill. She was impatient, bitchy, entitled; she said things she regretted. She was mean to Drum; she accused him of wasting his life. Instead of growing angry at her, instead of telling her to go jump in a big pool of fuck you, which was what he should have done, he kowtowed to her even more. He texted her forty or fifty times a day; he told her he loved her; he filled their apartment with fresh flowers; he threw her a surprise birthday party at Bill's Bar and Burger; he booked a family trip to Japan. No skiing, no surfing, he said. We can do whatever you want to do—the cities, the gardens, the pagodas. You always said you wanted to go to Japan.

Margot made him cancel the trip immediately. She told him she'd wanted to see Japan because that was where he had grown up. She had wanted to see it for Drum's sake. But that desire had faded as well.

She started going to a therapist even though she didn't really have time. She admitted to the therapist that she didn't think she loved Drum anymore.

If you could change five things about him, the therapist asked, would that make a difference?

Would it? Margot wondered. What if he landed a job as a TV anchorperson and he was on the news every night at six o'clock? What if he became a professor of Japanese at NYU? What if he invented something, started a company, made millions? What if he wore Robert Graham shirts and Ferragamo loafers? What if he took up golf and followed the stock market? What if he read Tolstoy, Dashiell Hammett, Norman Mailer? What if he listened to opera, subscribed to the *Wall Street Journal,* smoked a pipe?

But Drum didn't need to change; Drum was happy the way he was. Drum was, in fact, the happiest person Margot knew. Margot wanted to change one thing about herself. She wanted to be a woman who loved Drum the way he was.

What do you do when the love is gone? Margot asked the therapist. She was in tears. She wanted it back. She wanted to feel.

Where does it go?

The morning of the surfing lesson, Margot's father, Doug Carmichael, piled her three children into the back seat of his Jaguar. He was taking them to the Downyflake for doughnuts and pancakes and hot chocolate. Doug Carmichael was a prominent divorce attorney in Manhattan, but Margot hadn't told her father how close she was to jumping off the cliff of marriage into the churning sea of divorce. She didn't want to be work to him. When the time came, he would give her a colleague's name; she knew she would be in the very best hands.

Margot said, "Okay, I'm going for a run. Enjoy the sugar!"

Drum had left a few minutes before, his surfboard strapped to their Land Rover. Margot had kissed him goodbye as though for the last time. He was going to meet Hadley Axelram and her son at the beach. Hadley Axelram, Hadley Axelram, Hadley Axelram. Nothing; Margot felt nothing. How was this possible?

On her run, Margot imagined a scene between Drum and Hadley Axelram. Hadley would be in her bikini, her bones jutting out. She would give Drum the big-brown-eyes stare because she was so grateful he had shown up to teach Curtis to surf. Curtis needed a father figure; everyone else had failed her, but not Drum, never Drum, he was the one she still thought about, he was the one she had wanted all along. If Colin hadn't shown up in Aspen claiming to have a gun, she and Drum would be married by now; Drum hadn't ever been serious about pursuing the other girl in New York. How could he have been, when he was permanently under Hadley's spell? She would have given birth to a whole passel of little surfers. Hadley still thought about him every time she had an orgasm. Did he know that?

What would he say? Margot wondered. How would he respond? He would buckle, right? He would kiss Hadley; the kiss would ignite a spark; he would see the whole world differently, the way he used to see it when he was in love with Hadley. He would remember what it felt like when he'd dropped her off at Terminal E at Logan for her flight to Florence, where she would spend an entire year studying Giotto. She had taken his heart along for the ride, nestled among her cashmere sweaters inside her steamer trunk. But now she had been returned to him. He had finally, finally gotten her back.

Margot thought about all of this but felt nothing. How was this possible?

She decided to run to the beach to see for herself. If she saw Drum and Hadley together with her own eyes, if she spied on their private moments, she would feel something, she would be jealous, she would be heartsick, and the marriage would be saved.

Nobody *wanted* to be divorced—this was something Margot's father had always said. People *needed* to get divorced.

Margot ran up Main Street to the monument, past the lovely historic homes on Milk Street. Hydrangea bushes, weathered fences, brick sidewalks, leafy trees. She was moving and she felt great, healthy; she loved being out of the city, she loved being on Nantucket. She had thought that maybe being on Nantucket would do the trick for her and Drum—maybe they needed a change of scenery. This was where they'd met, fallen in love, conceived their first child. *Help me, Nantucket!*

Margot hadn't run in months; there had been absolutely no time. She spent her days at the office, and when she got home, she wanted to be with her children. They had grown masterful at the guilt trip. *We never see you, you're never home, and when you're home you're always on your phone. We want you. We can't stop wanting you.* Margot was running hard; she was in the sun now, headed up the hill by the Maria Mitchell Observatory. She didn't feel winded at all; that was the kind of person she was—when she said she was going to do something, she did it and she did it well. She didn't quit things. Was getting a divorce quitting? Her therapist said no, but Margot felt the answer was yes. Yes, getting a divorce was quitting. She should do what countless others before her had done and stay for the sake of the children, stay until Ellie graduated from Fieldston, only fifteen years from now. Could she stay for fifteen more years?

Nope, no way. She needed to follow her mother's advice and allow for her imperfect moments. The past year and a half had been a study in imperfection. But now, maybe Hadley Axelram could help. *Help me, Hadley!*

Margot was sweating buckets by the time she got to the dirt road that led to the antenna beach. This was the newly popular beach for serious surfers—Cisco had been overrun by college kids with cases of Budweiser. Margot saw their Land Rover parked at the beach entrance and next to it, a turquoise-blue Mini. Of course that would be what Hadley drove.

Margot stopped to stretch behind the cars. Some water would be nice; she was hot now and she still had to run all the way back. She surreptitiously opened the passenger door of the Land Rover, hoping that Drum had brought a bottle of water—of course he had, he was a Boy Scout that way, always prepared. She lifted it out of the console. Nice and cold.

She walked around the dune so that she could see the action on the beach without being seen herself. Drum was in the water waist-deep and Curtis was on the board next to him. Hadley was standing at the shore, watching. She wore a long sheer white cover-up over her bathing suit. When a wave came in, Drum positioned Curtis's board and yelled, "Go!" and Curtis paddled like crazy, then got into his crouch, then stood. He stood! He rode the wave to shore, and Hadley cheered madly. Drum said, "Let's do it again!"

Margot watched as a few more sets rolled in. She marveled at how Curtis's body moved just like his father's. He gritted his teeth in determination; his eyes bulged. He stood time after time after time; he had it down. Drum had taught him or had been able to coax out Curtis's natural ability. Hadley clapped and danced; she got the hem of her cover-up wet in the froth of the waves.

Drum came in, and Hadley handed him a towel. He wiped at his face and pointed at Curtis. Curtis was going to try it by himself. This was good; this was great. Margot focused on Drum and Hadley standing side by side on the beach. If Drum turned and saw her, he would realize she was spying on him, but he would think it was for a different reason. He would think she wanted to catch him at something; he would think she had come out here to confirm her worst fears. He would never guess that she was wishing for something to happen; he would never predict her hunger to feel jealous.

Curtis paddled out. Hadley turned to Drum, she raised her face to him; she touched his bare chest with one Concord grape–painted finger. She was thanking him, telling him how miraculous he was, telling him how he had saved the day, telling him how amazing it had been watching Drum out in the water with her son. She drew a line from his heart down his chest, then down to his stomach, then down to his...

Drum grabbed Hadley's hand. This was it! Margot thought. They were going to kiss!

Drum dropped Hadley's hand; he didn't exactly shove it away, but it was definitely a gesture of dismissal. He was giving her her hand back, saying, *Please don't touch me like that, I'm a married man.*

Hadley tried again. Maybe her luck with men was based on pure persistence. She took a step closer to Drum and turned up her face, pursing her lips. One of the straps of her cover-up slipped off her shoulder. There could be no mistaking her intentions. Margot thought, *Take the bait, Drum! This is the woman who taught you to love pistachio ice cream, who encouraged you to make "In the Blood" your own personal anthem.* But Drum stepped back, shaking his head like he couldn't believe her gall; he walked a few yards away, spread out his towel, and sat down. He pulled his cell phone out of his backpack.

Hadley called out something to him, but he didn't even bother looking up.

Margot's heart plummeted. Her eyes filled with tears. And at that second, her phone buzzed. She had a text message from Drum. I love you, it said. I wish you were here.

Margot looked up in alarm, thinking he must have seen her and *that* was why he hadn't kissed Hadley, *that* was why he'd walked away. But when she checked, Hadley was staring at Drum, and Drum was resting his forearms on his knees, watching Curtis surf. He hadn't seen Margot. If he had seen her, he would have beckoned her down. He didn't play games like this.

Suddenly a man came up behind Margot and she nearly jumped out of her shoes. He was a couple years older than she was, and he wore only a pair of orange swim trunks; he was carrying a longboard. His bare torso was tanned the deep brown of a tobacco leaf; his hair was black and wavy with a few strands of gray in the front. He stopped next to Margot when he saw the scene transpiring down on the beach.

He said, "Holy Mother of God, look who we have here."

Margot didn't respond. The man sounded like a carnival barker who smoked a hundred cigarettes a day.

He turned to her. He said, "That there is the girl of my dreams."

Margot nodded. The girl of everyone's dreams. She said, "You're Elvis?"

His eyebrows lifted in surprise. He held out his hand, fingers stained with nicotine. "Do I know you?"

"No," Margot said. "No, I don't think we've met. I just...well, I've heard about you. You teach surfing?"

"At Cisco," he said. "To the punks with rich mothers."

"Oh," Margot said. She crunched her water bottle, which was now empty. "Do you know who the guy is?"

"That guy there?" Elvis asked. "Yeah, I know who that is. Everyone knows who that is."

"Who is he?" Margot asked. Thinking: *Boy Scout, good guy, doting father, amazing cook. He speaks Japanese and gives great foot rubs.* Thinking: *Nobody knows where it comes from and nobody knows where it goes.*

"It's Drum...Drum...shit, I forget his last name. But I'll tell you what—" Elvis leaned closer to Margot as if to let her in on a secret.

"What?" Margot said.

"He's the greatest surfer this island has ever seen," Elvis said. "Watching him is like watching fucking Baryshnikov."

Margot nodded, wishing Elvis had been able to tell her something she didn't already know.

At that moment, Drum stood up and grabbed his board, which was sticking straight up out of the sand. He ran with it to the water and began to paddle out.

"Lucky you," Elvis said. "You're going to witness."

Margot took a deep breath. Curtis had come in off the water, and he was now standing next to his mother, both of them watching Drum.

Drum let a few waves go. He had always been picky. Because of her vantage point up on the dune, Margot saw the one he would take even before he did. She watched him sense its approach; she saw his muscles tense. She knew the man so well. If they separated and divorced this year and he moved to the West Coast, and she next saw him on a surfboard twenty years from now, she would still know which wave he would take. *You need to be your own best friend,* her mother had told her. But Drum was her best friend, Margot couldn't deny it, and she was going to lose him.

"There he goes!" Elvis said.

Drum was moving—he was up, riding the wave low and sweet all the way across the break, going for maximum speed rather than flair. He made the board act like a razor, cutting the wave cleanly across the middle. Margot was sure Hadley was swooning on the beach the way Margot used to swoon and wanted to swoon now. Elvis let out a whoop, and the sound attracted Drum's attention. He looked up at the dune and saw Elvis—and Margot—and something in his face changed. He lost his balance and tumbled headfirst into the crashing foam.

Elvis turned to Margot. "You don't know him, but he sure seems to know you."

Margot didn't have a reply to that, but none was needed. Elvis rushed down to the beach to greet Hadley.

Margot waited until Drum surfaced. His head popped up and his eyes sought hers. She thought, *Yes, I'm here. I'm still here.*

He waved to her. She gave him a thumbs-up and

called out, "Good ride!" Later, when she talked to him, she might use those very words, she might say, *We had a good ride, Drum. We had a good ride.* Or she might come up with better words. She had plenty of time to think about it on the hot, lonely run for home.

The Tailgate
(Read with *The Matchmaker*)

This is a prequel story, set decades before *The Matchmaker* takes place. Dabney Kimball is a student at Harvard, and her longtime boyfriend, Clendenin Hughes, is at Yale. Dabney has an unusual aversion to traveling but she is determined to go to New Haven for the Harvard-Yale football game (aka "the Game"). I loved delving into the traditions of this game and into the details of the mid-1980s. I was able to incorporate my love for a cappella groups, tailgate picnics, college life, J. D. Salinger, and football into this story. Ultimately, however, the story's purpose is to give a richer background to the characters we grew to love in *The Matchmaker*.

Dabney had no problem finding a ride to the game; everyone on campus owed her. Three weeks out, it looked like she would be driving to New Haven with two seniors from Owl, but she didn't know how to announce this fact to Clendenin without making him uncomfortable. Though he tried to hide it, he clearly felt threatened every time Dabney mentioned another boy's name. She and Albert Maku, for example, were *just friends,* but Clen was jealous because Dabney, apparently, went "on and on" about how much she enjoyed Albert's accent.

"I could never be romantically interested in Albert," Dabney said with a laugh during one of their Tuesday-night phone calls.

"Why not?" Clen challenged. "Because he's *Black?*" Clen was studying journalism and was obsessed with probing issues.

"Because he's Albert," Dabney said. "You know Albert."

"Yes," Clen said. "I do know Albert." His tone was accusatory, meant to emphasize the fact that Clen had traveled to Cambridge four times during their freshman year, had seen her dorm room and strolled her campus and met her friends, while Dabney had yet to visit New Haven even once.

There was a reason for that, one they left undiscussed.

But at the start of their sophomore year, Clen had announced that he would not set foot in Cambridge again until Dabney came to New Haven.

She had promised to come the third weekend of September and canceled, then promised again the long weekend in October and canceled, saying she had too much studying to do. Her father paid eighty dollars a month so she could park her car on campus. But every Friday afternoon when Dabney got behind the wheel of the Nova, it took her to Hyannis, where she caught the ferry home to Nantucket.

It was pathological; both Dabney and Clen knew this, but they did not speak of it. Or rather, they did not speak of it *anymore.* The topic was exhausted. What else could they possibly say? Dabney had been seeing a therapist since she was twelve years old, but aside from the fact that she had matriculated at Harvard, not much had changed since then. Harvard was a big step, and from this big step, Dabney felt, might be born smaller steps. Such as a trip to New Haven. But not yet.

November, however, presented a unique opportunity: the game. Clen had come north for the game the year before with a carful of his new friends from Morse, his residential college. It had been strange to see Clen among all those other…guys/boys/men—Dabney was never sure how to refer to males between the ages of eighteen and twenty-two—piling out of the beat-up woody. Clen had been part of the group, right there in the scrum, although throughout high school he had been friendless except for Dabney.

She had felt oddly betrayed by his having these friends, by his new membership in a group, a place where he clearly belonged and fit in. The guys/boys/men were all tackling one another in Harvard Yard, holding each other in headlocks, calling one another raunchy names. Dabney had watched from the steps of Grays Hall, thinking, *He's become someone else.* He had sounded the same in his letters and during their weekly phone calls from the dormitory pay phones. But in that moment, Dabney had seen that he was different.

After a while, he noticed her and trotted over. His bearing was more confident than she remembered, and he was growing a beard.

"Hey, Cupe," he said. He kissed her deeply, theatrically, dipping her backward. The guys/boys/men whistled and hooted.

"So that's her, Hughes?" one called out.

"Well, let's hope so," another said.

Dabney reached up to touch Clen's face. "Beard?" she said.

"No," he said defensively. "I just haven't had a chance to shave. Deadline, deadline, deadline."

Right—because, even as a freshman, Clen had secured a spot as a feature writer for the *Yale Daily News*. He had been a superstar in high school—a "hundred-year genius," their English teacher Mr. Kane had called him—and apparently his star shone just as brightly in New Haven. Dabney had been salutatorian to Clen's valedictorian, although she had gotten into Harvard and Clen had not. But at Harvard, she found that her skills and intellect were average, nothing special. Her only standout talent was her matchmaking; she had already set up two couples in Grays Hall and had another potential match brewing. This hobby of hers was local legend back home and the source of Clen's nickname for her: "Cupe," short for Cupid.

The game, the game! It was the perfect opportunity for Dabney to visit New Haven. *Everyone* from Harvard was going. By the time the week of the game rolled around, Dabney was able to tell the guys from Owl that she had found another ride, one that would be far more palatable to Clen. She would drive to New Haven with her roommate, Mallory, and Mallory's boyfriend, Jason, who was first line on the hockey team.

"Just like Oliver Barrett!" Dabney had swooned the morning after Mallory hooked up with Jason.

Mallory had looked at Dabney with the vacant expression that occasionally overcame her pale, pretty face. Once or twice a week, Mallory exhibited behavior that made Dabney question how she had gotten into Harvard. She was from Bozeman, Montana; that was, quite possibly, the answer.

"Oliver Barrett? From *Love Story*?" Dabney prompted.

Mallory shrugged. She was tired and hungover; her impressive mane of permed hair was mussed from love gymnastics with Jason the hockey player. "Never seen it," she said.

Dabney didn't know why she felt surprised. She had found few of her classmates were versed in the classics. Like much of the student body, Mallory was more interested in Howard Jones and *The Breakfast Club*.

Dabney later discovered, on a weekend when she gave Jason a ride to visit his sister at Tabor Academy, that Jason hailed from Ipswich, Massachusetts—*just like Oliver Barrett!* Dabney started calling Jason "Preppie." Mallory didn't like when Dabney used this nickname for her boyfriend, nor did she like it when Jason offered to take Dabney to the game. But, as Jason pointed out, he owed Dabney a ride.

Dabney thought that riding to the game with Mallory and Preppie would be fun. She would do it.

She would do it!

Every Monday afternoon, Dabney spoke on the phone for fifty minutes with her therapist, Dr. Donegal. These calls she took on a private line in the office for student life. Unlike Clen, Dr. Donegal never tired of discussing Dabney's issue—a rare form of agoraphobia—or maybe he did, but it was his job. He couldn't fix the problem—after eight years, they had learned it was something that couldn't be fixed—but he helped Dabney manage it.

"I'm going to New Haven," she announced to Dr. Donegal the Monday before the game.

"Excellent," Dr. Donegal said. "It's a big step. I'm proud of you. Are you driving?"

"No," Dabney said. "I'm afraid if I drive myself, I'll panic and head for home. So I'm going to catch a ride with my roommate and her boyfriend."

"Mallory and her boyfriend? The hockey player?"

Dabney loved how Dr. Donegal remembered the details of her life. He was a very good therapist. "Yes," Dabney said. "His parents just gave him a Camaro for his birthday." Dabney had a bit of a car fetish and was a devoted Chevy girl. In truth, the idea of riding in Jason's new Camaro thrilled her, even though she would be smushed like a thirteenth doughnut in the back seat. "Camaros are actually very safe cars."

"Indeed they are," Dr. Donegal said. "You'll be fine."

"Fine," Dabney said.

In her weekly call from the pay phone at the end of the third floor of her dorm on Tuesday evening, she told Clen, "I'm coming."

He said, "I hear you saying that."

She said, "You think I'm going to cancel."

There was silence on his end. He was debating, she knew, whether to state the obvious truth—she always canceled—or prop her up with false confidence.

He chose the latter. "I know you're coming," he said. "I know there is no way you would cancel on coming to the game. You go to Harvard and I go to Yale. I am your boyfriend. You love me, and you'll be safe."

"Safe," she said.

She planned a picnic for the tailgate party: chicken salad sandwiches, a caramelized onion dip made with real onions and *not* dried soup mix, some crackers and good cheese—aged Cheddar, soft Brie—a jar of salted almonds, some plump Italian olives shiny in their oil, and several bunches of good-looking grapes. On Thursday, Dabney prepared everything in the sad, small communal kitchen in the basement of her old freshman dorm, Grays Hall, then posted signs threatening severe consequences if anyone touched it. She could just imagine the softball players on the second floor coming home after a party and devouring the chicken salad.

Next, Dabney considered her outfit. She always wore jeans or a kilt, although for the game, she considered jazzing up her look. But it was November and the forecast for New Haven was sunny and 46 degrees. Jeans, Dabney thought. White oxford shirt, navy peacoat, pearls, penny loafers, headband. That was fine for the game, but Clen had made them a dinner reservation afterward at Mory's Temple Bar, and Dabney needed something fancier. Luckily, she lived just down the hall from Solange, a sophisticate from New York City who had gone to Spence and whose wardrobe included vintage YSL and Valentino pieces that she'd either stolen or salvaged from her mother's closet.

Solange was eager to help Dabney find a new look, not only because Solange liked dressing up her housemates like life-size dolls, but also because Dabney had set up Solange with her current boyfriend, the fabulous Javier from Argentina, whose family owned a ranch bigger than the five boroughs and who, like Solange, was majoring in Romance languages. Dabney had seen a rosy aura around Solange and Javier as they walked out of a Camus seminar together, which meant they were a perfect match. Dabney's special vision had yet to be proved wrong.

Solange rummaged through her closet. Dabney loved how Solange's room was decorated like something from *Arabian Nights*—jewel-toned Persian rugs, a silk pillow the color of a persimmon that was big enough for Dabney to sleep on, and an elaborate hookah that the resident dean did not know about.

Solange produced a black sequined batwing-sleeve blouse. When Dabney tried it on, Solange smiled. "Yes," she said. "Sexy." Dabney had never worn black in her life—Dabney's grandmother had been of the opinion that a woman should not wear black until she turned twenty-five.

"And here," Solange said. "I can't let you wear that blouse with your Levi's." She pulled a pair of velvet cigarette pants out of her closet and a pair of black suede kitten heels with dangerously pointy toes.

Dabney practiced walking around the room in the heels. Was she asking for trouble? Would she trip over herself at Mory's Temple Bar and face-plant in someone's cheese soufflé?

"We're going full throttle here," Solange said. "There is no way you're carrying your Bermuda bag. I want you to take this." Solange handed Dabney a silver cocktail purse that was fringed and beaded like a flapper's dress. "My grandmother carried this as a debutante in 1923. Look!" From out of the purse she produced a silver dollar from that year. "This is my lucky charm. I want you to take it with you on your special weekend."

"Okay," Dabney said. She wondered if lucky charms were transferable. Solange was offering it so earnestly, Dabney decided to believe it would work.

Dabney gazed at herself in the mirror, fully dressed in black. She swished the beaded fringe of the purse so that it looked like the purse was dancing. Dabney no longer resembled herself; she had become someone else—someone exotic and sensual, someone who wasn't afraid to go new places. Someone who wasn't afraid of anything.

On Friday afternoon, Dabney was in her room, starting her paper on J. D. Salinger's *Franny and Zooey*, when there was a knock on the door. It was Kendall from down the hall.

Kendall said, "There's a call for you."

"Call?" Dabney said.

Kendall nodded and tapped the toe of her raspberry-pink Chuck Taylor with clear impatience.

"Is it Clen?" Dabney asked.

"I think so," Kendall said. "Sounded like it."

This was highly unusual. Clen and Dabney spoke only on Tuesday evenings. On Friday afternoons, Kendall spoke to her "best friend," a girl named Alison who went to UNC. Everyone knew that Kendall and Alison were more than just friends. Their phone calls were routinely eavesdropped on because Kendall liked to talk dirty, and every so often Kendall and Alison would have a fight that would be explosive enough to count as high entertainment.

It was ten minutes to four.

"I won't be long," Dabney said. She ran down the hall in her socks to where the receiver was dangling from the pay phone. It looked ominous, like a noose.

"Clen?" she said.

"Hey, Cupe," he said.

"Is everything okay?"

"Yeah," he said. There was a pause, during which Dabney realized he meant just the opposite. "What is it?" she said. "What's wrong?"

"Uh," he said. "Well."

"What?" Dabney noticed that Kendall was lurking in the hall about ten feet away, gazing out the window toward Harvard Yard, ostensibly riveted by the campus visitors heading there to rub the foot of the John Harvard statue, which was supposed to bring applicants good luck. But really Kendall was there so that Dabney did not linger on the phone. Kendall played water polo. She had ten inches and fifty pounds on Dabney and was not unintimidating.

"Well," Clen said again.

Dabney's palms started to sweat. Unlike Kendall and her "best friend" in Chapel Hill, Dabney and Clen never fought on the phone; they never fought, period. All through high school it had been wedded bliss. They had always been in sync, navigating their emotional, physical, intellectual, and sexual blossoming side by side. Their only stumbling block now was the 140 miles that separated them. Despite the fact that they existed in two separate elitist bubbles of higher learning—one crimson, one blue—they had decided to keep up their relationship because to do otherwise was unthinkable. Freshman year had taught them that long-distance relationships were an art and a discipline. The weekly phone calls were part of the discipline. The art came in the letters. Dabney was more prolific, Clen more creative. He had once traced his hands on paper, cut them out, and sent them to Dabney so that she might place them on her shoulders when she needed comforting.

"Clen," Dabney said. "What's wrong?"

"You're definitely coming this weekend, right? There's no chance you're going to cancel?"

Dabney would be lying if she said the thought hadn't crossed her mind a thousand times. She had lain in bed panicking about the trip for over an hour the night before. Despite the carefully prepared picnic and the curated outfit, Dabney's overwhelming urge was to head back to Nantucket for the weekend the way she always did. She sometimes thought of herself as a humpback whale. She could hold her breath for the four and a half days a week she spent in Cambridge, but eventually she had to come up for oxygen. Nantucket Island was her oxygen. It was the only place she felt safe, healthy, whole. The weekends the year before when Clen had come to Cambridge had been torturous, despite his presence, simply because Dabney had to stay on campus instead of going home. Two of those weekends she had actually gotten sick, and Clen had spent hours at her bedside, reading and bringing her soup from the dining hall.

But now that Clen was expressing doubt, Dabney redoubled her fortitude. She would go to New Haven no matter what.

"Yes," she said. "I'm definitely coming. We're leaving here at seven thirty in the morning. I'll be there by ten, just like I said."

"Okay," Clen said. "Because some things have come up."

Kendall emitted a loud, exasperated sigh. Dabney turned around and forced a smile at Kendall, holding up a finger indicating *Just one more minute*. The hall clock said 3:53. "Things like what?"

"I have to cancel dinner at Mory's," Clen said.

"Why?" Dabney said. She felt a sharp sting of

disappointment, and not only because she wouldn't get to wear the fabulous borrowed black outfit or carry the debutante purse. Mory's was a legendary Yale supper club. Dabney had envisioned cold martinis, shrimp cocktail, and dancing to Sinatra between courses.

"Turns out, I'll be on deadline," Clen said. "I have to go back to the paper right after the game."

"You're *kidding* me," Dabney said. "I thought we agreed I was staying over. What about the postgame party at Morse? Are we doing that?"

"We can go for a little while, I guess," Clen said. "I don't know how long I'll be at the paper, though, Cupe. It might be late."

"So you're telling me I'm on my own?" Dabney said. "You're leaving me after the game and you won't be back until late?"

"It's work," Clen said. "I'm writing a big story."

It's work, Dabney thought. *He's writing a big story.* It was a college newspaper — granted, the oldest newspaper in the country — so how big a story could it be? Dabney didn't want to be the kind of girlfriend who complained. Clen had wanted to be a journalist his whole life; it was a consuming passion, and wasn't that one of the things she most loved about him? Nevertheless, a part of her wanted to scream: *Screw the deadline! I have finally mustered the courage to travel to New Haven and you should have cleared your plate!* Clen knew Dabney would not do well with being *left alone* for ... what? Seven hours? Ten hours?

She flashed back to her eight-year-old self at the Park Plaza Hotel. *Where's my mama?*

Your father's on his way, May, the Irish chambermaid, said. Then she sang "American Pie" to Dabney in a lilting accent.

Clen must have known this news would be a deal breaker and that once he announced that he had to work, Dabney would cancel altogether.

He *wanted* her to cancel, she realized.

Kendall cleared her throat. The clock said 3:58.

"No problem!" Dabney said in a false, chipper voice. She would not let this flare up into a loud, messy, emotional brouhaha for Kendall and the other students on the floor to appreciate. "You do what you have to do. I'll see you tomorrow at ten at the east entrance, okay?"

"Okay," Clen said. His voice still held a strain of uncertainty, she thought. What could this mean?

"Okay," Dabney said. She paused, waiting for him to say it first.

"I love you, Cupe."

"And I you," Dabney said. "Bye-bye."

She replaced the receiver at 4:00 on the nose. "It's all yours," she said to Kendall.

Her small overnight bag contained her nightgown, toothbrush, clean underwear, and a pink oxford shirt for Sunday. Dabney had returned the black outfit and purse to Solange with a heavy heart.

"I won't need it after all," Dabney said. "We aren't going out."

"*Merde!*" Solange said. "How come?"

Dabney shrugged. She was too dejected to explain.

Solange, realizing this, pulled the silver dollar out of her grandmother's cocktail purse and pressed it into Dabney's palm. "Take this though, okay? You can give it back to me on Monday."

Dabney put the chicken salad sandwiches and the rest of the picnic in her laundry basket with some strategically placed ice packs. She took one of the Valiums Dr. Donegal had prescribed for emergencies. The silver dollar was deep in the front pocket of her jeans.

She was ready.

Jason had a sign in the window of his Camaro that said YALE BOWL OR BUST! Mallory was already in the front seat working the radio when Dabney climbed in. Mallory was wearing a crimson Harvard hooded sweatshirt and she had woven crimson ribbons through her blond hair. There was a cooler of beer in the back seat, a fact that Dabney initially found alarming—for the past few years the most popular public service announcement had been *Do not drink and drive*—but all around them, people in similarly decorated cars were waving cans of Miller Lite out of windows, and strains of very loud Tears for Fears competed with even louder Spandau

Ballet. It was a tornado of crimson-red fun and Dabney was in the swirling middle of it. This was a novelty; in going home to Nantucket every weekend, Dabney had missed much of college party life. She occasionally went to a party at Owl or Porc on a Thursday night, but that usually meant a disjointed conversation with a couple of upperclassmen/guys/boys about whether Simone de Beauvoir was a genuine intellect or just a slut. Dabney was always back in her room by midnight.

Now Dabney let herself be swept away. She reached over and grabbed a Budweiser from the cooler. "Yale Bowl or bust!" she cried out.

"Whoa there, sister," Mallory said. "Easy now." She settled the radio on "The Boys of Summer," which was a pretty good choice for Mallory.

Jason said, "I like seeing your wild side, Dab." He grinned at her in the rearview mirror.

Mallory swatted Jason's arm. Dabney cracked open her beer and sucked off the foam. She hadn't eaten any breakfast; the only thing in her stomach was the Valium. Jason pulled onto the Mass Pike.

"Better Be Good to Me," Tina Turner.

"Material Girl," Madonna.

"Change this, please," Dabney said. "This song makes me ill."

"Summer of '69," Bryan Adams.

"California Girls," David Lee Roth.

"He ruined a perfectly good song," Dabney said.

"Agreed," Jason said. "You know, I was thinking of writing my thesis on the phenomenon of the cover song—which artists enhanced the originals, which artists desecrated them, which artists equaled them. Do you think that's meaty enough?"

Like many athletes at Harvard, Jason was an American studies major, which was another way of saying "anything goes." But a thesis about *cover songs?*

No, Dabney thought. However, her brain had been hijacked by the Valium and the beer, so the answer that came out of her mouth was "Yes! That's so creative. It will definitely get approval."

Mallory said, "I hate it when you guys talk over me."

Dabney said, "Oops, sorry, you're right." She sank low in the back seat, resting her legs over the cooler.

"Careless Whisper," by Wham!

Something was up with Clen, but Dabney couldn't figure it out. It wasn't as though she had expected a parade—but yes, she had expected a parade. She had expected dinner at Mory's, she had expected Clen to hold her arm proprietarily and introduce her to everyone he knew. *My girlfriend, Dabney Kimball.*

She had not expected to be left to her own devices for seven to ten hours.

"What are you guys doing after the game?" Dabney asked.

"I figure, get drunk before the game, take a flask

into the game, nap in the car, then go find the parties," Jason said. "But we're leaving tomorrow morning at ten o'clock sharp. I have a paper to write on Mark Twain."

"Ten o'clock sharp," Dabney confirmed.

"You must be excited to see Clen," Mallory said. "You guys go, like, months. I'm impressed by the level of trust."

"Trust?" Dabney said.

"Me too," Jason said. "I mean, you're both in college. Does he ever worry that you're going to cheat on him?"

"Cheat?" Dabney said.

"Do you, like, have an understanding?" Mallory asked.

Dabney wasn't sure how to answer this. Words like *trust* and *cheat* didn't really apply to Dabney and Clen. They were melded together; they were, essentially, the same person in two different bodies. It would never occur to Dabney to cheat, and she knew Clen felt the same way. They did have an understanding, which was that they were an unsplittable unit. After college, they would get married.

"Don't You (Forget About Me)," Simple Minds.

Dabney finished her beer, crumpled the can, and closed her eyes.

She awoke as they pulled onto Yale's campus. As far as the eye could see, there was an ocean of blue and crimson.

"Wow," she said. "Wow."

People were everywhere. There were the current students, who came in one of the two color palettes, and then there were alumni—couples in their early thirties with kids in strollers and retrievers on leashes, middle-aged couples with sullen-looking teenagers, and older couples, the men wearing blazers and school ties, the women in wrap dresses and sensible shoes. There was no reason for Dabney's anxiety; what she was witnessing was continuity and tradition. The Harvard-Yale game had been played since 1875. Watching the alumni was like watching different versions of herself and Clen—ten years from now, twenty years, forty years. They had already decided that, no matter what was happening in their lives, they would always attend the Harvard-Yale game. The years the game was held in Cambridge, they would root for Harvard, and the years it was held in New Haven, they would root for Yale. Presumably Yale would, in time, feel comfortable and familiar to Dabney. Safe. Not like now.

"East entrance," Dabney said. "That's where I'm meeting him. Where is it? Do we know where it is?" She felt her angst mounting, straining against the muting effects of the Valium like a bulging tummy against a girdle. She did not like new, unfamiliar places. They terrified her. The only person who halfway understood was her friend Albert Maku, who came from Plettenberg Bay, South Africa.

Were you afraid to come to Harvard? Dabney had asked him.

Yes, afraid, very afraid, Albert said. *It's like setting foot on another planet, where no one is familiar and I do not know the rules.*

Planet New Haven was overwhelming, even for sane people like Jason and Mallory.

"Jesus," Jason said. "I'm just going to park here."

"Is this near the east entrance?" Dabney said.

"I don't know," Jason said. "But it's a parking lot and there are other Harvard cars here. This is where we're parking."

Dabney squeezed her eyes shut and wished that she had gotten a ride from the guys at Owl. Clark, who wore horn-rimmed glasses in a perfect imitation of Clark Kent, had promised to hand-deliver Dabney to Clendenin. Now Dabney would have to find him on her own while lugging her picnic-in-a-laundry-basket.

She climbed out of the car and smoothed the legs of her jeans, straightened her pearls, and took a deep breath. Clen was here. He was at the east entrance. All Dabney had to do was find it and she would be safe.

She looked down at her penny loafers. They were resting solidly on the earth.

Jason and Mallory offered to walk with Dabney, which really meant that Jason offered. Mallory seemed put off by Jason's show of gallantry; in fact, she seemed downright jealous, huffing under her breath that she didn't see why they had to do this; Dabney had gotten into Harvard, she could find the east entrance herself.

Jason forged ahead, undeterred. He was carrying the laundry basket, which got him a lot of attention.

"Hey, man, you looking for the Wash 'n' Dry?"

"No, man, it's a picnic," Jason said. "Chicken salad, the best you ever tasted."

"I don't know why you would say that," Mallory snapped.

"It *was* really good," Jason said. "I gave you a bite." He offered Dabney a look of apology. "I ate one while you were asleep. I didn't want to stop at Burger King."

"No problem, Preppie," Dabney said.

They stopped and asked a young man in parachute pants for directions. He pointed them the right way.

"Clen better be on time," Mallory said. "Because I'm not waiting around."

Dabney scanned the surroundings. So many people.

"Cupe!"

There he was, standing alone, wearing his brown corduroy jacket with the fake shearling collar. He'd owned that jacket forever.

Dabney ran to him.

She was safe. Clen was real and strong and warm; he had a body and eyes and a voice. He had shaved. He smelled like himself. He picked Dabney up off the ground, and the days and weeks and months that she had pined for him evaporated. He was her oxygen. She could breathe.

"I can't believe you're here," he said in her ear. "I. Can't. Believe. It." He set her down. "You are in New Haven, Connecticut." He looked genuinely shocked and delighted, like she was Santa Claus or the Tooth Fairy or the Easter Bunny. Dabney was embarrassed. The other ten thousand people present had managed to get here without fanfare. Why was her arrival such a big deal?

But she knew why. She felt like she had flown without wings. It was that astonishing.

"You remember Mallory," Dabney said. "And this is her boyfriend, Jason."

Clen stepped forward and shook hands with Mallory and accepted the laundry basket from Jason.

"You're a lucky man," Jason said. "That's some picnic."

Dabney pulled out sandwiches for Jason and Mallory. "I'll see you tomorrow at ten sharp," she said. "I'll meet you right here."

"See ya," Mallory said. She handed Jason her sandwich and turned to go.

Jason, however, being a properly raised Ipswich preppy, offered a farewell. "Have fun, Dab. Thanks for the sandwiches. And hey, nice to meet you, Clen. Great girl you've got there."

Clen said, "I know. Thanks for the safe delivery."

Elation! They were arm in arm; he was happy to see her. The confusion and hesitancy she had heard in his voice over the phone the day before had been a figment of her imagination or caused by Kendall's stalking. The first thing Clen did once Mallory and Jason walked away was set the laundry basket down, hold Dabney's face, and kiss her deeply. God, the rush, the chemistry— it was the same now as it had been during their first kiss at the top of the hill at Dead Horse Valley during an early snowstorm. December 1, 1980, when they were freshmen in high school.

"I want to take you back to my room right this instant," he said.

"Yes," she said. "Take me, take me."

"But I can't," he said. "Because the *Daily News* has a tailgate all set up and we're expected."

Dabney felt cranky about the tailgate, even though Clen had warned her this was the first thing on the docket. She wanted him to herself; a ludicrous wish, she realized, as nearly the whole point of her coming to New Haven was to witness his life here, and the *Yale Daily News* was a large part of that life. The paper. It was as important as his coursework, possibly more so.

She said, "Maybe we can cut out on the game and go to your room?"

He said, "Cut out on the game?"

Ridiculous, right; she still wasn't thinking clearly— the Valium, the beer. She sounded like a sex-starved fiend; she should explain, perhaps, that it wasn't the sex she wanted as much as the time behind closed doors, alone—Clen had a single—his attention shining solely on her.

"We're over here," Clen said. He picked up his pace, the laundry basket held out in front of him. Dabney should have scoured the storage closets for a proper cooler. She hurried along, trying to keep up. There was the same woody Clen had driven to Harvard the year before, and next to it was a cluster of card tables that looked like a raft cobbled together by desperate castaways.

"There you are, Hughes!" A guy/boy/man stepped forward. "And you brought your wash!"

"Shut up, Wallace," Clen said.

It was Henry Wallace, Dabney realized, the editor in chief of the *Yale Daily News.* Clen never stopped talking about him. Wallace had been the one to recognize Clen's talents and make him a features editor as a freshman.

Clen set the laundry basket down on the tailgate of the wagon and ushered Dabney forward. "My girlfriend, Dabney Kimball."

Henry Wallace was tall with curly brown hair and square black glasses. Like so many people Dabney had met in the past year, he had the unmistakable air of the well-bred prep-school eternally privileged set. He took Dabney's hand and kissed it.

"A real live Cliffie in our midst," he said. "I'm Henry David Thoreau Wallace, fellow citizen of your fine commonwealth. Lovely to meet you."

"Lovely to meet *you*," Dabney said. "I've heard all about what a genius you are."

"Cupe," Clen said. He sounded embarrassed, and Dabney grinned at Henry.

"He talks about you all the time," she said. "I've grown quite jealous of you, you know. Although I'm mad as the dickens that you have my beau on deadline this weekend."

"Deadline?" Henry said. "The only person on deadline this weekend is the sports editor." He searched over Dabney's head. "Reese better be in the stadium getting his pregame interviews, not out getting wasted on bloodies."

No deadline? When Dabney turned to Clen with the question in her eyes, he shook his head and handed her a plastic cup. "Vodka tonic," he said. "For my Cliffie."

Dabney said, "Are you still on deadline?"

But before Clen could answer, they were interrupted. "You brought a picnic to a picnic?" A girl with long, dark, straight, shiny hair was peering into the laundry basket. Her hair was so beautiful it was impossible not to stare. If Dabney had hair like that, she would have felt immodest leaving it loose.

"Maybe you think a Harvard picnic is naturally superior to a Yale picnic," the girl said. "But I don't think anything from Harvard is superior."

Dabney immediately felt defensive. This girl wore jeans, a camel-colored cashmere wrap, and large gold hoop earrings. She was pretty—gorgeous, actually. Her eyes were dark blue. Some of her luscious hair fell over her face as she gazed up at Clen.

"Aren't you going to introduce me, Hughes?" she said.

Dabney glanced at Clen. He looked supremely uncomfortable, and Dabney felt an unfamiliar rumbling in her gut. Jealousy, she realized.

"Jocelyn Harris, this is Dabney Kimball. Dabney, this is Jocelyn. Our arts editor."

"Hi," Dabney said. She offered a hand and Jocelyn shook it quickly, as though a Harvard hand might give her a communicable disease. Then she reached into her buttery leather shoulder bag and brought out a pack of Newports and a matchbook that Dabney couldn't help noticing was from Mory's Temple Bar. Jocelyn lit two cigarettes and held one out to Clen, but he waved it away.

"No, thanks."

"What, all of a sudden you don't smoke?" Jocelyn said. She offered Dabney a poisonous smile. "You don't smoke, do you, Dabney?"

Mute, Dabney shook her head. She wanted to say, *Clen doesn't smoke either.* Except clearly he did smoke. He smoked with this girl, Jocelyn. Dabney located a second Valium in her jeans pocket, right next to the lucky silver dollar. She didn't want to be here. She would rather have been at Harvard in Solange's room, sitting on the persimmon silk pillow. Dabney washed the

Valium down with some of her vodka tonic. She had consumed nothing that day except pills and booze; she was turning into the Joan Collins character in *Dynasty*, minus the glamour.

Jocelyn shook the cigarette insistently at Clen. "Just take it, Hughes."

"I don't want it, thanks."

Jocelyn scoffed. "I don't get it. You're afraid to smoke in front of your friend here?"

His girlfriend, Dabney thought. *I'm his girlfriend.* It suddenly seemed imperative that Jocelyn know this. She realized that Clen had not introduced her as such. He had just said, *This is Dabney Kimball.*

Clen sighed. "Be nice, Jocelyn."

At that second, Henry Wallace swooped in and took the cigarette from Jocelyn. He grinned at Dabney. "Our arts editor has a flair for the dramatic," he said. "Which is why I hired her. I, for one, can't wait to taste a Harvard picnic."

Dabney set out her picnic on the rickety card tables with a sense of purpose, relieved to have something to do with her hands while her thoughts fell to pieces. Clen didn't have a deadline, at least not one the editor in chief knew about. Or maybe Dabney had misunderstood. The Valium was making her fuzzy. She felt like she was forty years old, matronly and persnickety; at that point, she would be in charge of children's birthday parties and soccer-team potlucks while this Jocelyn roamed the streets of Florence antiquing or hopped

from gallery to gallery in SoHo. Jocelyn had glamour —
that hair, that sneer, those eyes like pure, hard sap-
phires. And the way she'd pushed a cigarette on Clen,
something she had held briefly in her mouth that would
then go into his mouth. Dabney got it, or at least she
thought she got it. *Trust. Cheat.* Jocelyn and Clen had
been together.

She set out the sandwiches, the chips, the onion dip,
the cheese and crackers, the salted almonds, the grapes,
the plump, glistening olives. This *was* a better picnic
than the Yale picnic, she thought. The Yale picnic con-
sisted of tortilla chips and jarred salsa, a box of Triscuits,
and a bowl of microwaved popcorn.

Glory was hers when the flocks descended on her
sandwiches, devoured her dip. "God, what is *in* this?
Heroin? It's out of this world!"

Clen wolfed down two sandwiches without even
breathing, saying, "Really good, Cupe. Really damned
good." He went over to the bar that was set up on a
card table to make them some more drinks, and Dabney followed him. Somewhere, a marching band played.

She said, "So tell me about Jocelyn."

Clen filled their cups with ice and poured generously from the Popov bottle. He shrugged. "Tell you
what? She works on the paper. Arts editor, flair for the
dramatic." Clen was overly enthusiastic with the tonic
and the first cup bubbled over. "She can be a real bitch."

Dabney accepted her drink and reached for a wedge
of lime. "Well, yeah. I noticed."

"Your picnic is beautiful, Cupe," Clen said. "I mean, look, it's almost gone." He gazed off in the direction of the stadium. "Jocelyn's just jealous."

"Jealous of what?" Dabney said. She wanted clarification. Was she jealous that Dabney went to Harvard? Was she jealous that Dabney could cook? Or was there some other reason, something that had to do with Clen?

Clen didn't have time to answer, because at that moment, voices filled the air. The Whiffenpoofs were forming a semicircle in front of the *Daily News* tailgate. The Whiffenpoofs! Dabney felt a flutter of celebrity awe. She loved traditions like this; the most famous a cappella group in the country was *right here!* Dabney forgot about Jocelyn—she had disappeared into the crowd anyway—and grabbed Clen's arm.

"The Whiffenpoofs!" she said. "They're going to sing!"

"That's what they do," Clen said. He bent down and whispered in her ear. "Wallace's twin brother is the one in the middle. Ralph, his name is. Ralph Waldo Emerson Wallace."

"You're kidding me," Dabney said. Sure enough, the tall guy in the center looked exactly like Henry—same hair, same smile, same glasses.

"Henry asked Ralph to stop here," Clen said, "because I told him you would want to see them."

Dabney felt a thrill run up her backbone and explode in euphoria at the base of her neck. The Whiffenpoofs were here . . . to sing to her!

Ralph leaned in and hummed to give everyone the key, then they launched into "Ride the Chariot."

Dabney swooned. The voices blended and separated and blended again, melodies, harmonies, top lines, bass lines.

Next "The Boxer." Then "Is She Really Going Out with Him?" And one more—"Brown-Eyed Girl," which was Clen and Dabney's song. Clen led Dabney to a clearing a short way from the car and they danced.

"Did you ask them to sing this?" she asked.

"What do you think?" he said.

Dabney looked down at her penny loafers. This time, she was surprised when she saw they were touching the ground.

It was almost a disappointment to head into the stadium. Dabney had managed to eat one chicken salad sandwich and grab a few bites of the onion dip before the bowl was licked clean. Everything she had brought had been devoured. *So there!* Dabney thought.

Harvard 1, Yale 0.

Dabney saw Jocelyn again inside the Yale Bowl. She was sitting three rows ahead of Clen and Dabney and five seats to their left. She was with a girl with curly blond hair and two guys/boys/men, one of whom was wearing a white cardigan sweater with a blue Y that looked like it had been rescued from a 1952 time capsule and the other of whom wore a plain gray T-shirt and a baseball hat and seemed like he had just rolled out of bed.

Dabney prayed that either Letter Sweater or Boy Who Just Woke Up was Jocelyn's boyfriend.

There was a lot of fanfare before the game began. The Class of 1935 ran out onto the field—seventeen men were remaining, more than double that were killed in World War II, a moment of silence. The presentation of Handsome Dan, the bulldog—wild applause. Then the Spizzwinks sang the national anthem; the Spizzwinks were the underclassman version of the Whiffenpoofs. The person who named these groups must have been smoking opium with Lewis Carroll, Dabney thought.

Then...kickoff! The crowd went bananas. Dabney and Clen stood up along with the rest of the stadium and cheered.

Jocelyn turned around and appeared to be searching for someone. She was wearing brown cat's-eye sunglasses.

The kickoff returner for Harvard was tackled on the twenty-five-yard line, and the crowd sat down.

Clen turned to Dabney. "Do you want anything?"

She said, "Nope, I'm good."

He fidgeted in his seat. For all his enthusiasm about the game, Clen didn't really like to watch football, or any other sport. Dabney was much better at that. She had been the head of the pep squad at Nantucket High School and the editor of the yearbook, had played tennis and sailed at the Nantucket Yacht Club, and had surfed every beach on Nantucket that could possibly be surfed. She had fished for stripers off the tip of Great Point and hunted for ducks on Tuckernuck with her father. She had written her college essay about the duck hunting, actually, tying it into her relationship with her father, which was important and special, since her mother had left when Dabney was eight years old.

Abandoned her.

Half the crowd was cheering, the crimson half. Harvard's quarterback, Blood Dellman, had completed a seventeen-yard pass for the first down. Dabney bowed her head. Something was still off. Why this gnawing sense of insecurity? Why did she feel the need to mentally list all of her accomplishments and assure herself of her own value? And why, at this particular moment, when she and Clen were finally together, did the memory of her mother leaving have to steal in—the one thing certain to make her feel worthless? Goddamn it—tears were now blurring her eyes. This was ridiculous and uncalled for. Dabney did not do drama. Along with Most Popular, Smartest Girl, and Most School Spirit, Dabney had been voted Most Comfortable in Her Skin on the senior-class superlative page.

Dabney raised her head in time to see Jocelyn leave the stadium without looking at Clen or Dabney. Her eyes stayed forward, her chin raised, her camel-colored cashmere wrap flowing off her like cool water. Dabney gazed at the empty seat Jocelyn had left behind with the kind of relief one felt upon having an aching tooth pulled.

A minute later, Clen stood. "I have to go to the john," he said. "And I might get a Coke. Do you want one?"

Dabney stood. "Yes," she said. "I'll go with you."

"You stay here, please, and enjoy the game," he said. "Protect our seats. I'll get you a Coke. Anything else?"

"No," she said. She sank down into her seat. She thought, *He's going out there to see Jocelyn. To smoke a cigarette with Jocelyn.* He smoked cigarettes now. It was no big deal, except he hadn't told Dabney, and he told her everything. Or he used to. Probably he was ashamed about it. But Dabney understood that he was under a lot of pressure with the newspaper, and pressure led people to smoke.

Dabney watched Clen head up the concrete steps, out of the stadium. She redirected her attention to the game, but she could focus only long enough to watch Blood Dellman—whose given name was William Youngblood Dellman, a young aristocrat just like everyone else—throw an interception, which the Yale cornerback returned for a touchdown.

The blue half of the stadium was cheering.

Advantage Yale.

Suddenly, Dabney heard her name being called, and she saw Mallory and Jason picking their way across rows of people—*Sorry, 'scuse me*—toward her. Jason took Clen's empty seat and Mallory took the empty seat next to him.

"We found you!" Jason said. He seemed ecstatic about this fact, as though their plan all along had been to meet up, but Dabney knew this had not been their plan. "Where's the big guy?"

"I don't know," Dabney said. "He went to get a Coke or something, I guess."

They all watched Yale kick the extra point.

"This sucks," Jason said. He stood up, cupped his hands around his mouth, and yelled, "Come on, Harvard, you pussies!"

Dabney looked past Jason at Mallory. Mallory was so cold, her lips were blue. "Are you having fun?" Dabney asked.

Mallory shrugged. "No," she said.

Dabney wasn't having fun either. She admired Mallory for just being able to admit it. Maybe that was the Montana girl in her. Dabney had inherited the stiff upper lip, but today it wasn't doing her any good.

Mallory said, "I think Jason likes you."

"What?" Dabney said. She looked up at Jason, mortified that he might have overheard this, but Jason was wholly absorbed in the game.

"I think he, like, *like*-likes you," Mallory said.

Dabney was impressed that Mallory had managed to use the word *like* three times in a row and still make sense.

"No, he does not. Don't be stupid. You're beautiful, Mallory. He likes you."

"You were gone for, like, five minutes before he wanted

to try and find you. We've been searching for, like, half an hour. And he kept telling me how you loved the idea for his thesis."

"Oh my God," Dabney said. She did *not* love the idea for Jason's thesis; at best, she thought it might make an amusing party game at four in the morning while drunk or stoned. *Which is better, original or cover?*

"And when he was eating your sandwich?" Mallory said. "He was making *noises*. It sounded like...like he was having an *orgasm*."

"You have to stop," Dabney said. Jason was standing right between them, although she could tell he wasn't paying attention. He let out a loud, piercing whistle for something that happened on the field.

"I'm serious," Mallory said. "You somehow managed to steal my boyfriend."

"I did no such thing!" Dabney said.

"I really like living with you," Mallory said. "But I don't want you to ride home with us tomorrow."

Before Dabney could respond with the obvious question — *How will I get home, then?* — Jason plopped down into the seat between them and wrapped one arm around Dabney and one around Mallory. "How are my best girls?" he said.

Dabney stood up. "I'm going to find Clen," she said.

She headed up the stairs toward the concession area. Jason did *not* like her. Or rather, he liked her, most people liked her, but he was not interested in her romantically. Possibly he thought she was smart or interesting or a good cook. Jealousy was making Mallory irrational. Dabney had not *stolen* her boyfriend! She erased from her mind the time when she drove Jason to visit his sister at Tabor Academy and he had noticed Dabney chewing on her pearls and had, gently, removed them from her mouth and arranged them back around her neck. His hand had lingered on her clavicle for an extra second or two. Dabney laughed and said, "Thanks, Preppie."

Now she would be stuck here in New Haven unless she could talk Mallory out of her nonsense or find Clark from Owl. How would she ever find Clark?

There were many scary things about new places, the scariest perhaps being all the people Dabney didn't know. So many people. On Nantucket, Dabney knew nearly everyone; she had known most of them since she was born, and those she didn't know knew her father or her grandparents or her great-grandparents. Even in her second year at Harvard, she knew approximately one out of every four people she saw there. But here at the Yale Bowl, she faced a mass of unrecognizable humanity.

Until she spotted Clen and Jocelyn.

They were standing together, an island in the shifting sea of crimson and blue. Dabney blinked. Jocelyn had her arms around Clen's neck; her fingers were deep in his thick, dark hair. He looked like he was trying to pull away; his hands were on her shoulders but he seemed to be trying to keep her at bay rather than bring her closer. Dabney's eyes saw a green cloud, like tear gas, hovering above them.

Well, she thought, they weren't a perfect match. Green clouds like that were a very bad sign.

Clen was telling Jocelyn something. She nodded, then she said something, and Clen shook his head and said, loud enough for Dabney to hear, "I'm sorry, Joss. No."

Jocelyn slapped him.

Slapped him. Dabney was close enough to hear the sound it made. Close enough to feel the sting, and although Dabney did not do drama, she could say without much exaggerating that it felt like Jocelyn had slapped her heart.

Clen remained still. He didn't move anything except his eyes, which somehow found Dabney's in the crowd. He said something to Jocelyn and moved toward Dabney.

She thought, *What have you done?*

She wanted to run away, but where would she go? She reached into her pocket and rubbed the silver dollar. *Be a lucky charm for me,* she thought. *Please!*

In the stadium, the crowd cheered. Something had happened. Dabney no longer cared what.

She couldn't imagine how Clen would explain himself. She certainly did *not* expect him to smile. But that was what he did. He grinned at Dabney and reached for her hand and said, "I have good news."

Dabney stared at him. Her hand was numb; it was

like it wasn't even attached to her body. She thought of the paper hands Clen had sent in a letter. She had done as he had instructed and placed them on her shoulders when she felt lonely. She was such an idiot.

"And what," she said, "would that be?"

"I don't have to work at the *News* tonight," he said. "We can go to Mory's like we planned."

A small part of Dabney felt cheered by this news. She thought, *The lucky charm worked!* Now her only regret was that she'd returned the sultry black outfit to Solange.

But who was she kidding? There would be no Mory's—no ice-cold martinis, no colossal shrimp cocktail, no dancing to Sinatra.

"You never had to work at the *News,*" Dabney said.

"I . . . yes, I did."

"No, you didn't. I heard what Henry said, Clen. The only person on deadline today is the sports editor. You were never on deadline; you made it up. You lied to me. You had plans with Jocelyn. Are you dating her?"

"Not dating her," he said.

"She had her hands in your *hair,*" Dabney said. "She lit you a cigarette. She looked at me like I had a raging case of hives, and she just slapped you."

"She was angry."

"About what?"

Clen blew air out his nose. This was what he normally did when he was upset or frustrated; Dabney had seen it hundreds of times. She knew him so well.

For the years they were in high school, she knew every book he'd read, every record album he owned and his top three favorite tracks on each; she knew every movie he'd seen, she knew about every fight he'd had with his mother, she knew what he would order off any menu, she knew he sneezed in threes, she knew the way his face looked when he was sleeping. She would have said there was nothing she didn't know about Clendenin Hughes, but she was wrong. It was natural, she supposed. They were in college, they were forging identities. When Dabney had gotten into Harvard (she hadn't applied anywhere else) and Clen Yale, people said it would be healthy for them to be separated, to have some space. Space—140 miles. Space—room to lie.

"Tell me why she's angry," Dabney said.

"Because," Clen said.

"Because why?"

"Because she asked me to go to this alumni event tonight, a formal thing, a dinner-dance thing. Her parents are in town, apparently, and her father is top of the masthead at the *Wall Street Journal,* and…I told her I'd go. I thought for sure you were going to cancel on me, Cupe. You always cancel. But then you showed up and I do love you so goddamned much, but it's hard being apart, and I get lonely and Jocelyn is persistent, she doesn't hear the word *no.* She's used to getting what she wants."

"And she wants you."

"I guess so," Clen said. "But I told her, I mean, I was *clear* that I'm taken. I belong to you, Dabney Kimball."

And yet he had planned on leaving her for seven to ten hours while he went to a formal alumni dinner-dance thing with Jocelyn and her influential parents. Dabney caught a glimpse of herself in Clen's dorm room, lying on his bed, sniffing his pillowcase for his scent. She would have read *Franny and Zooey* for the umpteenth time and tried again to figure out why Franny never made it to the football game with Lane Coutell, why she never took a bite of her chicken sandwich but felt okay enough to smoke seventeen cigarettes in a forty-page story. She would have waited, thinking how dedicated Clen was to the newspaper, while in reality Clen was eating bloody prime rib and stroking Jocelyn's long hair and trying to sound impressive for Jocelyn's father. Dabney felt sorry for the girl who would have waited alone in Clen's dorm room, but that girl was not her—because she was leaving.

Jealousy, cheat, trust, *like*-likes, crimson and blue, Harvard, Yale, Spizzwinks, Whiffenpoofs, Henry David Thoreau, Ralph Waldo Emerson, the transcendentalists, Handsome Dan, nearly fifty Yale graduates killed in World War II. People had problems, Dabney thought. Her father had fought in Vietnam, and he came back different. Dabney's mother couldn't handle it. *She didn't leave because of you, honey. She left because of me.* Dabney's father had told her that once when they were duck hunting.

But she did leave me, Dabney thought. Her own daughter, her only child.

There was a game taking place on the football field, and there were, Dabney supposed, other games being played here in the Yale Bowl.

She turned away from Clen. He said, "Wait a minute, where are you going?"

Back to Jason's car, she thought, even though Mallory didn't want her. *To find Clark from Owl. To find a pay phone.* She would call Solange and go back to Cambridge. Or she would call Dr. Donegal and go back to Nantucket. Where was she going? Anywhere but here.

She started walking and people rushed past her, so many people, they swallowed her up, making her invisible. If Clen didn't move right this minute, she knew, he would never find her.

It's like setting foot on another planet, where no one is familiar and I do not know the rules.

Yes, Dabney thought. That was it. That was it exactly.

Barbie's Wedding
(Read with *The Rumor*)

This story was written as a bonus chapter for my 2015 novel *The Rumor*. It takes place after the novel has ended and focuses on one of my favorite minor characters of all time, Barbie Pancik, the tough, street-smart sister of Fast Eddie Pancik. In *The Rumor,* Barbie is something of a mystery. She doesn't discuss anything "P"—for *personal*—with anyone, including her brother. Barbie is a savvy, even ruthless, businesswoman and is intent on making money in her and Eddie's real estate company—but we find out in the novel that she is also secretly dating their business rival, Glenn Daley. In "Barbie's Wedding"—you guessed it—Barbie and Glenn are about to get married.

But it's complicated.

I absolutely loved telling this story from Barbie's point of view. It was great fun for me to delve into a minor character's head and tell a story that fleshes out the world I created in *The Rumor.*

Because Eddie is in jail, there is no one to give her away. That's the first thing she thinks after Glenn slips the ring on her finger.

The second thing she thinks is: *I'm too old for a big wedding, but I'm going to have one anyway.*

Glenn lays a big, juicy kiss on her in front of everyone in the office — which, as she's worked there scarcely a week, she still thinks of as *Glenn's office*. Everyone claps even louder than they did when Barbie said yes. Another woman might have been annoyed at the public proposal, but, especially since Glenn and Barbie had been so dead set on (and so successful at) keeping their relationship a secret, Barbie likes finally having everything out in the open. She feels honored that Glenn would want to put his love for her on display. She is forty-one years old, and most of this island certainly thought she would go to her grave a spinster.

The ring is an absolute stunner — three point one carats (as Glenn whispers in her ear only seconds after it's on her finger; he's a stickler for details like that, and he knows Barbie is too. If he hadn't told her, she might have run right into Jewel of the Isle and had it appraised). It is nearly as big as the black pearl Barbie wears around her neck, a pearl she bought with her first five-figure commission because she could. She'd lied and told Glenn that the pearl had been given to her by a man named Earl Fischer, a hedge-fund manager who retired to the north shore of Oahu to surf and play golf. Earl Fischer doesn't exist. Barbie made him up in order to make Glenn jealous and also to hide the fact that, aside from Glenn Daley, she's never been in a real, adult relationship.

There was Tony Harlowe in high school — too upsetting to think about — and a few one-night stands with men she didn't know and would never see again. One of the one-nighters was named Comanche Jones. This she remembers because who could forget *that* name? Comanche Jones had a bald spot the size of a drinks coaster on the back of his head and a bit of a paunch; he was the "head manager" at the Sports Authority in Hyannis. Barbie had met him at the bar at Not Your Average Joe's at the mall when she was stranded during a snowstorm, and one thing led to another, aided by five or six prickly pear margaritas. To be painfully honest, the best thing about Comanche Jones had been his name; Barbie later suspected he had made it up, although this hadn't stopped her from telling Glenn that she had "dated" a man named Comanche Jones.

There had been many, many lies and exaggerations to Glenn in the eighteen months of their dating, mostly harmless fibs about Barbie's romantic past, but some lies were bigger, the most troubling among them Barbie's claim that she had had no involvement in the prostitution ring on Low Beach Road. The conversations Eddie had had with his attorney were confidential, but Barbie knew that word on the cobblestones was that Eddie had offered a confession as long as Barbie was spared.

He would be in jail for three and a half years.

Glenn had asked about this point-blank. "Did you know what your brother was doing out there? Those poor, innocent girls! Jeez, it turns my stomach to think about it."

Barbie said, "I had no idea, obviously. I'm a woman myself, Glenn. Do you think I would have allowed Eddie to debase them like that?"

"One was only seventeen years old," Glenn says. "A baby. And so far from home."

Barbie could never have admitted her involvement— the whole thing had been her idea!—nor could she point out that the girls, although young and far from home, were hardly victims. They were willing participants who had been more eager for the money than even Eddie or Barbie. The cash they pocketed had improved their quality of life, and they'd gotten to meet some interesting men. Barbie had overheard Gabrielle talking to Nadia about IPO offerings and stock options and a prospectus for a company she was considering investing in.

"I thought Eddie was hiding something," Barbie said to Glenn. "I wish I'd paid closer attention. I would have stopped him before he started."

Glenn had kissed the tip of her nose. "That's my girl."

Barbie had sensed his palpable relief. She and Glenn were madly in love, but nobody wanted to propose marriage to a felon, even an unconvicted one.

After the public proposal in the office, Glenn announces that he and Barbie are taking the rest of the day off. Barbie notes the baleful expression on Rachel McMann's face, so Barbie treats Rachel to a view of her nostrils, an upturned nose. Rachel is a hemorrhoid. She reminds Barbie of the girls she used to fight in high school. However, Rachel is one of Glenn's favorites in the office — why, Barbie isn't quite sure. Maybe because she's both anal about her work and a kiss-ass.

But Glenn hasn't proposed marriage to Rachel McMann, has he? He has proposed to Barbie Pancik, and they are taking the rest of the day off!

They leave the office and climb into Glenn's Cadillac Escalade. The weight of the diamond on Barbie's finger is delicious. She wishes she could call Eddie.

Glenn says, "Now that we're getting married, you can sell your Triumph. I'll buy you something more practical."

Before Barbie can stop herself, she says, "No, that's okay. I'll keep the Triumph."

Glenn is silent, and Barbie thinks that they've been engaged for five minutes and already there are territory wars.

Glenn knows that Barbie loves her Triumph, and Barbie knows that Glenn hates it because he's too big to fit in it. He chews on his knees and the seat belt doesn't clear his girth. On the one hand, Barbie feels she should concede and let Glenn buy her a car that he will be comfortable in. On the other hand, the Triumph is Barbie's ride. It's a signature piece in the life she has painstakingly curated.

"That car needs too much maintenance," Glenn says.

"It's good on gas," Barbie says. "And it's impressive to clients."

"Clients don't like to be squished," Glenn says.

Barbie stares out the window at the streets of Nantucket. It's the last week of August and the island is jam-packed with summer visitors. Barbie would like to put her window down and flutter her ring at everyone. She sees Roy Weedon, another real estate agent, standing on Broad Street with a couple who look like potential buyers—the woman carries a Nantucket Lightship basket, and the husband's hands are stuffed deep in his pockets (Barbie's guess is that the wife is dying for a house but the husband doesn't want to spend the money). Barbie waves at Roy, but he doesn't see her.

"That's something you and your brother have in common," Glenn says. "You're both wavers."

Barbie lets this comment slide. She loves Eddie to

death but Glenn pointing out their commonalities will only lead to a complex conversation. "Where are we going?" she asks.

"Yacht club," Glenn says. "Lunch."

It's almost embarrassing how excited Barbie is. She has lived on Nantucket for over twenty years and has never been invited inside the yacht club. Dating Glenn Daley was her best chance to go, but in the eighteen months that they've been together, he's never once invited her. Their relationship was under wraps, but Barbie hinted that Glenn might bring her there as a colleague. Real estate agents have lunch together all the time. But at the Nantucket Yacht Club, business is verboten, so if Glenn had taken Barbie to lunch there, it would have to have been as a friend, and then, possibly, people would have figured out their secret.

"Why do you want to go to lunch there so badly, anyway?" Glenn had asked.

Barbie shrugged. We all want what we can't have. Eddie had sat on the waiting list of the Nantucket Yacht Club for over ten years until he eventually joined at Great Harbor. Eddie told Barbie once, in confidence, that he knew he would never get into the Nantucket Yacht Club. He'd said, "They don't want people like us."

Barbie didn't have to ask what he meant; she knew. He meant they didn't want people with Slavic last names. They didn't want kids who had grown up above a dry cleaner's in New Bedford. The Nantucket Yacht Club was for blue bloods. Glenn Daley was a member because his ex-wife, Ashland Daley, was old summer money, and when they'd divorced and Ashland moved to California, Glenn wisely held on to the membership.

Glenn parks the Cadillac and escorts Barbie inside.

Barbie tries to absorb every detail; she had such elevated expectations that even if it looked like the Hall of Mirrors at Versailles, she might be disappointed. The inside of the Nantucket Yacht Club is unremarkable, although Barbie realizes the word she should use is *understated*. She clicks in her heels down the blond polished-wood floors, past a glass cabinet that displays sailing and tennis trophies. In front of her is a ballroom where, at the moment, children are playing badminton. The whole place smells of bacon and French fries; Barbie's stomach rumbles.

The receptionist smiles at them and says, "Good afternoon, Mr. Daley. A little lunch?"

Glenn leads Barbie through French doors to the back patio. Here is the true beauty of the yacht club, Barbie sees: the brick patio with wrought-iron tables under navy-blue canvas umbrellas. At the end of the patio is a thick green lawn that reaches all the way to the harbor. There are sweeping views of the Brant Point lighthouse. The sky is bright and cloudless; the flags snap; sailboats bob in the harbor.

A raven-haired woman whom Barbie recognizes from an exercise class she took a million years earlier is playing "Falling in Love Again" on an upright piano.

Barbie waves at her enthusiastically and thinks of say-ing, *I didn't know you worked here!* She hadn't expected live music at lunch, but she sees how civilized it is.

Civilized had been Mrs. Schaffer's favorite word. Bar-bie wishes Mrs. Schaffer were still alive so that Barbie could tell her about her engagement. Mrs. Schaffer had worried about Barbie ending up alone.

Barbie scans the other tables for people she recog-nizes. There is no one. But is this *possible?* No, wait—there's a retired lawyer at a corner table; they did at least a dozen real estate closings together, but Barbie doubts he will recall her name. Barbie sees the smart-looking woman who was married to the late superintendent of schools. Everyone else is unfamiliar. Most of the people are older, although there is one convivial table of beau-tiful mommies all wearing tennis whites. The members aren't as dressed up as Barbie thought they might be; in her mind, this place had taken on such a grandeur that she expected couture. She is definitely among the best dressed of the women in her DVF wrap dress and nude Manolo stilettos. If anything, she is overdressed; she wonders if it looks like she's trying too hard.

Glenn pulls out a chair for Barbie at a table for two. He says, "Can you see yourself being a member here, Mrs. Daley?"

Mrs. Daley. Barbie's head spins. *A member here.* When Eddie gets out of jail, the first thing she will do is bring him here for lunch.

"I think I *will* sell the Triumph," she says.

*   *   *

Part of Barbie thinks that, before she makes a single wedding arrangement, she should right her wrongs and tell Glenn the truth about everything: There is no man in her past named Earl Fischer, and she "dated" Comanche Jones for all of twelve hours. And she *was* involved in the prostitution ring on Low Beach Road; in fact, the whole thing had been her idea. She tries to remember if she'd lied to Glenn about anything else.

There was the matter of the crystal ball.

Barbie's crystal ball has created more problems than it's solved. It told her flat out that Grace would cheat on Eddie and that Madeline would do something unspeakably awful to Grace. Glenn has expressed what Barbie considers an "unhealthy interest" in her supernatural powers in general and the crystal ball in particular.

A few weeks earlier, Glenn had run his hands over the crystal ball and said, "Do you ever ask this thing about us?"

"About us?" Barbie had said, gently lifting Glenn's hands off the globe. Other people's energy *could* disrupt the ball the same way a magnet made a compass go haywire.

"Yeah," Glenn said. "Do you ever ask about our future?"

"Yes," Barbie said. For a long time, she had been afraid to get a read on her relationship with Glenn. She was so happy, and if the relationship was doomed, she didn't want to know. But one night, after too many prickly pear margaritas, she cuddled the ball in her lap like it was a baby or a puppy and asked about her and Glenn.

The ball had glowed as it did when it was thinking for Barbie, but the answer it had eventually arrived at was...muddled. It was a mass of thick gray clouds; it was a pea-soup fog. Indecipherable.

"What did it say?" Glenn asked.

"It said we're going to be very happy," Barbie answered.

At lunch, Glenn introduces Barbie to an endless stream of people. "Please meet my fiancée, Barbara Pancik."

He uses the name Barbara, not Barbie, and Barbie can't really blame him. *Barbie* is the name of a doll.

The men slap Glenn on the back; the women squeal. There are congratulations all around. As much as Barbie enjoys being introduced to Glenn's friends, she bristles at all these people she hadn't even realized Glenn knew. It's like he had a secret life. Barbie wonders if any of the people she's meeting are Ashland's friends. She has to assume some of them are, and she wonders how she measures up in their eyes.

Everyone seems genuinely happy for Glenn. He did survive a hellish divorce. It's amazing that Glenn wants to get married again. Amazing!

Barbie wonders if Glenn will ask her to sign a prenup.

One of the women from the beautiful-mommy table

approaches. "Glenn Daley!" the woman says. "I didn't think you ever left your desk in the middle of the day!" The woman is blond and very tall, and her voice is so loud that Barbie wouldn't be surprised if she's breaking the yacht club's decibel rule.

"I'm celebrating today," Glenn says. "Sharon Rhodes, please meet Barbara Pancik, my fiancée."

Sharon arches her eyebrows. "Pancik?" she says. "Are you by any chance related to Grace and Eddie?"

Barbie smiles at the woman in a way that says, *Maybe I am, maybe I'm not.*

Glenn says, "I couldn't have special-ordered a more beautiful day to get engaged. It was nice seeing you, Sharon."

Sharon nods in slow motion, her eyes not leaving Barbie's face. "Good to see you, Glenn. Congratulations."

As Barbie drives home from the office later, she decides that she'll tell Glenn about everything except her involvement in the prostitution ring. She will tell him that she exaggerated about her relationship with Comanche Jones and wholly made up Earl Fischer.

But as Barbie pulls the Triumph into the crushed-shell driveway of her adorable cottage — which she and Glenn have decided they will rent once Barbie moves into Glenn's upside-down house in Tom Nevers — she thinks, *Why bother?* It's not as if Earl Fischer will ever show up to call Barbie out. And she's pretty sure that

Comanche Jones was lying not only about his name but also about the fact that he was single. If Barbie ever does bump into Comanche Jones again, say, while shopping for a kayak at Sports Authority, she's certain he will treat her like a complete stranger. Her romantic life before Glenn was pathetic indeed. But it hardly matters now—she's getting married!

She runs inside the house to call Grace.

Barbie wants a big wedding, and Glenn wants to get married as soon as possible, as if Barbie is indeed being pursued by past lovers who might snatch her from his grasp at any moment. Glenn would get married tomorrow in the Nantucket town hall. September is too soon, so Barbie suggests October. But October is a popular wedding month on Nantucket, and with a few exploratory phone calls, Barbie realizes that every church, every restaurant, every venue is booked and has been for at least a year.

Their only option is to get married on the beach on a Wednesday during the last week of October and have their reception dinner at the Company of the Cauldron, which seats forty-two people. Forty-two people does not constitute a "big wedding," and Barbie doesn't know how she feels about getting married on a Wednesday afternoon only a few days before Halloween (bad luck, her gut tells her)—but she supposes it's better than waiting an entire year. God only knows what might happen over the course of a year.

"Let's do it," Barbie says.

"That's my girl," Glenn says.

Grace is a huge help with wedding arrangements. She accompanies Barbie to Parchment, the stationery store, where they pick out invitations. For someone who wants a big wedding, Barbie has very few people to invite. Her parents are dead; Eddie is in jail. Grace will come, and Allegra and Hope will serve as Barbie's bridesmaids. Barbie will invite Uncle Andy and Auntie Guinevere, who live in a retirement community in Fall River. She will invite her best, most loyal friend, Molly Brimmer-Crawley, from high school, and Molly's husband, Jimmy Crawley, whom they used to call Jimmy Creepy-Crawley, although he has turned out to be a winning choice in the husband and father departments.

Who else? Madeline King and Topper Llewellyn for certain, as well as all the staff from the office of Bayberry Properties. Glenn has a huge family—he's one of six children—but he informs Barbie that only his two brothers will show up.

"My sisters don't speak to me," he says.

"They *don't?*" Barbie says. This is news to her. Whenever Glenn talks about his siblings—his brothers Bruno and Leon, his sisters Angela, Carrie, and Libs—he does so with equanimity. But now that Barbie thinks of it, all of Glenn's stories about his sisters are from childhood. Glenn is originally from Chicago, and the siblings live in places like Evanston and Winnetka. Barbie took a trip to the Windy City with him right after they started dating. They stayed at the Drake Hotel downtown and had drinks with only Glenn's brother Bruno, who lived in a Frank Lloyd Wright house in Oak Park, a fact he mentioned three times in an hour. "Why don't they speak to you?"

"Oh," Glenn says. "It's a long story."

"Tell me," Barbie says. It never occurred to her that at the same time she was lying to Glenn, he might have been lying to her. Lying by omission! Why didn't his sisters speak to him? Did it have anything to do with his former drug use? Or did his sisters take Ashland's side in the divorce? How could they have taken Ashland's side? Barbie had witnessed the woman with her own eyes, albeit from afar—documented psychopath.

"Money," he says. "My parents' will."

"Oh," Barbie says. She breathes a sigh of relief.

Barbie spends a very pleasant Saturday afternoon with her nieces shopping online for bridesmaid dresses. Barbie tells them they can get whatever they want, and she will pay for it.

"Mom already said no black," Allegra says.

Hope elbows Allegra. "Only you would even *consider* wearing black to a wedding."

Allegra is a fashionista, there is no denying it, and Barbie figures she'll pick something by Carmen Marc Valvo or Parker from Neiman Marcus, but both girls turn out to be surprisingly conservative. They pick the same strapless silk shantung sheath from J. Crew—Allegra in dove gray, Hope in dusty pink.

Barbie likes the color of Hope's dress so much that she calls Flowers on Chestnut and orders three bridal-party bouquets in roses just that color.

She contemplates her own dress. She's forty-one years old, hardly an ingénue, and it's a midweek, midafternoon ceremony. She should probably wear a suit. But Barbie doesn't *want* to get married in a suit! She wants a dress. She could ask Grace to go with her to Boston to the Vera Wang boutique or Musette on Newbury Street. But that feels like too much—a beaded bodice, a train, even a veil.

She decides to stay within her comfort zone. She orders a long lace gown from Diane von Furstenberg in a color called blush, which is the palest, palest pink. The gown has an open back, which is perfect—Glenn always says he loves Barbie's back. He's mentioned it so often that Barbie has contorted herself to get a glimpse of her back in the full-length mirror.

The dress problem is solved. Barbie will go barefoot at the beach, and she buys a pair of shocking-pink patent leather Manolos with four-inch heels for the reception.

She and Glenn meet with the chef-owner and the chef de cuisine at the Company of the Cauldron. They pick out a lavish menu: an appetizer of lemon-thyme linguine with pan-roasted lobster, followed by a seasonal salad of greens, roasted butternut squash, and warm goat cheese coated in spiced pepitas, followed by grilled sirloin, rosemary potatoes, and asparagus drizzled with maple-bacon hollandaise. The cake will be a triple-layer devil's food with two layers of mocha mousse and house-made chocolate buttercream icing.

Barbie is excited. This is starting to feel like a wedding!

Barbie picks out favors: hand-milled pillar candles in three autumnal colors—pumpkin, burgundy, and caramel. She orders fireplace matches with her and Glenn's joint monogram on the cover—GDB—and secures a box to each candle using gold wire ribbon.

Responses to the invitations start to arrive. Glenn's best friend from college declines, which seems to bum Glenn out. Madeline and Timothy are coming as well as everyone from the office. Glenn's brother Bruno has a business trip to Dallas that can't be rescheduled. He calls Glenn and says, "Who the hell gets married on a *Wednesday?*" Glenn's brother Leon can come with his wife and their grown son, Bodie, who is unemployed and living in their basement. Barbie's friend Molly Brimmer-Crawley is coming alone—Jimmy Crawley has to work—but Molly seems to be happy to be flying solo, and she offers to take Barbie out drinking the night before the wedding.

"A little bachelorette party!" Molly says.

They end up with *exactly* forty-two people attending. What are the chances?

To celebrate hitting their mark, Glenn takes Barbie

out to dinner at Le Languedoc. They sit at an intimate corner table overlooking Broad Street. Their relationship has been secret for so long that going on a date like this still feels illicit. Le Languedoc is romantic; the service is impeccable; the French food is exquisite. It's *civilized.* Barbie orders the chopped salad and the steak frites; Glenn orders the escargots and the duck and he selects an expensive bottle of Bordeaux.

Once their food is ordered and their wine poured, Glenn pulls a velvet box out of his blazer pocket and sets it on Barbie's bread plate.

"For my beautiful bride-to-be," he says.

Barbie gasps. He's already given her a diamond ring worthy of Marilyn Monroe. What could *this* be? She opens the box. It's a delicate gold chain with a gold, diamond-encrusted sand-dollar pendant.

"Oh my," Barbie says. "You…"

Glenn puts his hand over hers. "First of all," he says, "you're getting married, and every bride needs a 'something new.' And second, I can't tell you how damn jealous it's made me that you still wear the necklace that Earl Fischer gave you. But then I said to myself, 'Now, Glenn, you can't expect her to take *that* necklace off until you give her something to replace it with.' So will you please, please take the pearl off and put this on?"

Barbie blinks. Now is the time to tell him that not only did Earl Fischer not give her the pearl, Earl Fischer doesn't exist. *Tell him now!* Barbie commands herself.

Glenn notices her hesitation. "Do you not like it?" he asks.

"Like it?" she says. "I love it." She hurries to unclasp the chain that her pearl hangs from. She hasn't taken the necklace off since the day she bought it, eight years ago. She can't *believe* she is doing so now. The necklace—like her Triumph and her cottage, both of which she is relinquishing—*defines* her. It was the first nice thing she ever bought herself.

She should never have told Glenn that a man bought it for her. She should correct that misconception right now; she won't get a better opportunity than this.

But...if she tells Glenn, the evening will be ruined. Barbie lays her pearl next to her bread plate and secures the sand-dollar pendant around her neck. The chain hangs longer than Barbie likes and the sand dollar feels light and insubstantial compared to the heft of the pearl.

"How does it look?" Barbie asks.

"Beautiful," Glenn says.

Between dinner and dessert, Barbie rises and goes to the ladies' room. As she's washing her hands, she gives herself a long, hard look in the mirror. Without the black pearl, she feels like another person. But, she reminds herself, she is still the same. She is not defined by her possessions.

When Barbie emerges from the ladies' room, she finds a tall brunette standing in the narrow hall, waiting. The woman looks *very* familiar. It's...it's...

"Barbie," the woman says. "Hi."

It's Andrea Kapenash, the police chief's wife.

Barbie smiles. This is the civilized thing to do. "Hello, Andrea," she says, and she scoots past.

Barbie can't keep herself from peering into the other dining room. Sure enough, there's the Chief, checking his phone. Barbie tries to steady her breathing, which is becoming rapid and shallow. The Chief definitely knows that Barbie was involved in the shenanigans on Low Beach Road. (*Shenanigans* makes it sound like a sorority prank. What Barbie was involved in was *international underage sex trafficking!*) Has the Chief told his wife? Has he told *anyone?*

The Chief looks up, sees Barbie, and offers half a wave. Which means...what?

Barbie can't stand to think about it. She heads back to her table.

She is still the same person she ever was. She is a woman who lies to the man she loves.

Later that night, after Glenn is asleep and snoring in her bed, Barbie tiptoes out to the living room and takes the crystal ball off the top shelf of her coat closet.

She puts her hands over the globe until it starts to glow.

Barbara Ann Pancik and Glenn Harlan Daley, she thinks. *What does the future hold?*

The ball glows with a dull gray light, just as it did the one other time that Barbie asked. Dark, thick clouds, like the kind one sees from an airplane, obscuring what's below.

She won't get a clear read until she tells Glenn the truth.

Barbie tries not to feel hurt that no one is throwing her a bridal shower. Her only close friend is Molly, who lives off-island, and her bridesmaids are seventeen years old and can't know what's expected. Barbie thought perhaps Grace would organize something, but Grace is busy packing and moving as well as raising the girls and dealing with all the matters that Eddie left behind.

Barbie also thought maybe one of the women in the office might throw together a tea or a luncheon. Rachel McMann *lives* to plan happy events like that, and for a while, Barbie enters the office each morning anticipating a surprise. She wouldn't even care if Glenn told the associates they *had* to plan something. Barbie would still be thrilled.

A week passes, then another, and no shower. Barbie decides that she can't expect the women in her office to feel anything toward her but jealousy and resentment. She was hired one day and proposed to the next and she receives the best listings because she's the boss's fiancée.

She reminds herself that a shower would be pointless anyway. Any household item Barbie might receive, she already owns. She has a KitchenAid mixer in bright pink, she has maple cutting boards in three sizes, she has Henckels knives and a full set of All-Clad stainless-steel pots and pans. She has a French mandoline, a potato ricer, a chinois strainer, a Crock-Pot. She has sumptuous bath towels and Frette linens on her bed.

Possibly everyone thinks that, at the age of forty-one, a successful woman like Barbie has everything she could want.

Barbie makes a series of appointments at R. J. Miller — one to get her hair frosted, one for a facial, one to get her eyebrows and bikini line waxed. On the Saturday before the wedding, she and Grace and Hope and Allegra all go and get their nails done, and afterward, Barbie suggests they go to the Nantucket Hotel for lunch.

"My treat," Barbie says.

"You can't pay," Grace says. "You're the bride." Then her eyes grow wide with guilt. "I should have thrown you a shower. I'm so sorry, Barbie. I dropped the ball."

Barbie waves a hand through the air as if this is the most ridiculous thing she's ever heard. "A shower?" she says. "For what? I have everything a woman could want."

"And now you have Glenn," Hope says.

Molly Brimmer-Crawley arrives the afternoon before the wedding, and Barbie drives to the airport in her Triumph to pick her up.

"You still have the Triumph!" Molly says. "I adore this car!"

Molly hasn't been to Nantucket in three or four years, and the last time she came, she was with her kids, one of whom was teething. She is free as a bird now, and she announces that there is no need to stop by Barbie's cottage to drop off her suitcase. "Let's go straight to the bar," she says. Then she puts her hands in the air and whoops.

They head to the Pearl for passion-fruit cosmos — three, in fact, in rapid succession. Whoa! Barbie hasn't felt this *loose,* this *light* in a long time. Molly Brimmer is the one person other than Eddie who has been a constant since childhood. Barbie and Molly sang into hairbrushes in front of a mirror to the *Grease* soundtrack; they smoked cigarettes for the first time outside the ice-skating rink; they bleached their jeans and pierced their ears with a needle, an ice cube, and a bottle of Jack Daniel's. They were perceived as bad girls — Molly was shanty Irish and Barbie a gypsy Slovakian, both from the most undesirable part of a dying town — but they were smart girls. They took honors classes; they were secretly intent on doing their homework, getting into college, and leaving New Bedford forever.

Molly and Jimmy live in Newport, Rhode Island, where Jimmy owns a marina. Molly insists on paying for their drinks.

"All of our drinks," Molly says. "All night. This is your bachelorette party."

Barbie went to Molly's bachelorette party sixteen years earlier, when they were both twenty-five. Barbie had been one of Molly's bridesmaids, but Molly's college roommate Amber had been the maid of honor, and Barbie's feelings were hurt. The other bridesmaids were also Molly's college friends, so Barbie had suffered from a bad case of odd man out. She marveled that Molly had been able to make close friends so easily out of high school. Barbie hadn't been successful at it; she had never found a friend as good, fun, and loyal as Molly.

They go to Lola for ruby-red grapefruit martinis.

Then to 56 Union for espresso martinis.

And then Barbie surrenders. "I can't drink any more," she says.

Molly smiles triumphantly.

They end their evening at Steamboat Pizza with a couple slices of pepperoni, olives, and mushrooms. From there, they can walk home to Barbie's cottage; she has to remove her Manolos and go barefoot, but she's so drunk, she doesn't care. They leave the Triumph in town; Barbie will walk back in the morning to get it.

It's on the walk home that Barbie decides to confess. "I lied to Glenn," she says.

"About what?" Molly says.

"Oh," Barbie says, swinging her Manolos by the straps in a wide circle. "Everything."

"Everything like what?" Molly says.

"Like I made up an old boyfriend and told Glenn that he was the one who gave me the black pearl necklace. And I made up other men. Just, you know, so

Glenn would be jealous and wouldn't think I was a loser who had never had a boyfriend."

"You're not a loser," Molly says. "You dated Tony Harlowe."

Barbie winced. She had never admitted, even to Molly, the brutally honest things Tony Harlowe had said to her after the senior prom. He loved her, he said, but his parents didn't think Barbie Pancik was good enough for him and he knew in his heart that they were right. Tony Harlowe had gotten into UPenn and had his sights set on law school after that. He wanted to be a judge someday.

"I never told Glenn about Tony Harlowe," Barbie says.

"You didn't?" Molly says. "Why not? Tony Harlowe was a catch."

"It was high school," Barbie says. But the real reason she never told Glenn about Tony Harlowe was that Tony Harlowe had been the person who made Barbie believe she would never measure up.

"What else have you lied to him about?" Molly asks.

"The thing Eddie went to jail for?" Barbie says. "I was involved in that, and Glenn doesn't know."

"The prostitution ring?" Molly asks.

Barbie nods. She says, "Do you think I should call Glenn up tonight, right now, and just *tell* him?"

"No," Molly says. "There's no need for any night-before-the-wedding drama. Listen, you have your past transgressions, and Glenn, I'm sure, has his. The important thing is that the two of you are going to leave those behind and start a life of eternal bliss tomorrow." She stops in her tracks. "Jeez, I sound like a Hallmark card."

"That's okay," Barbie says. "I like it."

When Barbie wakes up, she can't believe how stunning the day is. It's unseasonably warm—nearly 65 degrees—and the sky is a bright, cloudless blue.

Molly makes a breakfast of poached eggs on rye toast and wedges of honeydew melon. She pours them each a mimosa.

"Hair of the dog," Molly says. Molly looks *very* hungover.

They eat on Barbie's back deck, enjoying the sun. Barbie plays the *Grease* soundtrack on her iPod speakers and they sing along. *Summer lovin', had me a blast.* Barbie can't remember ever being this happy.

Molly's words from last night have put Barbie's mind at ease. As of today, her life is a tabula rasa, a clean slate; this is a fresh start.

There is only one sore spot for Barbie. She misses her brother.

Because Eddie is in jail, there is no one to give Barbie away, so Barbie will walk by herself up and over the dune, then down to the waterline, where forty chairs are set up, twenty on each side of the white wooden trellis that has been pounded into the sand. Judith, the

Unitarian minister, will marry them in her flowing white robe. There will be a classical guitarist.

It feels like a wedding!

Barbie is "hiding" behind the tinted windows inside Grace's Range Rover, which is parked at the far end of the beach lot. She has carefully arranged her blush-pink lace gown around her. She wears her new gold sand-dollar necklace and old button-stud earrings— replicas of the ones she and Molly pierced each other's ears with decades earlier. Barbie never wears anything more than mascara and lipstick on a regular day, but today her something borrowed is Allegra's makeup; her stylish niece has done Barbie's face. Her hair has been smoothed and twisted into a chignon. For her something blue, there are discreet violets embroidered on her underthings.

She's ready to go!

From behind the tinted windows of the Rover, Barbie catches glimpses of the guests as they pull up. They are escorted over the dunes by two brokers at Bayberry Properties, Gary and Chris, and Glenn's brother Leon, all of whom look dashing in pink Vineyard Vines ties and navy blazers.

When it's five minutes to three, Grace and Molly climb out of the car, and then they too are escorted over the dunes. Allegra, Hope, and Barbie remain in the back seat, awaiting Leon's signal. One finger means they are to get out of the car, two fingers means the processional music has started.

They wait, and they wait. It's ten after three, then three fifteen. Barbie isn't sure what's causing the holdup, but she doesn't like it. The sun is sinking in the sky. It will set in a little over an hour, another disadvantage to getting married in late October.

Hope tugs at the top of her dress. Allegra sighs with impatience. "Maybe they forgot about us," she says.

Finally, Leon appears at the top of the dune. He holds up no fingers. He hurries down.

Carefully, Barbie climbs out of the car, and the twins follow.

Leon looks at Barbie. "Can I talk to you for a second?"

His voice contains bad news. Did the altar blow over? Barbie wonders. Did the classical guitarist break a string? "What's wrong?" she says.

"Glenn isn't here," Leon says.

"What?" Barbie says. She glimpsed the setup on the beach when they first arrived, but then Barbie was so intent on not letting anyone see her that she didn't notice exactly who had come and who hadn't. She just assumed Glenn was on the beach, waiting for her. "Where *is* he?"

"Right before he left the house," Leon says, "he told me he had to go on a special mission and that he'd meet me here."

"A special *mission?*" Barbie says.

"His exact words."

Well, all Barbie can think is that a "special mission"

is Glenn's nifty euphemism for cold feet. He doesn't want to marry Barbie after all. He found out about Earl Fischer or, worse, about Barbie's part-time job this summer as a madam. The thick fog inside the crystal ball meant this: a botched wedding, a bride left standing at the altar. Tony Harlowe had been right; Barbie Pancik wasn't good enough.

Leon puts a strong hand on Barbie's bare shoulder, and the kindness and pity contained in this gesture is what makes Barbie cry. Just a few salty tears—she's too tough for anything more. Plus, there's her makeup.

"I tried his cell phone," Leon says. "But he's not answering."

Barbie can't believe this. She spoke to Glenn at noon, and he'd sounded happy, even joyful.

Allegra and Hope close in.

Hope says, "Auntie Barbie, what's wrong?"

Barbie opens her mouth to explain, to tell them sometimes in life, lots of times, in fact, things don't turn out the way they're supposed to. Barbie should never have lied. She could have told Glenn about everything, she realizes now, and he would have loved her anyway.

But before Barbie can figure out how to explain the inevitable disappointments of the world to her nieces, Allegra shrieks. There is a car barreling down the dirt road toward the beach.

"Daddy!" Allegra says. "I swear, *I see Daddy!*"

Barbie squints. The car, she sees, is Glenn's Escalade, and in the passenger seat is . . . is . . .

Barbie cries out, "It's Eddie!"

Glenn screeches to a stop in a cloud of dust and sand. He hops out of the car and so does Eddie. A third man climbs out of the back seat. He's wearing a uniform, and there's a gun in his hip holster.

Glenn waves at Barbie. "Get-out-of-jail-free card," he says. "For twenty-four hours!" He gives Barbie a big grin. "What do you get the woman who has everything?"

Barbie's vision is blurred with tears. She and Hope and Allegra run to give Eddie a hug.

"You look just beautiful, Barb," Eddie says.

"Doesn't she?" Glenn says. He kisses Barbie and wipes away one of her tears with his thumb, then he turns to Allegra and Hope. "I'm going up now. You two follow behind me, just like we practiced."

"Okay," Hope says.

"Okay," Allegra says.

The girls line up with their bouquets in front of them, then process up and over the dunes.

Eddie offers Barbie his arm. "It's our turn," he says.

The Country Club

(Read with *The Identicals*)

This short story, "The Country Club," is a prequel to *The Identicals*. I wrote it in November of 2016 after I had turned *The Identicals* in to my editor and was waiting for her revisions. Revisions are the trickiest part of writing a novel. The first draft is complete, the characters and plot and "world" have been established, but there are often significant changes to be made. I have described it as a puzzle, taking the novel apart and putting it back together differently. Because the work is so challenging, I rent an apartment in the Beacon Hill neighborhood of Boston for six weeks (for maximum concentration, it's important to be away from home). I wrote this story during a weekend of exceptional weather; temperatures were in the high sixties, and I took long walks through Beacon Hill, admiring the town houses, especially the grand homes surrounding Louisburg Square. It also happened that I had just gotten back from a short trip to Dubai and was horribly jet-lagged.

The owners of my rental apartment had a wonderful book about the history of the homes in Beacon Hill and I would read it at two and three in the morning as I lay awake. It was around this time that I learned that the country club in Brookline was referred to as simply "the Country Club," and I thought, *I must set a story there.*

In *The Identicals,* much is made of the fact that Billy Frost and Eleanor Roxie Frost come from different backgrounds—one quite fancy, one modest. I wanted to delve into the 1960s Boston that created both Eleanor and Billy; I wanted to describe the night they met; I wanted to establish Eleanor as a bit of a rule breaker, a woman who longed for a career. I wanted to discuss the effect of the Vietnam War on the characters (I would get into this in more depth in *Summer of '69*). But most of all, I wanted Eleanor and Billy to fall deeply and genuinely in love.

The result was "The Country Club," set at Eleanor's parents' Christmas party in 1968. I hope you enjoy it!

Because her mother is the most unreasonable of WASPs, Eleanor is required to stand in the foyer of the Country Club and greet every last one of the guests attending her parents' Christmas party, held each year on December 22. This receiving-line duty—or "doody," as Eleanor's younger sister, Flossie, calls it—can last up to an hour. Eleanor's parents invite three hundred people to the party, and few dare to decline. The Roxies' Christmas party is known throughout Boston and its suburbs as simply "the Christmas Party," the same way that the country club in Brookline is "the Country Club." Are there other Christmas parties, other country clubs? If so, it hardly matters.

Eleanor is twenty-one years old, a senior at Mount Ida, where nearly all of Eleanor's classmates are engaged to be married, many of them to boys at Babson, many of them in June, right after graduation. The mere concept of marriage is nauseating to Eleanor. Her parents have set a miserable example. Eleanor can count on one hand the number of times she has heard her mother,

Vivian Harper Roxie, laugh. Eleanor's father, Edgar Winford Roxie, "Win" for short, is the president of Boston's oldest bank. He flirts with whatever woman is in front of him, an attempt, Eleanor supposes, to find validation of his masculine charms. He teases waitresses, jokes with coat-check girls. Has he ever been unfaithful? Ever taken one of the sweet young tellers or his secretary—whom he always refers to as Miss Pitch, though, as Eleanor knows, her name is Jennifer—to lunch at the Marliave? It's not impossible.

Eleanor herself has been dating a boy named Glendon Bingham; he attends Harvard Business School. When Eleanor's mother met Glen, she awarded him a genuine smile, as rarely seen as the California condor. Glen is appropriate in every way—handsome, pedigreed, from a suitably but not ostentatiously wealthy family. However, he is also a terrific bore. When Eleanor looks at Glen, she sees in his dull brown eyes a center-entrance colonial in Wellesley or Weston, summers spent by the pool at the Country Club, dutiful attendance at this very party every year, two children (a boy and a girl), a golden retriever, a woody wagon, and the missionary position. Eleanor will be expected to serve on committees, bring a fruited Jell-O mold to potlucks, and organize the carpool.

She has no interest. She wants to work. She wants not only a job but a career. In fashion design. Her idol is Priscilla Comins Kidder, otherwise known as Priscilla of Boston, the woman who designed the wedding gowns of Princess Grace and President Johnson's daughter Luci.

Eleanor's parents know nothing of her ambitions. She is an art history major at Mount Ida, specializing in Rembrandt and Rubens—two vastly different artists. She brings home respectable A minuses and B pluses even though her notebooks are filled with sketches of dresses, skirts, blouses, pantsuits, even shoes.

In fact, Eleanor has designed the dress she is wearing this evening, a strapless black velvet sheath. It's probably snugger than her mother cares for, but it does hit below the knee, an anachronism in this, the age of mini-skirts. Vivian doesn't know the dress is her daughter's design and creation, sewn on a turquoise Singer sewing machine that Eleanor bought in Chinatown and keeps in her dorm room; Eleanor told Vivian that she bought the dress at Filene's. She is wearing it with black sling-back heels and—her nod to the holiday—a crimson velvet ribbon tied around her neck as a choker. Her mother cast a jaundiced eye at the ribbon, saying, "Pearls would have been better."

Eleanor had merely rolled her eyes. Pearls—how unimaginative.

Flossie, who is thirteen but, because she has a baby complex, acts eight, takes advantage of the lull after greeting the Dennis Paiges, the Thomas M. J. Kingslands, and the Paul Henry Koglers. "I'm thirsty," she says. "And my feet hurt."

"Your shoes are too small," Eleanor points out. Here

is one example of Flossie's childishness—her insistence on wearing last year's Mary Janes instead of the black silk ballet flats that their mother had bought for her in Paris last fall. (What had Eleanor received from Paris? An umbrella.)

Flossie ignores Eleanor. "Daddy, may I please get a Shirley Temple?"

"Go on, then," Win says.

"I'd like a drink as well," Eleanor says. "Something stronger."

"All in good time," her father says. He gives a sky-ward glance that lets her know he, too, is dying for a drink. Since Eleanor has been home on holiday break from college, Win Roxie has been educating her in the world of spirits, a paternal duty he seems to particu-larly relish. Each night before they watch *Bewitched* (Eleanor's favorite) or *The Red Skelton Hour* or *That Girl* (her father's favorite; he likes looking at Marlo Thomas's legs, Eleanor suspects), Win pours himself a drink and brings a scant finger in a highball glass for Eleanor as well. Mount Gay rum is her favorite so far, especially after her father added tonic and a wedge of lime.

Vivian doesn't know about these tastings. She would not approve. She believes that ladies drink wine and, on special occasions, champagne.

"Where is Glen this evening?" her father asks. His voice contains a hint of playfulness. The evening that Win Roxie introduced Eleanor to bourbon—or truth serum, as Eleanor now thinks of it—she confessed to her father that she was more than ready to break things off with Glen. She doesn't want to spoil his holiday, however, so she has decided to wait until the new year to drop the ax, which her father agreed was the politic thing to do.

"He's working on a project about franchises," Eleanor says now.

"And he couldn't leave it just for one night?" Win asks.

"Alas, no," Eleanor says. Harvard's semester doesn't end until after the holiday break, a brutal cruelty if ever there was one. Eleanor is secretly thrilled that Glen can't make it. She plans on drinking as much as she wants—it will have to be champagne; her mother is watching—and dancing to the Philip Becker Orchestra.

Who will she dance with? None of her parents' friends; the men are all hands. Maybe her childhood friend Topher. His girlfriend, Liesl, is here tonight, although she has a sprained ankle.

"Are we done?" Eleanor asks her mother as they stand on the receiving line.

"A roast is done," her mother says.

"Are we *finished*?" Eleanor asks impatiently. She wants a flute of champagne and a chance at a canapé or two. The shrimp will be gone, as they are every year, but she might get salmon mousse on a Ritz cracker or a stick of celery stuffed with pimento cheese if they end this pointless formality right now.

"We still have more guests, darling," Eleanor's mother says, turning the word *darling* into a pitchfork and offering her phony smile, her lips tight across her teeth.

The Nutcracker Suite, which her mother insists on, ends and the Philip Becker Orchestra launches into "Mistletoe and Holly." Eleanor is certain that Mr. and Mrs. Charles Eaton, Mr. and Mrs. Richmond Collier, and Aunt Lizbet and Uncle Myles have started dancing. That's one good thing about WASPs, Eleanor thinks. The instant the band starts playing, they get up to dance. Probably it's their frugality surfacing; they can't stand to think of the money their parents spent on years of ballroom-dancing lessons going to waste.

"Daddy?" Eleanor implores.

Win Roxie straightens up—shoulders back, hands clasped in front of himself, eyes resolutely forward. "Look," he says. "Your cousin is arriving."

Her cousin? Eleanor raises her eyes to see Rhonda Fiorello slink through the door with a young man at her side.

What? Eleanor thinks.

Her mother exhibits a rare failure of composure; her gasp is audible, but probably only to Eleanor. Then a whispered "Good God."

"Now, now," Win Roxie murmurs.

It's approximately twelve steps from the front door of the club to the receiving line, and in the time it takes Rhonda Fiorello and her date to cover those twelve steps, Eleanor has the following thoughts:

1. Rhonda has come to the Christmas party wearing a floor-length lavender (out-of-season) dress that is (basically) see-through and a pair of leather thong sandals. Over the top of the dress is a threadbare white "wrap"—honestly, for all Eleanor knows, it might be a towel stolen from the Holiday Inn, but she is grateful for its presence because Eleanor fears her cousin isn't wearing a bra. Rhonda has not seen fit to wash her hair; it hangs in dark strings around her sallow, pinched face.

2. Rhonda has never been a pretty girl, but this evening she looks particularly ghastly.

3. Eleanor is not supposed to have uncharitable thoughts about her cousin. Rhonda's mother, Cressida Roxie Fiorello, Win's younger sister, got pregnant at nineteen, endured a shotgun marriage at Eleanor's grandfather's insistence, gave birth to Rhonda, then promptly left the city of Boston, the Commonwealth of Massachusetts, and the East Coast altogether. She became an activist for a Sioux Indian tribe in South Dakota, leaving Rhonda to be raised by her father, Sal Fiorello, a car salesman on Route 1 in Revere.

Win Roxie tried to intervene. He offered to pay to send Rhonda to Winsor with Eleanor; he offered to let Rhonda move into the house on Pinckney Street. She could stay in the fourth bedroom, he said, the one with the best view of their hidden garden out back. *She'll be like another sister!* Win had said to Eleanor as if this were something she might have wanted. Rhonda was only two years younger than Eleanor, far too close in age to remain uncompetitive. Eleanor enjoys being her father's favorite and resents the soft spot he seems to have for Rhonda. Eleanor realizes it is merely hand-me-down affection—his younger sister, Cressida, was his favorite of his four siblings for reasons Eleanor doesn't understand—and now that Cressida is effectively *gone,* he has transferred his tender feelings to Rhonda.

Thankfully, Sal insisted on keeping Rhonda in Revere to attend Immaculate Conception; however, Rhonda got expelled by the nuns for smoking marijuana. That was in her junior year, and although it had been possible for her to finish up at the public school, she chose to drop out. She took a job as a chambermaid at the Sheraton Commander and started dating a boy who worked as a bellhop. The boy's name was Frank Paley. Rhonda had brought Frank Paley to the previous year's Christmas party and he had presented himself well, which is to say better than anyone thought a special friend of ne'er-do-well Rhonda's might. He had held his liquor and ended the evening sitting in the men's bar with Win, teaching him magic tricks—he took a dollar bill from Win, then produced the same dollar bill from inside a lemon, a trick that had confounded Win.

The boy's going to be famous! Win said.

But shortly after the new year, Frank Paley enlisted

and was deployed to Vietnam. He was killed in July during Operation Buffalo—and that was when Rhonda went from being a black sheep to a full-blown off-the-rails lunatic. She became a war protester, the tenacious, unruly kind. She was photographed marching outside the Massachusetts State House, and the photo was published on the front page of the *Boston Globe*—Rhonda with her mouth open, fist in the air, sign thrust in front of her: CHILDREN ARE NOT FOR BURNING. Vivian, who believed that a lady should appear in the newspaper only three times in her life—her birth, her marriage, and her death—was fit to be tied. She was relieved there was no common last name linking the angry young woman in the photograph to the Roxie family of Pinckney Street.

No time for further thoughts; Rhonda and her date are upon them.

"Hello, Rhonda," Eleanor's mother says. "Welcome to the Christmas party."

"Happiest of holidays, Rhonda," Win says. "Would you care to introduce your guest?"

Rhonda stares at Win and Vivian with glassy eyes, then starts to cackle. She's on drugs, Eleanor thinks. She wonders if her parents are going to let Rhonda stay or if they will ask Frederick, the club's social director, to find someone to discreetly escort her out.

The young man speaks up for himself. "I'm William Frost, sir," he says, offering a hand. "But please, call me Billy."

Win shakes Billy Frost's hand, clearly relieved that the young man is upright and coherent and speaks English. "How do you do, Billy Frost. Welcome to the Country Club. Is this your first time?"

"Yes, sir," Billy Frost says. "However, I have long dreamed of playing the Primrose course."

"A fellow golf enthusiast!" Win says. "How marvelous!"

Eleanor takes a look at this fellow, Billy Frost. He's tall and well built with sandy hair, recently barbered. He's wearing a navy blazer and a standard red-and-blue rep tie, a webbed belt, penny loafers. The outfit, at least, passes muster. Where did Rhonda find this fellow? Surely not at one of her protests or sit-ins. Possibly she stationed herself outside the Hasty Pudding Club and waited for a suitable escort to emerge.

At that moment, Billy Frost turns to Eleanor, and her heart swells enough that she is aware of it there, in her chest, beneath the black velvet. Billy Frost's eyes are so intensely blue that Eleanor feels as if she has never seen blue eyes before. As she is noticing this, he appears to be noticing her. His eyes flick to her décolletage — *Rude?* she wonders, even as she knows that the entire point of décolletage is to be noticed — then back to her face, and he gives her a prizewinning smile.

"Oh, hello," he says, and the rest of the world — her parents, her mousy cousin, the orchestra, the canapés, the evergreen garland spiraling down the banister of the main staircase emitting the scent of Fraser fir, the entire Country Club—evaporates. Eleanor is suspended in a silvery mist. Billy Frost extends his hand. "I'm Billy Frost. And who might *you* be?"

"I'm Eleanor Roxie," she says. She nearly adds *Rhonda's cousin,* but she stops. She will *not* define herself in terms of Rhonda. Rhonda, Eleanor decides at that moment, is irrelevant.

She takes Billy's hand.

Rhonda, perhaps realizing she is about to be cast aside, snaps to attention, but her focus is not on the thrum of energy between her date and her cousin; her focus is on her uncle.

"How *dare* you!" Rhonda says to Win. She swallows, and her eyes blaze like trash fires. "How dare you throw a party, a party as sparkling and frivolous as this one, when our boys are dying in the rice paddies! How dare you, Uncle Win! Tell me, is President Johnson in attendance tonight? He is a *war criminal.* A murderer."

Win laughs uncomfortably and takes a breath to respond, but Vivian whispers, "She's high as a kite, Win."

"I can hear you," Rhonda says, now addressing Vivian. Eleanor has to admit, she's impressed. Vivian is fearsome to one and all, and especially, Eleanor would assume, to someone as disenfranchised as Rhonda. But Rhonda is giving Vivian her full ferocity. Maybe that's easier to do when you have nothing to lose. One can't fall farther than the floor. "I'm standing right here, *Vivian.*"

"But not for long," Vivian says. She signals to

Frederick, who has sensed trouble and is posted nearby. "Frederick, please ask our driver to deliver Miss Fiorello home immediately."

Before Eleanor can think better of it, she says, "But Mr. Frost can stay, can't he, Mother?"

"Of course!" Vivian says, and the miraculous happens: her face lights up with a natural smile. Whether this is because Vivian relishes the act of separating Rhonda from her date or because Vivian senses her daughter's utter captivation by Billy Frost, Eleanor doesn't know, nor does she care. She takes Billy Frost by the hand and leads him into the ballroom.

Later that night, after procuring a glass of champagne for herself and a Jameson, neat, for Billy; after snatching up the last Ritz cracker with salmon mousse from the tray; after sitting next to Billy for a dinner of prime rib, Yorkshire pudding, and peas; after dancing with him to over a dozen songs, including "At Last," "Boogie Woogie Bugle Boy," and "Fly Me to the Moon," which Billy croons in Eleanor's ear, immediately making it "their" song, Eleanor and Billy leave the party in Billy's car, a Plymouth Valiant convertible, the vinyl top of which is not quite flush, so that even when Billy cranks the heat, there is still a blast of chilly air leaking into the passenger side.

Does Eleanor care? No!

"Where do you live?" Billy asks. "Around here?"

"Here? Brookline?" Eleanor says. "No." She lives with her parents on Pinckney Street on Beacon Hill in one of the houses that face Louisburg Square. They have a key to the garden, although the novelty of that wore off years ago. Eleanor and Flossie have been trained never to reveal their exact address. This started in June of 1962 when Eleanor was sixteen and the Boston Strangler was on the loose. The whole city had been in a panic, but Vivian doubly so because Win was a bank president, and one of Vivian's most frightening childhood memories had been of the Lindbergh baby's kidnapping in 1932. "I live in the city, but let's not go there."

"Okay, where to, then?" Billy asks. "My place? I have an apartment in Dorchester."

Eleanor closes her eyes. *An apartment in Dorchester*—those four words would fell Vivian Roxie like a tree. As much as Eleanor pretends not to care what Vivian thinks, she can't, under any circumstances, spend the night in *an apartment in Dorchester.*

But then Eleanor gets an idea.

She directs Billy onto Mount Ida's campus. The college is deserted but technically open because there are a handful of students who live too far away to leave for Christmas break—Washington State, Mexico City, Jordan—and another handful who are willfully staying on campus to avoid or annoy their families. All of the women on Eleanor's floor are gone, however. Her roommate, Ann-Lane, is safely in Memphis.

Once in the dorm room, Eleanor wonders what she's really prepared for. All she wanted was a warm, quiet place to talk.

The first thing Billy notices is her sewing machine.

"Is this yours?" he asks. "You sew?"

She nods, suddenly shy. "I want to be a fashion designer." She plucks the velvet of her bodice. "I made this dress."

"You did not."

"I did."

"Come here," Billy says. He takes his overcoat off and lays it across Ann-Lane's bed, but he leaves his blazer on, like a gentleman. Eleanor walks over to him and raises her face.

He pulls the red ribbon at her neck. "It's like opening a present," he says. He kisses the hollow at the base of her throat.

Just like that, Eleanor is in love. She suspects it's a condition from which she will never recover.

William O'Shaughnessy Frost. O'Shaughnessy is his mother's maiden name. He's Irish Catholic, grew up in the Mission Hill section of Boston, attended Boston Latin.

Eleanor silently celebrates. Her mother can't argue with Boston Latin.

His college was in Amherst, and Eleanor gets ready to marshal a parade until she realizes he means UMass, and in any case, he dropped out after two years when he decided he didn't want to be an engineer after all. He now attends trade school in Southie. In eighteen months, he will be a licensed electrician.

Trade school, Eleanor thinks. She imagines Vivian pursing her lips.

"Family?" Eleanor asks. They are lying naked under the sheet, wool blanket, and Amish quilt on Eleanor's bed. She did not, however, sacrifice her virginity. She wanted to, but Billy said she was too fine a girl and they should wait until they knew each other better.

Billy's father is a doctor, a general practitioner on Mission Hill. His mother is a librarian, a slave to the card catalog. The physician father will meet Vivian's standards, although a hospital position would have been better. But what will Vivian think of a mother who works? Vivian sits on the ladies' auxiliary committee for the Boston Public Library, so she might consider being a librarian noble work in the name of literacy for the masses or she might consider a woman who gets paid for finding call numbers and locating microfiche a travesty.

There are no siblings. Apparently, Billy had had a complicated birth.

An only child is preferable to a squawking Irish household of twelve, Eleanor supposes, although she herself has always longed for a bigger family—brothers, more sisters. Not, however, an adopted sister such as Rhonda.

"How do you know my cousin?" Eleanor asks. This is the answer she dreads the most.

"I was a chum of Frank Paley," Billy says. "We were altar boys together at the basilica. He introduced me to Rhonda, then told me to look out for her while he was overseas. I saw her again at his funeral, and last week out of the blue she called me up and invited me to the party. She was afraid to go by herself, she said. I went partly as a favor to her but more as a favor to my old buddy Frank, may he rest in peace."

"So you don't . . . *like* her?" Eleanor says. "The two of you aren't . . . you haven't . . ."

"No," Billy says, kissing Eleanor's left eyelid. "And no," he says, kissing her right eyelid.

She feels it again, the heart swell. She had worried that Billy held back in bed because he was in love with Rhonda. But he barely knows her! He was a childhood friend of Frank Paley's! Eleanor wonders if Billy knows any magic tricks. His eyes are a magic trick all their own.

Billy Frost, Eleanor decides, is on the edge of suitable. She breathes in deeply, then exhales. She is ready to live on the edge. It's what she's been waiting for, she realizes.

"It's amazing that a girl as beautiful as you doesn't already have a boyfriend," Billy says.

Eleanor manages to suppress a spurt of nervous laughter. She has *completely forgotten* about Glen Bingham and his franchise project!

"Not so amazing," she says.

They are to be married June 22 on the "flat of the hill," at the Church of the Advent, where everyone in the Roxie family has been baptized, confirmed, married, and memorialized for nearly a century. Eleanor will be attended by her Mount Ida roommate, Ann-Lane Crenshaw, and Flossie will be a junior bridesmaid.

But before this is set in stone, there is a discussion about Eleanor asking cousin Rhonda to be an attendant.

Win Roxie says, "Would you consider it?"

Vivian stands in silence at Win's side. On this rare occasion, Eleanor's eyes seek out her mother's. There is *no way* Vivian wants Rhonda at the altar with her daughter.

"I'd rather not," Eleanor says—diplomatically, she thinks.

"Technically, she is the one who introduced you to Billy," Win says. "I think it would be a nice gesture to ask."

"If it were only a gesture, that would be one thing," Eleanor says. "But what if she says yes? I can't have Rhonda all strung out on drugs, tripping on LSD or high on PCP at my wedding."

"I have taken measures to neutralize Rhonda," Win says. "Set her on the straight and narrow."

Vivian flinches almost imperceptibly. Clearly, this is the first she's heard of these "measures." There is more than one way to be unfaithful, Eleanor realizes.

"I'm sorry, Daddy," Eleanor says. "I won't do it."

This is a gamble. Win is, of course, footing the bill for the nuptials and the honeymoon to Nantucket and Martha's Vineyard. But if he gives her an ultimatum—ask Rhonda or the wedding is off—then Eleanor will elope. Billy would prefer that, she's certain.

Win nods, accepting defeat. "All right," he says.

*   *   *

Not only does Eleanor not want Rhonda as a bridesmaid, she doesn't want to invite her to the wedding.
But this, she knows, is pushing things too far. She considers sabotaging Rhonda's invitation—dropping it
through the sewer grate on West Cedar on her way to
the Charles Street post office—but she worries she'll
be found out. What should concern her more than the
invitation addressed to Rhonda is the one addressed to
Win's sister and Rhonda's mother, Cressida. That envelope says simply *Flandreau Santee Sioux Reservation,
South Dakota.*

It's unlikely either Rhonda or Cressida will accept.
If Rhonda does come, Eleanor imagines she will be
there to make a scene. Rhonda might show up at the
church in an attempt to steal Billy back, like Dustin
Hoffman in *The Graduate,* which was, coincidentally,
the movie Eleanor and Billy went to see on their first
official date. Or Rhonda could create some other kind
of kerfuffle. Eleanor imagines protest signs, cherry
bombs, fire. She envisions Rhonda streaking naked
through the church—anything to call attention to herself, her pain, her beloved killed by the Vietcong. Anything to discredit the establishment, the world of power
and privilege that she has never had access to. There is
no possibility that Rhonda is as rehabilitated as Win
believes. She was too far gone to save. She was, Eleanor
thinks, doomed from birth.

Rhonda's invitation goes into the post with everyone else's, and a week later her response card comes back: *Miss Rhonda Fiorello will attend.* No mention of a guest, which is worrisome; a date might serve as ballast or buoy.

There are many other things to worry about, however. There's an iffy weather forecast for June 22, a fever that Flossie runs the week before the wedding, the failure of the church's air-conditioning, and whether or not Vivian will be civil to Billy's parents, Dr. James and Mrs. Tabitha Frost. ("Unusual name, Tabitha," Vivian remarks. "Is that *Jewish?*") Following the reception, photographs are to be taken in the Public Garden. Eleanor hears that a classmate of hers from Winsor and Mount Ida, Suzie Worth, is getting married at the Church of the Covenant in Back Bay and is planning on having *her* photos taken in the Public Garden at nearly the exact same time. Eleanor loathes Suzie Worth and has since ninth grade; this discovery causes Eleanor to dissolve into tears.

The one steadfast element amid all of the wedding planning is Eleanor's groom. Billy offers Eleanor a handkerchief, kisses her tenderly, tells her that if the wedding planning is making her upset, they can hop on a Greyhound bus to Vegas. All that matters is their love.

It turns out Billy is right. Eleanor puts faith in the *love* part of the marriage and things start to go smoothly. Three days before the wedding, Dr. and Mrs. Frost are invited to the house on Pinckney Street for a cold supper. Dr. Frost is a charming man, older than Win by ten years and avuncular; he smokes a pipe and wears a fine watch—a gold Omega 1954—that Win admires. Mrs. Frost is quieter; her voice still holds a tinge of an Irish accent. She came to the country as a child, she says; her father was an editor at Little, Brown.

This gets Vivian's attention. "The Little, Brown offices are right on Beacon Street," she says.

"That's right," Tabitha Frost says. "I visited them with my father. He used to show me the manuscripts he was editing in red pencil. Back then, I thought books were born whole, but he taught me about editing, how he would try to tease the best writing out of the author. It's a process, like anything else."

Vivian nods, and Eleanor can tell she's impressed.

Then Tabitha says, "Your daughters, Mrs. Roxie, are two of the most beautiful girls I've ever laid eyes on."

"Oh, stop," Vivian says. A blush creeps up her cheeks, and Eleanor notices the start of that most elusive of phenomena turning up Vivian's lips.

There is bright sunshine and low humidity on June 22. The church's air-conditioning works just fine. Flossie is the picture of good health, adorable with her blond curls and her blush-pink dress. Eleanor looks stunning in her gown (designed by Priscilla of Boston) and her veil. Her going-away suit is her own design—pencil skirt and bolero jacket in peach shantung silk. Once again, she told her mother she'd bought it at Filene's, and once again, Vivian believed her, which seems to bode well for Eleanor's future career.

Eleanor doesn't think of Rhonda at all until near the end of the service when Reverend Caruthers says, "If any man can show just cause why they may not lawfully be joined together, let him now speak or else hereafter forever hold his peace." The church is quiet. Eleanor scans the first few rows of the bride's side, but she doesn't see Rhonda, and the rest of the church is a swarm of faces, all of them beaming.

Eleanor and Billy are married.

They stand at the entrance to the Country Club to greet people as husband and wife. The guest list is much the same as it was for the Christmas party with the addition of Eleanor's friends from Mount Ida and Billy's friends from trade school, from UMass, from Boston Latin, from childhood—including his pal Ian, who lost his left leg in Vietnam at the Battle of Ia Drang. He labors up the front steps on crutches, but his countenance is bright.

Glen Bingham has come to the wedding, and as soon as Eleanor sees him, she introduces him to Miss Pitch, her father's secretary. They head inside together, and Billy turns to Eleanor. "Matchmaking, are we?"

Eleanor doesn't know what to say. She is so unimaginably *happy* that she wants everyone to feel as she does. She wants everyone to be in love.

The flow of guests has slowed to a trickle, and Eleanor is about to lead Billy inside for a glass of champagne—her mother will be watching—when she sees a young woman in a canary-yellow linen shift dress and a matching pillbox hat approaching. Eleanor's eyes widen. "Rhonda!" she says.

"Sorry I missed the service," Rhonda says. "I had to finish something for class."

"Class?" Eleanor says. She can't get over how different Rhonda looks. The dress is clean and pressed, the nude kitten heels are appropriate, and Rhonda has cut her hair to shoulder length. It flips up at the ends now, just like Marlo Thomas's. She is wearing a pearl necklace and pearl earrings.

"I go to Katie Gibbs now," Rhonda says.

"Good for you," Billy says. He reaches out to embrace Rhonda, then Eleanor does the same, although she feels discombobulated, nearly duped, by Rhonda's transformation. The real magician isn't Frank Paley, she thinks—it's Win. This is a better trick than pulling a dollar bill out of a lemon. Rhonda is presentable, nearly pretty!

Rhonda holds on to their hands and looks each of them squarely in the eye. "I am so happy for the two of you," she says. "You are a stunning, dynamic couple. People in this country need something to believe in, and I know that everyone in attendance today believes in the two of you. You radiate more than love—you radiate hope."

Hope, Eleanor thinks. She felt it in the church, all eyes on them. She felt the wedding guests' faith and their optimism — despite the war raging in Southeast Asia, despite the killing of President Kennedy's brother in California just a couple of weeks earlier. Some things are bigger than circumstance, bigger than history. Love is bigger. Resiliency is bigger.

Eleanor squeezes her cousin's hand. "Thanks, Rhonda," she says. "That means a whole lot coming from you." She eyes Rhonda's dress again and decides that although the dress is fine as it is, it would be even better with a belt, an obi belt, perhaps, like the Japanese geisha girls wear. *Yes!* Eleanor thinks. She will hunt down a matching shade of linen and make such a belt for Rhonda herself as soon as she gets home from her honeymoon.

She ushers her cousin forward and offers her new husband her arm. "Enough standing around," she says. "Let's get this new life of ours started."

Frank Sinatra Drive

(Read with *The Perfect Couple*)

This is a previously unpublished extra chapter!

When I was growing up, I loved Choose Your Own Adventure books. It was intriguing to me as a budding writer that in fiction, as in life, there are choices to be made—if you head in one direction, you will have a completely different outcome than if you head in another direction. "Frank Sinatra Drive" is an "alternative ending" to my novel *The Perfect Couple,* told from the point of view of Shooter Uxley. Shooter runs a company called A-List that sets up bucket-list trips and experiences for business executives. His job is to "work magic" and "make dreams come true." And in this story, he decides to manipulate the circumstances of the Winbury wedding—choosing a different path from the one described in the book—in an attempt to create his own "happily ever after." This story is set in Palm Springs, where

I went on a short vacation the week after I turned in the first draft of *The Perfect Couple*. Palm Springs is a unique place and I found it a terrific inspiration for this piece. Good luck, Shooter. I hope it works out!

Let's say it didn't happen that way.

Michael Oscar Uxley, known exclusively as "Shooter" since his senior year at St. George's School in Newport, Rhode Island, where he ran a dice game in a dark third-floor dorm hallway referred to as Lost Arden, is in the business of making dreams come true. He's the founder of a company called A-List that brings executives from overseas to experience the best of what America has to offer. He likes to tell clients that he can make anything happen. You want a spot with Jimmie Johnson's pit crew during the Daytona 500? He'll make a call. An eight o'clock Saturday night reservation at Le Coucou in New York City, impossible to get if you're a mere mortal? Shooter can arrange it in his sleep. Access to any experience is just a matter of knowing the right people.

Shooter wonders if it's possible to work a little magic on his own behalf. He wants to try.

Let's say Thomas Winbury is able to keep his on-again/off-again affair with Featherleigh Dale a secret—or, better still, let's say Thomas ends his relationship with Featherleigh the morning after his first date with Abby Freeman, when he has a pretty good idea that Abby is someone he would like to get serious with. (Thomas loves Abby's snub nose, her Southern sorority-girl accent, and the aura of easy entitlement that comes from being the daughter of the sixth-richest oilman in Texas.) If this were the case, then Abby Winbury, fifteen weeks pregnant with a boy who will no doubt be named Thomas Charles Winbury IV, would have no reason to drop Greer's sleeping pills into anyone's water, and chances are Merritt Monaco would still be alive.

"Chances are" isn't quite good enough for Shooter, however. Because there's still the slight possibility that if Merritt had chased the silver lace thumb ring, which fell off while she was rinsing the cut on her foot, into deep enough water, she might have been held hostage by the weight of her wet jersey dress and the exhaustion that comes with early pregnancy, especially at that late hour.

So...let's say Merritt and Tag Winbury do have a brief affair—face it, they are destructive magnets to each other's moral compasses—but Merritt uses birth control like a reasonable, responsible twenty-nine-year-old single woman. She does *not* get pregnant and she does *not* threaten to tell Greer anything about their liaison. By the time the wedding weekend is upon them, the fling is over. Do Tag and Merritt still harbor feelings for each other? Maybe so, but the only outward indication is a few sly glances.

There, Merritt is safe.

While Shooter is at it, why not make things better for Karen Otis? What if her secret is *not* that she illegally acquired euthanasia medicine off the internet from the mysterious Dr. Tang but rather that she has been part of a clinical trial at St. Luke's Hospital in Bethlehem, Pennsylvania, that has put her cancer into remission. She hasn't yet told Celeste because she doesn't want to get anyone's hopes up, but the fact is, she feels stronger.

Okay, Shooter thinks. *Great.* His work here is done.

Now it's time for the happily ever after.

When they get back from town the night before the wedding, Celeste heads upstairs. It's a quarter after one; she sets her alarm for five thirty. As she crawls into the bed in Benji's room—a bed with the most sumptuous sheets one can imagine—she looks at her wedding dress, which is hanging on the back of the closet door. Does she feel any regret about not wearing it? *Regret* is the wrong word. Mostly, she's sorry for the pain and heartbreak she is about to cause—to Benji, certainly, but also to Greer and Tag, who have been so generous. They have paid for everything, down to the monogrammed cocktail napkins, and they've asked for nothing in return except for Celeste to show up and say, "I do."

Celeste doesn't worry about anyone else. The other guests are about to have a story they can dine out on for the rest of their lives.

Celeste sends Merritt a text: When you wake up in the morning, I'll be gone. I'm fine. I'll explain later. She doesn't worry about Merritt. Running off the morning of her wedding to be with someone else falls squarely in Merritt's wheelhouse.

Celeste falls asleep, then wakes up and is dismayed to see that it's only ten past four. She has another hour and twenty minutes. Her blood tingles with the spice of her escape. She wonders about Shooter. He's in the first cottage with Benji, but she doesn't dare text him. If she were to text him, she would say, *Are we doing the right thing?* Because it's crazy, their plan. Run off, fly to Vegas, get married later today? That won't happen, she decides. They will get to Hyannis, rent a car, drive back to New York. Maybe they'll take a trip; Celeste doesn't have to be back at work for two weeks.

Her parents, though. Celeste needs to talk to her parents. She slides out of bed, tiptoes down the hall, and opens the door to their room. They're both sound asleep, of course; Bruce is snoring.

Celeste eases down next to Karen. Karen's face is twitching; she's having a dream. Celeste gently touches her mother's shoulder, and Karen's eyes fly open.

"Aaaaahhhh!" she cries out.

"Shhh!" Celeste says. "It's okay, Betty, it's me. I need to talk to you."

Karen blinks rapidly. Celeste watches her regain full consciousness; it's as though she's breaking through the surface of water. "Darling," she says. "What's wrong? Never mind, I already know."

"You *do?*" Celeste says. She doesn't want to sound like a teenager, but she's quite sure her mother does *not* know. Celeste has done far too fine a job of pretending for anyone to know the truth. Hasn't she?

"You don't want to marry Benji," Karen says. "You're running off."

Celeste stares at her mother and feels very, very exposed.

Karen takes Celeste's hand. She has grown frail since she's been sick but her grip is strong and warm. "It's okay," she says.

"Running off is only half of it," Celeste says. "I'm in love with Shooter."

"Ah," Karen says. The skin above her eyes — where her eyebrows used to be, before chemo — lifts. "That I didn't know. I mean, he certainly seems like he's crazy about you — that comment he made earlier tonight gave it away — but I didn't realize the feeling was mutual."

Celeste nods. Suddenly, the ugliness of her situation is magnified, like she's looking at it in a fun-house mirror. "Aren't you upset?" Celeste asks. "Aren't you...I don't know...*horrified?*" She has long suspected her parents love her so much that they would forgive her for anything — murder, grand larceny, arson.

"Everyone has secrets, Celeste," Karen says.

"You don't," Celeste says. "And Mac doesn't."

"Mac does," Karen says.

"He does?" Celeste says.

"Oh, yes," Karen says ominously. She pauses. "Your father's secret is that . . . he's pretending to be asleep right now."

"He is?" Celeste says.

"I can tell by the way he's breathing," Karen says. "He's awake, listening to every word we say."

"Mac?" Celeste says to her father.

"Go, sweetheart," Bruce says. "And remember we love you."

Celeste kisses her parents goodbye, then pads down the hall to her room and changes into her pale pink sheath with the nautical rope detail. This was supposed to be her going-away outfit, what she'd wear when she and Benji left for the airport after the Sunday farewell brunch. The trappings of this wedding have meant little to Celeste but she did love the old-fashioned elegance of a going-away outfit, and now, since she is going away, she will wear it.

Celeste grabs her yellow paisley Vera Bradley duffel bag and leaves the Winbury house. Her relief at a clean escape outweighs her regret at knowing she can never return.

At ten after six, Celeste and Shooter meet on the bench at the side of the Steamship terminal.

"How'd it go?" Shooter asks.

"Easier than I expected," Celeste says.

Which was exactly how Shooter had planned it.

Shooter doesn't take Celeste to Las Vegas; it's no place for a genuine lady. Instead, he books a suite at the Ritz-Carlton in Palm Springs. Shooter is a big, big fan of Palm Springs. He likes the midcentury vibe, the ghosts of old Hollywood, the endless emerald patchwork of golf courses (which he will ignore while Celeste is present), and, of course, the weather. There's never a cloud in the sky.

His enjoyment of Palm Springs is enhanced by Celeste's enthusiasm. She has never been anywhere with palm trees. She has never been in a desert or seen a cactus growing in the wild. She loves the street names—Gene Autry Trail, Bing Crosby Drive, Jack Benny Road, and, her favorite, which is felicitous because it's where their hotel is located—Frank Sinatra Drive.

"This is where they all hung out back in the day," Shooter says. "Bob Hope, George Burns and Gracie Allen, Dean Martin, Dinah Shore, and, of course, Frank."

He swings their rented Camaro, top down, into the circle in front of the Ritz.

"Welcome back, Mr. Uxley," the valet says as he opens Celeste's door.

Welcome back, welcome back, welcome back, the valet, the bellman, the front-desk clerk say. Shooter starts to feel uneasy. He knows that the staff has been trained to remember all of their repeat customers, but Shooter can't help feeling like a heel. He was here four weeks ago with Benji for the bachelor party and now he is here with Benji's fiancée. Former fiancée.

He wants nothing more than to get Celeste up to the room. Benji wouldn't believe it, nobody would believe it, but Shooter has not yet slept with Celeste. He wanted to wait; he wanted to be away, relaxed, out from under the blistering fire of this thing they've done. He hasn't checked his phone since leaving Nantucket and neither has Celeste; they agreed that would be best.

He sees a figure walking toward him in the hall, a man — tall, thin, blond hair, glasses.

Shooter's heart sinks.

"Mr. Uxley!" the man says.

"Hey, Frank," Shooter says. Frank is the concierge on the club floor; this is a relationship Shooter has given a lot of time and energy to. He and Frank shake hands. "And please don't ever let me hear you calling me Mr. Uxley again."

Frank laughs. "Okay, Shooter, sorry." He turns to Celeste. "And who have we here?"

"Celeste Otis," she says, shaking Frank's hand. "It's a pleasure." She offers him a smile so beautiful that Shooter's knees grow weak. She is happy, finally, and there is nothing more attractive on a woman than happiness.

"A pleasure to meet you, Miss Otis," Frank says. "Where are you visiting from?"

"New York City," she says.

"Very nice," Frank says. "And what do you do in New York?"

"I'm the assistant director of the Bronx Zoo," Celeste says.

Frank stiffens. Maybe. Or maybe Shooter is imagining it. Shooter is pretty sure Benji talked to Frank at length about his impending wedding and about Celeste's job. But does Frank remember? Does he retain stuff like that? Wouldn't it be virtually impossible with so many guests in and out of the hotel on a daily basis?

If Frank does put two and two together, what will he think of Shooter? It's cringe-worthy.

Frank says, "We actually have a wonderful zoo here in Palm Springs called the Living Desert Zoo and Gardens."

"You do?" Celeste says. She turns to Shooter. "Can we go?"

"Of course," Shooter says. He puts his hand on her back to usher her down the hall. "Good to see you, Frank."

"And you," Frank says. "Nice to meet you, Miss Otis."

When they are out of earshot, Celeste whispers, "Everyone knows you."

"Yes," Shooter says. He supposes that's why he brought Celeste here. Benji has money; Shooter has relationships. He should feel good about this, but instead he feels like a common thief.

*　　*　　*

Shooter and Celeste are perfectly compatible—better than compatible; they are greater than the sum of their parts. They give off heat and light. Shooter is relieved. He's aware that he could have been disappointed once the drama of their escape had passed. But he can't get enough of her. When she goes for a run the next morning, his heart aches with missing her. He falls back to sleep clutching her pillow.

When she returns, she calls her parents from the room, tells them she's safe. Her parents have made it home to Pennsylvania.

"Don't tell me anything else yet," Celeste says. "Please."

"Good for you," Shooter says when she hangs up. "What do you want to do today? Lunch by the pool? Massage? Hike in Joshua Tree?"

"Can we go to the zoo?" she asks.

It has been a long time since Shooter has been to a zoo. There was a field trip to the Franklin Park Zoo while he was a student at Fessenden, and he dated a girl who dragged him to the National Zoo in DC to see the pandas. The Living Desert Zoo and Gardens are small and manageable. Celeste studies the map; she's as eager as a little kid.

"They've obviously been well funded," she says. "Look how immaculate this place is. And they've stuck to what they know—animals from hot and dry climates."

Shooter and Celeste see the addax, the striped hyenas, and the serval. At the meerkat habitat, there's a silver-haired gentleman in suit pants and a tie holding a clipboard, and Celeste goes right up to introduce herself. Shooter hangs back, watching her in action. She and the gentleman — Jack, Shooter hears him say — point at the exhibit in front of them, then at Celeste's map, then they must get into shop talk because it seems like the conversation is never going to end. Shooter is torn between feeling jealous of this Jack guy and feeling awestruck by how smart and knowledgeable Celeste is.

When she finally breaks away from Jack, she has a business card in her hand. "He's the director," she says, grinning. "He offered me a job."

The business card of Jack Colgate, director of the Living Desert Zoo and Gardens, is like a silver ball bearing at the start of a Rube Goldberg contraption. Why don't they *move* to Palm Springs? It would be better if they left New York, right? Fresh start, et cetera. Shooter can do his job from anywhere; he travels so much anyway, and he's in Las Vegas all the time. He can be home with Celeste more once he cuts out the cross-country travel.

They talk about it over dinner at Jake's. They are seated in the courtyard with a couple of martinis. Celeste is wearing a green dress. Her hair is long and loose around her face; she doesn't wear any makeup. Her beauty is all natural, enhanced by moisturizer, Chap-Stick, and a light tan from the afternoon sun.

"What about your parents?" Shooter says. He paid enough attention over the truncated wedding weekend to realize that Celeste living three thousand miles away from her parents won't work.

"What if they sold their house and bought an RV and moved out here?" Celeste asks. "They've always dreamed of doing that."

"They have?" Shooter says.

"Well, no," Celeste admits. "But probably because they haven't thought of it. I bet they would quit their jobs, sell the house, take a nice long road trip out here, and relocate. My father can get a job at a men's clothier—"

"Wil Stiles," Shooter says. Now his wheels are turning.

"And my mother can work in a shop, maybe a place that sells home goods—"

"Just Fabulous," Shooter says. "Or Motif."

"You can teach my father to play golf," Celeste says.

"Would they live with us?" Shooter says.

"Only when they're not traveling," Celeste says.

Before Shooter met Celeste, his worst nightmare was being tied down, owning a house with a yard and a driveway, living with his girlfriend's parents. No one in his right mind wants to live with his girlfriend's parents. No one in his right mind wants to teach his girl-friend's father to play golf.

And yet, the visions Shooter has of this future fill him with exuberance. On the way home from Jake's that night, Shooter drives the Camaro through a residential neighborhood, and he and Celeste inspect the homes.

"I like that one," Celeste says. "That one right there."

The girl has taste, Shooter thinks. The house she has picked out is low-slung and modern with a sexy curved front porch. The yard is an artfully lit landscape of gravel and cacti (nothing to mow, Shooter notes). There's a tall fence around the backyard, meaning there's a pool and, likely, an outdoor bar, maybe even a pizza oven. If not, they can put one in.

Is the house for sale? Why, yes, there's a discreet sign with a broker's number. Shooter writes the number down, then spends another long moment staring at the front of the house. It's like looking into a crystal ball.

In his crystal ball, he sees Celeste hired as the assistant director of the Living Desert Zoo and Gardens, and nearly as soon as she is hired, the zoo is given an enormous donation that's earmarked for a primate exhibit, specifically for silverback gorillas, and this becomes Celeste's project. She loves the job, loves her coworkers, and flourishes in her new role in the community. She is asked to join the Palm Springs Chamber of Commerce.

She starts going to a barre studio in Palm Desert. She shops for clothes at the Trina Turk boutique and she looks so stunning in the clothes that they ask if she would be willing to model for them at a fashion show at L'Horizon to benefit the Bob Hope USO. Celeste says she would be honored.

Shooter shifts the primary locus of A-List from New York to Palm Springs. The golf, the swimming pools, and the weather can't be beat. He works out a deal with Frank, and all of the executives stay on the concierge floor at the Ritz. Shooter still has to travel, but no more than one week a month. Celeste isn't lonely, because her parents, Bruce and Karen—Shooter has been invited to call them Mac and Betty—now live in the east wing of the house.

How does Shooter feel about living with Mac and Betty?

It's a dream come true.

No, seriously.

Mac does every bit of handyman work that's needed around the house: He paints the trim, he cares for the pool, he washes Shooter's car. He works at Wil Stiles twenty hours a week and spends most of his paycheck buying clothes for himself. Shooter can say one thing: The guy likes to look good.

Betty, meanwhile, is in charge of feeding everyone, a responsibility she does not take lightly. The retro, midcentury vibe of Palm Springs is perfectly suited to Betty's culinary style. The very first thing she makes for Shooter is a layered meat loaf, which is essentially an inside-out hamburger: the two meat layers sandwich a filling of savory bread crumbs, celery, onion, and herbs. It's the most delicious meat loaf Shooter has ever eaten. He also loves the potato salad gelatin mold Betty makes to go with it, which initially he declared too pretty to eat—it was a wreath of creamy potato goodness studded with pimiento-stuffed olives and pale green chunks of cucumber and garnished with long, slender scallions.

"Did you eat like this growing up?" Shooter asks Celeste as they stand together at the sink doing the dishes. Shooter washes and Celeste dries because when Celeste was growing up, Bruce and Karen took those respective roles. After dinner, Bruce and Karen walk through the neighborhood hand in hand because Karen has grown fond of the desert sky at night. Sometimes they stop in at the Bigelows' house down the street for a cordial. Last week, the Bigelows invited Bruce and Karen over for fondue.

"Sort of," Celeste says. "She's definitely gotten more into it since we've moved here."

Right, Shooter thinks. Karen created something called a Luau Wheelbarrow Ice Bar that was a fruit phantasmagoria in a wheelbarrow full of ice—blackberry sorbet in hollowed-out cantaloupes, watermelon and strawberry kebabs, and lots and lots of pineapple. It was so visually stunning that Shooter took pictures.

He has gained eight pounds.

Sometimes when he is entertaining the executives, he will mention that he lives with his girlfriend and his girlfriend's parents and he will roll his eyes, which always evokes groans of sympathy. But the truth is, Shooter loves having Bruce and Karen around. They are...parents, real-life, hands-on parents, the kind Shooter never had growing up. He can spend an hour passing Bruce tools as Bruce reupholsters some swivel barstools he found at a yard sale, and he can let Betty push a third slice of her black-magic cake (made with canned tomato soup!) on him...because this is what he's been missing his entire life.

He is happy.

He is whole.

He pulls himself away from his imaginary crystal ball when he feels Celeste's hand on his arm. She yawns and then he yawns; they are not quite adjusted to the time change. Back in New York—and on Nantucket— it's two o'clock in the morning.

"Should we go back to the hotel?" Celeste asks.

The next day, they relax by the pool. Celeste is reading a novel called *The Heirs* about a wealthy family on the Upper East Side of Manhattan (gulp), and she's laughing every few pages—in recognition? he wonders. He also wonders if it's a novel Benji recommended or maybe even bought for her. Benji is an avid reader; he was always impressive when he talked about books, even in high school at St. George's. Shooter has brought along a copy of Malcolm Gladwell's *The Tipping Point* that he borrowed from the concierge floor so that Celeste wouldn't think he was a complete illiterate; he has no intention of reading it.

Instead, Shooter watches Celeste read. He notices the slight curve of her lips, the concentration that tenses her forehead, the movement of her eyes. Celeste told him the story of how Karen knows Bruce so well that she can tell when he's faking sleep. Shooter wants to know Celeste that well, and better.

He drifts off.

He dreams it's April. Coachella. Shooter has a group of fifty executives in from Hungary and Bulgaria. Fifty is a large number, but... Coachella. Shooter decides to do the previously unthinkable and marry his professional and personal lives: He invites all fifty gentlemen to the house for a barbecue.

It's funny — over the years, Shooter has come to understand that the biggest asset of the company is himself. The clients like him; they think he's fun and charming and suave. Near the end of a retreat, they often start peppering him with personal questions: Is he married? Does he have a girlfriend? Is she hot? Where does he live? What does he drive? Shooter has become skillful at deflecting such inquiries. This tactic has created a kind of mystique, but really, Shooter doesn't answer the questions because he knows his clients will find the answers disappointing.

But now—now the executive group appears at the front door of Shooter and Celeste's midcentury showpiece, and Shooter escorts them back to the pool, where Bobby Darin is crooning on the sound system, where Celeste is beaming and radiant in a Lilly Pulitzer patio dress, holding an ice-cold martini, where Bruce is manning the grill, wearing an apron over his orange-and-green psychedelic paisley pants, and Karen is offering the gentlemen cubed-cheese-and-salami kebabs, each one garnished with a cherry tomato that's garnished with an olive. In Karen's world, the garnishes have garnishes.

"Let's get this party started!" Shooter says.

Just then he feels a disruption to his right. Someone has taken the chaise next to his and is blocking his sun. Shooter opens his eyes, blinks. Is he still dreaming?

No.

It's Benji.

Shooter struggles to sit up. His mouth is dry, his ears are ringing. Benji, here. How did he find them? Well, it wouldn't have been hard. Benji knows the handful of places that Shooter frequents; all he would have had to do was make a few phone calls.

Shooter looks to his left. Celeste is gone. Her book is splayed open on her chaise.

"Here," Benji says. He hands one of the two beers he's holding to Shooter.

"Thanks?" Shooter says. He swings his feet to the ground, sets the beer down for a second, and pulls on his shirt. He's completely unprepared for this confrontation. But he knew it would come eventually, didn't he? He stole his best friend's girl. He broke up the perfect couple. "Benji, listen, I'm—"

"Don't apologize," Benji says.

Right, Shooter thinks. This isn't something that can be *apologized* away. Shooter has betrayed a fifteen-year friendship. What will settle it, then? A fistfight? No. This is Benjamin Winbury. Will Benji go up to the concierge floor and tell Frank that Shooter Uxley is a backstabbing Benedict Arnold? No chance of that. Whatever is going to happen will be private and deeply painful.

But wait, Shooter thinks as he picks up his beer and takes a long, cold swallow. What if it *didn't* happen that way?

"You actually did me a favor," Benji says.

"I did?" Shooter says.

"Celeste and I are so different," Benji says. "Different worlds and all that."

"Right," Shooter says. "But I thought that didn't matter? I thought you loved her?"

"Oh, I do love her," Benji says. "But loving someone doesn't bring automatic happiness. In fact, it can bring quite the opposite. When Celeste and I were together, I always felt like there was a part of her I wasn't reaching, a part she was holding back. And you know, practically better than anyone, that I'm a giver and a pleaser and a fixer...so life with a woman I couldn't make blissfully happy would have been torture for me." Benji takes a swig of his beer and Shooter studies his friend's face, trying to determine if Benji is kidding or being sarcastic. "I had a long talk with Reverend Derby and I think I've come to terms with this."

Come to terms with this? Shooter thinks. In only three days? Reverend Derby? The only thing Reverend Derby has been good for up to now has been giving the blessing before meals. Did he really lead Benji through the necessary soul-searching to reach this place of placid acceptance?

Shooter narrows his eyes. "So what are you going to do?"

Benji sighs. "Honestly? I'll probably get back together with Jules."

"Jules?" Shooter says. He fights to keep his tone neutral, but inside he's shouting: *No, man! Do not get back together with that miserable, shallow woman!* The thought of Benji resorting to a life with Jules Briar makes Shooter feel fresh regret about what he's done.

"I guess her friend Laney saw you and Celeste standing in line for pizza Friday night," Benji says. "And Jules texted me to say that if I was having second thoughts, she was still in love with me. She said Miranda still asks for me every night at bedtime."

Shooter nods. Laney was the one who took the

picture, then, he thinks. And Jules was the one who texted it to him, he's sure. She could tell, probably just from the look on his face, what the story was. Which is pretty intuitive for Jules; he has to give her credit. "What did your parents say?" Shooter asks. What he's really asking is: *What did Greer say?* Shooter doesn't give two shits about Tag's opinion.

"Well, you know how my mother feels about Jules," Benji says. "When she finds out we're back together, she'll make Jules the villainess in her next book."

"What did she say about me?" Shooter asks. "And Celeste?"

"She said she totally understands," Benji says. "She said she would have left me for you if she were Celeste."

"She did *not* say that," Shooter says.

Benji laughs. "No. But I could tell she was thinking it."

Shooter finishes his beer. He can't believe this is happening. He can't believe Benji is being so incredibly cool about this. He really is a prince. Actual royalty in the friend department. But his magnanimity makes Shooter feel like even more of a louse. Maybe that's the point?

"Let me buy the next round," Shooter says. "We can switch to vodka, if you want."

"No, thanks," Benji says. "I should go before Celeste gets back." He stands and then Shooter stands and looks around the pool at the other hotel guests, lounging in the sun, reading their books, or listening to music, completely oblivious to the incredible thing happening at the southwest corner of the pool. "I only came to clear the air with you. I figured you'd be feeling bad and I didn't want that to ruin things between us. It might take a little longer for Celeste to accept that there are no hard feelings. I get it. Love is a mystery. And not the kind of mystery that has a neat ending, like a Greer Garrison novel." He reaches out to embrace Shooter. "You deserve this. Just promise me you'll take good care of her. If I find out otherwise, I'm hiring a hit man, you hear me? Be true to her."

Shooter surprises himself by getting choked up. "I will."

Benji is gone by the time Celeste gets back.

"I went to the room to call Merritt and let her know what happened," she says. "She's my best friend and I couldn't just have her not knowing. I hope you aren't angry."

Shooter considers telling Celeste about Benji appearing out of nowhere, but he decides she would never believe it.

"Not at all," he says.

That night, as Shooter and Celeste are getting ready to go to dinner at Mr. Lyons, there's a knock at the door. Shooter, wearing only a towel, is standing at the sink, shaving. Celeste is wrapped in the white waffle-weave hotel robe, so she answers the door.

"Hi, Frank," Shooter hears her say. "Look at you! Thank you so much!"

Shooter hears the door close, then a second later, Celeste's face appears in the mirror. She's holding an ice bucket that contains a bottle of Veuve Clicquot.

"Look!" she says. "Someone sent us this."

Shooter steels himself. The bottle must be from Benji; it's the same champagne he chose when he took Celeste up to the Wauwinet to propose. Shooter has been thinking all afternoon that he got off way too easily. Benji must be planning some kind of elaborate revenge, and the visit by the pool was a trick to lull Shooter into a false sense of security.

"Who's it from?" he asks carefully.

"I'll look at the card, hold on," Celeste says.

Her face appears in the mirror a few seconds later. She's beaming.

"It's from Merritt!" she says. "The card says: 'Here's to your happily ever after.'"

Happily ever after, Shooter thinks. *This is it. Right here on Frank Sinatra Drive.* He decides to enjoy it.

While it lasts.

The Sixth Wedding

(Read with 28 Summers)

There's a way in which *28 Summers* leaves readers with a bunch of unanswered questions. Do Bess and Link get together? Do Jake and Ursula stay married? Does Ursula win the presidential election? What happens to Cooper, Leland, Frazier Dooley? I decided I would let these beloved characters go back to Mallory's cottage on the no-name road one last time—and, just maybe, catch one last glimpse of Mallory herself.

What are we talking about in 2023? Home robots, life on planet B20, the resurgence of "appointment television," an NFL team in Paris, a phone battery that holds a charge for one year, the Hamptons submarine, Elon Musk's moon colony, an eight-billion-sensor economy and... the end of the pandemic. Social distancing, quarantining, PCR and antigen tests, masks and PPE are in our collective rearview mirror. We can gather once again. Twenty thousand people pack into Madison Square Garden to hear Billy Joel segue from "My Life" into a cover of "Tenth Avenue Freeze-Out." Super Bowl LVII is held in Glendale, Arizona, and those who don't have tickets crowd around the bar at Kimmyz on the Greenway. Movie theaters are packed, people do the Electric Slide at weddings, and Viking River Cruises has a three-year wait list. Every treadmill at Orangetheory Fitness in Boca Raton is spoken for; all Peloton classes in both New York and LA are sold out. The late-night Jimmys perform their monologues in front of live studio audiences. The Broadmoor Hotel in Colorado Springs is at 95 percent occupancy and there's no

hope for getting a ticket to a Boston Pops Christmas per-formance unless you want to pay five thousand dollars on StubHub. Bingo night at Chai Point Senior Living in Milwaukee is back on, every Wednesday at six! We all go to have our teeth cleaned, our eyes checked. The theme of the Met Ball is Fashion Returns (people get dressed up, wear heels). The impossible-to-get item is no longer toilet paper, it's a seat on Alitalia's Friday-night flight from JFK to Rome. The online-dating scene rebounds with a fervor—people are meeting IRL!—with newcomer Fire-pink leading the way for Gen X and boomers. The Dow soars over 40,000—and we thought the 1920s were roaring!

Although we are relieved that life is "getting back to normal"—we have returned to our offices and in-person meetings and we're throwing away our ring lights; if we never Zoom again, it will be too soon—we have all learned some valuable lessons, and not just how to make sour-dough bread. We have learned to save and budget for the unexpected. We have learned to cherish all the things we temporarily lost: baseball games, author tours, Disney World, family reunions, charity benefits, college visits (col-lege, period), our sense of taste and smell, acoustic night at Frayed Edge Coffee, sitting next to a stranger on a bus or at a bar, seeing one another smile, and, most especially, the opportunity to hug our loved ones wherever we want, whenever we want.

We honor the ones we have lost.

What are we talking about in 2023? We are talking

about our shared grief. We are talking about our collective gratitude.

COOPER

In the summer of 2023, Cooper Blessing is fifty-six years old, and when he gets down on one knee on the sidewalk in front of the Red Star Bar and Grill in Fells Point, he's momentarily concerned that he'll need help getting back up. But he'll worry about that in a minute.

"Stacey," he says, prying the ring box open. The ring is a 1.75-carat ruby flanked by 1-carat oval diamonds set in platinum. Cooper bought the ring at Market Street Diamonds, which was where he bought rings for wives numbers one and four, but those had been diamonds only. The ruby is something new; it's Stacey's birthstone. "Will you marry me?"

Stacey Patterson's eyes widen. The people who are gathered outside the Red Star—couples dining at the café tables, people in line for the bar, an older gentleman out walking his Pomeranian—turn to stare.

Stacey takes the ring box and snaps it shut. "Let's go to the car," she says, and she offers Cooper a hand.

They're parked in the lot across Wolfe Street; the walk there is like an extended free fall. Cooper and Stacey have had a wonderful evening. The Red Star has been their place for the past eight months: the hostesses, bartenders, and waitstaff know them by name. They had drinks and dinner and they danced to the live band, Purple Porpoise, until they were sweaty and breathless, making Cooper feel like he was twenty-two again, a senior at Johns Hopkins out on a date with his Goucher girlfriend.

He's wise enough to keep his mouth shut until they reach Stacey's car, a sleek silver Audi A4. Stacey appreciates fine automobiles, one of the many things Cooper loves about her.

When they climb in, Stacey cranks the air-conditioning, which is a relief. The Baltimore night is hot, sticky, foul. "I'm not going to marry you, Cooper."

"You're not?" he says. He closes his eyes and tries to let the cool air soothe him. How did he misread this? At the risk of sounding sappy, he thought this would be his storybook ending.

Cooper first saw Stacey Patterson thirty-seven years earlier at a party in the basement of the Phi Gamma Delta house. It was early September, the first week of school. Cooper had the robust confidence of a sopho-more and he was finally in a position to chat up the freshman women from Goucher (they had all ignored him the year before). He picked Stacey like he was cut-ting the prettiest bloom off a rosebush. Stacey had long dark hair and she was wearing a yellow sundress. The other women in her cluster were in jean shorts, one in shorts overalls, reminding Cooper of his younger sis-ter, Mallory, who intentionally "dressed to distress."

Cooper's parents, Senior and Kitty, were formal people who believed in good grooming and strong first impressions. As enthusiastically as Mallory rejected these values, Cooper embraced them. He admired not only Stacey's dress but her pearl earrings, her sandals, her French manicure. She was put together. Cooper walked right up to Stacey and offered his hand and a smile, thinking how delighted Kitty would be when Cooper brought this young woman home.

Cooper and Stacey had dated for three years, until Cooper graduated from Hopkins, moved to Washington, DC, scored a prestigious job with the Brookings Institution, and decided that he had outgrown his college girlfriend. Stacey wasn't quite as upset as Cooper thought she might be. Because she'd been dating Cooper since her freshman year, she hadn't had the "full college experience," she told him. The breakup would be good for them both, she said—what she meant, it turned out, was that she wanted to date other people, starting with the captain of the Hopkins lacrosse team.

Okay, fine, Cooper thought. *Good for Stacey.* He could meet women at any of the trillion bars in Georgetown. The problem was that Cooper was back to being a freshman—a freshman at adult life—and the women that Cooper met at Clyde's and the Tombs were clerking for this judge, interning for that senator, researching those initiatives at the NIH, and they intimidated him. Often, when Cooper got home from the bars at night, he called Stacey.

Sometimes she answered; sometimes she didn't.

Cooper and Stacey got back together briefly ten years later when Cooper was home in Baltimore for Christmas and Stacey, still single, was working as VP of marketing at the Baltimore Aquarium. That interlude fell between Cooper's first and second marriages, and although Stacey had been eager to get more serious, Cooper was hesitant (though why, he can't recall) and he'd stopped calling.

Stacey married one of the marine biologists at the aquarium and had two children—first a daughter, Amanda, and five years later, a son, Alec. Stacey and her family lived in Ellicott City, the kids went to parochial school, and husband and wife presumably commuted to work together. Cooper received a Christmas card every year, the tasteful kind with carefully curated photos—skiing in the Poconos, on the beach in Rehoboth—and he thought, *Okay, fine. Good for Stacey.*

This past Christmas, however, the card included pictures of only Stacey and the kids; the husband, Lars, wasn't mentioned. A quick check of Facebook confirmed that Stacey was once again single.

At that point, Cooper had been divorced from Amy for nearly three years. He couldn't call Stacey fast enough—and they had been together ever since. Nearly eight months.

They were happy, he thought. They joked all the time about how their relationship was the "best use of Facebook." It was good that no one would ever forget your birthday again, but that didn't hold a candle to being able to reunite with your old flame.

"You've been married five times," Stacey says now. "And divorced five times. I love you, but you're a bad bet, and although I have some negative qualities, stupidity isn't one of them. The quickest way to put an end to this relationship is to get married."

Coop opens the ring box. The ruby is the color of a bleeding heart.

"But I like being married," Coop says.

"You don't, though," Stacey says. "You've failed at it five times, Coop. That isn't normal."

"Maybe the sixth time is the charm," Cooper says. He's trying for levity. Stacey has a great sense of humor; she's fun, she's smart and secure, she gets it—*it* being the world, life—in a way that none of his wives did, and Cooper wants to grow old with her. They can take Viking River Cruises, drive an RV across America, watch *Jeopardy!*, learn to play bridge.

Stacey starts the car. "There's something wrong with you, Coop. And I was mistaken before. The quickest way to put an end to this relationship is for you to propose on the sidewalk like that."

"That was impulsive. I'm sorry," Coop says. "What if I start over privately here and now? Please, Stacey, will you marry me?"

"No," she says as she feeds their parking stub into the greedy mouth of the machine at the exit. The barrier rises. "I'm sorry, but no."

*   *   *

There's something wrong with you, Coop. Stacey Patterson had the courage to state what no one else would. All his life, people have been telling Cooper he's an "old soul." He's been here before, he was born with an... *ease.* An... *understanding.* Who was the first person to tell him this? His mother? A teacher? Geri Gladstone from across the street? Well, whoever it was had done Cooper a great disservice. He'd always trusted his instincts—even after they turned out to be wrong again and again and again. (And again and again.)

Cooper's most recent ex-wife, Amy, is a psychologist in the District, and in order to find someone who isn't a close colleague of Amy's, Cooper has to look in Northern Virginia. Fairfax, as it turns out, where he makes an appointment with a woman named Dr. Theron Robb. Whereas Amy is known as a touchy-feely therapist, Dr. Robb is cool and reserved. Cooper appreciates this. He doesn't need someone to empathize with him; he needs someone to tell him what's broken and how to fix it.

Dr. Robb is in her late forties, Cooper would guess. She's tall, Black, and as slender and graceful as a ballerina—but Cooper must think of his therapist as a person, not a woman.

"You lost your parents in a tragic car accident in 2013 and your sister to cancer in 2020. You've been divorced five times." Dr. Robb pauses. "That's a lot of loss."

Cooper nods.

"It's no wonder you proposed to Stacey," Dr. Robb says. "I'm sure you were driven by a primal instinct for permanence. Someone who would stay."

"Maybe?" Coop says. "I'm not completely alone. My nephew Link is living with me this summer, doing an internship at Brookings. We're close."

"But he'll go on to have his own life," Dr. Robb says. "He won't be with you forever."

"True." Cooper doesn't like to think about this. Link is the only family he has left, and Cooper loves the kid like a son, always has.

"Why did your marriages end?" Dr. Robb asks.

"Various reasons," Coop says. "Sometimes it was them, sometimes me. The most recent divorce was me. I wanted out."

Dr. Robb studies Cooper frankly from behind her glasses. He would love to know what she's thinking. "When was the last time you were happy?" she asks. "When was the last time things felt right? Can you take me back there?"

"I'm not completely obtuse," Coop says. "I've given this exact question a lot of thought. The mistakes started on Nantucket Island in 1993."

Dr. Robb laughs, startled. "I hadn't anticipated *that* kind of archaeological dig, but I'm game. What happened on Nantucket in 1993?"

"I left my own bachelor-party weekend," Coop says.

"My sister, Mallory, was cool enough to invite me and my two best friends to visit her over Labor Day. And then she had *her* best friend from growing up come as well, so there were five of us around the dinner table. I can remember when we all hoisted our glasses, remember thinking how *lucky* I was. That moment was... *golden*." Coop sighs. "Then, later that night, my fiancée, Krystel, called to demand that I come home. She was jealous, she was threatened—"

"Controlling," Dr. Robb says.

"And I left," Cooper says. "I abandoned my sister, I abandoned my friends. But most of all, I abandoned myself."

Dr. Robb nods.

"So I guess if I could go back to any point, I would choose that night."

"I see."

"A bunch of things happened that weekend after I left," Cooper says. "*Crazy* stuff, like from a novel or a movie. And I set them all in motion by leaving. If I had stayed on Nantucket in 1993 instead of going home... my sister's life, my friend Jake's life, and my friend Fray's life all would have been different."

"That's a pretty big statement," Dr. Robb says.

"I know," Cooper says. "But it's true." He drops his head into his hands. "I can't tell you how many times I've wished I could go back and do it over."

URSULA

On Sunday evenings, Ursula stops working long enough to make two phone calls—the first to her daughter, Bess, and the second to her ex-husband, Jake McCloud.

This is what passes for Ursula's family life these days.

Bess lives in Washington, DC, at the Sedgewick in Dupont Circle, just like Ursula herself had thirty years earlier. She works for the National Council of Non-profits, an umbrella organization that consults with and advises nonprofits across the country, and it's her dream job; Bess has always wanted to save the world and empower the disenfranchised, and in this job she doesn't have to choose between the homeless and hungry children—she helps everyone who's in need. Ursula sends Bess money for rent and living expenses, and if and when Bess decides she wants to go to law school, Ursula will pay for that as well.

"How was your week, sweetie?" Ursula asks.

"Long," Bess says. "I'm working with the Red Cross on their national campaign."

"That sounds exciting," Ursula says.

"The director basically offered me a job," Bess says.

"I'm not surprised," Ursula says. More likely than Bess going to law school is that one of the nonprofits she's working with will snap her up as executive direc-tor. She has always been more like Jake than Ursula. "Did you do anything fun this weekend?"

"I had a date Friday night with some guy who works for the Nature Conservancy," Bess says. "I had to spend two hours pretending to be outdoorsy while he described climbing Denali. It was painful."

"DC is filled with men, sweetheart," Ursula says. "Find yourself a hot young lobbyist."

"I am *not* dating a lobbyist," Bess says. "But you're right, those guys are the hottest. Honestly, it's like hotness and social conscience are inversely proportional."

"Except for your father," Ursula says. "A do-gooder *and* hot."

"Ew, Mom, please."

"You're still so young," Ursula says. "You should wait at least another five years before..."

"I know, I know," Bess says. "How was your weekend, Mama? Did the great UDG do anything fun? Depose the bagel guy, maybe?"

Ursula smiles. She's standing in her living room in front of the floor-to-ceiling windows that overlook Central Park. She feels like she could dip her toe in the Bethesda Fountain. She's still in her running shorts and Lululemon tank, both damp with sweat. She did four laps around the reservoir as soon as the beastly heat of the day eased a bit. "I went for a run in the park," Ursula says. "So I'm feeling *very* outdoorsy. And I'm going to order up from Marea after I talk to Dad. The lobster and burrata salad. I've been thinking about it all day."

"You should start dating too, Mama," Bess says. "I

can make you a profile on Firepink? That's the new one for olds."

"Ha!" Ursula says. "Every man in this country already knows my profile. That's what happens when you run for president. You lose your mystique on the dating apps."

Bess laughs. "I love you, Mama."

"I love you too, baby," Ursula says. "Talk next week."

They hang up and Ursula stays at the window, watching the sky turn purple, and tries to judge how Bess sounded. A bit too much like Ursula herself: lonely, and working too hard.

Ursula and Bess hadn't always been this close; Bess's adolescence was a battlefield. Bess challenged Ursula's political views and called her out on her relentless ambition. *Achieving is the most important thing to you. It's more important than love,* Bess said when she was fifteen years old. And wow — Ursula had felt that comment like a slap in the face.

Bess has mellowed as she's gotten older. She approved of Ursula's vote against confirming Stone Cavendish as a Supreme Court justice, and when Ursula announced her bid for the presidency a short while later, Bess joined the campaign, courting Gen Z voters.

But the development that brought mother and daughter close, the event that finally made them *friends,* was Ursula's defeat on Election Day.

Ursula had been stunned when first Florida and then Ohio swung for her opponent, Fred Page. Ursula de

Gournsey and Fred Page weren't that dissimilar. Fred was a centrist who leaned a little left and Ursula a centrist who gravitated a bit toward the right, but they agreed on more than they disagreed on and their debates had been civil, even collegial. Ursula felt she could afford to be nice to Fred (she hadn't run a single attack ad) because she was dead certain that she was going to win. All of the polls had her ahead by three to five points. Her campaign had outspent Fred's campaign by 20 percent. Bayer Burkhart, who served as Ursula's shadow campaign manager, assured her daily that a de Gournsey presidency was a lock.

So what had happened?

All Ursula could come up with was that when people were alone in the voting booth, they couldn't bring themselves to vote for a woman.

The problem wasn't Ursula. It was American society.

Of course Ursula harbored plenty of private fears — that ultimately, she wasn't likable; that the country saw her naked ambition, her quest for power; that somehow she hadn't projected her desire to *serve* as effectively as Fred had. Ursula had focused too much on foreign policy and not enough on controlling the pandemic. She had mentioned Notre Dame too many times, and Georgetown Law; she had seemed like a braggart when she told Anderson Cooper that she was fluent in French, Spanish, Italian. She rarely attended church, despite her Catholic background. She hadn't seemed maternal enough or like a devoted-enough wife. So much more was expected of a female candidate.

It didn't matter. Fred Page had won fair and square. Ursula gave a beautiful concession speech wishing Fred the very best and encouraging her supporters to celebrate his victory.

She spent the next two days in their house in South Bend in a numb fog while Jake and Bess dealt with the news vans lined up on LaSalle Street. At night, Ursula would lie on the couch, clicking among the news outlets, listening to everyone's surprised reactions about the outcome. Bess brought Ursula mugs of tea that she didn't drink and made her sandwiches she didn't eat. Bess covered Ursula with a blanket at night and kissed her mother's temple.

"I'm proud of you," Bess said. "You're taking time to process. You aren't making excuses. You aren't *blaming* anyone. It takes an extraordinary person to handle this kind of loss as graciously as you are."

At these words, Ursula sat up and stretched out her arms. Bess came to her, and finally, Ursula cried. She cried for her broken dreams, dreams she'd nurtured since she was a child; she cried out of embarrassment; she cried for her dead father — she had wanted to make him proud. She cried from exhaustion and bone-deep weariness. She had given the campaign everything she had — nearly two full years of her life, trips to forty-three states, bus rides, flights, hotel conference rooms.

How many women, not to mention girls, had told her she was inspiring? How many virtual fundraisers had she attended where she had given some variation of her platform speech, "Straight Up the Fairway"? She spoke out for commonsense politics, against extremist agendas. Ursula would have been a moderate, clear-eyed president who used her intellect and her excellent judgment to govern.

She cried because she had been rejected, plain and simple.

"It hurts," she told Bess. "It really hurts."

"I know, Mama, but that's okay," Bess said. "Pain means you're growing."

The call came three weeks later while Ursula was still emotionally convalescing, still dismantling her campaign, and still working as a U.S. senator from Indiana.

It was Fred Page. He asked Ursula to serve in his cabinet. Attorney general.

This was, needless to say, unexpected. And it wasn't just a good-guy Fred Page promotional stunt. It wasn't a "nod to unity." Fred said, "You're the most accomplished lawyer I know. I would trust you above and beyond any other candidate on my list."

Yes, Ursula thought. *He's right. I would be the best at this job.*

Ursula told Fred she'd consider it, and she called her executive coach, Jeannie. After an hours-long conversation, Ursula and Jeannie reached some conclusions.

Ursula didn't want to be attorney general. She didn't want to stay in politics at all; when her senate term was up, she would return to private life. She wanted to go back into mergers and acquisitions. She wanted to live in New York City.

She would do both, she decided.

After she hung up with Jeannie, she went to the kitchen, where she found Jake walking in with a pizza from Barnaby's.

"We have to talk," she said.

"Jeannie and I decided—"

"You and Jeannie decided? You didn't bother to ask me what I thought? Because I don't matter, because you have no consideration for me or for this so-called family. Bess and I have always bent to your will and now your will is to be an attorney in New York and you think I'm just going to...what? Pick up and move my life there? I'm not, Ursula. I'm staying here."

Ursula had laughed. "I'm not staying here one day longer than I have to. South Bend is the last place I want to end up."

Jake stared at her. "I should have stood up to you long ago. Do you know why I didn't? Because I have always believed that you were special. But I'm not giving in on this. If you go to New York, Ursula, you go alone."

It was an ultimatum, but was he serious? Was Ursula serious? They let the topic drop; Ursula still had a year of her term left, so going anywhere was a moot point. Maybe Ursula was suffering from PTSD. Maybe she would change her mind and decide that it would be nice to stay in the Bend with her mother and Jake's parents nearby. Or…maybe Ursula and Jake would finally get divorced. While they were dating, they had broken up a handful of times and seen other people, but they had always gravitated back to each other. In the late nineties, Ursula had had an affair with an associate, Anders Jorgensen. Jake had conducted a one-weekend-a-year affair with a woman named Mallory Blessing for the entirety of their marriage. They had survived all that; surely they would survive Ursula's presidential loss.

Now it's four years later. Fred Page will sail easily into a second term, and Ursula is the managing partner at Hamilton, Laverty, and Smythe, the biggest M and A firm in the country. She bought a two-bedroom apartment on the seventy-eighth floor of 436 Park, which is the premier address in Midtown, maybe in all of New York. Ursula lost the presidency and lost her husband — but she's gained a city. She loves the noise, the taxis, the subway, the sushi restaurants that deliver twenty-four hours a day, the elegant hotel bars, the doormen, the bodegas with their rainbows of floral bouquets out front. She loves the Cuban coffee place and the Vietnamese food truck. She loves racing down to SoHo when she needs something new to wear; she loves the

FDNY; she loves the guys who drive the horse carriages in Central Park; she loves the Upper East Side mommies and nannies; she loves the ten-story-high screens in Times Square and the tugboats on the East River. She loves that while everyone knows who she is, nobody cares, because this city is also home to Alicia Keys, Yoko Ono, Sarah Jessica Parker, people far more exciting than Ursula.

Does she wish she had someone to share it with?

Yes, she does.

Maybe a dating app, then, after all?

Ursula laughs at herself and calls Jake. She's prepared to hear about his fun-filled weekend: sailing on Lake Michigan, meeting his parents for dinner at the South Haven Yacht Club, picking cherries, brunching in Saugatuck. At some point, she's sure Jake will start dating. Ursula will pretend to be supportive and he'll know she's pretending.

When he answers, he says, "You're never going to believe who just called me."

"Who?"

"Cooper Blessing," Jake says. "He has the craziest idea."

Cooper Blessing is hosting a bachelor-party weekend on Nantucket over Labor Day.

"Please tell me he's not getting married again," Ursula says. "What will that make it? Seven? Eight?"

"Six," Jake says. "And no, he's not getting married.

It's the opposite. He proposed to this girl named Stacey who was at Goucher when we were at Hopkins. She said no, and now, as part of the work he's doing with his new therapist, he wants to re-create the bachelor weekend—only make it all about the guys. Coop is single, Frazier Dooley is single..."

Yes, Ursula read about Frazier and Anna Dooley's divorce in *People*. Anna walked away with two hundred and eighty million dollars—and Ursula had thought fleetingly, the way one does, about dating Frazier Dooley.

"And *you're* single," Ursula says.

"I shouldn't say it's all about the guys, because Leland Gladstone is coming too," Jake says. "She was with us the first year."

"Wow," Ursula says. "That's going to be a veritable Who's Who of powerful Americans." Leland Gladstone is the founder of the huge women's lifestyle blog *Leland's Letter* and was recently chosen as one of *Time* magazine's Most Influential People of the Year.

Leland had been plenty influential in Ursula's life. She wrote an article in *Leland's Letter* entitled "Same Time Next Year: Can It Save Modern Marriage?" that had been Ursula's first hint about Jake and Mallory.

"Won't it be difficult for you?" Ursula asks. "Going back to..."

"Mal's cottage?" Jake says. He sighs. "I don't know, Ursula. Probably. I'd rather not get into a big fight about it. I just got off the phone with Coop and I thought I'd let you know that I'll be on Nantucket next weekend."

"You're letting me know now, but not for the twenty-eight years that you went to see Mallory."

"Ursula. We aren't doing this."

"Right," Ursula says. "Well. Please give everyone my best."

"Oh, I will."

"And report back."

"Of course, Sully."

She smiles at the nickname. "Come see me sometime. I miss you."

"That's sweet of you to say. Talk next week."

They hang up and Ursula presses her phone to her heart and stares out at the city beneath her; it's dark enough now that lights are starting to come on.

Back to Nantucket for Labor Day. It sounds like fun, actually, and Ursula half wishes she'd been invited. She pours herself a glass of wine, orders up her lobster and burrata from Marea, and downloads the Firepink app on her phone. She will create an online dating profile.

Ursula de Gournsey

Age: 56

This is going to hurt, Ursula thinks. But that's okay. Pain means she's growing.

LINK

"So it's okay with you if we invade the cottage?" Uncle Cooper asks.

"Yeah, of course," Link says. When Uncle Coop said he was planning to head up to Nantucket for the weekend, Link was afraid he'd be expected to go along, and that was the last thing he wanted to do. He'd flown back to the island over the week of the Fourth of July, when he'd hung out with his friends from high school and even hooked up with his ex-girlfriend, Nicole, the one who'd ditched him on day six of her Italian semester abroad. While it had been fun, it also made Link unbearably sad. Link missed his mother every second of every day, but when he was on Nantucket, the memories were everywhere, especially in the cottage where Mallory had raised him for eighteen years. Mallory was present everywhere he looked—her books were on the shelves, her favorite green pans were in the kitchen cabinets; the quilt she made out of Link's old T-shirts was smoothed across his bed. Link could see the spot on the front deck where Mallory used to sit when she watched Link and his friends swimming or when she drank her wine as the sun went down. Mallory and Link had their usual seats at the narrow harvest table— Link at the head, Mallory next to him in the chair closest to the kitchen, because she was often up to get extra napkins or more ice or second helpings for Link. They had their designated spots on the sofa—Link would do his homework there while Mallory graded papers. On Sundays during football season, they watched games. His mother was a Baltimore Ravens fan, something he teased her about relentlessly.

Swim in a little, please! Link! Lincoln Dooley, swim in!

Did you brush your teeth?

Where are you with your history project?

Wanna kayak? We'll be back in an hour, then I'll drive you to Dylan's.

Did you put on sunscreen?

Why the long face, handsome? Talk to Mama.

Call your father, please, he's been texting me and I'm afraid he's going to send drones next.

There's a card from your grandparents on the counter. I bet it has money in it!

You know what makes everything better? Guacamole.

I will never be disappointed if you strike out swinging. That means you tried.

My eighth-period class was a bitch today—come give your mom a hug.

You will never, ever understand how much I love you until you have children of your own, and then every word I've ever said will make perfect sense.

Link is relieved that the weekend Uncle Coop is planning is just for old people. Link's father is flying in from Seattle, Leland is coming from New York, and... Jake McCloud is traveling to the island from South Bend, Indiana. It's supposed to be a reunion of some weekend that happened before Link was born. Link doesn't ask too many questions; he's afraid he'll get roped in.

Jake McCloud, though, has always intrigued him.

When Mallory was dying, she asked Link to call Jake, and Jake and his daughter, Bess, had left the Ursula de Gournsey campaign so Jake could come say good-bye to Mallory. He brought a guitar and sang to her.

Link and Bess McCloud had taken a walk on the beach and Link said, "I feel like something's going on that I don't understand."

Bess said, "My dad told me Mallory is an old friend of his."

"Oh," Link said.

Bess had laughed. "Do they think we're naive? They're more than friends."

"Are they?" Link said. "I've never heard my mom mention his name before, and I would have remembered that. Your family is a very big deal."

"My mother is a very big deal," Bess said. "My dad and I are just…infantry soldiers." She picked up a quahog shell. "Look!"

Link smiled. "You don't get to the beach much?"

Bess examined the inside of the shell, the swirls of blue and purple—once used in wampum beads, which were traded like money. "I'm taking this home." They kept walking. "I like thinking that my dad had something of his own, a secret friendship or whatever. Or maybe they're in love. Maybe they've been in love all these years."

"Maybe?" Link said. The thought was, frankly, absurd.

Link won't lie—he's psyched to have his uncle's place in Georgetown to himself for the weekend. It's a bachelor's *paradise.* The town house on Q Street is three stories tall with a finished media room in the basement, and it's decorated like something out of a design magazine. The whole house is done in black and white with pops of color—in the living room, there's a curvy flame-orange sofa and two lime-green cup chairs. There's a sweeping staircase with a curved black banister. Coop has huge abstract paintings and modern sculpture on pedestals—it's real art; he goes to the galleries and gets into complicated negotiations with the owners. And then there are antiques scattered throughout—some of the pieces are from Link's grandparents' house in Baltimore and some are from the far-flung countries Coop has visited. There's a chess set from India that resides permanently in the sunny breakfast nook with windows that overlook the back courtyard, and every morning, when there's time, Coop and Link play. Link has gotten pretty good.

Link is thinking about having a party—just some of the other interns from Brookings and a fraternity brother, Woj, from USC, who's working on Capitol Hill this summer and who knows a crazy number of smart and beautiful women. It won't be a full-blown banger—the last thing he wants is to trash Coop's space—but he's thinking about some good people and good whiskey (Coop has a wine and whiskey cellar tucked behind the home gym in the basement) out back in the courtyard. He'll pick up some tacos and banh mi and play some music and generally flex like the place is his own.

Before Coop leaves on Friday morning, he hands Link three hundred bucks, because that's the kind of awesome uncle he is. Link spends his entire walk to work reminding himself that he has to be a responsible adult and not act like a kid in a movie whose parents are away for the weekend. He'll cut the party off at fifty people, sixty max.

But when Link gets to the office and starts firing off texts—Party at my house tonight at eight—he gets a rude awakening. It's a holiday weekend, the last before people go back to college, graduate school, et cetera, and everyone is leaving town. Woj is going to Fenwick Island; the other interns are heading to Dewey, Ocean City, Cape May.

His buddy Oliver is going home to his parents' house on the Eastern Shore of Maryland and asks if Link wants to go with him. "My dad has a sailboat," Oliver says. "And my parents are having a cocktail party on Sunday with a tent and a Dixieland band. It'll be fun."

Sailing, cocktails, a Dixieland band. It does sound kind of fun, but it's not what Link had in mind. If he wanted to be on the water, at the beach, he would have gone with his uncle. He wants city life. "I think I'll stay put, thanks, man," Link says.

His idea for the weekend instantly changes. He'll just hang out at the house, play loud music on Coop's state-of-the-art sound system, watch movies in the home theater, sip the whiskey and cognac alone. He was raised an only child; he can entertain himself.

But once Link gets home from work and takes a shower—the city is a smoking griddle; why did he not go to the beach?—he can't settle down. He feels like a friendless loser, sitting home alone. He should go out. He will go out. He remembers his mother's story about going to Nantucket when she was his age without knowing a soul.

Honestly? she said. *It was liberating. I was in control of my future.*

He heads to a place he and Woj sometimes went called Roofers Union in Adams Morgan, and he finds it pumping—there are people his age drinking and laughing at the tables on the street, and there's a line of young, beautiful people snaking out the door. He waits his turn, presents his ID to the bouncer, and heads inside. He goes to the upstairs bar; it's normally a little less crazy than the one downstairs.

There are three free seats at the far end and beyond those sits a girl with dark hair and glasses, absorbed in her phone. She has a glass of wine in front of her. Is she alone? Link gives her a couple seats as a buffer, orders a Stoli tonic with a twist of lemon, and after his drink arrives and he's had a sip, he glances over. At the same time, she looks up at him.

He knows her. It's . . .

"Oh my God," she says. "You're . . ."

"Yeah!" he says. "Wait, this is weird. I was just thinking about you." It's Bess McCloud. This is surreal—although Link has just learned that this phenomenon has a name, when you think about someone or something and then, out of the blue, the person or thing appears.

"My dad went to Nantucket with your uncle and your dad," Bess says. "He just texted to say he landed."

"That's crazy," Link says. He drinks in the sight of Bess McCloud; she's just as pretty as he remembers. Nerdy-pretty, with glasses and hair that hangs in her face a little. "Are you waiting for someone?" Link asks.

Bess rolls her eyes. "I'm supposed to be on a Bumble date, but the guy is stuck on the Metro." She holds up her phone. "It says he's sixteen minutes away."

Link slides down the bar next to her. "I can hang with you for sixteen minutes," he says. "Then when your boyfriend gets here, I'll leave quietly."

Bess laughs. "He's not my boyfriend," she says. "I don't even know him. He's a lobbyist for the alcohol industry."

"A *lobbyist?*" Link says. "Legal bribery."

"Exactly." Bess sighs. "I normally stay away, but..."

But the dude is probably good-looking and rolling in cash, Link thinks. "Looks like I have sixteen minutes to try and lure you away from the dark side," he says. "I'm working for Brookings. Domestic policy. I analyze the impact of policy decisions on the least served among us and suggest ways to make them more effective."

"I work in nonprofits," Bess says.

"Sexy!" Link says.

"Yeah, as sexy as being a producer for public television," Bess says.

"Hey, do you still have that shell?" Link asks. "That quahog shell that you found on the beach on Nantucket?"

Bess sips her wine and nods. "It's on my dresser, actually."

"No ... seriously?"

"Swear to God."

"And did you ..."

"Did I what?"

The thing that Link wants to ask might take another drink, but the clock is ticking. The lobbyist will show up with his American Express Obsidian card in eleven minutes. "Did you ever ask your dad what was going on between him and my mom?"

Bess's green eyes find Link's from behind her glasses. Her eyebrows raise. "I did." She swivels her head to take in the raucous bar scene beyond them. "Do you maybe want to go someplace quieter and I can tell you about it?"

Link laughs. "What about your date?"

Bess checks her phone. "The pin hasn't moved. He's stuck on the Metro. I'll cancel him and we can go over to Lapis for Afghan food. Does that sound okay?"

Link doesn't care if they go to McDonald's. There's no way he's going to miss a chance to sit across the table from this beautiful nerdy girl and learn something new about his mother. "Sounds great," he says.

LELAND

When Leland's JetBlue flight from JFK touches down on Nantucket, she looks out the window and takes note of the rows and rows of private planes, including an impressive jet with the Frayed Edge coffee logo on the side. She experiences a childish burst of excitement: Fray is here!

She pulls down the front of her denim cloche hat and puts on oversize sunglasses. There are some young women farther back on the plane who recognized Leland at the gate in New York; they asked for a selfie with her, which she indulged, even though she's more than over it. But Leland's brand and *Leland's Letter* are all about women lifting up other women, so she can hardly refuse these girls.

She hurries down the plane's stairway and practically runs across the tarmac. Nantucket Island — the name speaks of wealth and entitlement, though to Leland, the idea of Nantucket is inextricably tied to memories of the best friend she has ever had in her life, Mallory Blessing. The first time Leland set foot on this island was Labor Day weekend of 1993. She had been *so young,* only twenty-four years old. In those days, she lived on the Upper East Side and worked as an editorial assistant at *Bard and Scribe.* Leland had thought she was special. She imitated the lockjaw of the Vassar girls she worked with, she dyed her hair pink, she bought all her clothes from thrift shops in the Village, everything except for a stiff leather jacket from Trash and Vaudeville that she spent a whopping nine hundred dollars on because Ray Goodman himself said that Leland reminded him of a young Patti Smith.

When Leland came to Nantucket on that first trip, she had behaved...atrociously. She kissed Fray—Frazier Dooley, her first love—in the back seat of Mallory's car, but then once they got to the bar, she bumped into an acquaintance from New York—Kip Sudbury, whose father was in commercial real estate and who had a yacht at his disposal—and Leland left Mallory and Fray and Cooper without a word of explanation. She'd *ditched* them; it made her cringe to remember it now. The only excuse she had was youth.

She returned to Nantucket a few years later with her girlfriend at the time, the novelist Fiella Roget—Fifi— but things hadn't gone much better. That was early on in Leland and Fifi's relationship, back when Leland was still threatened by Fifi's fame and was alternately possessive and bitter. It didn't help that Fifi shamelessly flirted with Mallory, maybe as a way of reminding her who in the couple had the allure, the power. Leland should have laughed off Fifi's behavior—Mallory was so hopelessly straight that she would have seen the sexual overtures as Fifi being friendly—but instead, Leland had lashed out by tearing Mallory down. Mallory had overheard Leland insulting her, and the weekend had been ruined.

Leland had read an interview with Toni Morrison in which the author said she regretted a third of her life. Leland's percentage was running a bit higher than that.

The last time Leland had been on Nantucket was four years earlier, when Mallory was dying. She'd had skin cancer that she thought had been successfully treated, but it metastasized to her brain. It wasn't fair — Mallory was a good person, a mom and a teacher, a reader and a thinker, the most generous friend in what she was willing to accept and forgive. It should have been Leland in the bed. Leland deserved little mercy from the universe. Her life had been a cakewalk by comparison. She had always been free to be self-absorbed.

She gets a text. It's Coop: I'm out front in Mal's Jeep.

Leland's fellow New Yorkers are all looking very self-consciously Nantuckety in their faded red pants and straw hats. Leland has made a concession to the season by wearing Eileen Fisher, the queen of black linen. Unlike these weekend warriors, Leland feels she belongs here because, while they all check their Ubers, she has some-one waiting for her out front in a seen-better-days Jeep.

The girls who approached Leland at the gate in JFK are right behind her. She can hear them checking the address of their Airbnb and then one of them says, "Oh my God, look — I think that's Frazier Dooley."

Leland raises her eyes. Sure enough, Fray is walking out of the private-jet terminal wearing his usual uniform of white T-shirt, jeans, Ray-Ban Wayfarers, and a messenger bag strapped across his chest. His blondish-gray hair is long and unkempt. The hair is his signature; it's what makes him the most recognizable CEO in the country. When he raises his arm and calls out, "Lee!," it's all she can do to stop herself from running into his arms.

"I'm jealous AF right now," one of the girls stage-whispers. "He knows Leland Gladstone."

Leland is tempted to turn around and say, *He was my boyfriend in high school. That* would have given them something to talk about—but Leland is well beyond defining herself by any relationship she's had with a man. "Hey, Fray," she says with a coy smile. They embrace and kiss, gestures of fondness that Leland missed during the pandemic years. Fray smells like some kind of heavenly expensive aftershave. He's so delicious that Leland would like to take a bite of him, a reaction that thoroughly surprises her.

Cooper honks the horn. "Let's go, kids!" he says.

Fray gallantly takes Leland's bag and tosses it into the back of the Jeep, then opens the passenger door so Leland can hitch her skirt and climb in. She sees her fans gawking from the sidewalk and she can't help herself: she gives a four-finger wave.

"Woo-hoo!" Coop shouts. He turns up the radio, which is playing the top five hundred rock songs of all time in honor of the holiday weekend, and number 426 is Van

Halen's "I'll Wait." It has been a very long time since Leland listened to Van Halen (she sticks with female artists—Alison Krauss, Norah Jones, Lizzo), and the song delivers her right back to Deepdene Road in 1984:

She and Mallory are freshmen in high school, and Cooper and Fray are juniors. Even though Leland has been around both boys all her life, they attain a new mystique that year because they get their driver's licenses. Cooper is the good boy—clean-cut, preppy—and Fray is the bad boy. Fray's hair is long; he wears red parachute pants and walks around with a permanent scowl, flipping his bangs out of his eyes. Leland finds him mesmerizing (but she doesn't tell Mallory, because Fray is like a brother to her, and...eww). Fray is the arbiter of everyone's musical tastes. He listens to Van Halen, Twisted Sister, Honeymoon Suite. Fray lives with his grandparents around the corner on Edgevale but he's always at the Blessing house with Coop, and because of this, Leland and Mallory start spending all their time there as well.

Leland and Mallory ask Coop and Fray for rides, even though there's nowhere to go. Inner Harbor is a destination but the shopping is touristy and expensive, and Fells Point is one bar after another that they can't get into. Still, they beg to be allowed to ride around in the back seat—anything to get them out of the house. They're sick of watching movies in Leland's basement rec room and listening to records. They both know there's life out there somewhere and they're ready for it.

"Sorry," Coop says. "Riding around with my little sister and her best friend isn't my idea of a good time. It's babysitting."

At the end of October, Coop starts dating a girl named Alana Bratton, who's a senior at the Bryn Mawr School. Alana is beautiful, and when she snaps her fingers, Coop does her bidding. The person who is left out is Fray; his buddy has ditched him for a girl.

At the beginning of November, Mallory gets the flu. Leland is under strict orders from her parents, Geri and Steve, as well as from the Blessings to stay away from the Blessing house until the contagious period is over. Leland's parents are leaving for the weekend on a leaf-peeping trip through the horse country of Virginia, and Leland thinks how unfair it is that she will now have the house to herself but nobody to enjoy the freedom with.

In her bedroom, as she's watching Coop pull out of the driveway—he's probably off to pick up Alana—Leland gets the idea to call Fray.

"Mal is sick and my parents are away," Leland says. "Want to come over and use the hot tub? My dad has a fridge full of beer in the garage."

Fray says, "Won't he notice if some is missing?"

"No," Leland says. "I drink it all the time. We just have to be careful with the cans. I normally ditch them in the dumpster behind Eddie's." This is a complete lie. Leland has never drunk her father's beer—she can't stand the taste—and she has no idea if Steve

Gladstone will notice cans missing, though there are at least two cases in the fridge, so she kind of doubts it.

"Cool," Fray says. "I'll be over in a little while."

Leland races up to her room to pick an outfit and curl her hair. She puts the Police album *Ghost in the Machine* on her turntable and dances around. He's coming! Fray is coming!

"A little while" ends up being two hours, nine o'clock, late enough that Leland has already spiraled through self-doubt and convinced herself that Fray won't show. She's wearing her red bikini under her Jordache jeans and a velour top; she cracked open one of her father's beers—she pulled six out of the back; when you open the fridge, you don't even notice any missing—and she poured a bag of Utz chips into a bowl and opened a container of onion dip because her mother, Geri, says people always appreciate a snack. The hot tub is bubbling like a witch's cauldron under the cover and it's this that Leland suspects might get her in trouble—the oil bill; her father is energy-conscious—but why even *have* the hot tub if they can't use it?

When the knock finally comes, Leland's heart leaps. She has finished one beer and feels as light and floaty as a spirit in the material world. "Hey," she says when she opens the door. Fray looks so fine—he has on a gray hooded sweatshirt under his Calvert Hall lacrosse jersey, jeans, and high-top sneakers, which are, as ever, untied. He's holding a pair of swim trunks.

"Hey, Lee," he says. They lock eyes and Leland

wonders why it took them so long to shed the Blessings and acknowledge what has been true for a while now: they are meant to be together.

When Leland looks back on that night, it seems painfully romantic in a nostalgic 1980s way. They each crack a beer; Fray changes into his trunks in the powder room, then helps Leland lift the top off the hot tub. They climb in and sit on the same bench but not touching. Leland has the stereo in the rec room cranked to 98 Rock and the back sliding door is open so they can hear strains of "Radio Ga Ga" and "When Doves Cry." They tap their cans of Natty Boh together and drink.

They start kissing during "We Belong," by Pat Benatar. It happens naturally, like a magnet is drawing them together. It isn't Leland's first kiss or even her first tongue kiss—that was Jay Pitcock after the eighth-grade dance back in May—but this is different. Fray is skilled with his tongue; he tastes like beer, and he knows to put a hand on the back of her neck and pull her toward him.

When they finally break apart, Leland is dizzy, dazzled.

"I'll grab more beers," Fray says. He hoists himself out of the tub and Leland watches him leave wet footprints on the rec-room floor. When he disappears from view, she gets a crazy idea, then talks herself out of it, then decides to just go for it. Tonight is the night her life changes.

She takes off her bikini top.

Fray reappears holding a six-pack by the plastic rings. Leland raises her bare breasts above the water. Her nipples are instantly hard.

"Whoa," Fray says. He leaves the beer to the side and starts kissing Leland again. One of his hands finds her nipple and he rubs it back and forth, a feeling so exquisite that Leland thinks she's going to dissolve. Then he lowers his mouth to her nipple and gently sucks. She can see his erection poking up in his trunks. She wants to touch it but doesn't because her mother gave her all kinds of instructions about what can happen if you let a boy go too far. She will hold Fray at second base tonight. Second base with Frazier Dooley. It's so crazy, Leland can hardly believe it.

A few weeks after Leland and Fray start dating, Coop and Fray are invited to a high-school party thrown by a friend of Alana Bratton's whose parents are away. It will be mostly Bryn Mawr girls and Calvert Hall boys—Leland and Mallory go to Garrison Forest, so they won't know anyone, but Leland wheedles them an invite anyway. Once they get to the house—a mansion on Roland Park Drive—Coop and Fray disappear to do beer bongs, leaving Leland and Mallory to fend for themselves in the kitchen. The good news is that Alana spots them and takes them under her beautiful blond wing. She gets the girls glasses of real champagne, Moët et Chandon, that someone lifted from the wine fridge.

"I'll introduce you around," Alana says.

"I should probably go find Fray," Leland says.

Alana laughs. "Let him come find you."

Which is exactly what happens an hour later. Leland and Mallory are in the library playing a drinking game called three-man with two Calvert Hall seniors. One of them, a kid named Penn Porter, drapes his arm over Leland's shoulders just as Fray walks in.

"Get your hands off her, Porter," Fray says.

Leland jumps to her feet. "We weren't doing anything," she says. She's so drunk, her words are slurred, and Mallory is slumped over on the green velvet sofa, eyes at half-mast. Fray storms out of the library. Leland wants to chase after him but she can't leave Mallory drunk and alone with two senior boys; that's how date rape happens.

She appeals to Penn Porter. "Can you help me get her to her feet? She's Cooper Blessing's sister."

Penn rolls his eyes but obliges. He and Leland ease Mallory up. "Are you dating Frazier Dooley? That guy has issues. Seems to me you can do better."

Leland leads Mallory through the house. She finds Fray in the kitchen, swigging from a bottle of Jim Beam. "We're ready to go," Leland says.

"Great," Fray says, his eyes flashing with what Leland understands are his "issues" — rage, jealousy, alcohol. "Ask your buddy Penn to get you home."

"Fray," Leland says. "We weren't doing anything."

"He had his arm around you," Fray says, swigging

from the bottle again. Just the smell is enough to make the room spin. "I didn't see you fighting him off."

"You *left* me by *myself* for over an *hour!*" Leland says. "What did you *think* would happen?"

He shrugs. "Just goes to show I can't trust you."

Leland would like to say that this is an isolated incident, but the entire three years that Leland and Fray date are marked with similar explosions, like firecrackers on a string. She becomes only too used to what she comes to think of as Fray's "white-hot sulk."

But there is love too, real love, desperate love, Frazier clinging to Leland, pressing his face into her neck and murmuring, *Please, baby, don't ever leave me.*

Now, as Cooper turns down the no-name road that leads to Mallory's cottage and she sees the ocean glittering in the distance, Leland marvels at how much time has passed—and how much has *happened*. Leland went on to have a decade-long relationship with a woman. Fray became a billionaire. (A *billionaire!* What must Penn Porter think about *that?*) Leland's father, Steve Gladstone, divorced Leland's mother and married Fray's mother, Sloane Dooley. Technically, Leland and Fray are stepsiblings! These are the kinds of things that only happen in novels. In fact, Fifi wanted to write about it—but Leland put her foot down.

"Where's Jake?" Leland asks when they pull up to the cottage.

"Inside," Coop says. "He wanted some time to himself."

No doubt, Leland thinks. If what happened between her and Frazier is one novel, then what happened between Jake McCloud and Mallory is another. Oh, boy, is it.

When they walk in, there's music playing—Cat Stevens singing "Hard Headed Woman"—and Jake McCloud is standing at Mallory's bookshelves, running a finger over the spines.

"I'm glad you're listening to this song now," Frazier says. "Get it out of your system so we don't have to hear it again."

Jake turns and smiles, and the men shake hands. Leland follows up, hugging Jake and kissing him on the cheek. "Don't listen to him," she says.

"Leland, you're in Mal's room," Cooper says.

"You can have Mal's room," Leland says to Jake.

"I'm in the guest room," Jake says. "That's where I was the first summer."

"Fray, you can take Link's room," Coop says. "I'll take the sofa."

Leland carries her bag into Mallory's room and shuts the door behind her. The room is lovely, with its huge white canopy bed and peach and green attached bath. Leland kicks off her shoes, sits on the bed, and stares at the ceiling. "Can you see us, Mal?" she whispers. "I hope so. I very dearly hope so."

JAKE

He reminds himself that this weekend is for Cooper, not him.

He also reminds himself that, although it's Labor Day weekend, it won't be like any other Labor Day weekend that Jake has spent on this island. Mallory isn't here, and nobody else knew about their rituals but her.

Friday night, they eat at home, just like Jake and Mallory always did — only instead of simple burgers, corn, and sliced tomatoes, Cooper goes to the Nantucket Meat and Fish Market and returns with thick, marbled rib eyes, blocks of ruby-red tuna, half a dozen twice-baked potatoes, colorful vegetable skewers, a Caesar salad, two pies (peach and blueberry), and a container of vanilla Häagen-Dazs.

"And a charcuterie and cheese platter," Coop says. "In honor of my mother and her penchant for hors d'oeuvres. I also got a case of wine."

Coop pours glasses of some obscure Riesling that he was tickled to find (although Fray has water) and they all go out to the porch that faces the ocean.

Cooper raises his glass. "To Mallory," he says.

Jake has trouble swallowing. It's a clear evening, warm and summery. Jake watches the waves curl and crash and he feels that Mallory is here somewhere, but where? In the golden sand, in the soft quality of the light? Jake is sure she would want them to be swimming—they're not *that* old, after all, and it's not *that* cold. Jake sets his glass down, heads inside to change into his suit, then comes out and goes charging past everyone down the slope of the beach and into the water.

Cooper joins Jake a few minutes later and the two men bob in the waves as they gaze up at Fray and Leland, who are deep in conversation on the porch.

"I just remembered that Mallory told me those two used to have a thing," Jake says. "'A thing that refused to die,' she called it."

"That was back in high school," Coop says. "It's dead, believe me. Long dead."

"Thanks for inviting me here, man," Jake says. "I know you didn't like what your sister and I had going on..."

"You loved her," Coop says. "That's all that matters to me. I'm the last person who gets to comment on what kind of relationship is right and what kind is wrong."

"The minute I realized I'd fallen in love with her, I was right here," Jake says. "It was maybe year three or four, in the morning, and I was swimming when your sister got home from her run. She came out to the porch to stretch and she didn't see me, so I could appreciate her without her knowing it. And I remember thinking, *I love that girl.*"

"She had a light inside her," Coop says. "A funny, innocent light. A good-person light."

"I should have left Ursula and married her," Jake says. "There were dozens of times I wanted to do it, but I was afraid. I was afraid of life without Ursula, I was afraid your sister would turn me down, and I think we were both afraid that once we were officially together, our love would seem regular, and, like regular love, it would die."

"Remember that one year Mal and I met you at PJ's at Christmastime and the two of you were dancing by the jukebox? I should have figured out what was going on back then."

"You should've," Jake says. "But you were too busy chatting up Stacey."

Coop splashes him. "I've got first shower."

Right before dinner, Jake gets an idea. He searches through the cabinets until he finds a mason jar and then he goes out the back door and snips the last remaining hydrangea blossom off the bush and puts it on the harvest table as a centerpiece.

Now it feels like Mallory is there.

They all sit at the narrow table, which is lit only by votive candles. Jake recalls the year Mallory decided to use tapers and one fell while Jake and Mallory were in the bedroom fooling around, and the cottage nearly burned down, and one of the firemen who showed up was Mallory's ex-boyfriend JD.

After he finishes his second glass of wine, he considers telling this story, but it feels too precious to share.

Leland says, "Let's go around the table and say which of Coop's wives was our favorite. My favorite was Tish."

Cooper laughs. He really is a good sport, Jake thinks. "Tish was my least favorite," Coop says. "She was in love with someone else when she married me—her 'family friend,' Fred from San Francisco. They've been happily married for over twenty years and have a business flipping houses in Nob Hill. Their daughter goes to Stanford."

"My favorite was Valentina," Fray says. "She was a sweet woman."

"Sweet," Coop says. "But using me to escape an arranged marriage."

"Did she go back to Ecuador?" Jake asks.

"Oh, yes," Cooper says. "I'm not sure if she ended up with Pablo. That was the guy her parents wanted her to marry. I haven't heard from her in nearly twenty-five years." He stabs a piece of steak with his fork. "It seems surreal that I could have stood at the altar at Roland Park Presbyterian and taken a *lifelong vow* to stay with someone and then that person and I split a few months later and I never see or hear from her again."

Leland digs into her twice-baked potato. "I hate to say this, but I can't even remember who wife number four was. Did I meet her?"

"Tamela," Coop says. "Poli-sci professor at Georgetown. She had three teenagers that took up a lot of her time and energy. One was gender-transitioning. Her first husband was killed in a highway crash; the kids were devastated, and they resented me. We eloped in Antigua. That was romantic, but then it was back to reality, and reality was challenging."

"How long did that one last?" Jake asks. He can't remember much about Tamela either. He *does* remember Coop eloping, because Ursula had been relieved to be spared another wedding, and Jake had felt robbed of a chance to see Mallory.

"Two and a half years," Cooper says. "The irony is that I'm still in touch with the kids. They love me now."

"Amy was nice," Jake says. He met Amy at a Johns Hopkins alumni event in DC. She had kind brown eyes and a way of tilting her head to let you know she was really listening to you.

"That was the problem," Coop says. "Amy was nice, sweet, accommodating, eager to please. There was no mystery, no intrigue, no edge."

"And that's what you're attracted to?" Leland asks. "You fall in love with the edge? The crazy parts, the dangerous parts?"

"I'm not sure," Coop says, draining his wine. "I'm not sure what's wrong with me."

"There's nothing *wrong* with you, Coop," Leland says. "I mean, this group isn't exactly filled with spokespeople for successful relationships."

Jake frowns at his plate. It's true that he and Ursula are divorced—but that they stayed married for so long feels like a success. However, he would say his most successful relationship was the one he had with Mallory. He's probably deluding himself.

"I notice nobody chose Krystel as his or her favorite," Fray says.

Coop groans. "Krystel." He whistles. "In some sense, Krystel is the reason we're all here. Thirty years ago, when we did this the first time, Krystel called and demanded I come home."

Oh yes, Jake remembers it well. He's always wanted to send Krystel a thank-you card. It was because of Krystel that he and Mallory got together.

Cooper says, "I wonder how life would have been different if I'd just ignored Krystel when she called. What if I'd stayed and gone to the Chicken Box like I was supposed to? Maybe she would have called off the wedding, and maybe without making that first mistake, I could have avoided the others as well." Coop leans in toward the candlelight; his face, now weathered with age and experience, glows a pinkish orange. "If I'd stayed on the island on this night thirty years ago, so much would have been different."

Jake nods slowly. He can't bear to imagine things unfolding any differently than they had. "It's probably safe to assume things worked out the way they were supposed to."

"Amen," Fray says.

"Well, I'm not sure about you guys," Coop says, standing up and tossing his napkin on his plate, "but I'm not missing out on the Chicken Box tonight."

The Chicken Box looks exactly the same. The concrete floor is sticky with beer and there's a crush of people at the bar. The only difference between tonight and the first time Jake set foot in the place in 1993 is that now, every single person is holding a cell phone. The band is singing "Just the Two of Us," by Grover Washington Jr., a song so old it's new again, apparently, and up front there's a group of people dancing and taking videos of themselves dancing.

Leland and Fray opted to stay home, so it's just Jake and Coop on this nostalgic adventure. They're by far the oldest people here. They are gray-haired geezers, and Jake trains himself to keep his eyes off the scantily clad girls his daughter's age.

"I'm going up front to dance," Coop says.

"Have fun," Jake says. "I'll be at the bar." He chooses the less populated side, over by the pool tables, where there's a bit of breathing room. It takes so long for the bartender to notice him that when she finally does, Jake orders four Coronas, two for him and two for Coop. Cooper, however, is nowhere to be seen, and Jake doesn't want to try moving four beers through this crowd, so he stays put and starts drinking.

A female voice says, "I'll give you twenty bucks for one of those."

Jake turns. There's a woman standing next to him in a white T-shirt and cutoff jean shorts with a long blond braid. She's in her forties somewhere, maybe even her late forties, though he'd be too afraid to hazard a guess.

"Have one," he says. "Please, my treat."

"You're my hero," she says. She takes one of the cold bottles and rolls it across her forehead. "It's my girlfriend's birthday and she dragged me here. It's fun to dance but it's hard to not feel completely geriatric."

"Tell me about it," he says. He offers his hand. "I'm Jake."

She has a nice, firm shake. "Brooke Schuster," she says. "You look familiar to me for some reason. Have we met before?"

Jake stares at the lime wedge choking the neck of his bottle. "No, I don't think so."

"Are you sure?" she says. "Because I swear..."

"I'm Jake McCloud," he says, and when that doesn't clear up the confusion on her face, he adds, "My ex-wife, Ursula de Gournsey—"

Brooke snaps her fingers. "Yes! That's where I know you from." She takes a sip of her beer. "Well, if it makes a difference, I voted for her and I was sorry to see her lose."

"Everything in life works out as it should," Jake says.

"Spoken like a man who wants to change the subject," Brooke says. "And I can't blame you. What are you doing here at the Box?"

"Ah," Jake says. "Reliving the past with a buddy of mine from college." He takes another quick look at Brooke. She's pretty, he decides, and the cutoff shorts are giving him strong Mallory vibes. He checks her left hand — she's wearing a lot of silver but nothing that looks like an engagement ring or wedding band. So here it is, finally — an opportunity to have a conversation with a grown woman in real life. He can practically hear Bess urging him along: *Come on, Dad, you have to get back out there!* But dating, or even chatting up someone, feels like so much effort — getting to know someone from scratch, starting all over with personal histories, figuring out what makes someone else tick. He's not sure he's up for it.

Brooke sets her beer firmly down on the bar. "I'll probably regret saying this in the morning, but I had something of a celebrity crush on you."

"On *me?*" Jake knows he sounds surprised, though he's aware there was a small part of the female electorate across the country who turned a Jake McCloud crush into a thing. (There had been an article in *The Cut* entitled "The Very Real Sex Appeal of Mister UDG.") At nearly every event Jake did on behalf of his wife, someone would slip him a note or brazenly approach his security detail and ask for a "private meeting." Jake always told Ursula about these overtures, and when she could spare a few moments of her attention, she would pat his cheek and say, "I'm well aware how appealing you are, the adoring, devoted husband, handsome and well spoken, and I'm grateful." This patronizing response had stoked Jake's resentment—Ursula cared only about how Jake's persona reflected on her—but in the name of propriety, Jake had continued to be up front about every woman who approached him.

Brooke says, "You're the executive director of the CFRF. And my nephew Charlie..." She stops and her eyes shine with tears. "We lost him to cystic fibrosis a few years ago."

"I'm so sorry," Jake says. "And I didn't mean to be flip when I said everything works out the way it's supposed to. In my business, I know that's not the case. How old was he?"

"Twenty-six," Brooke says. "He was my sister's only child."

"That's so difficult," Jake says. "I lost my twin sister to CF when we were thirteen."

"I know," Brooke says. "I read the profile of you in *Time*. I just want you to know how grateful I am for all the work you've done, the money you've raised for research. You became my sister's personal hero." When she blinks, a single tear rolls down her flushed cheek. "I can't believe I'm talking to you *here,* at the Chicken Box."

Jake wants to take the conversation in a lighter direction, but how? He has no experience talking to women like this, as evidenced by the fact that Brooke is now crying. "Do you live here year-round?"

"I do," Brooke says. "I teach English at the high school."

"You...what?" Jake says. He feels a surge of energy course through him. "Did you know my friend Mallory Blessing?"

Brooke's face falls. "I only knew *of* her," she says. "Dr. Major hired me to replace Mallory."

Before Jake can react—this is Mallory's *replacement?*—Cooper appears, sweaty and grinning. "Why'd you leave?" he asks Brooke. "Band's just getting started."

"I was thirsty," Brooke says. She looks between Cooper and Jake. "Do you guys know each other?"

"Best friends," Coop says. He lifts one of the unclaimed Coronas off the bar and takes a swallow. Coop looks at Jake. "Brooke is here with Mallory's friend Apple. It's Apple's birthday."

Whoa, Jake thinks. It's a small island. He listened to Mallory talk about Apple for years and years—her best friend, the guidance counselor at the high school, married to Hugo, mother of twin boys who might be in high school or even college by now. But Jake never met Apple, and Apple doesn't know Jake exists.

"I'm sure Apple is wondering where I've gotten to," Brooke says. She offers Jake a tentative smile. "Want to join us on the dance floor?"

Jake knows the fun, good-sport answer is *Sure, why not?* But dancing up front at the Chicken Box is too far out of his comfort zone. "You kids go have fun," he says, and he feels only the slightest pinch of regret when Cooper takes Brooke by the hand and leads her away.

*   *   *

When the lights come on and the bell rings for last call, Jake wanders through the bar, weaving around couples making out, taking selfies, drunkenly debating where to go next, until he finds Coop standing with Brooke near the exit. The three of them step out into the warm, dark night.

"We closed the Box!" Coop says.

"A dubious distinction," Brooke says. "Especially if one of my students finds out."

"Brooke is a high-school English teacher," Cooper says. "She was hired to—"

"Yes," Jake says. "She told me."

"That's crazy, right?" Coop says. "So should we go get pizza?"

Brooke laughs. "I'm afraid I have to call it a night." She twirls her braid and looks up at Jake in a way that seems meaningful. "I hope to see you both on Sunday."

"What's Sunday?" Jake says.

"Apple is hosting a beach picnic at Fortieth Pole," Brooke says. "She invited you both."

"We'll be there," Coop says. "Let me walk you to your car."

"I'll be fine," she says. "I'm just across the street." She looks at Jake again. "It was nice meeting you guys." With that, she slips across the street, and both Coop and Jake watch her until she disappears.

"Is it Sunday yet?" Coop says.

*   *   *

In the morning, Jake tiptoes out of his room so as not to disturb Coop, who is sprawled across the big white sofa that Mallory nicknamed Big Hugs. Jake pours himself a cup of coffee—it's the Frayed Edge Platinum that Fray brought as a gift, which was an excellent surprise because it retails for forty-five dollars a pound—and steps out the back door to tie his running shoes. Thanks to the wine, the beers, and the late night, Jake feels like his head is stuffed with cotton batting, but the morning is clear, with just a hint of coolness in the air—autumn is coming—and Jake doesn't want to waste another second sleeping. Back when he used to visit Mallory, he would sleep only a few hours per night. The rest of the time he would spend watching Mal, memorizing her face, drinking her in—and yet he was never tired. He always left the island with his emotional batteries recharged. Perfect love existed, he would think. It existed here on Nantucket.

He sets his cup of coffee on the porch railing and listens to his joints pop as he touches his toes. Then he sets off running down the no-name road, which meanders along Miacomet Pond.

He goes all the way out to Surfside Road, then loops around to the other side of the pond, and only then, when he's hot and sweaty and parched, does he realize he's come too far. He can't get back to Mallory's cottage this way without a significant beach walk. This, however, will be shorter than retracing his steps, so he sits on a rock to take off his shoes. He becomes mesmerized by the clear green water lapping at the muddy shore. Is he thirsty enough to drink a handful of pond water? No, but close.

He's just about to head up over the dunes to the beach when he sees a woman walking a Bernese mountain dog, holding the dog's leash in one hand and a bottle of water in the other. She looks like a goddess from a Greek myth.

"Hey!" the woman calls out. Jake wonders if he's trespassing.

When she gets a few steps closer, Jake sees that it's Brooke. Her hair has been let out of its braid, and it's long and wavy under a navy-blue Nantucket Whalers baseball cap.

"Oh, hey," Jake says. *This is like magic,* he thinks. He would be lying if he said he hadn't thought about Brooke the night before and again during his run. He was looking forward to seeing her on Sunday and even toyed with inviting her to the CFRF gala in Boston at the end of October. He's not sure what he's thinking; he lives in South Bend, Indiana, and has no plans to move to Nantucket. No, if he wanted to do that, he would have done it thirty years ago. He waves at Brooke and pushes himself to his feet. He's so overheated, he's seeing stars.

"This is Walter Cronkite," Brooke says, indicating the dog, and Jake laughs. "You can call him Walt."

Jake spends a minute rubbing Walt's head. He's always

wanted a Bernese mountain dog, but Ursula pointed out that they didn't have time to take care of a pet. Jake thinks it's telling that Brooke has the exact kind of dog that Jake wants. Cool woman, cool dog.

"Would you like some water?" Brooke asks. She hands him the unopened bottle that she's holding. It's seductively frosted with condensation.

"Yes, please," Jake says, and he downs half the bottle in one gulp. "Thank you. You just saved my life."

"I'm glad I bumped into you, actually," Brooke says. Her expression grows a little shy. "I had a question."

"Oh, yeah, what's that?" Jake says. The water has revived him like a plant. He's sturdy, upright, ready to get to know this woman better. After all, the connection is uncanny — she said she had a celebrity crush on him, she lost a nephew to CF just as he lost a sister, and she took Mallory's job at the high school. For all Jake knows, Mallory has somehow sent this woman to him. Because what are the chances that he would meet her in a crowded bar last night and then see her again this morning?

"I was hoping you would give me Coop's cell phone number," Brooke says. "He was really great."

FRAY

He wakes up on Saturday to two missed calls and three texts from DEAD TO ME, who is Anna, his ex-wife. Fray won't take the bait. He sets his phone down on the nightstand, rolls over, and gathers Leland up in his arms.

She stirs as he kisses her shoulder. "Good morning," she whispers. "I'm happy to see this wasn't all just a dream."

"Not a dream," Fray says, and he moves his mouth from her shoulder to the curve of her neck. "I'm real."

They make love again, quietly, because the cottage is small, and despite the grand renovation, you can still hear people thinking in the next room. Fray hasn't felt this kind of unbridled desire in four decades; it's like he's back in high school. In the summer of 1985, Fray and Leland used to sneak out in the middle of the night, skinny-dip in the country club pool, then have sex on the tennis courts. The difference between now and then is that Fray knows what he's doing, and so does Leland. She spent over ten years in a relationship with a woman, an idea that Fray finds sexy.

When Cooper told Fray that Leland would be coming on this reunion weekend, Fray never imagined they would end up in bed together. He'd been too wrapped up in the drama and pain surrounding his split from Anna. Getting involved with another woman, even his long-ago first love, was the furthest thing from his mind.

But chemistry is chemistry—and Fray and Leland have always had it.

Things had started to seem promising the night before, after Jake and Coop left for the Chicken Box. Fray didn't have many rules when it came to his sobriety, but *no bars* was one, and Leland said she didn't want to go either. Fray thought maybe she was just tired — they were older now; at home, Fray liked to be in bed by nine, something Anna found maddening — but as soon as they heard the Jeep rumble off down the no-name road, Leland grabbed a blanket from a basket by the sofa and said, "Come with me."

She spread the blanket out on the beach. She lay down and patted the spot next to her.

The second Fray opened his eyes to the starry sky above and listened to the crash and roll of the waves, he decided to share a realization he'd had earlier but that had seemed too private to talk about at dinner.

"It's the thirtieth anniversary of my sobriety," he said.

"Tonight?"

"The Friday of Labor Day weekend thirty years ago, yes," he said. "Do you remember that night? You and I and Mal and Jake went to the Box, and Coop stayed home to talk to Krystel. I went to the bar to get you a chardonnay. You very specifically asked for one from the Russian River Valley — I'll *never* forget that. They didn't have it, of course, they didn't have any white wine, only wine coolers, so I got you a beer, but then I couldn't find you. So I checked outside and you were with that preppy kid from the city. You left with him."

"That was Kip Sudbury," Leland said.

Kip Sudbury. The name rang a bell, one more recent

than that night thirty years ago. Was he a Wall Street guy? A hedge-fund guy?

"He was involved in that bond scandal back in—"

"Oh, right," Fray said.

"He took me to Twenty-One Federal to meet his friends and the next day we went sailing on his father's yacht."

"Well, I sat in the back of Mal's Blazer and drank by myself until the bar closed," Fray said. Memory was a slippery thing. Fray couldn't remember what he'd been served for lunch on his plane earlier that day but he could vividly picture himself in his Nirvana T-shirt, smoldering like a red-hot coal in the back of Mal's car. He remembered being tempted to go with Leland and her New York friends because he'd thought he read some apprehension in her expression—but then Fray realized that what Leland feared was him coming along. She didn't want him to embarrass her and expose her for the regular Baltimore girl she was. "And then when we got back to the cottage, we realized Coop had left the island and I snatched a bottle of Jim Beam and headed down the beach."

Leland turned on her side toward him and laid her fingers across his biceps. He inhaled her scent. She had always smelled spicy, like sandalwood and ginger, rather than sweet or floral. That was one of the many things he loved about her.

"I stripped down to go for a swim," Fray said. "At

least, I think that was my intention, because when the paramedics found me, I was buck naked, passed out in the sand."

Leland moved her hand down to Fray's thigh and leaned in so that her chin rested on his shoulder and her words breathed straight into his ear. "I'm glad nothing happened to you."

"I wouldn't say nothing happened. The next morning when I woke up, I realized I had a problem." Fray often wondered why *that* had been his aha moment. It wasn't the drunkest he'd ever been. He used to black out all the time at the University of Vermont. And there had been one fateful night during a summer home from college when he bumped into Leland and Mallory at Bohager's downtown. Leland had spent the whole evening talking to Penn Porter, who had been a classmate of Fray's at Calvert Hall, and Fray was jealous. He'd done at least six shots of Jägermeister at the bar, and the next thing he knew, he was waking up in Latrobe Park robbed blind with bruises all over his body and two teeth knocked loose. "I decided I would take a break from drinking." That was all Fray had intended to do: take a break. He certainly hadn't meant to go the rest of his life without tasting the first sip of an ice-cold beer or the velvety warmth of a good red wine on his tongue. But once the alcohol had cleared from his system, he liked how he felt. Powerful. In control. The control was its own high, and—if you listened to

Anna—he was addicted to it. "The break has lasted thirty years."

Leland kissed his cheek. Her hand remained on his thigh, which could only be interpreted one way. Fray felt himself stiffen beneath his jeans. Anna had convinced him he was washed up sexually, but that had been an excuse she invented so she could justify sleeping with Tyler.

"I'm sorry for my part in it," Leland whispered.

Fray shook his head. "I blamed you initially because you were the easy target. My first love, the one I couldn't get out of my system."

"When I landed here this afternoon, I was thinking about our first date in the hot tub."

Fray was so hard he had to adjust himself, subtly—the last thing he wanted was for Leland to move her hand. "You'd probably be uncomfortable to know how many times I've played back that scene in my head when I'm alone."

"Fray! Seriously?" Leland Gladstone the feminist might have been offended to know that she was the subject of his sexual fantasies, but Leland Gladstone the woman lying next to him sounded...flattered.

"It was a horny teenager's wet dream," Fray said. "Coming back out to the hot tub to find you topless?"

Leland propped herself up on her elbow and gazed down at him. He could see that she was older—there were lines by her eyes and around her mouth—but she was still the same smart, sassy, complicated person he'd fallen in love with a lifetime ago.

Fray's upbringing, seen through the lens of 2023, might be described as compromised, meager, possibly even traumatic. His mother, Sloane, was wild and rebellious. She got pregnant with Fray when she was twenty-one and couldn't identify the father; there had simply been too many men, many of them sailors who'd been in port in Baltimore for a few days before shipping out. Fray's maternal grandparents, Walt and Ida, took on the job of raising Fray. They were kind, but their household was abstemious. Walt and Ida didn't drink, didn't smoke, didn't swear. They didn't allow Fray to eat potato chips or Cap'n Crunch, drink Coke, or chew bubble gum. His bedtime was nine o'clock sharp; he had never once been allowed to stay up to watch *Taxi, Barney Miller,* or *Magnum P.I.* If Ida could hear his music playing through his bedroom door, it was too loud. Sloane would live with them periodically when she was between boyfriends and had nowhere else to go, and she acted more like an older sister than a mom. It was Sloane who had offered Fray his first cigarette at fourteen, his first drink at fifteen, his first toke of marijuana at sixteen. She did these things only when Walt and Ida were away or out of the house. "Your grandparents," Sloane would say—she always referred to Walt and Ida as "your grandparents," as though they were not related to her—"think I'm a bad influence on you."

She was, of course. His own mother was a bad influence.

In the face of that, Leland's love had been a life raft. As soon as Fray and Leland started dating, Fray stopped spending so much time at the Blessing house. Senior and Kitty had always been welcoming and inclusive, though Fray suspected they pitied him. He'd once overheard Kitty refer to Sloane as a "perennial party girl," a term he knew was unflattering but also not the worst thing she could have said. Fray found he felt more comfortable across the street with the Gladstones. Steve Gladstone took Fray under his wing, often bringing Fray along on errands to the hardware or auto-parts store, saying he was grateful to have "another man around." Steve and Geri came to every single one of Fray's lacrosse games junior and senior year, cheering for him as loudly as real parents might have.

When Fray left for college in Burlington, he and Leland broke up for the first time. She was still only a junior in high school and they both agreed the mature decision was to split up and see what happened. What happened was that they spent a small fortune on long-distance calls, and there were plenty of conversations that ended with one or the other of them slamming down the phone. But every time Fray returned to Baltimore, his first stop was the Gladstones' house, even before his own.

Frazier Dooley had loved Leland Gladstone. She was

a key part of his personal history. Last night on the beach there was nothing to stop them from making out on the blanket like the crazy kids they once were, then standing up, going back inside, and locking themselves in Mallory's bedroom.

Fray's phone rings again when he's underneath the covers, gently nibbling on Leland's hip bone, a sex move he feels like he invented because Leland says, "God, nobody has ever done that to me. Please don't stop." He hears the vibrating of his phone on the nightstand and when Leland says, "Who's 'Dead to Me'?," Fray tells her to ignore it.

After making love, they decide to go out for breakfast. Leland scurries into the bathroom to freshen up and Fray checks his phone. Anna didn't leave a message. It's nine thirty in the morning on Nantucket, six thirty in Seattle. He clicks on her texts in case there's an emergency with Cassie, their ten-year-old daughter.

You're unbelievable.

Talk about a HYPOCRITE.

Check Page Six.

Whaaaa? Fray thinks.

Leland comes out of the bathroom. She's glowing — as luminous as he's ever seen her. "Everything okay?"

"Yeah," Fray says. He plucks his underwear from the floor.

"Let's not bother showering," Leland says, tousling

his hair. "We're just going to swim when we get back anyway, and I'm *starving*."

"Me too," Fray says. "I just need to stop and get a copy of the *New York Post*."

Leland laughs. "I thought I was the only person I knew who read the *Post*," she says. "Fifi used to give me so much jazz about it."

"Everyone reads the *Post*," Fray says. "But only the brave admit it."

Coop is passed out on the sofa and Jake is nowhere to be found, so Fray scribbles a note saying he and Leland are taking the Jeep and going to breakfast. He drives to the big mid-island grocery store and leaves Leland in the car as he runs in to get the newspaper. Page Six? Is *he* on Page Six? Talk about a HYPOCRITE. What does *that* mean?

Leland had asked about Anna the night before, but Fray dodged the question; his divorce was the last thing he wanted to talk about. He imagined that getting divorced as a regular person — an accountant in Cheyenne or a florist in Shreveport — would be painful and difficult enough, but as a very wealthy, semi-famous person, it was a whole other circle of hell. Fray and Anna's story, although not unique, was a source of endless tabloid fascination. Anna had cheated on Fray with Tyler Toledo, the manager of her former band, Drank. They had been spotted having dinner at L'Oursin by one of Fray's vice presidents while Fray was down in

South America on business and Cassie was home with a sitter. When Fray asked Anna about it, she broke down in tears and said that yes, she and Tyler had been seeing each other for nine months and it was all Fray's fault because he had robbed Anna of any identity except for that of "Frazier Dooley's wife" and "Cassie Dooley's mother." She used to be interesting, she said. She used to be cool. Now she was just another Botoxed Seattle socialite with a private Pilates instructor and a twelve-thousand-square-foot glass house on Puget Sound.

Fray asked Anna if she was in love with Tyler and Anna said she was, though it was clear from both her facial expression and her tone that she was lying. She didn't love Tyler Toledo; sleeping with him was an act of rebellion, a cry for attention. Fray did a little investigative work and found out that Tyler's best days had been when he was managing Drank. Since then, he had couch-surfed his way around Queen Anne and Capitol Hill; he'd even been homeless for a while. Certainly reuniting with Anna, Drank's former bassist, had been a huge boost to him, especially since she was married to the eighth-richest man in Seattle. Fray thought maybe he could pay Tyler off to make him go away, but when this was intimated to him, Tyler doubled down and leaked his affair with Anna to Google News, and in a nanosecond, it was everywhere. It was the news of the scandal rather than the scandal itself that led to the divorce. Fray could have forgiven the infidelity. What he could not forgive was Anna on TMZ both disparaging him and shamelessly promoting old songs by Drank. (It worked; their song "Back It Up" surged on iTunes.) The tabloids gobbled up the seedy aspects of the story, which was bad for everyone involved but especially Cassie. Ten was such a tricky age. Cassie was old enough to understand what was going on but not old enough to understand why, and Anna had broken every single rule in the Evolved-Parenting Handbook. She thought nothing of badmouthing Fray in front of Cassie any chance she could get.

Fray agreed to a two-hundred-and-eighty-million-dollar settlement only because he wanted the whole thing to be over.

He grabs the last copy of the *Post* at the Stop and Shop and somehow resists looking at the paper while he's waiting in line. When he gets back to the car, Leland has the radio cranked to the rock station playing the top five hundred songs of all time and she's singing along to "Heaven" by Bryan Adams.

"You're all that I want! You're all that I need!" She turns down the music and grins at him. "This song has always reminded me of the Calvert Hall junior prom. Remember my lavender dress?"

Fray shakes his head but he can't stop his smile. "I need coffee," he says.

Frazier Dooley loves nothing more than a good breakfast place and as soon as he sees Island Kitchen, he knows he's found one. It's mid-island, right across the street from the Stop and Shop, as it turns out, so it doesn't have a water view, but the place is loaded with character. The post-and-beam construction is charming; there are lush pink impatiens in the window boxes; it feels rustic and homey—like the island's kitchen.

Fray and Leland are seated at a two-top inside, where Fray immediately detects the scent of Frayed Edge Classic Black. This comes as no surprise because it was his New England sales manager who'd given him the name of this place.

A server who is girl-next-door-pretty with a dark ponytail and freckles—her name tag says SARAH—comes over, holding the signature Frayed Edge silver pot, and says, "Coffee?"

"Please," Fray says, nudging the chunky ceramic mug forward.

"I'll have tea," Leland says. "Herbal, if you have it."

"Right away," Sarah says. She pours Fray's coffee, and despite the steam, Fray can't get it to his mouth fast enough. He looks at Leland. "You're on a date with me and you're ordering *tea? Herbal* tea?"

Leland laughs. "I did it just for that reaction."

"Excuse me!" Fray calls out. "My beautiful friend here will have coffee as well. It's Frayed Edge, right?"

"That's all we serve," Sarah says. She takes a second look at Fray and he watches recognition cross her face. "Oh my God, you're…"

Leland hoots. "Do you get recognized everywhere you go?"

Sarah pours Leland's coffee and lowers her voice. "Someone called us yesterday to say you might be coming in. They wanted to make sure we had the signature pots and all the signage."

"It looks great," Fray says.

Sarah turns her attention to Leland. "Oh!" she says. "You're the woman from the *New York Post*!"

"I don't work at the *Post*," Leland says. "I'm Leland Gladstone, of *Leland's Letter*?"

Fray gets a sinking feeling. The *Post* is folded in half on the bench next to him. "We'll be ready to order in just a minute," he says.

Fray finishes his first cup of coffee and decides to distract Leland with another topic they've been avoiding—their parents. Twenty-five years earlier, Steve Gladstone and Fray's mother, Sloane, had an affair. Steve ended up leaving Geri Gladstone and marrying Sloane. Fray speaks to his mother sporadically but he hasn't seen her and Steve in a few years. He gathers that Leland keeps contact to a minimum as well; she aligned herself staunchly with Geri.

He reaches for Leland's hand. "How funny would it be if we called Steve and Sloane on the way home and told them we're back together?"

"I'm trying to forget the unfortunate fact that we're actually step-siblings," Leland says. At that instant, Leland's phone pings and she checks the text. "It's my mother. She—I kid you not, just *look* at this—she says, 'Are you with Frazier Dooley?'" Leland holds up the screen of her phone. "Tell me that's not spooky."

Sarah shows up with the silver pot and refills both their cups. Fray is starting to sweat.

"We're ready to order," he says. "I'll have the Panko Eggs Benedict."

"And I'll have the Bananas Foster French Toast," Leland says.

Sarah leaves and Fray feels his phone buzz again: DEAD TO ME. He declines the call and sighs. "I got the *Post* for a reason. I think there might be something about me on Page Six."

"Eeeeeeee!" Leland says. "Let's look together, come on." She slides around to his side of the table, picks up the *Post*, and slaps it down in front of him. "You do the honors."

Fray stares at the paper. What is he going to find? He tries to remember if he heard any drones during the night.

"Or I can?" Leland says.

"No, I'll do it." He opens the paper to Page Six— and there is a photograph of Fray and Leland kissing outside the Nantucket airport. The headline reads: "Frazier Dooley's Tony Island Getaway with Feminist Icon Leland Gladstone."

To her credit, Leland doesn't shriek or scream, but when she pulls her reading glasses out of her purse, he notices her hands are shaking.

" 'Coffee mogul Frazier Dooley greets paramour Leland Gladstone outside Nantucket Memorial Airport. The couple were then whisked away by a private vehicle.' "

Leland turns to Fray, and all he can think is how sexy she looks in her glasses, like a naughty librarian. "That's why our server said I was from the *Post*," she whispers. "And that's why my mother texted. They've already seen this."

Everyone reads the Post, he thinks. *But only the brave admit it.* He can't gauge where Leland is going to land on this. He's pretty sure her brand depends on her sexual identity, which is...well, whatever it is, it's probably not compatible with a weekend rendezvous on the arm of a white male billionaire.

"I'm sorry," he says. "I attract all kinds of attention because of the business. And the whole thing with Anna has made things exponentially worse."

"Has Anna seen this?" Leland asks. "Was that her calling this morning?"

Fray nods.

"*I'm* the one who's sorry," Leland says. "I know who took this picture. There were two women on my plane who asked for a selfie, and then when we were walking out of the terminal they were behind me and I overheard them saying they recognized you."

"So they took our picture and sold it to the *Post*," Fray says.

"I'm sure they think they won the internet jackpot,"

Leland says. She picks up the paper. "Does *feminist icon* make me sound old?"

"*Icon* is better than *mogul*," Fray says. "*Mogul* is such an ugly, hobbity word."

"I can't believe this," Leland whispers. "I mean, it wouldn't be funny except it's *true*. I *am* your weekend paramour."

"Will you get ... canceled?" Fray says. "Will you be hounded by trolls? Do your readers think you sleep with women?"

"My sexuality is considered fluid," Leland says. "It's 2023. Everyone's sexuality is considered fluid, Fray."

"Oh," Fray says. *His* sexuality doesn't feel fluid; it feels very Leland-specific. "So this isn't necessarily *bad* for you, then?"

"I don't know and I don't care," Leland says. "I've been happier the past twenty-four hours than I've been ... maybe ever."

This statement nearly brings Fray to tears. He hasn't been this happy maybe ever either. He thinks back to his much younger self, glaring at the pay phone in his freshman dorm after just having hung up on Leland, who was back in her bedroom on Deepdene Road in Baltimore. What had they been arguing about? Who knows—maybe Fray told her he was pledging a fraternity, maybe she told him she and Mallory were going to a party with boys from Gilman. He then pictures himself in the back of Mallory's Blazer, calling Leland every swearword he knew under his breath after she strolled off to 21 Federal with Kip Sudbury.

He had no idea then that all he needed for things to finally be perfect between the two of them was patience. A lot of patience.

BESS

Everything about her Friday evening improves all at once. Not only has she traded up in the date department—she bumped into Link Dooley, a boy she has thought about ever since she met him on Nantucket three years ago—but she is also leaving behind the Drake-and-buffalo-wings scene at Roofers Union for Lapis, her favorite restaurant in the District.

Lapis is quiet and elegant; it gives off strong bistro vibes, only with sitar music. The owner, Shamin, gives Bess a smile when she sees her enter with Link. Shamin leads them to one of the tables in the window. Bess thanks her profusely even though, because of the conversation she's about to have, she would prefer a table tucked behind one of the latticed wooden screens.

"Wow," Link says. "You get star treatment."

"I come here a lot," Bess says. She doesn't mention that this was the one place in DC where Ursula would eat in public while she was campaigning. Shamin made every accommodation to ensure that Ursula, Jake, and Bess were comfortable.

"I love bolani," Link says. "And qabuli palau."

"The palau here is off the chain," Bess says. "It's made with cinnamon rice."

"We have to get the halwa for dessert," Link says.

Bess beams. Link really does like Afghan food. All she can imagine is the lobbyist looking at the menu and ordering a chicken kebab and French fries.

"Let's get the pakoras to start," she says. She wants to pinch herself. How did she get so lucky?

Once they're settled with a glass of Albariño for Bess and a beer for Link, Bess realizes this happiness comes with a price: She has promised to tell Link what was going on between her father and his mother.

Link tears a piece off his flat oval of bolani and dips it in yogurt sauce, then raises his eyes to Bess. He's better-looking than any lobbyist, she decides. She loves his shaggy blond hair and his bluish-green eyes that remind her of the ocean the day she first met him.

"So your dad told you what was going on?" Link says.

"He told me on the way back to St. Louis after we saw you," Bess says. She busies herself with her own bolani. Her father made her solemnly swear never to tell a soul, and she had promised. She understood the gravity of the situation at the time: Her mother was running for president and there could be no scandalous family secrets floating to the surface. If Bess told her best friend, Pageant, or Kasie, the campaign manager, in a moment of weakness, it would be all over. Her father was entrusting her with a secret he'd kept longer than she'd been alive. She realized that he was telling her because she was the one who had made the trip to Nantucket with him, because she'd asked him what the whole thing meant, because he loved her, because he was sodden with emotions when he left Mallory's bedside, holding the rented guitar, because Mallory was a day or two from death and by telling Bess what had happened between them, he was keeping Mallory alive.

Their circumstances were different now, of course. Ursula had lost the election and she was no longer in public life. No one cared about Ursula de Gournsey and Jake McCloud anymore. It wouldn't matter who Bess told about this secret now, but she still felt guilty because it was her father's story to tell and not hers. What would he think about Bess sharing it with Lincoln Dooley?

Well, either he would be appalled or he would think that Link deserved the truth, just as Bess did. She'll go with the second choice, since she can't very well back out now. Link is looking at her expectantly.

"They had an affair," Bess says. "One weekend a year. Labor Day weekend, actually."

Link's brow creases. "Does that have anything to do with why everyone is up on Nantucket this weekend?"

"They're reliving the summer of 1993—that's when your mom and my dad met. Your uncle and your dad were there too."

"Ahh," Link says. "Thirty years ago."

"Yup."

"So did they see each other only on Labor Day weekend?"

"Yes. Always on Nantucket. From 1993 until, well, 2020."

"Where was I when this was happening?" Link asks. He looks at Bess as though she might have the answer. "You know what? I always, always spent Labor Day weekend out in Seattle with my dad. All through growing up, I did that. Except for one year, when I went to DC to see my uncle. And another year, I went with an old girlfriend to New York City."

Bess feels herself bristling at the mention of an old girlfriend. "My dad said they met every single Labor Day weekend no matter what. Always at your cottage. They never missed a year."

"And nobody found out?" Link says. "Your mom never found out?"

A server sets their order of pakoras on the table; they're golden brown, fragrant, and too hot to touch, never mind eat. Bess thanks him and points to her wineglass. She's definitely going to need another.

"My mom found out, or suspected, anyway. She went to Nantucket in 2019 to confront Mallory."

Link's eyes widen. "She..."

"She was running for president. She didn't think she could have that coming to light."

"Why did she go to Nantucket? Why didn't she just talk to your dad?"

"She was afraid my dad would leave her," Bess says. "She believed the only person who could put an end to the affair was your mom."

Link leans back in his chair and takes a sip of his beer. Bess nudges the plate of pakoras toward him. He takes one and blows on it.

"I'll ask the obvious question. Why didn't your dad just leave your mom earlier? Why didn't he leave her in year five or ten or fifteen? My mother—" Link sets the fritter down without tasting it and stares out the window. "She never got married. She had boyfriends when she was young, and she hooked up with my dad, obviously, and there was a guy she was serious about when I was little, but that didn't work out. She was alone. I could never understand it. My friends didn't get it— so many of them thought she was super-hot. My grandma used to get on her case all the time about meeting someone." He sets his elbows on the table and drops his head in his hands. "Now all I can think is that she wasted her life, year after year, waiting for Labor Day weekend to roll around. How do you live like that? Only seeing the person you love three or four days a year?"

"My dad said it was...well, *excruciating* was his exact word."

Link gives a short, bitter laugh. "Excruciating for him? No offense, Bess, but he was married. He went right home to your mother." Link pushes away the pakora on his share plate and Bess thinks, *Oh, no, no, no!* She only wanted to tell Link what she knew. She didn't mean to hurt him or make him angry. "You can see how this little arrangement..."

"Same time, next year," Bess says. "It was the title of a movie they used to watch."

"Yeah, well, the same time next year was profoundly unfair to my mother."

"That's what I told my dad," Bess says. "The arrangement was lopsided. And sexist." Bess remembers how Jake had patiently endured her tirade about white male privilege. "He assured me that the arrangement was Mallory's choice. I guess there were a couple of junctures when my dad said he wanted to be with her on a permanent basis and she turned him down. She didn't want to leave Nantucket."

"She never would have left the island."

"He said she was happy. He told me she had a full life." Bess's second glass of wine is dropped off by none other than Shamin herself.

"Is everything okay here?" Shamin asks, eyeing the untouched pakoras. "We are busy preparing your entrées."

"Delicious!" Bess says too eagerly, and she takes a perfunctory bite of pakora.

"Very good," Shamin says, smiling, and thankfully, she leaves them.

Bess turns back to Link. "I'm not pretending to know

what your mother's life was like. You would know that far better than me. But my dad claims she had her job, her cottage, friends, a community... and you."

Link looks at her incredulously and she can't help but agree with him. She's ridiculous! She's trying to justify what happened between their parents when it was, quite clearly, unfair to Mallory. But then Link does an amazing thing. He reaches across the table for her hand. Bess tries to act natural but she instantly flushes from the neck up. She likes Link so much — okay, she realizes she doesn't really know him, but she's been drawn to him since she first set eyes on him stepping out of the cottage on Nantucket. He'd looked so forlorn, a boy on the verge of losing his mother. He'd been trying to escape the adults inside, and, like Bess, he was probably wondering what the hell Jake McCloud was doing there. But he was kind and funny with Bess, and she thought she'd seen a spark in his eyes, like maybe he thought Bess was pretty, and then he offered to show her the beach. She'd wanted him to ask for her number before she left but her dad had been standing there and it wasn't clear if she and Link would ever see each other again, so what would be the point?

"Don't you think everyone deserves to find love?" Link asks. "Isn't that what we're all programmed to search for? Someone we can connect with — a lover, a friend — someone to build a life with?"

Bess nods but is afraid to speak. She isn't sure if Link is trying to tell her she might be that person for him (could she be so lucky?) or if he's blaming Jake for keeping Mallory from finding such a person.

They found love, she wants to say. Maybe it didn't look like other people's love—a split-level house with a two-car garage, family road trips in the summer, date night on Saturdays—but that doesn't mean it wasn't romantic or real. That doesn't mean they weren't devoted. Something about the way her father described his time with Mallory made it sound very real and very romantic. And if twenty-eight consecutive summers *no matter what* wasn't devotion, then what was?

But before Bess can articulate any of this, two things happen. The first is that a server arrives with their entrées and the second is that Link's phone plays Toto's "Africa"—Bess loves that song too—and the screen lights up with the name Stacey.

Link stands up as his plate of palau lands. "I have to take this."

Bess blinks. "Okay?"

"Outside," he says. "I'll be right back."

Who is Stacey? she wonders. An old girlfriend? A current girlfriend? She tries not to worry. It might be his boss or a coworker or a friend. She feels relieved that they are finished with the Jake and Mallory story. Maybe when Link gets back, they can eat and talk about their own lives like two normal people on a date.

Bess watches Link on the sidewalk on his phone, his head bent, one ear plugged. She considers the food. It would be rude for her to start without him, but she's hungry, so she helps herself to one of the pakoras, which have finally cooled enough to eat. She devours one and is reaching for another when a guy takes Link's seat.

"Uh..." Bess says, her mouth full. She swallows. "Wrong table?"

"You're Bess, right? Bess McCloud?" The guy looks like a Hollister model or like the lead actor in a sexy HBO series about the Ivy League's secret societies. And then, of course, it dawns on Bess: It's the lobbyist.

"Aidan?" she says.

"You ditched me," he says. "I finally made it to Roofers Union and you were gone."

Bess stares at Aidan Hydeck's perfectly coiffed dark hair, his sleepy brown eyes, and his square shoulders, and she realizes that, in the excitement of leaving Roofers Union with Link, she forgot to cancel this date. And not only that, she'd continued to share her location with Aidan.

"I'm so sorry," she says.

He tilts his head and gives her a slow smile. "It's okay, I was the one who was late."

"Yeah, but that wasn't your fault. You got stuck on the Metro."

"That I did." He looks at the food on the table. "I don't mean to be a poor sport but I don't like Indian food."

"It's Afghan."

"Even worse," he says. "I was really looking forward to wings at the Roof." Only then does he seem to notice

Link's empty beer glass and the share plate with the now-cold pakora. "Oh, snap, are you here with somebody?"

Bess is utterly at a loss. She checks out the window. Link is still on the phone, standing just off the curb in the street between two parked cars.

Aidan follows her eyes and taps the glass. "That guy?"

"He's...an old friend. He showed up at Roofers Union and...oh God, Aidan, I'm so sorry. I meant to let you know I was leaving. I'm not like this, I swear."

Aidan gets to his feet. "It's fine," he says. "I would suggest that we reschedule when you're not quite so busy, but now that I've seen you in person, I don't think I want to bother."

Bess recoils. Did he just say that? She knows he's angry, but that was dirty.

He leans down by her ear and says, "I only asked for this date because I know who your mother is."

Link approaches the table. "Hey?"

Aidan turns around and smirks at him. "She's all yours, bro."

Bess is so angry she wants to dump her palau all over Aidan's gorgeous lobbyist head. Instead, she stares at the table and waits for Aidan to leave the restaurant; she can't make a scene, not here. She wants to ask Shamin to wrap everything to go so that Bess can eat it alone in her apartment. Link was on the phone with Stacey for so long that all Bess can imagine is he's about to offer an excuse to cut dinner short so he can meet her.

How can she live in a city filled with men and still not be able to meet anyone suitable?

When she raises her head, Link has retaken his seat. He's leaning forward, staring at her. "Friend of yours?"

"That was Aidan," Bess says. "The lobbyist." Aidan was the last man on earth she should have chosen off Bumble. *Now that I've seen you in person, I don't think I want to bother. I only asked for this date because I know who your mother is.*

"He seemed like a real peach and I'm sorry you missed out on spending the evening with him, but I'll try to make it up to you." Link reaches for Bess's hand again.

Link doesn't seem like he's in a particular hurry to rush out, but Bess is wary. "Everything okay with your phone call?"

Link shakes his head. "It was my uncle's girlfriend. Ex-girlfriend? Almost fiancée? The woman who turned down his marriage proposal, which was what made him want to organize the Nantucket weekend? Yeah, that was her. She's had time to process and she decided she wants to marry him after all, so she showed up at the house but he wasn't there, so she called him and it went straight to voice mail and she's convinced he blocked her, which he probably did, because what else would you do to the woman who turned down your proposal? And she wanted to know if I knew where he was."

Bess is overcome with relief. Stacey isn't Link's girlfriend. Stacey is his uncle's girlfriend! "Did you tell her?"

Link shrugs. "I said I wasn't sure but I thought he'd made plans out of town with a friend."

"Aaaaahhhh!" Bess says. "Did she think you meant a female friend?"

Link squeezes Bess's hand, then lets go so he can dig into the palau. "I don't want to worry about Coop's romantic life," he says. "I'd like to focus on my own."

After dinner, Link asks if he can walk Bess home and she says yes, and they stroll the streets of Washington, holding hands. When they reach the Sedgewick, Link escorts her to the door and Bess says, "Thank you for saving me from the lobbyist."

Link lays a gentle hand on the side of her face and then leans in and kisses her. It's the best kiss Bess has ever received—sweet, warm, just enough to leave her aching for more.

"Oh," she whispers.

Link kisses her again. He pulls her to him and soon they are making out while moths beat around the light over their heads.

Bess pulls away. "Would you like to come up?"

Link takes a breath, and Bess wonders: *Does he not want to come up?* Was something wrong with her kissing?

Link says, "I feel like I should let you know something."

"Okay?" Bess says.

"Seeing you once a year isn't going to be enough for

me," he says. "So if we're following in our parents' footsteps or fulfilling their thwarted destiny or whatever, that part has to change."

Bess pulls out her key. She can't hide her smile. "Deal," she says.

COOPER

On Saturday, Cooper wakes up at noon. Noon! When was the last time he'd done *that?* College? High school? He's an up-at-the-crack-of-dawn, seize-the-day kind of guy. A morning person. But when he finally unsticks his eyelids, he can't deny he lacks any motivation to get up off the wide, comfortable sofa.

Except that he's the host here.

Ever so gently, he lifts his head from the cushion and gazes around the room. Nobody is in the cottage, though he hears voices on the beach. Coop swings his feet to the floor and stands up. He overdid it — drank too much, stayed out too late. Deep inside him, like a coin dropped in a well, rests a small sense of accomplishment: He closed the Chicken Box!

The person he would like to tell this to is Stacey.

He pours himself a giant glass of ice water and heads out to the beach, where Jake, Leland, and Fray are enjoying the sun. Jake is in his trunks, sitting in a chair with a book open on his chest; his hair is wet. Fray and Leland are lying side by side on a blanket. Leland is in a black tank suit and a straw hat, and Fray is beside her. Something is funny about that. Cooper squints. It's bright outside, and he goes inside for his sunglasses. When he comes back out, he sees that Fray's and Leland's legs are intertwined in a way that looks more than friendly.

"Hello, all," Coop says, collapsing in an empty chair.

"How you feeling, old man?" Fray asks. Coop can see that Fray is also stroking Leland's shoulder. *Ohhhhkay.*

Jake says, "Want me to make you an omelet? You must be starving."

Coop feels queasy. "I think I'll go for a swim first, then see if I can handle food."

"So listen," Fray says. "I booked a sunset sail on the *Endeavor* for Leland and me tonight and then I got the two of us a highly sought-after reservation at the Boarding House. I've heard their lobster spaghetti absolutely *slaps.* So I hope that's cool with you…"

Sunset sail? Lobster spaghetti? What does that mean, it "slaps"? The "for Leland and me" part he understands; Fray and Leland want to go to dinner alone. Coop made a nine-thirty reservation for the four of them at Nautilus, but who is he kidding? He's not up for sitting down to dinner at nine thirty; he'll fall asleep in his bao buns. He'll cancel Nautilus. He and Jake can get a pizza and watch college football. He feels a bit bummed that they aren't doing something all together, but he can't ignore his relief. He has been set free from expectations.

Coop spends the afternoon waiting for the fog in his head to clear. The swim helps a little, and the pillowy omelet that Jake serves him with two pieces of toasted Something Natural herb bread soaks up the beer and the shot of tequila he did the night before. (The tequila had been handed to him by a member of a bachelor party who called him "Pops.")

He sits on the beach for a while but the sun makes his headache worse. Jake suggests hair of the dog—he's drinking a Dark and Stormy—but Coop can't think about alcohol.

Fray and Leland disappear inside and Coop says to Jake, "Did something happen between them?"

"They have a thing," Jake deadpans. "A thing that refuses to die."

"Since the mid-eighties," Coop says. He lowers his voice. "I thought Leland liked women?"

Jake shrugs.

Jake dozes off in his chair and Coop heads inside to grab a Coke, thinking some caffeine might help. He sees Fray and Leland pop out of Mallory's bedroom all dressed up. "Dressed up" for Fray is jeans and a white button-down shirt that looks like it could have been pulled off the rack at Sears but is probably by an Italian designer and costs eleven hundred dollars. Leland is wearing a fitted black dress; after only one afternoon in the sun, she's tan.

"Have fun, kids," Coop says. He is looking at Frazier Dooley and Leland Gladstone in 2023, but he's also having a flashback to Fray and Leland standing up against the cinder-block wall outside the Calvert Hall boys' locker room after one of Fray's lacrosse games. Rumor around the school was that Leland gave him special "favors" if he scored a goal.

"Hey, you can sleep in Link's room tonight," Fray says. "I've been upgraded."

Leland kisses Fray's cheek. "Damn straight."

Coop laughs and shakes his head. He loves them both. If they're happy, he's happy.

After they leave, Coop thinks maybe he *will* go into Link's room and lie down—but he stops in front of the bookshelves, which hold not only Mallory's impressive library but also a bunch of framed photographs. Many of them are of Link growing up and of Mallory and Link together, though there are also some wonderful photos of Mallory and Cooper as children that Mallory must have taken when they cleared out the house on Deepdene Road after Senior and Kitty were killed.

There's a shot of Cooper, Mallory, Senior, and Kitty taken during brunch in the Green Room at the Hotel Du Pont in Wilmington, Delaware. The Blessings always went the Saturday after Thanksgiving, because that was the first day the hotel was decorated for Christmas.

Kitty used to go to the Green Room with her own parents, so the brunch tradition was *very* important to her. Coop recalls suffering through it his junior and senior years in high school following the epic Friday-after-Thanksgiving parties he used to attend. That was definitely the case in this picture—Cooper's eyes are bloodshot; his hair is uncombed and his tie crooked—but what makes him laugh out loud is Mallory in her kelly-green monogrammed sweater and kilt (a kilt!) and knee socks. She must be fourteen and she's wearing knee socks.

Tears burn his eyes as he laughs. She was *such* a nerd! Before she had braces, she used to have buckteeth, and Cooper would tease her relentlessly. He also teased her about her adoration of Rick Springfield, her addiction to *General Hospital,* and the stubborn cowlick in her hair that she would spend the moments before leaving for school fruitlessly trying to tame.

Coop knows that, growing up, Mallory resented him. Things came easily to him—good grades, sports, charming all the adults in his life so that he got pretty much whatever he wanted. Mallory was shyer, a bit socially awkward; she preferred to stay in her room, lounging on her fuzzy purple beanbag chair, reading. Oh, and she ate saltines with butter. Coop closes his eyes. He hasn't thought of her saltine-and-butter addiction in decades.

He picks up another picture where he is maybe ten and Mallory eight. It's Easter. Coop is in a navy blazer,

Mallory in a pink dress and headband (buckteeth protruding from her smile). They're standing in front of the fireplace at their grandparents' house, holding baskets filled with candy. Coop can practically smell his grandfather's pipe smoke. The next picture he picks up moves him even further back in time. Coop is maybe seven, Mallory five, and they're wearing the lederhosen that their grandparents brought back from a trip to Munich. This picture is *serious* blackmail material. They look *ridiculous!* Coop laughs until he cries, and then he's bawling like a baby because Mallory was his kid sister and he misses her. He sets the lederhosen picture next to a picture of Aunt Greta and Uncle Bo, who were the original owners of this cottage. Cooper remembers when Mallory was "sent to Nantucket" for the summer as a kid; he thought she was being punished. Little did he know.

There are no pictures of Mallory with Jake, obviously, since their relationship was like a state secret, and no pictures of Mallory with any other men. Coop wonders, as he often has, if there was something *wrong* with him and his sister. Mallory had a child but never married; Coop has been married five times, but none of the unions lasted and he never had children. Was it random luck that things ended up that way or had they both been defective somehow? Kitty and Senior, although they had their faults, set a wonderful example. They were devoted and attentive and respectful of each other. Cooper Senior could be impenetrable emotionally but he had a soft spot for his wife. There had always been romance in the house—long-stemmed roses "just because" and evenings spent on the couch in front of the fire, Kitty lying with her head in Senior's lap. Maybe they set an example that was too hard to live up to.

Cooper thinks of Dr. Robb's point that he has suffered a lot of loss. It was all weighing on his shoulders now. He missed his family. He would give everything he owned to be back in the Green Room at the Hotel Du Pont.

He's overtired and growing very emotional. He needs a nap. Coop slinks into Link's room and crashes facedown on the bed.

When Cooper wakes up, the sun is setting in a blaze of pink on the horizon. Link's room, which has a window onto the beach, is suffused with rose-gold light.

Coop finds Jake in the living room drinking a beer in front of the Clemson–Ole Miss game.

"Hey," Coop says. "Should we order a pizza?"

"There's something I forgot to tell you earlier," Jake says. "Do you remember that woman Brooke from last night?"

"Yeah?" Coop says. "The teacher who was friends with Apple?" He's having a hard time coming up with Brooke's face, though he recalls thinking she was pretty.

"I bumped into her this morning on my run," Jake says. "She was walking her dog."

"Wow, small island," Coop says, then he wonders if maybe Jake found Brooke attractive too. That would be great. Jake needs to get back in the game after losing Mallory and splitting from Ursula. And it would be so fitting, him dating the woman who replaced Mallory. Or would it be weird?

"She gave me her number," Jake says. "And she told me to tell you to call her."

"Me?" Coop says, laughing. This is unexpected. Or is it? Now that he thinks of it, he was dancing with her pretty exclusively.

"Do you remember that they invited us to that beach picnic tomorrow?"

"That's right!" Coop says. He forgot about the beach picnic. But they were definitely invited. "Send me her number now. I'll text her and find out what time."

Coop marvels at how well Sunday's schedule works out. At eight o'clock, Coop, Jake, and Fray play nine holes of golf at Miacomet while Leland bikes to a hot-yoga class. They all meet back at the cottage for bagels and fruit salad and coffee (of course), and after a swim and a nap in the sun, they get ready for their respective afternoons. Fray and Leland are biking out to Sconset for a late lunch in the garden at the Chanticleer. Cooper and Jake put on polo shirts and swim trunks and drive out to a beach called Fortieth Pole, stopping at Cisco Brewery on the way for beer so they don't show up empty-handed.

It's been an A-plus day so far—Coop shot a 45 in golf, he was sharp and clearheaded, and he loved hanging out with his two best friends for three hours. He feels even more excited about this picnic and the chance to reconnect with Brooke. They had a flirty text conversation the evening before. Brooke was making a blueberry pie to bring to the picnic and she would be wearing a blue bikini.

They drive the Jeep up over the soft sand road that cuts between the dunes and come down onto a flat curve of beach.

"Jake!" a woman calls out. "Coop!" The woman is blond and wearing a blue bikini, so Coop figures it must be Brooke. She's with a group of people camped off to the right. She shows them where to park, and when Cooper climbs out of the Jeep, she throws her arms around his neck and gives him a big hug.

Okay? he thinks. When they separate, he studies her face. She's pretty, smiling, and he does vaguely remember her from the other night. Vaguely.

Apple is at the picnic with her husband, Hugo, and their twin boys, Caleb and Lucas, who are going to be seniors at the high school, and a bunch of other people whose names Coop tries to retain but loses after ten seconds. He knows he doesn't have to worry about Jake; the guy raises money for a living and can talk to anyone about anything.

Coop throws their case of beer into the tub of ice and cracks open one for himself and one for Jake. *This is the life,* he thinks. "Upside Down" by Jack Johnson is playing on the portable speaker; the grills are smoking; and there's a table laden with food, including a blueberry pie with a lattice crust. Apple holds out a platter of oysters sitting in rapidly melting crushed ice.

"Hugo just shucked these," she says. "Please, have one."

"Then you two come play some bocce," Hugo says. "Jake, you're on my team."

"No wonder my sister loved it here so much," Coop says to Apple.

"You know something funny I remember about Mallory?" Apple says. "She never once came to our Labor Day picnic. She always claimed she was busy. Every year."

"Oh, she was busy, all right," Coop says.

"Bocce," Jake says.

Coop hopes that he will be as impressive at bocce as he was at golf that morning—but he's the weak link, probably because he's distracted by Brooke, who is waving her drink around, chanting his name: "Coo-per! Cooper!" He wonders how much she's had to drink and then reminds himself not to judge. She's a teacher, and this is her last full day of freedom; she's allowed to be enthusiastic.

The tenth-grade history teacher whose name Cooper thinks is Nancy comes around with a tray of pink cocktails in plastic cups.

"Madaket mysteries," she says. "A Labor Day tradition."

Coop tastes one—it's strong and goes down way too easily. The Spanish teacher, Jill, comes by with buffalo chicken dip and Fritos, and Cooper is a sucker for Fritos. Then the ribs and jumbo shrimp come off the grill. This is the best day he's had in a long time—even though he loses, badly, at bocce.

"Want to go for a walk, handsome?" Brooke asks. She has pulled on a diaphanous white cover-up and she hands him another Madaket mystery.

"Sure," he says. He checks on Jake, who is deep in conversation with the biology teacher over by the deviled eggs. He catches Jake's eye, waves, and points to Brooke.

They head down the beach, walking past kids building sandcastles and collecting shells and past a teenager on a skim board who looks at Brooke and says, "What's up, Ms. Schuster?"

Without missing a beat, she says, "See you Tuesday, Liam."

"I love it," Cooper says. "You see your students at the beach."

"I see my students everywhere," Brooke says. "It's a small island."

She tells Coop her basic story: She's forty-eight years old and has two kids, a son who's a sophomore at UMass and a daughter who will be a senior at the high school, in the same class as Caleb and Lucas. She lives on the island year-round in a rental that she fears the owners will someday sell out from under her, but she doesn't make enough on her teacher's salary to buy her own home. "I always wondered how Mallory did it," she says. "She was a single mom too, right?"

"She was," Coop says. "She inherited the cottage from our aunt when we were in our twenties. It's on the beach but it's simple and pretty small. When my parents died, she had the money to finally renovate."

"Well, sadly, I don't have a rich aunt to leave me a beachfront cottage," Brooke says. She goes on to tell Coop that all of her family is in New Hampshire, which was where she lived before she got divorced from the children's father and decided she needed a change. She sighs. "So, what do you like to read?"

Coop scrambles to think of one of the titles on Mallory's bookshelves, but he draws a blank. He was always the kid in English who skimmed the CliffsNotes five minutes before class. "I don't read for pleasure because I do so much policy analysis at work." This answer is lame, and to distract Brooke, he reaches for her hand. It works—maybe too well. Brooke pulls him into the water. He manages to shuck off his shirt but she goes in with her cover-up still on, which strikes him as a little unhinged. Brooke paddles out, then turns to splash him right in the face, and when he sputters, she says, "Oh, I'm sorry, baby," and while Coop is thinking, *baby?*—he hardly knows this woman; he wasn't even sure it was her when they pulled onto the beach, and he never would have recognized her on the street—she swims into his arms and starts kissing him.

Whoa, he thinks. *That was fast.* "We should probably get back," he says.

She splashes him again, right in the face. "You're no fun."

As they're walking back, she says, "So how do I convince you to move into your sister's cottage and stay on Nantucket year-round?"

Coop laughs, even though he is now officially uncomfortable. "Hopefully in a few years when I retire, I'll be able to spend more time here."

"A few years?" Brooke says. "I'll be off the market by then."

At a loss for how to respond, Coop quickens his pace. He's relieved when they get back to the party and Jake says, "Leland called—we have to go."

"Did something happen?" Coop asks.

"She didn't say. She just told me we were needed at home."

Coop and Jake say their goodbyes and Coop gives Brooke a hug and a quick kiss goodbye. "I have your number," he says. "And you have mine if you ever get to Washington."

Brooke waves like crazy until the Jeep is up over the dunes.

"You like her?" Jake says.

"Perfectly nice woman," Coop says. "And attractive. But we had exactly nothing in common and I'm not unhappy to be leaving."

"That's good to hear," Jake says. "You two were gone so long, I was afraid you'd proposed."

As they head down the no-name road, Coop wonders if he should be concerned. Fray and Leland both seemed giddy about their reunion, but all Coop can think now is that they had an argument (this would be par for the course with them) and Fray lost his temper and is threatening to leave. It would be sort of like what happened thirty years ago.

But when they pull up to the cottage, Coop hears laughter and conversation coming from inside. He hears a woman who is *not* Leland. It sounds like...

Coop throws open the screen door and steps inside. Fray and Leland are sitting at the narrow harvest table with Stacey.

Stacey?

She stands up and smiles at him. She's wearing a flowing white strapless dress and a pair of barely there sandals. She's every bit as captivating to Cooper as she was the first time he saw her, in the basement of the Phi Gamma Delta house.

"Stace?" he says. "What are you doing here?"

"I've had a change of heart," she says. "So if your offer still stands..."

Coop sweeps her off the ground. He grins at his friends. "I'm getting married!" he says.

"For the *last* time," Stacey says.

JAKE

On Monday, Fray generously offers to fly Jake back to South Bend on his private jet.

"It's on my way home," he says. "It's no problem to make a stop. I'll have my pilot add it to the flight plan."

Fray and Jake part ways with the others outside the terminal. Leland is heading to New York, Cooper and Stacey back to DC. Jake gives Coop and Stacey each a hug as Fray and Leland share a very long kiss goodbye.

"Wow," Stacey says, elbowing Coop. "Why don't you ever kiss me that way?"

"I do!" Coop says and he pulls Stacey closer.

"Time for me to get out of here," Jake says. He feels a lump rising in his throat as he recalls all the Labor Days that he kissed Mallory goodbye. No offense, but they put Fray and Leland to shame.

Jake has never flown private before. It isn't something he ever aspired to, and even when Ursula was an arm's length from the presidency, he never pictured himself aboard Air Force One.

Good thing.

Fray's plane is a Gulfstream 550, which Jake understands is a big deal. The plane has a pilot, a copilot, and a bubbly flight attendant named Heather. After Fray and Jake take seats in the living area — they're facing each other in buff leather chairs with a high-gloss table between them — Heather asks what they would like to drink.

Jake is about to ask Heather for a Bloody Mary — why not celebrate this crazy experience? — when she says, "We have Classic Black, the Platinum, and —" She pauses dramatically. "This jet is one of the few places in the world where you can get a bottomless cup of Frayed Edge Select Reserve."

Coffee. She's talking about coffee — of course.

"We'll have two cups of the reserve, thanks, Heather," Fray says. He looks at Jake. "Do you take anything in it?"

"Cream, two sugars." As soon as the words are out, he wonders if Fray will disapprove. Maybe drinking the reserve with cream and sugar is like dropping an ice cube into a glass of Château Lafite.

Takeoff is smooth. Fray gazes out the window as Nantucket slips from view.

"Now, *that* was a good weekend," Fray says. "I had no idea that was how things would turn out."

Heather appears with two mugs, the signature silver pot, and, for Jake, a pitcher of cream and a tiny bowl of organic sugar cubes. She winks at Fray. "I saw you on Page Six, Mr. Dooley."

"That was me with Leland!" he says. "I can't wait to introduce you to her."

"I've subscribed to *Leland's Letter* for over ten years," Heather says. "I didn't know the two of you were friends."

"It's a long story," Fray says. "Literally."

Jake sips his coffee. It's by far the best coffee he's ever tasted.

Fray says, "Heather, would you pack up a couple pounds of the reserve for Jake to take home?"

"Yes, sir, Mr. Dooley."

Once Heather leaves them, Jake says, "So, will you and Leland continue to see each other? Aren't you worried about the distance?"

"I'm going to New York next weekend," Fray says. "I renovated a brownstone on East Third Street and have yet to spend the night there. That's about to change."

A brownstone in the East Village that he's never even slept in? It's only sinking in now just how wealthy Fray is. This is *his* jet; those pilots are *his* pilots; Heather is *his* flight attendant. Whenever Jake has thought about Frazier Dooley in the past thirty years, his mind always conjured the angry young man who disappeared down the beach with a bottle of Jim Beam. Now he's a billionaire who sells the world's finest coffee in the coolest cafés in the country. Jake has heard that the flagship Frayed Edge café in Burlington, Vermont, has live music twenty-four hours a day. Billie Eilish has played there, and Luke Combs, Ingrid Michaelson.

"I could use your help with something," Jake says.

"Anything," Fray says.

"I'm going to need a date for Coop's wedding."

"Sorry, man, I already have a date," Fray says, and they both laugh.

Jake pulls out his phone. "Have you ever used a dating app?" He figures this is a stupid question. Fray is a billionaire, so, before Leland, there must have been a line of eligible women after him.

"No, man, but I'm friends with the woman who created Firepink, and that's the app you want. It's for users over forty and it's marketed for professionals."

"Firepink?" Jake says. "What about Bumble or Match dot-com? Is Match still a thing?" He laughs. "Honestly, I'm used to meeting women the old-fashioned way. I met Ursula in sixth grade."

"I hear you," Fray says. "I met Leland when we were kids and I met Anna at the café. Her band played there one night and I fell in love." He's quiet and Jake wonders why it's no longer popular to meet someone in real life. "But trust me, you want Firepink. Here, I'll download it for you." Fray takes Jake's phone and taps and swipes, then hands the phone back to Jake and says, "Fill out the answers to these questions and click the Fire Up! button. This app goes through tens of thousands of profiles in lightning speed and picks the top three women. I've heard you should always choose number one. They have the highest success rate in the business with the first match. Their algorithm is magic."

Jake chuckles. "All I need is a date for a wedding."

Still, he fills out the answers for his profile and then, once he's double-checked his responses, he presses the Fire Up! button. The phone flips through faces like a Vegas dealer through a deck of cards — Jake thinks he sees a bunch of attractive women but it's moving too fast and he can't make it stop — until finally a face appears on the screen and remains there.

Jake blinks. It's a striking dark-haired woman in what he recognizes as an Alexander McQueen suit.

Ursula de Gournsey. Age: 56. Nickname: Sully. Height: 5 foot 6. Hair: dark brown. Eyes: brown. Occupation: attorney, M&A. Address: New York City. Political party: Independent. Birthplace: South Bend, Indiana. Favorite pastime: work.

Jake laughs. "We're supposed to go with the first choice, huh?"

"Yeah," Fray says. "Did you already match with someone? Let me see."

"Not yet," Jake says. "I'm going to ask her out and I don't want you to jinx it."

"Yeah, bro, go for it," Fray says. "You're a boss."

Jake doesn't reach out to his ex-wife via Firepink. He texts her instead.

Heading back to the Bend, he says. Guess what? Coop is getting married again. His sixth wedding! Next June in DC.

Jake sees the three floating dots, indicating that his number-one match — maybe Firepink does know best after all — is writing back.

Need a date? she asks.

The Workshop
(Read with *Golden Girl*)

This extra chapter has never been published!

People often ask what I do when my editor suggests changes or revisions that I don't agree with. The answer: I make them anyway. One edict I have sworn by for the twenty-two years I've been publishing is that my editor is always right.

In the original draft of my novel *Golden Girl*, my main character, Vivian Howe, attends the University of Iowa's Writers' Workshop, just like I did. I wrote what I thought was a vivid (and very funny) chapter where finally, *finally*, I got to describe my experiences at Iowa—the good, the bad, and the ugly. I thought the chapter was brilliant. My editor, Judy Clain, found it distracting and maybe a bit "inside baseball." She suggested I cut the chapter, and, obediently, I did. (I saved it and later sent it to one of my dear Iowa chums, the writer Jonathan Blum, and he enjoyed it, which was all the validation I needed.)

I was able to rewrite the chapter into a prequel—this story takes place long before the action in *Golden Girl*. I changed the Iowa Writers' Workshop to a shorter workshop I had attended—Bread Loaf at Middlebury College in the summer of 1995—and much of the brutal, juicy, fun workshop details remain here.

It's the summer of 1992. Vivian Howe and J. P. Quinboro are to be married in the fall—but already, Vivi has done something behind JP's back.

Their wedding is scheduled for Saturday, October 17. The ceremony will be held at St. Mary's, with a reception following at the Field and Oar Club. Because Vivi's mother, Nancy Howe, died of a massive coronary only two weeks after JP proposed, Vivi finds herself working with JP's mother, Lucinda, on the wedding. *Working with* is a generous way to phrase it. What's actually happening is that Lucinda is making decisions and Vivi is doing a lot of nodding.

That's fine; Vivi is emotionally exhausted from dealing with the business of her mother's death. She organized her mother's funeral and burial at St. John Bosco back in Parma, Ohio, sold her childhood home, and donated all the contents to the church. (There wasn't a single item in the house that Vivi wanted to keep.) After all the debts were paid, Vivi was left with…three thousand dollars. (Nancy Howe had taken out a second mortgage and accrued a wild amount of credit card debt.)

Three thousand dollars. It's Vivi's inheritance, and though it's meager, she puts it to good use. She spends twelve hundred dollars on her wedding dress, veil, and shoes (Vivi and her best friend, Savannah, go to Priscilla of Boston).

Then Vivi takes seven hundred and fifty dollars and enrolls in a ten-day session at Bread Loaf, the legendary writers' retreat at Middlebury College in Vermont. Vivi submitted a writing sample and has been accepted into a workshop led by her literary heroine Caroline Corrigan.

What is outlandish, and even scandalous, about this is Vivi hasn't told JP, her own fiancé, that she's going to Bread Loaf—because she fears he might discourage her.

But she can't wait any longer.

"What would you say if I told you I wanted to go to the Bread Loaf Writers' Conference for ten days next month?" Vivi says. She has to speak loudly and clearly in order to be heard above the wind. She and JP have taken Lucinda's sloop, *Arabesque,* out for a day sail.

"I'd say I can't live without you for ten days," JP says.

Vivi stretches out on the long bench of the cockpit, crosses her tanned legs, and folds her arms behind her head in an attempt to look like someone asking a hypothetical question. The day is sublime, sunny and warm, with enough wind that they skate across the surface of the water. It's just the two of them. Vivi has packed a picnic, and they have nowhere they have to be and no one they have to see. Today is as close to heaven as Vivi has ever been, she decides. Does she really want to leave Nantucket for ten days in August?

Yes.

"I feel like everyone who looks at me these days sees me only as your fiancée." Vivi sits up. "I want to forge my own identity."

JP lets out a little sail. There's a deep rumble of canvas and the plash of the waves against the hull of the boat. He's intentionally not answering; he's focusing on his man-work. This is what he does.

"Caroline Corrigan is teaching one of the workshops," Vivi says. "With a little luck, I could study with her. You know she's my favorite."

"What would you do about your job? They're never going to let you leave for ten days in August, Viv. It's a nice idea, and I know how much you love Caroline Corrigan, but it's just not practical."

"You're right, I'd have to see what they say at work." Vivi is the assistant manager at Fair Isle Dry Cleaning. The owner, Mr. Santamaria, is a man of letters. He loves Melville, Vonnegut, John Irving. He was the one who handed Vivi the brochure for Bread Loaf in the first place! He encouraged her to apply! "If I can persuade them to give me the time off, then I think I'll probably go."

"Vivi…" JP says.

Vivi jumps to her feet, throws her arms around JP's midsection and rests her cheek against his sun-warmed back as he stands at the wheel. "Thank you, Jackie," she says. "Here's what will happen: I'll go to Bread Loaf and find my voice, then someday I'll write a bunch of books and they'll become bestsellers and I'll be able to keep you in the lifestyle to which you're accustomed. And I'll keep on paying you even after you leave me for a younger woman because you're so threatened by my success."

JP laughs. "You have a good imagination, anyway," he says.

There are different ways to enjoy summer, Vivi thinks, as the share van from the Burlington airport pulls onto the Middlebury campus. The college is tucked in among the Green Mountains, and the section of campus claimed by Bread Loaf is rustic and bucolic. There are rolling green lawns backed by woods, dotted here and there by cabins with screen doors and Adirondack chairs thoughtfully placed for a productive afternoon of writing in the golden sunshine.

Vivi is about to spend ten days living in a Robert Frost poem!

She has been assigned a room in one of the "summer dormitories," buildings that feel more like camp than college. There are double rooms with a communal bath at the end of the hall. The air smells like mildew and moss and damp. Vivi doesn't mind it one bit.

Vivi has been quietly taking note of her fellow attendees, trying to determine who's a poet, who's a memoirist, and who's a fiction writer like herself. In her share van was a contingent from New York City. The men wore fedoras or porkpie hats, the women granny glasses and fringed shawls, as though they all *wanted* to look eighty years old. They'd chatted among themselves without acknowledging Vivi, and Vivi shoved away the adolescent feeling of being excluded from the cool group by writing a short story in her mind called "The Share Van." She was relieved that their conversation focused mostly on Sharon Olds and Jorie Graham because this telegraphed that they were poets, a different species from Vivi.

Vivi had seen a woman about her age crossing the emerald-green lawn wearing white face makeup and a long black coat whose tails flew out behind her the way that Charles Dickens's might have. And then Vivi noticed a woman in dramatically ripped jeans and a Bon Jovi concert T-shirt, one with the band members' faces silkscreened on the front and the tour dates listed on the back. These women looked—if not exactly *promising,* then at least intriguing. Vivi has a notion that the second most important aspect of Bread Loaf (the first being dedicated time to write in a creative atmosphere) is who she meets. She dreams of being part of a group of friends who are all so talented, they become a literary brat pack. But even one or two friends will suit her, preferably people who seem like they have bright futures, so that someday Vivi will have an esteemed author chum to blurb her novels and meet her for cocktails at the Miami Book Fair: *I've known Gillian since 1992. We were at Bread Loaf together!*

Vivi is hopeful about her roommate, a woman listed on her housing form as Darla Kay Bolt.

When Vivi walks into room 12 of Beacon House, she finds the woman she presumes is Darla Kay Bolt taping pictures to the cinder-block wall above her bed. The pictures are of a baby, and when Vivi says, "Hey, Darla Kay, how are you, I'm Vivian Howe, you can call me Vivi," Darla Kay turns around and Vivi can see Darla has just been crying.

"Oh, is that your baby?" Vivi asks, like a moron.

"Yes," Darla Kay says. "His name is Pinto."

"Like the bean?"

"Yes, and like the horse." Darla Kay sits heavily on the thin mattress, made up with what Vivi sees are threadbare white sheets and a pilled, dun-colored blanket. A quick glance to the other side of the room confirms that, unfortunately, Vivi's bed has identical linens. "I left Tallahassee at five this morning, so it's been only ten hours without him but I don't think I'm going to make it."

Vivi isn't sure what this means. Will Darla Kay... expire? Or will she toss the seven hundred and fifty dollars she paid in the trash and go home?

Vivi says, "I don't have a baby but I do have a cute fiancé who I miss a ton." This is an exaggeration; Vivi hasn't started to miss JP yet. "So I definitely know how you feel. I think this will be just like summer camp. The homesickness will go away."

Vivi sets her yellow Pierre Deux duffel on her bed (the bag was a present from Lucinda last Christmas). "Are you a fiction writer or a poet or a memoirist?" Vivi asks. Darla Kay has a wan, nearly jaundiced complexion. She looks like she's been living in a meerkat burrow. Her hair is dyed a flat yellow and she has a pointy nose. She's wearing a brown tank top and black genie pants that billow out before tapering above her Birkenstocks.

If Vivi had to guess... no, she's at a loss; she can't guess. Darla Kay doesn't look like a writer. She looks like a sad mother and housewife from Tallahassee.

"Fiction," Darla Kay says. "I'm studying with Grady Coyle."

Vivi's first reaction is relief that Darla Kay won't be in the workshop with Vivi. Her second reaction is pity. Grady Coyle is the only genre writer on the faculty at Bread Loaf this year. He writes horror, gore. Darla Kay must have signed up late, and Grady Coyle was the only instructor with room left in his class.

"Was that your...first choice?" Vivi asks.

"Oh, yes," Darla Kay says. "I have this idea for a series of books set in purgatory. It's called the Gruesome Goth series."

Vivi's eyes widen. *This* is certainly unexpected! Vivi wonders if Darla Kay has met the vampire girl in the long black coat and death-mask face paint. Vivi starts to unpack her things. She supposes they'll find each other soon enough.

"So, how is it?" JP asks.

It's the morning of the third day and Vivi has just gotten back from her run. She is the sole runner here at Bread Loaf, and she appears to be the only early riser as well. The past two mornings, she has tiptoed out of her room at five thirty, tied her shoes, and hit the winding mountain roads before the sun burned off the mist.

"Vermont is beautiful," Vivi says.

"I've been to Vermont," JP says. "I'm curious about the program. What's it like?"

"It's..."

"Come on, Vivi, you're the writer. Describe it."

"It's intense," Vivi says. "I thought it would be nurturing, but there's a pervasive sense of competition. There's a pecking order. For example, we're served in the dining hall by waitstaff who were selected to attend the conference for free. They're the elite talent." Vivi drops her voice because she's on one of the pay phones outside the dining hall and people have finally started to show up (in their pajamas), searching for coffee. "One of the waiters, this guy named Mike, goes to *Iowa*."

JP gasps melodramatically. "Not *Iowa!*"

"The best pieces from the conference are being published in the *Bread Loaf Review*," Vivi says. "So everyone is acting quite cutthroat about being chosen."

"Have you gotten any writing done?" JP asks.

Vivi has claimed one of the Adirondack chairs as her own (it's not as comfortable as it appears), but she's been doing more editing than actual writing. The first story she's submitting for the workshop is an incarnation of a short story she started writing back in high school, "Coney Island Baby." Her original story was about a woman who thinks her husband is having an affair but discovers he's attending rehearsals for a barbershop quartet. In this new draft, the protagonist is a teenage girl, Deneen, whose father commits suicide. Their regular breakfast waitress, Cindy, comes to the funeral and tells Deneen that she *had* been having an affair with the father (Vivi deleted all the barbershop-quartet references). Then Deneen and Cindy forge a friendship that is comforting to them both.

The new title is "Meeting Cindy."

Vivi worries about the ending. Should Deneen and Cindy become friends, or should the relationship be fraught in some way? Vivi tries to imagine how she would feel if she learned that her father and the real

Cindy-from-Perkins were having an affair and Cindy was every bit as devastated by his suicide as Vivi.

Yes, they would be friends. Friends forever.

"I go to my workshop for two hours every morning," Vivi says, "then there are seminars and lectures in the afternoons, and they offer activities like hiking and fly-fishing, but I don't do any of that."

"Fly-fishing, though," JP says. "I should have come!"

"There are readings at night. We all pack into a small theater and the instructors read and some of the wait-staff do as well." Vivi pauses. "Everyone is so good, JP."

"How is Caroline Corrigan?" JP asks. "I bet you're her favorite student."

Vivi laughs because this is so far from the truth. The most unsettling thing about Bread Loaf has been the two workshops with Caroline. She's a…bitch. There's just no other way to phrase it. This is profoundly upsetting because Vivi *adores* her work. *Cleaning House* is Vivi's all-time favorite book, and *By Myself in a Tree* is in her top five.

But how does the old saying go? *Never meet your heroes, lest they be found to have feet of clay.*

Or just otherwise suck, Vivi thinks.

Caroline Corrigan looks exactly like the picture on her book jacket. She has long silver-blond hair that she wears loose around her face like an aging folk-rock star. Despite the heat of the summer mornings, she wears jeans and white blouses that are as crisp as paper. She unbuttons the blouses to reveal the barest hint of cleavage. (Vivi can't decide if this is alluring or slutty.) Caroline Corrigan has a raspy edge to her voice. Out of class, she is *always* smoking. What makes her such a bitch is the way she delivers her scathing criticisms with a huge smile. She's like some kind of evil queen, the Marie Antoinette of writing workshops. The one time she offered praise, she appeared abjectly miserable.

"She doesn't know me from Adam," Vivi says. Caroline's manner is so severe and her comments so unflinchingly cruel (yet intelligent and spot-on) that Vivi hasn't once summoned the courage to raise her hand to offer her own thoughts. "I count that as a good thing."

It's Darla Kay's idea to read each other's stories the night before they will be respectively workshopped. Vivi can't bring herself to say no — and besides, she has little else in the way of friends. Both the vampire girl — whose name is Katelyn — and the Bon Jovi woman, Beth, are in Vivi's workshop, but Katelyn is a sex-obsessed whiner and Beth is a Caroline Corrigan kiss-ass who says things like, *I just didn't feel any sense of narrative tension. What's at stake? Why should I care about these people?*

Reluctantly, Vivi hands Darla Kay "Meeting Cindy" and accepts a copy of Darla Kay's story, "The Stairwell," in return.

"The Stairwell," by D. K. Bolt (Darla Kay says that in horror writing, androgyny is best), is, essentially, unreadable. The language is overwrought, cartoonishly

Victorian. Two characters named Elgin and Piccolo are vying for control of the staircase that leads to the underworld, which Darla Kay has described in vivid, horrific detail. Vivi has to press her eyes closed against the language; if she continues, she'll be sure to have nightmares about skinned...no, stop. She can't believe that sad, mousy Darla Kay writes this stuff (although Darla Kay has seemed less sad recently, Vivi notes. She has two male buddies from her workshop and she's been hanging out in their room until well past midnight). Vivi skims the story to the end, then says, "Wow, Darla Kay."

Darla Kay is crying again—forget what Vivi said about her seeming less sad—and she clutches Vivi's story to her chest. "This is just...beautiful. What a moving story about a girl and her father. The details are so...well curated. You didn't fall back on cliché even once. And the ending is poignant. It's pitch-perfect, Vivi." She blinks. "I can't believe I'm your roommate. You're going to be famous."

"And you..." Vivi says, trying to muster up matching enthusiasm for "The Stairwell," even though it's so creepy and awful that Vivi can't wait to hand it back. (Is that maybe the point? Would Darla Kay take this as a compliment?) "This is remarkable."

"Maybe we'll both be famous someday," Darla Kay says.

"Wouldn't that be crazy?" Vivi says.

*   *   *

The feedback from Darla Kay gives Vivi the moxie she so badly needs. (It does occur to Vivi that maybe Darla Kay was flattering her, maybe she found "Meeting Cindy" as offensive to her sensibilities as Vivi found "The Stairwell" to hers and was pretending to like it only to preserve Vivi's feelings. But Darla Kay had been crying real tears, so Vivi dismisses these doubts.)

To workshop, Vivi wears a red sundress. Red is the color of confidence.

By now, Vivi has allies in the class—John, Jay, and Ray. The three of them have a little bromance going and Vivi has somehow been included as "one of the guys." John hails from the Chicago area, where he's a pharmaceutical rep; Jay is a high-school principal from Lafayette, Louisiana; and Ray is divorced from his college sweetheart and lives somewhere in New Jersey, where he's some kind of foreman. (Vivi has to keep Ray at a distance because he's single and stares at Vivi all through workshop.)

First up in the day's workshop is John's story, which is about a baseball game at a juvenile detention center. It's a bit predictable—a Christian youth group of (white) kids come to play baseball with the (predominantly Black) kids in juvie and there's a lot of tediously technical baseball-driven plot, and at the end of the game, it's a tie until one of the most problematic juvie kids hits a home run and becomes the hero and is celebrated for the first time in his life.

The story gets generally praised, and Vivi, frankly, can't believe it. She's shocked that Bon Jovi Beth hasn't mentioned the blatant racial stereotypes. Neither has Jay, who is Black himself. But Vivi likes John, so she doesn't mention them either. She doesn't want to be the only naysayer, especially not when her story is up next.

Will Caroline Corrigan drop the guillotine blade on the story, as she always does? Apparently not. She offers an indifferent shrug and says, "Okay, good discussion. Let's move on. 'Meeting Cindy' by Vivian Howe. Who would like to start?"

John starts by saying he "really admired the palpable sense of grief" in the story, but then vampire girl Katelyn pipes up to say she found the characterization of the breakfast waitress "classist."

"The author is sneering at her because she's in the service industry."

"Agree," Caroline says. She's beaming. "It does real damage to the story. The elitist, pitying tone when describing Cindy has to go. But then again, this story is so flawed, it's hard to say what the biggest problem is."

Other people chime in, and not one positive word is uttered. The class is a pack of jackals feasting on the pinned prey that is Vivi's story. Ray, who Vivi was so sure was in love with her, delivers the death blow.

"The author treats her characters with such contempt, they might as well be cockroaches. The girl's father dies and she goes right up to the point with her boyfriend and loses her *virginity?*"

"That part felt authentic to me, actually," Katelyn says. "Sex and death are *always* connected."

"Agree," Caroline says. "If there's *anything* to be salvaged from this story, it's the protagonist's relationship with the boyfriend. It felt a bit like it was cribbed from a Springsteen song, teenagers out driving around at night and all that." The class titters. "But there are glimmers of some actual human emotion. The ensuing relationship between the protagonist and the breakfast waitress is…*blech,* treacly regurgitation of a dozen mindless sitcoms." Caroline beams at the class as though she has just learned she's won the Pulitzer. "Beth and Ray are up tomorrow, yes? Until then, ta."

The rest of the class slide their annotated copies of Vivi's stories across the table like they're dealing her a losing hand, and she stacks them in a nice, neat deck as though she plans to read through them, take suggestions, and glean ideas for a future revision — instead of throwing them all in the dumpster outside the dining hall.

She's numb. She can see her arms, see that they end in hands, but she can't feel them. Red is the color of the bloodbath she just endured.

John, Jay, and Ray are waiting outside the classroom for her.

"Are you coming with us to the How to Get an Agent seminar?" Jay asks. Jay offered no opinion during the workshop of her story. He had been parented well.

"No."

"Oh, come on," Ray says, thumping her shoulder. "You survived your first workshop. And you'll need an agent if you want to be published someday. Just come with us."

"I'll take a pass," she says. "I'm going to call my fiancé."

And pack my bags, she thinks.

JP picks up on the first ring. "How'd it go?" he asks. "Did she love it? Are you going to be in the literary magazine?"

Vivi bursts into tears. The pain she's feeling is so... foreign. She's used to doing well in school, being celebrated for her intelligence. She won the creative writing award at Duke! She feels like she's been kicked in the gut, the teeth. The class *hated* it, and because it was a story *so close to her heart*—about her *father!*—it feels like they hate *her.*

Vivi is crying so hard she can't breathe. She can hear JP on the other end of the line trying to soothe her, but surely he can sense she's beyond being consoled by him telling her he loves her, that she's his shining star. She needs more than that right now. Or maybe she doesn't. Maybe she should just give up and go home.

"Talk to me about something else for a minute," she says. "Tell me what's happening there."

"Here?" JP says. He's been working all summer for a real estate agency as a glorified gofer, but he likes it, and, as everyone knows, real estate is where the money is. "Well, Mattie met me for a swim after work yesterday and then we went down to the Rope Walk for dinner, sat on the deck, had steamers and beers, and then Mattie went to the Muse to see the Radiators, but I didn't have a ticket, so I went home."

"What are you doing over the weekend?" Vivi asks, snuffling.

"I'll probably sail on Saturday, maybe drive out to Madequecham for a beach party on Sunday. My mother is having some people for cocktails tonight, so I'll swing by. And I have to get fitted for my tuxedo at Murray's." He pauses. "I'm getting married to this really hot chick in October."

Vivi can't even smile. "I wish I were there."

"Me too, Vivi," JP says. "I know that all sounds like fun, but the truth is, I miss you like crazy."

Vivi hangs up the phone. Through the door to the dining hall, she sees the waitstaff setting up for lunch and Vivi tries not to hate them. *They* are the ones who will be published in the literary magazine, and, ten years from now, theirs will be the novels on the front pages of the *New York Times Book Review*. She trudges back to her room, where she finds Darla Kay and two of her workshop cronies — Vivi thinks their names are Matt and Max; they look like slightly older versions of the boys back at Parma High who were obsessed with Dungeons and Dragons — popping open a bottle of sparkling wine. (Where did *that* come from?)

"Hey," Vivi says. She would like to liquefy and seep through the floorboards. "I take it your workshop went well?"

All Darla Kay can do is squeal.

"It was complete domination," Matt/Max says. "Grady *loved* DK's story."

"He's hooking me up with his *publisher!*" Darla Kay says.

Don't sound bitter or surprised or jealous, Vivi thinks, though she is experiencing all three emotions in abundance. "Yahoo!" Vivi says. "Amazing! And so well deserved, Darla Kay!" Behind Darla Kay, one of Pinto's baby pictures is crooked, clinging to the wall by only one corner. Vivi can't believe Darla Kay hasn't noticed this.

Darla Kay says, "I wish we'd brought an extra cup so you could have some bubbly."

Vivi waves away the suggestion. "You enjoy. This is your celebration."

Darla Kay gasps. "I'm so thoughtless. How did *your* workshop go?"

"Mine?" Vivi says. She pauses long enough that Darla Kay and Matt/Max turn back to the task at hand—toasting DK's success!—and Vivi doesn't have to answer.

My fiancé's mother is sick is the excuse Vivi comes up with. If the timing works out, she might be able to slip away without anyone noticing. She will call a private taxi to take her back to the airport. Who will even notice she's gone? Well, Darla Kay and John, Jay, and Ray. Darla Kay will, most likely, alert the office—but there are deserters all the time, people who can't handle the pressure or the criticism.

Vivi will be one more person who quit.

How will she ever become a writer if she quits now? She won't, she surmises. If she leaves Bread Loaf, she can just forget the idea of ever finishing a book, because that requires discipline, grit. Doesn't Vivi have both of these things? Yes! So she had a bad workshop—who cares? She will stay and fight. She won't go home to Nantucket.

She will bring Nantucket here.

For the next four days, Vivi writes like a fiend. Every morning after her run, she grabs a banana from the dining hall and claims her Adirondack chair. She leaves only to go to workshop. In workshop, she starts sharing her honest opinion. Sometimes Caroline Corrigan agrees with Vivi, sometimes she doesn't, but at least she learns Vivi's name.

Vivi is so focused on her work that it takes her a little while to realize that her industriousness is garnering attention. One of the women in the fringed shawls from New York City who were in the share van with Vivi introduces herself. Her name is Annabelle and she and her roommate, Loredana (peasant blouse, wide-brimmed felt hat), were wondering if Vivi wanted to come over that evening after the readings for some wine.

Vivi smiles gratefully at Annabelle. "No, thank you," she says.

Vivi's second story for workshop is entitled "The Powder Room." It's about a young woman who thinks she's spending the summer at her best friend's home on Nantucket until she realizes her friend's parents have other ideas.

Vivi is savvy enough this time to go into workshop expecting the worst. The class is going to trash her story, tear it to messy shreds, and, being prepared for this, Vivi feels lighter, nearly nonchalant. It's just her heart and soul on the page, no big deal. By criticizing her writing, the class is, essentially, disapproving of her very being, but that's the risk that every writer in the history of the world has taken. Vivi isn't special.

Jay starts off by running his hands lovingly over the first page and saying, "I *felt* this story."

"Me too," Bon Jovi Beth says. "The sublimated loneliness was palpable when the protagonist was in the powder room surrounded by pictures of her best friend's family."

"Agree," Caroline Corrigan says. "Powerful imagery, the use of that powder room. Our protagonist is masterfully positioned as the other — an outsider without a family history of her own to claim. And yet it's clear the protagonist has a soul, whereas the family — it's a brilliant portrayal of her best friend's mother, by the way — might have been more troubled than they appear."

"Those parents seem like the kind who never have sex," Katelyn says.

"I loved the dog," John says. "And how the dog followed the protagonist everywhere. It's a subtle way to let the reader know whom to root for."

"Disagree," Caroline Corrigan says, and her expression is gleeful. Finally, a bone of contention! "Children and animals in fiction smack of an easy device. The dog was the only element of this story I objected to. I say euthanize the dog."

The class is quiet. This is not a popular opinion.

"I have questions about her decision to stay at the end," Ray says. "How is she going to make it work?"

"You're supposed to have questions," Jay says. "I like that not everything is spelled out for us."

"Agree," Caroline Corrigan says. She frowns. "I think this might be the strongest story we've seen. I'm recommending it for the *Bread Loaf Review*."

*　　*　　*

When JP pulls up in front of Nantucket Memorial Airport in his Blazer, Vivi runs to him, her yellow duffel thumping against her side.

"I'm so happy to be home!" she says.

Vivi has kept another secret from JP, but once they're lying on Steps Beach with sandwiches from Something Natural and a bottle of sparkling wine to celebrate Vivi's return, she shares the news of her triumph. Not only was Vivi's story "The Powder Room" chosen to be in the *Bread Loaf Review,* but Vivi was asked to read it aloud on the final evening of the conference, and she received a standing ovation.

JP doesn't react quite the way she hoped he would. He looks...concerned.

"So, wait," he says. "You wrote a short story about Savannah's powder room?"

"I did what all writers do—I took an experience that had emotional resonance and transformed it so that it made narrative sense."

"I hope you won't ever write about me," JP says. He clears his throat. "About us."

"Don't be silly, Jackie," Vivi says. "I wouldn't dream of it."

Summer of '79

(Read with *Summer of '69*)

As some of you know, I was very close friends with the novelist Dorothea Benton Frank, who passed away suddenly in the summer of 2019. (I dedicated my 2020 novel, *28 Summers,* to Dottie.) Dottie's novel for 2020 was supposed to be called *Reunion Beach,* and in Dottie's honor, her publisher asked her writer pals to contribute a short piece with the theme "reunion beach." I desperately wanted to do it, but because I work on such a tight schedule (at that time, I was writing two novels a year), I decided that, rather than starting from scratch, I would piggyback off a novel I had already written. I decided to reunite my characters from *Summer of '69* ten years later. I loved placing the Foley-Levin-Whalen clan against the backdrop of the late '70s. And once again, I used song titles to evoke the mood.

1. Hot Child in the City

Jessie Levin (rhymes with *heaven*) is drinking an ice-cold can of Tab on the northwest corner of Washington Square Park when her sister, Kirby, pulls up in her butterscotch-colored Ford LTD with the sun roof open; strains of Lou Reed float out like a haze.

Hey, babe, take a walk on the wild side

Reed must have been talking about Washington Square Park in this song, Jessie thinks. She has done a fair amount of studying in the park while she's in law school and she's seen it all: punk rockers with purple hair and pierced lips walking their dachshunds, drag queens eating knishes, a couple painted gold who set a boom box on the lip of the fountain and discoed to Chopin's Polonaise in A-flat Major.

"Get in!" Kirby shouts. "Just throw your suitcase in the back seat."

Jessie does as she's told — Kirby's back seat is as big as Grand Central Terminal — but even so, the cars lining up behind the LTD start honking and someone yells, "Move your tush, sweetheart!"

Kirby pulls away from the curb before Jessie even has her door closed. Jessie sets her macramé pocketbook on the front seat next to a tray of hot dogs from Gray's Papaya. She kicks off her Dr. Scholl's and puts her feet on the dash.

"I know I shouldn't feel happy," she says. "But I do. I took my last exam this morning, I have a full week off before I start my internship, and we're going to Nantucket."

"I'm happy too," Kirby says. "Or I would be if I weren't so hungover." She pulls a cigarette out of a pack of Virginia Slims with her lips and leans over to Jessie, who rummages through her pocketbook for a light. She finds a matchbook from McSorley's. Jessie's ex-boyfriend, Theo, basically lives there.

Jessie lights Kirby's cigarette and fights the urge to throw the matches out the open window—the city is so dirty, what difference would it make?—because she has taken great pains to rid her tiny studio apartment and her carrel at Bobst Library of everything Theo-related.

"I need to get out of this city," Jessie says at the same time that Kirby says, "I need to get out of this city."

"Jinx," Kirby says. "You owe me a Coke." She blows smoke out the window without taking the cigarette from her mouth.

"Why do *you* need to get out of the city?" Jessie asks. Kirby's life in New York is glossy and fabulous. She's the sex and relationships editor at *Cosmopolitan*. She lives rent-free in a loft down on Broome Street, babysitting the paintings and sculptures of the artist Willie Eight while Willie travels the world. He's in New York only one week per month, and it's during those weeks that Kirby's life gets even more enviable. Kirby and Willie and Willie's boyfriend, Tornado Jack, have long, lavish dinners at Mr Chow and the Quilted Giraffe — and then go to Studio 54. Through Willie, Kirby has met Baryshnikov, Farrah Fawcett Majors, Richard Pryor! It seems outlandish that Kirby, Jessie's own sister, has rubbed elbows with such celebrities, though, as Kirby says with her usual world-weariness, "They're just people, Jess."

In Kirby's own pocketbook — a tan suede fringed hobo — she keeps a Polaroid picture in an envelope. The picture is of Kirby linking arms with Willie and Tornado Jack, and sitting in front of them, with his signature platinum mop and clear horn-rimmed glasses, is...yeah.

Andy Warhol. Kirby has met Andy Warhol.

Kirby sighs. "I've been burning the joint at both ends."

Well, yes, so has Jessie. But whereas Jessie goes to Torts and Contracts during the day and studies at night, Kirby strolls into the Hearst offices at the crack of ten fifteen with her sunglasses still on and is congratulated for it. Kirby reports directly to Helen Gurley Brown, who has assigned Kirby the task of writing about the after-hours lives of young urban women—which means spending night after night out on the town.

Jessie isn't naive. Kirby said "joint," but Jessie knows she's drinking every night—tequila sunrises that become more tequila and less sunrise as the hour grows later—and she also snorts cocaine. Probably a lot of cocaine. Kirby may even be a cocaine addict; the edges of her nose are pink like a rabbit's and she keeps sniffing. Jessie wonders if she should express her concern, maybe tell Kirby the story of poor Cesar Coehlo, her fellow second-year law student who also liked to frequent Limelight and Studio 54. A few weeks earlier, Cesar overdosed and died. The next day, in Jessie's property law class, a girl said she'd heard the cocaine made Cesar's heart "pop like a balloon."

The song changes to Player, "Baby Come Back."
Any kind of fool could see
There won't be any cocaine on Nantucket, Jessie thinks, though there will be drinking, starting first thing in the morning with mimosas. Jessie has vivid memories of her grandmother, Exalta, sucking down two or three mimosas on the patio of the Field and Oar Club while Jessie took her tennis lessons.

Despite the ungodly heat of this sweltering June day, Jessie gets a chill.

Exalta is dead.

She died in her sleep two days earlier in the house on Fair Street while Mr. Crimmins, their former caretaker, slept beside her. Jessie and Kirby are heading up to Nantucket for the funeral tomorrow, which will be followed by a reception at the Field and Oar Club, which will be followed by a bonfire on Ram Pasture beach. The bonfire is Kirby's brainchild. She's calling the gathering Midnight at the Oasis, and it's for family and close friends only, although Kirby pointedly has not invited their parents, saying, "They won't want to come anyway."

Jessie and Kirby sit in traffic on the Cross Bronx for what feels like days—Jessie drifts off for a second and she thinks maybe Kirby does as well—but then I-95 clears. Kirby puts the pedal to the metal and the LTD goes sailing right up alongside a tractor-trailer. Jessie yanks her elbow down once, twice, three times, and the trucker honks his horn, which gives Jessie a silly thrill. She feels like a character from *Smokey and the Bandit*.

"Flash him!" Kirby says.

Jessie considers it for a second, then remembers that her older sister is a terrible influence.

They have more fun on the drive up to Hyannis than they should under the circumstances. They devour the hot dogs—Kirby doctored them with just the right amount of mustard, relish, onions, and sauerkraut—and the radio gods are with them because they hear one great song after another.

"Lonesome Loser." *Beaten by the Queen of Hearts every time*

"One Way or Another." *I'm gonna get ya, get ya, get ya, get ya*

"Knock on Wood." *It's like thunder, lightning / The way I love you is frightening*

After they finish singing at the top of their lungs with Bonnie Tyler's "It's a Heartache" — *Nothing but a heartache* — Kirby turns down the radio and says, "So, what happened with you and Theo?"

Jessie doesn't want to talk about Theo but she needs to come up with some kind of answer for her family.

Jessie met Theo her first week at NYU. She'd done her undergraduate work at Mount Holyoke, and so New York City — and men — were a dramatic change. Theo Feigelbaum had thick dark hair, green eyes, and remarkably long dark lashes. He sat next to Jessie in their lawyering seminar and asked to borrow a pencil and a piece of loose-leaf, which Jessie gave him while wondering what kind of bozo showed up to the first day of class unprepared. But when he raised his hand and offered an example of jurisprudence, Jessie fell in love.

They dated the entire first year, through the summer, and into the autumn of their second year, when they basically cohabited. But the second year of law school was more difficult than the first, just like the second year of a relationship. The things that had been fun, even blissful—studying together in the park, getting pizza at St. Mark's Place, splurging on a foreign film at the Angelika, sneaking into the Metropolitan Museum of Art (it was easy enough to find discarded metal buttons on the steps and attach them to their collars)—lost their luster. And there was no time, anyway. Besides which, Theo grew increasingly jealous of how well Jessie was doing in class and how easily she had landed a summer associate's job at Cadwalader. He started to turn mean and surly. He put Jessie down in public—at McSorley's, for example, in front of their mutual friends—and argued with every single point she made in class.

Jessie would have been embarrassed to admit to Kirby how she backed down, how she *apologized*, how her main objective became placating Theo and defusing his growing anger, how she intentionally turned in a sloppy opinion so that he would get a better grade than her. Jessie watched herself make concession after concession even as she yearned to be strong and stand up for herself like a proper women's libber. But she wanted Theo to be happy. She wanted him to love her. And so she yielded; she flattered him, diminished herself to make him appear bigger.

And what had this gotten her? It had gotten her a kick to the gut, a fat smack to her pride. One night,

Jessie spent the last dollars of her monthly stipend on Reuben sandwiches at the Carnegie Deli, where Theo was supposed to meet her. He never showed up. The sandwiches, which Jessie had transported back downtown on the subway as carefully as she would have a newborn baby, grew cold and greasy. Jessie left them in the white paper bag and stormed down to McSorley's, where she found Theo at a back table with a girl named Ingrid Wu, a first-year. They were all over each other.

"He cheated on me," Jessie tells Kirby. "So I threw him out."

Kirby is smoking again in a more relaxed way, her elbow hanging out the window. "Good for you," she says. "You deserve better."

Jessie rummages through her macramé pocketbook for her sunglasses because suddenly, she feels like she might cry. She'd wanted to call Theo when Exalta died but she hadn't because she was afraid it would sound like a plea for attention. A dead grandmother, how unoriginal. And yet, Exalta *is* dead, and it hurts. Jessie and Exalta hadn't been *close,* exactly, but there had been something—a mutual respect and admiration that was, in a way, more meaningful to Jessie than the more typical variety of grandmotherly love. Exalta was proud of Jessie's accomplishments—her impeccable grades at Brookline High and Mount Holyoke, her high LSAT score, her admission to NYU's law school. Exalta could be stingy with praise, but she had, more than once, said that Jessie was a young woman with a good head on her shoulders who had a very bright future.

Along with her cutoffs and her crocheted tank, Jessie is wearing the gold-knot-and-diamond necklace that Exalta gave her for her thirteenth birthday. Jessie lost the necklace the very first time she wore it, and she'd spent one fraught week of her thirteenth summer in a state of agitated panic. Mr. Crimmins found the necklace—thank God!—and Exalta kept it in her custody until Jessie turned sixteen. At that point, Jessie put it on—and she has never taken it off. It has been witness to every second of the past seven years. It's a talisman and a reminder of Exalta's belief in her. *Good head on her shoulders. Very bright future.*

Theo Feigelbaum be damned.

"You're right," Jessie says, thinking maybe her sister isn't such a terrible influence after all. "I do deserve better."

2. Baby, What a Big Surprise

Over her mother's protests, Blair tells her nine-year-old twins, George and Gennie, to climb into the once red, now nearly pink International Harvester Scout, their family beach vehicle that refuses to die. Blair is taking the twins into town for hot fudge sundaes at the Sweet

Shoppe. They arrived on Nantucket an hour ago and ice cream sundaes are their first-afternoon-on-island tradition.

"Your grandmother's body isn't even cold yet," Kate says before Blair heads out the door after the twins. "What are people going to say when they see you and the children with whipped cream all over your faces?"

"They'll think we're trying to cheer ourselves up," Blair says. She gives Kate a pointed look. "The kids have been through a lot recently."

"Well," Kate says, and she meets Blair's gaze. "Whose fault is that?"

"Mmm," Blair says. She has been waiting for this exact confrontation, the one where Kate blames Blair for her divorce from Angus, even though their split was hardly Blair's fault. Angus dragged Blair and the children down to Houston for the most miserable year of their lives so that he could work at NASA on the Viking mission to Mars. The children despised their new school—the other kids made fun of their "accents"—and Blair felt adrift in the astronaut-wives society. It was as though she had stepped back in time rather than forward. The astronauts' wives didn't have careers. They spent their days getting manicures and planning fondue parties. When Blair mentioned, at the one "garden lunch" she attended—which was held looking at the garden through a plate-glass window because it was too beastly hot to eat on the patio—that she resented having to give up her adjunct professor job at Radcliffe, all the women at the table had stared at her, forks suspended over their cottage cheese as though Blair were speaking in tongues.

Blair hadn't made a single friend and neither had the children. Even a swimming pool in their backyard didn't cheer them up. The kids sat in front of the color television and started speaking to each other in a new language they called Brady, saying things like "George... Glass" and "Marcia, Marcia, Marcia!" in a way that seemed to have a secret meaning.

Angus was, of course, never around. He had a cot at NASA and spent the nights there.

In a moment of desperation, Blair decided to get the children a dog, thinking this might help. And it had, initially. They went to the SPCA and picked out a mutt, some kind of spaniel-terrier mix. The children named him Happy, which made Blair melt a little—her twins were remaining optimistic!—but Happy was not happy once they brought him home. He was lethargic; he slept twenty-two hours a day, rising only to limp over to his bowl of chow.

A trip to the vet revealed that Happy was a very sick dog. He had tumors all down his spine—Blair could see them in the X-ray, evenly spaced like pearls on a string. The vet said the kind thing would be to put the dog to sleep.

The death of the dog brought Blair to the end of her

rope. She surprised Angus at his office and begged him to return to his job at MIT in Cambridge. Angus was his usual opaque and uncompromising self. He had a project here in Houston. The Viking mission. Mars.

"Then the children and I will go back alone," Blair said.

She hadn't necessarily meant to ask for a divorce. She had imagined they could work out some kind of long-distance marriage. But Angus said he planned on staying in Houston. In addition to the Viking mission, he was in on the ground floor of the space-shuttle program. His future was at NASA, and if Blair and the children refused to support him, well, then, he supposed that constituted irreconcilable differences.

"There's no reason we can't work out a civil arrangement," Angus said. "You and the children will be well cared for."

And they have been, financially. Blair took sole ownership of their home in Chestnut Hill; the children are enrolled in public school. Blair will return to Radcliffe in the fall. Their life is remarkably similar to what it was before they left. The interlude in Houston was like the pain of childbirth; as soon as it was over, Blair forgot about it.

This is not to say all is hunky-dory. Angus hasn't flown up to see the children even once since they left. They have a Sunday-evening call scheduled. This consists of Angus asking the children how they're doing ("Fine"), then how things are going in school ("Fine").

Are they getting good marks? ("Yes.") Then he tells them, "Be good for your mother." ("We will.") And then, with what seems like enormous relief, one or the other of them will hand the phone back to Blair, who will listen to Angus say, "This month's check is in the mail. We'll talk next week."

Being a divorcée at Radcliffe is no big deal. Cambridge is filled with "Free to Be...You and Me" families — divorced mothers and fathers, unmarried couples with children, gay and lesbian couples, biracial couples, married couples with adopted children. Blair's best friend from her Wellesley days, Sallie, has given up on ever finding a suitable man and is now a "single mother by choice." She used a sperm donor — a six-foot-two engineer with dark hair and dark eyes — and now has a four-year-old son, Michael.

However, Chestnut Hill, the affluent Boston suburb where Blair lives, is another story. Everyone is married, everyone drives a woody wagon with the back seat and the backety-back crowded with kids and at least one dog, a golden retriever or Irish setter. Blair has a circle of lovely, well-meaning friends who were thrilled when Blair and the kids moved back. But once Blair admitted that Angus wouldn't follow in six months or a year — he was staying in Houston permanently; they were getting a divorce — she sensed everyone pulling back a few inches so they could better judge her. They were "sad" for her, they said, even though she herself was much happier. The truth, Blair knows, is that her so-called friends see divorce as a virus, and if they get too close, they might catch it.

Tom Murray from three houses down offered to mow Blair's lawn, which was very kind, but Blair felt she had to say no. The last thing she wanted everyone to see was another person's husband mowing her lawn or shoveling her snow.

She hired a gardener, a twenty-four-year-old Puerto Rican named Jefe. He was handsome and friendly and the kids loved him, especially George, once Jefe admitted that he had been a baseball star back in Ponce. Blair once looked out the window to see George and Jefe playing catch in the front yard, and, in a moment she regretted perhaps more than any other in her life, she told Jefe that she wasn't paying him to play games and that he should leave immediately. Jefe had been hurt, George had stormed off in a sullen rage, and Blair ran up to her bedroom to cry. She knew that George needed a man around but she couldn't bear to have the neighborhood whispering about exactly what role Jefe the gardener was filling over at the Whalen house.

Being divorced is a social stigma; there's no denying it. Blair thinks about dating again, but how to go about it? Back in April, she let Sallie talk her into an outing with Parents Without Partners, which Sallie called "PWP." Blair and the twins and Sallie and little Michael had joined the other single mothers and fathers and their children at Fenway Park to see the Red Sox play the Philadelphia Phillies. It was meant to be fun, Blair knew, like a grown-up version of a mixer in college. The weather cooperated; it was sunny and warm enough to sit in the bleachers without a jacket or sweater. But Blair found herself preoccupied with what was wrong rather than what was right. On the one hand, Sallie had chosen well. Because it was a baseball game, most of the other participating parents were men. However, Blair couldn't find a single candidate she would consider dating. Some men were fat and sloppy, some had stringy comb-overs, some had facial hair that reminded Blair of Charles Manson. But it wasn't only appearances that put Blair off—after all, Angus had looked like a central-casting poindexter. The problem was that the PWP fathers carried the stench of desperation. Most of them slouched, and those who did stand up straight seemed angry at the world.

The gentleman closest to Blair—he introduced himself as Al Sparks and stared at her chest—wasn't bad-looking, but he jumped out of his seat after nearly every pitch and cursed at the umpires. He swore in front of his two sons, though they didn't notice because they were too busy tussling over the bucket of popcorn he'd bought for them to share until the older son pulled a little too hard and the bucket upended all over the seat in front of them, which was occupied by a toddler who had fallen asleep with his head cocked at an unnatural angle while his oblivious father kept track of the stats in a spiral-bound notebook.

The children at this outing seemed like ragamuffins. Blair didn't like to be ungenerous but she couldn't help noticing a little girl with tangled hair and a boy, nearly obese, whose father had stuffed him like a sausage into a Yastrzemski jersey. The children looked... motherless, and this made Blair suspect that, although she was here looking for someone who would trim the hedges and take the car for an oil change, the gentlemen were looking for a woman who knew how to French-braid and who might be willing to cook a hot breakfast every morning.

If Blair were to, God forbid, *marry* one of the men in PWP, she would become... a stepmother. This wasn't something she had considered.

Of course Blair had been raised by a stepfather— David Levin, who had been perfect in nearly every way. But that felt different somehow. Kate had been tragically widowed; David had swooped in to save the day. It hadn't been two broken families awkwardly trying to fit themselves together.

Blair is too much of a feminist to admit that she's now looking for a David, a single man without children who will love Blair, George, and Gennie unconditionally—but secretly, she fears she is.

The Red Sox game was Blair's one and only foray with PWP. Sallie dated angry Al Sparks for six weeks before declaring him an "absolute psychopath" after he got drunk at a Memorial Day picnic and lost his temper over a Frisbee that landed on the grill.

Blair is irritated with her mother's comments about the propriety of her taking the children to the Sweet Shoppe, although as she parks the car on Main Street in front of Bosun's Locker, she does in fact worry that she will bump into someone she knows who will want to express his or her condolences about Exalta—and how will Blair explain that they're on their way to get sundaes?

"Let's hurry along," Blair says. The twins are in the back seat, completely oblivious to their surroundings despite the rumbling of the Scout over the cobblestones. Gennie is immersed in her book of science experiments, and George is doing the crossword puzzle from the *Boston Herald*.

They are, Blair thinks somewhat mournfully, *Angus's* children—obsessed with the world of the mind.

But then she brightens, because at least the twins *look* like Blair. They're both blond, pink-cheeked, nicely proportioned, and they have straight white teeth. Gennie is an inch or two taller than George, but that will soon change. Next month, they'll be ten. How did that happen?

"You know," Blair says, "I went into labor with the two of you on this very street."

"We know," they say in unison.

Of course they know; it's part of Foley-Levin-Whalen family lore. In the summer of 1969, while Angus was in Houston working on the Apollo 11 mission to the moon, Blair went into labor right in the middle of Buttner's department store. She had taken Jessie in to be fitted for her first bra and that's where her water broke. Blair had waddled up Main Street, leaking amniotic fluid all over the brick sidewalk, while Jessie ran ahead to get Kate, who appeared moments later in the Scout. Because Blair couldn't possibly endure a trip over the cobblestones, Kate had driven down one-way Fair Street in reverse. The twins had been born the next morning, a scant hour before the moon launch.

Blair climbs out of the car and has to snap her fingers through the open back window to get the twins to move. "Let's go," she says. "Hot fudge."

"Blair?" a voice says. "Blair Foley?"

Blair has been inside the Sweet Shoppe for ten seconds, just long enough to shepherd the twins to the end of the line. The Sweet Shoppe never changes. It's still deliciously cool and smells like vanilla waffle cones.

Blair turns. A man is standing at the cash register holding a double scoop of rocky road in a sugar cone. He accepts a quarter in change, grabs a napkin from the dispenser, and heads right for Blair with a sly smile on his face.

Blair tries to prepare herself. Who is this? The man

is her age. He's wearing a powder-blue leisure suit and blue gradient-lens glasses; his reddish hair is long and feathered. Surely this isn't someone she knows?

"It's Larry," he says. "Larry Winter."

Larry Winter! Blair dated Larry Winter for three consecutive summers when she was a teenager. In those days, Blair, Kirby, and Tiger lived in the guest cottage of Exalta's house, called Little Fair. At night, Larry Winter would ride over from Walsh Street on his Schwinn, throw a pebble at Blair's bedroom window, and the two of them would neck, Larry perched on the top rail of the fence, Blair tucked between his legs. To this day, it was some of the loveliest kissing Blair can remember, and some of the purest desire. They had been caught once by Mr. Crimmins, the caretaker, who had passed down the side street, Plumb Lane, late at night on his way home from somewhere, probably Bosun's Locker. He'd stepped out of the darkness, startling them both, and said, "Time to call it a night, kids." Then he continued on in the direction of Pine Street, where he lived in an efficiency. Blair remembers wanting to chase after him to beg him not to tell her mother or—horrors!—her grandmother. But Blair needn't have worried; Mr. Crimmins kept her secret.

"Larry!" Blair says. "What a surprise! I thought you were a Floridian these days."

She hopes she has this right. Larry Winter went to Georgetown to study political science, but somehow he'd ended up as the food and beverage manager at a private club in Vero Beach. He'd risen to general manager and then had started a venture of his own somewhere else in Florida. The Everglades, maybe?

"I'm up for a couple of weeks," Larry says. "The heat in Florida this time of year, even in the Keys..."

Key Largo, Blair thinks with a mental snap of the fingers. *He owns a nightclub in Key Largo.*

"Plus, Grandma isn't getting any younger—" Larry stops himself. "Which reminds me, I heard about Exalta passing. I'm so sorry."

Blair feels tears burn her eyes. The Sweet Shoppe is only a few blocks away from Exalta's house on Fair Street and it's inconceivable that if Blair and the twins ventured up there after their sundaes, the only person they would find would be Mr. Crimmins, who had become Exalta's devoted companion.

Unlike Blair, Exalta hadn't given one whit what people thought about her shacking up with the caretaker. She and Bill Crimmins had fallen in love. For the past ten years, Exalta had been a different woman. Gone was the stern, judgmental blue blood and in her place was a fun-loving old lady who listened and laughed.

When Blair last visited Exalta, she had meant to tell her grandmother that she and Angus had divorced. But Exalta was so sick and frail at that time, swimming in and out of lucidity, that Blair couldn't bear to bring it up. Exalta had adored Angus. Why burden her with news that would only make her sad and disappointed?

At that point, Exalta had still been living in her house in Boston, on Mount Vernon Street in Beacon Hill, but a few days after Blair's visit, Exalta sat bolt upright in bed and clearly announced that she wanted to spend her final days in the house on Nantucket. And so Bill Crimmins arranged for a door-to-door ambulance transfer — the ambulance even went over on the ferry — and they installed Exalta comfortably in the house on Fair Street, where she died two days ago, none the wiser about Blair and Angus.

Blair leaves the twins in line and steps away a bit so she can talk to Larry more privately. "As I'm sure you've heard," she says, "I got divorced."

Larry turns his head so he's looking at her with only one eye; this, she recalls, is a gesture of his. "I had *not* heard that, actually."

Ah, right. Larry lives in Florida. The only person who would have told him is Mrs. Winter, his grandmother, and she would only have heard it from Exalta. Blair is glad she came out with it before Larry had a chance to ask about Angus.

Blair shrugs. "Didn't work out, but the kids and I are fine. We live outside of Boston. Everyone's happy." She flashes Larry a smile that she hopes indicates *happy*, or *appropriately happy*, considering they're on island to attend a funeral. "How about you? Married? Kids?"

Larry stares at the ice cream cone that is slowly melting in his hand. "Not married, no kids," he says. "Haven't met the right woman."

Blair feels herself flush. "Oh. Well, I'm sure it's only a matter of time."

Larry stares at his cone for a few more seconds; he must be finding this experience as surreal as she is. "So, listen, I'm planning on coming to the funeral and the reception. Escorting my grandmother."

"Of course," Blair says. "You belong there. And Kirby has planned a bonfire tomorrow night at Ram Pasture. Young people only."

Larry laughs. "That leaves me out."

"And me," Blair says. "I'm thirty-four. Twice as old as I was the last summer we dated."

"I've got a year on you, don't forget. And you, Blair Foley, are far more gorgeous now than you were at seventeen."

Flush turns to blush. He's lying, though Blair *has* lost a lot of weight since the divorce and now might be nearly as slender as she was in high school. "Thank you, Larry. I needed to hear that."

"I'll see you tomorrow," Larry says. "Enjoy your ice cream."

Blair is as preoccupied as the twins as they sit and eat their sundaes. Blair made George and Gennie leave their projects in the car, so they've moved on to their second-favorite pastime—dissecting a special trilogy of episodes of *The Brady Bunch*. The Bradys go to Hawaii, they find a tiki that appears to be cursed—Greg Brady has a surfing accident; a tarantula crawls on one of the other brothers—but Blair loses the plot when they start talking about a cave and someone (or something?) named Oliver. Doesn't matter. Blair is doing her own dissecting. Larry Winter, of all people! Single and without children, telling Blair she looked "more gorgeous" than she had at seventeen. And she'll see him tomorrow at the funeral, the reception, and the bonfire.

"Time to go," Blair says, though she has barely touched her sundae.

Blair drives back to her mother and David's sprawling beachfront compound on Red Barn Road, listing Larry Winter's pros and cons. The only con she can come up with is that he lives in Florida and owns a nightclub, which might explain why he looks like one of the Bee Gees. Well, another con is that Blair felt no particular emotion when she saw him other than a fondness for the kissing. And she'd liked being complimented, of course, because who didn't? But there was definitely something missing—a zing, a ping, a tingle. They had broken up, Blair remembers, because she had grown tired of him.

The pros are that he's single and without children. But surely she's entitled to ask for more than just that?

Blair wonders if the divorce has turned her heart to ice. Look at how she spoke to poor Jefe. Maybe she'll feel differently about Larry tomorrow night at the bonfire once she's had a few drinks. Maybe her running into Larry was meant to be, orchestrated by Exalta, who is watching out for Blair from above.

The driveway of Kate and David's compound is crowded with cars. Blair sees the Trans Am that Tiger drives; he'll have to give that thing up once he and Magee finally have children. She sees Kirby's LTD and Mr. Crimmins's pickup truck. And she sees a turquoise Porsche 911 with the top down.

Blair freezes. Only one person she knows would drive a car like that.

"Looks like we have company," Blair says.

Kate and David bought the sprawling old house on Red Barn Road ten years earlier, right after the twins were born, back when Tiger was still over in Vietnam. They lived in it for five years without making a single change. Then, once Jessie left for Mount Holyoke and Kate no longer had children at home, she and David sold the big house in Brookline, rented an apartment in Charles River Park, and poured their time, energy, and resources into the Nantucket property. The main house got a complete face-lift — a new roof; new doors and windows; new wood floors throughout, except for the family room, which they carpeted; paint for all the bedrooms; an updated kitchen with avocado-green appliances and bright pink-and-orange wallpaper, so when you were at the counter making a sandwich, you felt like you were standing in the middle of fruit ambrosia. (Only Exalta was brave enough to say to Kate, "You might have chosen something more classic, darling.") But Kate wanted a happy, modern house as a counterpoint to the staid, history-laden confines of All's Fair. She and David built a guest cottage on the back edge of the property — two bedrooms, one bath. (This was where Blair and Angus had always stayed with the children; now it's just Blair and the children.) Between the guest cottage and the main house, they built a clay tennis court and a turquoise lozenge of an in-ground pool that had a curved fiberglass slide at one end. There was a concrete patio for barbecuing and even a portable tiki bar that David hauled out of the shed every Memorial Day for the summer. Kate had discovered frozen blender drinks — strawberry daiquiris and margaritas — which she served in obscenely large glasses that she got on sale at Kmart.

If the whole thing sounded out of character for Kate, well, it was, a bit — but Kate made no secret that she wanted the compound filled with grandchildren someday.

On that front, Blair had done her part. The onus now fell on her three siblings.

Kirby, Tiger, and Jessie are all out on the patio, sitting under the awning by the pool. Mr. Crimmins and Kate and David are there as well, and Magee, Tiger's wife, who quit her dental hygienist's job to care for Exalta when she first fell sick. (Kate had been relieved, Blair knows. She was certain that Tiger and Magee didn't have children because Magee worked too hard.)

The blender isn't purring, the grill isn't smoking; there isn't a drink in sight, not even iced tea. Kate is holding tight to her principles. They are a family in mourning; no one will enjoy him- or herself. Blair's not sure how she'll explain that she and the children have just been to the Sweet Shoppe, though perhaps Kate has already announced this. Perhaps everyone has been discussing Blair's blasphemy, her loosened morals since getting divorced.

Tiger moves to the edge of the patio to light a cigarette and he's joined by a dark-haired gentleman wearing a white polo, madras shorts, and Wayfarer sunglasses.

Blair's heart isn't frozen after all, because suddenly it revs like a race-car engine. She will be taking a ride in that Porsche later, her face raised to the night sky, her hair streaming out behind her.

It's Joey Whalen, Angus's little brother and Blair's boyfriend before (and after) she met Angus.

"How about that, my darlings," Blair says. "Your uncle is here."

3. SAD EYES

Magee hasn't stopped crying since Exalta died, and finally, on the morning of the funeral, Tiger realizes he can't ignore it any longer. This isn't normal, run-of-the-mill grief. Something else is going on with his wife.

They're in their summer bedroom, getting dressed. Kate has okayed navy blazers instead of suits for men. Tiger is still in just khaki pants and an undershirt. Magee is in her slip, her hair in the pink spongy rollers she sleeps in when she wants waves. She's sobbing into Tiger's pajama top, presumably so no one else in the house will hear her.

"Mags," he says, sitting next to her on the end of the bed. "What's wrong?"

She raises her face, and her sweet, soft pink bottom lip quivers. "I can't believe you have to ask that. Your. Grandmother. Is. Dead."

Tiger is careful how he proceeds. Yes, Exalta is dead. Exalta was sick for months, her internal organs shutting down one after another like someone shutting the lights off in a house before bed. It wasn't a violent death or even gruesome and it wasn't a surprise. Exalta was eighty-four years old. Tiger had watched men die nearly every day in Vietnam, some of those men only eighteen years old, some still virgins. Exalta had lived a full and privileged life. She had known love not only with Tiger's grandfather Pennington Nichols, but also with Mr.

Crimmins. She had one child, four grandchildren, two great-grandchildren—with more, presumably, on the way.

This, Tiger knows, is the real reason Magee is crying. She and Tiger will have been married for nine years next month, and although they've been trying since day one, she hasn't been able to conceive a child.

At first, they were too busy to notice. When Tiger got home from his tour, he was eligible to inherit his trust from Exalta. The first thing he did was buy a house in Holliston, thirty miles southwest of Boston. The house had been built in the 1840s. It was three stories and had plenty of charm—five bedrooms and a finished playroom in the attic. (In retrospect, Tiger wonders if buying such a big house jinxed them.)

The second thing Tiger did was open a bowling alley on the Holliston-Sherborn line that he called Tiger Lanes. Tiger had spent countless hours in-country, dreaming about the perfect bowling alley. He would have twelve state-of-the-art lanes on one side of the building and a pinball arcade on the other, with a soda fountain and snack bar in the middle. There would be music and party lights. It would be a hangout for teenagers and adults alike, a place to bridge the widening generation gap. He would start a Tiger Lanes bowling league for veterans.

Tiger is aware that he was lucky to come home in one piece, not only physically but mentally. Lots of veterans found themselves at loose ends. They were traumatized; they'd become drug addicts; they'd become *adrenaline* addicts, in search of the high that was part of being on the front lines. When every day was a struggle to stay alive, coming home to conveniences like ten kinds of bread at the supermarket and Johnny Carson every night at eleven thirty felt like sleeping in a bed that was too soft. Where was the action, the danger, the purpose? Some soldiers came home from thirteen hellish months of defending the ideals of American democracy only to be spit upon, harassed, and called "baby killers."

None of this happened to Tiger, but that didn't mean he was unaffected by the war. He'd watched his best friends, Puppy and Frog, get blown to bits. They hadn't had a chance to make something of their lives, but Tiger did, and he'd be damned if he was going to waste it. He would be enough of a success and bring about enough positive change in the world for all of them — Puppy, Frog, and every other person of service in the United States who died in Vietnam.

Tiger bought a defunct shoe factory and transformed it into the first Tiger Lanes. It was such a success that Tiger opened a second location in Franklin the following year, followed by one in Needham and one in Mansfield. He then opened the grandest of them all, a flagship with twenty lanes, a disco floor, and a full bar, in Newton. At that point, Tiger sold the five-bedroom in Holliston and bought a brick center-entrance colonial in Wellesley that had four bedrooms and a finished basement rec room with shag carpeting and a wet bar. The house also had a detached two-car garage, where Tiger kept his Trans Am and Magee's hot rod, a Datsun 240Z.

At that point, Magee still worked as a dental hygienist for Dr. Brezza in Waltham. She'd been working there since Tiger met her, and she told Tiger she would only leave once she got pregnant.

There had been some tense discussions — spurred by visits to Tiger's parents — about Magee's job being the reason they didn't yet have a baby. Kate Levin felt that Magee should stay home and develop a nurturing side. She should do the things that mothers did — go to the salon, volunteer, redecorate, take a pottery class at the community center. Kate privately asked Tiger if it wasn't difficult for poor Magee to clean the teeth of sixteen children a day, none of whom were her own. And how did she handle the busybody mothers, who must be wondering when Magee would have good news to share?

Magee held up to Kate surprisingly well. She loved her job, loved her patients, loved Dr. Brezza. There had been one agonizing moment when Tiger wondered if maybe Magee actually *loved* Dr. Brezza, that maybe they were having an affair and Magee was secretly on the pill so as not to become pregnant with Dr. Brezza's baby. When Tiger came home (after a few too many beers following the Vietnam veterans' bowling league championship) and asked Magee if this was the case, she crumpled.

She wasn't having an affair with Dr. Brezza or anyone else. She loved Tiger; she wanted a baby with Tiger more than she wanted to breathe. She didn't know what was wrong. She didn't drink, didn't smoke, and didn't take Quaaludes like so many other Wellesley women did.

Magee quit her job and gave Kate's method a try. She joined the ladies' auxiliary, audited an anatomy class at Pine Manor, learned to roller-skate because she heard it was good for physical fitness.

When there was still no sign of a baby, Magee agreed to see a doctor. Magee's own mother had a theory that radiation from all of the dental X-rays that Magee had taken had somehow fried her insides. Magee knew this wasn't the case but she nonetheless submitted to a complete physical exam at the Brigham, which involved a lot of poking and prodding of both Magee's body and her psyche. Magee waited three days for the results of the exam—all she could think of was Jennifer Cavalleri in *Love Story* learning that she had leukemia—but when the call finally came, it was with the news that she was in perfect working condition.

Then it was Tiger's turn. He'd been at war. He could have been exposed to chemicals or gases that affected his sperm count or motility. And so he went to the Brigham as well and gave the doctor a specimen (that was weird), but his sperm count was high, his swimmers veritable Olympians.

The problem then became that there was no problem. The problem was lack of patience and high expectations. The problem was that sex stopped feeling like a natural manifestation of Tiger's love for his wife and more like a test he was failing. Magee started going to the public library to research fertility issues. There were options — medical procedures, drugs — that could be pursued right there in Boston, right at the Brigham! The science, Magee said, was remarkable. A baby had been conceived *in a test tube!*

Tiger didn't want his child conceived in a laboratory. Call him old-fashioned, call him stodgy, but he'd rather adopt one of the hundreds of thousands of children orphaned in Vietnam than be subjected to "drugs" and "procedures."

Before Magee could get too carried away, life intervened. Exalta got a head cold that turned into pneumonia. Before she was fully recovered, she suffered a minor stroke and became bedridden. Bill Crimmins was good for handholding but not much else. Kate was alternately too worried and too impatient to be helpful, so she looked into hiring private nurses, but it was very expensive for round-the-clock care. Magee saw a chance to put to use all the love and attention she had been storing up for their future children. She spent countless hours caring for Exalta. She fed her soft foods, made sure she took her pills, read to her, plumped her pillows, sat with her through endless episodes of *The Flying Nun,* consulted with Exalta's doctor over the phone and with the night nurse each morning.

Now that Exalta is gone, Magee's newfound purpose is gone too. And what's left is not only Exalta's absence, but the absence of a baby as well. Tiger gets it.

He hasn't been inside a church in over ten years. Even when he and Magee got married, it was outside on the front lawn of his parents' Nantucket home. He can't quite explain why he's avoided it. He certainly has a lot to be grateful for—his success in business; his beautiful, devoted wife; hell, the mere fact that he's alive. A lot of guys Tiger knew in the war became either atheists or born-again Christians. If there's one thing Tiger has learned, it's that God doesn't live in a church. For Tiger, God lives in the shaking hands of a U.S. Air Force fighter pilot who needs Tiger to tie his bowling shoes but who can somehow send a ten-pound ball down the boards for a strike. God is in the illuminated windows of Tiger's neighborhood, homes occupied by Americans who are safe and sound inside, enjoying pot roast and *Donny and Marie.* God is in the Firestone tires of Tiger's Trans Am, in the gravelly voice of Wolfman Jack on the radio, in four-year-old Joey Bell from down the street who saluted when Tiger marched past in the Memorial Day parade. God is in the glove of Carlton

Fisk. God is in the ocean he sees from the windows of their summer bedroom.

God is in all these places, so why would Tiger—or anyone—need to go to church?

Well, today he needs to go so his mother doesn't wallop him. She spies him smoking outside the front door of St. Paul's Episcopal and perhaps suspects that he'd like to skip the service altogether, because she plucks the cigarette from his mouth and grinds it out beneath the sole of her black slingback heel.

"Get inside," she says, "and pray for your grand-mother."

"Too late now," Tiger deadpans. Then he grins. Will his mother find this funny?

Kate shakes her head before letting a fraction of a smile slip. "Pray for yourself, then. And your sainted wife."

Maybe he should go inside and pray for a baby, he thinks. It couldn't hurt.

4. HEART OF GLASS

With Exalta's death, Kate is now the matriarch of the family. Along with her deep sorrow, she feels a rush of power, of agency. There's no one left to please, no one left to placate, no one left to impress.

There is no one left to judge her.

She's free.

"Is it horrible to feel this way?" Kate whispers to David in the car. "I loved her—"

"You worshipped her," David says.

"I respected her—"

"You revered her."

"I even liked her at times."

"She *was* a great deal easier to deal with once we bought our own house," David says. "And once she and Bill got together."

Bill Crimmins, yes. Kate owes a tremendous debt to Bill—not only for four decades of service to their family and the house but for the past ten years as Exalta's companion. In her will, Exalta granted Bill lifetime rights to All's Fair and Little Fair. Only when Bill dies will Exalta's Nantucket home pass to Kate. This was an appropriate gesture, and yet Kate can't help but worry that Bill will mend his relationship with his daughter, Lorraine, who is responsible for every bit of heartbreak Kate has known in her life, and Lorraine Crimmins will end up spending time, maybe even entire summers, in All's Fair.

Bill Crimmins wouldn't encourage this, certainly. However, if Lorraine discovers—from one of her former chums at Bosun's Locker, let's say—that Exalta died and Bill has been granted residency, and she decides to simply show up, would Bill have the willpower to turn her away?

Kate fears the answer is no. So many of us are powerless when it comes to our own children.

*   *   *

Kate tries to push all unpleasant thoughts from her mind in order to be properly attentive during the service. She, David, and Mr. Crimmins sit with the twins in the first pew, while Kate's four children and Magee sit behind them.

Exalta wanted zero frills. Straightforward service, no poetry, no eulogizing, no dreadful receiving line where Kate and the children would have to, in Exalta's words, "listen to everyone lie about what a wonderful woman I was."

Reverend Meeker conducts a proper Mass (without Communion, also Exalta's choice), and during his rather bland homily, Kate's mind wanders. Exalta built an extraordinary family, although really, it was Kate, Exalta's only child, who built it. She had her first three children with Lieutenant Wilder Foley and then, after Wilder confessed to an affair with Lorraine Crimmins, got Lorraine pregnant, and shot himself, Kate married David Levin and had Jessie.

Each of her four children has something that sets him or her apart. Blair has the twins, Kirby the glamour, Tiger the money, and Jessie the smarts.

They also each have problems. Blair is divorced, Kirby wild, Tiger and Magee can't seem to conceive. And Jessie—well, Jessie is a long way, still, from being settled.

Reverend Meeker lifts his palms to the sky. They stand for the creed, segue into prayers, sing the final hymn—"I

Am the Bread of Life" — then await the benediction. Exalta's casket is so close to Kate, she can reach out and touch it, but Kate doesn't feel even the faintest vestiges of her mother's spirit hovering. To haunt one's own funeral, Exalta might say, just isn't done. Better to make a complete and graceful exit. Think of me fondly, but for heaven's sake, don't cry.

Kate doesn't cry. Exalta raised her sensibly. However, Kate does notice Mr. Crimmins pulling a handkerchief from his pocket and dabbing at his eyes, which is sweet. Magee's muffled sobs are less so, though understandable considering how much time she spent with Exalta at the end. One of Exalta's last clear-minded quips to Kate was a sotto voce comment after Magee left Exalta's bedside to go fetch Exalta some tapioca pudding: *I see I have a new best friend.*

All in all, Kate is relieved when the service is over — and she's even more relieved once the casket is lowered into the ground in the cemetery on Hummock Pond Road and the rich, fresh dirt is smoothed over the top. Gennie squeezes Kate's hand so tightly she nearly fuses Kate's fingers. Cemeteries are scary for children; nobody likes to think about being put in a box and buried for all eternity. Kate nearly says, *We can come visit Grand-Nonny here whenever you want,* but she doesn't want Gennie to think for one second that Exalta is actually *here* — and so she says nothing at all.

Kate can't get to the Field and Oar Club fast enough. She's in desperate need of a drink.

*   *   *

She sucks down a Mount Gay and tonic—this has been the favorite cocktail at the club in recent years—and makes sure that all four of her children are present and accounted for on the lawn between the clubhouse and the waterfront before she begins the odious business of socializing. It's a brilliant day with deep blue skies and a tennis wind—enough to be refreshing but not so strong that you wished you were out sailing. There seem to be more people at the reception than were at the church, and isn't that just typical of their set—skip church, how dull, and choose instead to pay respects over cocktails and the lunch buffet on someone else's chit.

Kate sees Bitsy Dunscombe step onto the brick patio with her second husband, Arturo, her identical twins, Heather and Helen, and their husbands. Heather and Helen are Jessie's age, twenty-three; they both went to Briarcliffe; and they are both new housewives of just under a year. Bitsy and her loathsome first husband, Ward Dunscombe, threw the twins a double wedding here at the club last July. Kate and David had attended, mainly because Bitsy declared it would be the "wedding of the decade," and Kate wanted to see what that looked like. For Kate, the best part of the wedding wasn't the girls in matching dresses—they looked lovely, though the double vision came across as something of a sideshow spectacle—but rather when Bitsy's first husband and second husband had a fistfight in the parking lot. By all accounts, it was Ward who threw the first punch (he was a notoriously nasty drunk), but, alas, it was Arturo who had gotten posted. Ward was the sixth-wealthiest man on Nantucket and was a life-long member of the Field and Oar, whereas Arturo was a Panamanian national who had come to the island to work as a waiter at the Opera House restaurant.

Technically, Arturo isn't allowed to set foot in the club, but Kate won't say a word. It's a funeral reception.

"Kate," Bitsy says, her arms open in a V and her head cocked back. "I'm so sorry for your loss. Exalta was one of a kind."

These are probably the nicest words Bitsy could say about Exalta without lying, because for seventy-four of her eighty-four years, Exalta was imperious, judgmental, and cold. That she had thawed late in life was the only thing that kept today from being a celebration. *Ding-dong, the witch is dead.*

Out of the corner of her eye, Kate sees Bill Crimmins standing out on the dock, hands crammed into his pockets, gazing at the water. He might feel more uncomfortable here at the Field and Oar than even Arturo. Kate should go over and bring Bill into the fold, but she can't dismiss Bitsy quite so fast.

"Thank you for coming, Bitsy," she says. "Of course Mother adored you." This isn't true, but Kate treads lightly where Bitsy is concerned. Ten years earlier, Kate and Bitsy had had a fight in the middle of dinner at the Opera House — the night Bitsy revealed that she was sleeping with Arturo — because Bitsy accused Jessie of stealing from her daughter Heather. Kate had stormed out, indignant, only to find out later that it was true. Jessie had stolen five dollars and a lip gloss from Heather Dunscombe's Bermuda bag.

That had been a tumultuous summer for them all, 1969. Kate wouldn't relive that summer for anything.

Kate had never apologized to Bitsy the way she should have, but by the next summer Ward had found out about Arturo, and a messy divorce followed. Kate made amends by supporting Bitsy and inviting her and Arturo to their new house on Red Barn Road for cocktails. Bitsy loved the house and intimated that she, too, might leave the socially suffocating cobblestoned streets of downtown and move to a place that was secluded and private, a place where "not everyone knows what you had for breakfast."

In the intervening years, Kate and Bitsy have handled their relationship like some kind of fragile family heirloom that will shatter if they aren't careful.

"I'm sorry we didn't make it to the church," Bitsy says. "Robert had a call with his law firm that ran longer than we expected." Robert was one of the twins' husbands, the lawyer, and the other husband was a doctor. Both twins now lived in Westchester County — one in Rye, one in Ardsley. "But I knew you wouldn't mind. Exalta wasn't particularly *religious,* was she? She used St. Paul's like the rest of us—for networking."

Networking? Kate thinks. What a bizarre thing to say! Their family attended St. Paul's for one reason only—because they were Episcopalian.

"Mother loved the music," Kate says.

"Speaking of," Bitsy says. "The girls tell me there's to be a bonfire at Ram Pasture tonight in Exalta's honor. For the young people?"

"Bonfire?" Kate says. "Ram Pasture? I think you must be mistaken. I've heard nothing about this."

"Helen?" Bitsy says, calling over one perfectly coiffed twin, who's wearing a Lilly Pulitzer patio dress printed with turquoise giraffes. "Didn't you tell me there was a bonfire tonight at Ram Pasture?"

"Yes," Helen says. "Midnight at the Oasis, Kirby is calling it. Heather and I have been discussing what to wear. It sounds vaguely Moroccan, so we were thinking caftans." When Helen brings her Mount Gay and tonic to her lips, Kate can't help noticing the enormous diamond on her left hand, resting over a simple gold wedding band. She fights the jealousy she feels that Bitsy has two married daughters and Kate has zero. Zero married daughters out of *three!* "Kirby is so clever. So...sophisticated."

"Yes," Kate says. "Isn't she just."

Kate finds Kirby looking deceptively wholesome in a sleeveless navy silk sheath with one of Exalta's brooches at the neck, eating finger sandwiches and chatting with Reverend Meeker. Kate wonders what Kirby and the reverend could possibly be talking about; they have exactly nothing in common. Kirby's life in New York, as Kate understands it, includes a lot of expense-account lunches with that dreadful Gurley Brown woman and then it's off to the disco every night, wearing gold-lamé jumpsuits. Kirby sleeps with men but doesn't date them; she flits from one to the next like a child who grows bored with her toys. This is her excuse for not settling down: she can't find anyone who holds her attention. She thinks marriage should be one episode of *Laugh-In* after another, which it most decidedly is not.

"Reverend," Kate says. "I need to borrow Katharine for a moment."

"Uh-oh," Kirby says. "If she's calling me Katharine, I'm in trouble. Pray for me, Reverend."

Kate leads Kirby into the snack bar, where it's shaded and quiet and smells like French fries. "Did you plan a bonfire for tonight?" Kate asks. "At Ram Pasture? In your grandmother's honor? Did you do this and not *inform* me? Not *invite* me?"

"Mom," Kirby says.

5. Night Fever

They drive the Scout right onto the sand, near the spot where Tiger dug the giant hole and filled it with stacked wooden pallets that he took from the back alley behind Charlie's Market. Jessie and Kirby set out thin kilim rugs that Kirby transported from New York in the back of the LTD. There was a place downtown that practically gave them away, she said. They cover Kate's long folding table with a tapestry and arrange a row of votive candles down the center. They set out the refreshments: whole salted almonds, dates, dried apricots, an assortment of olives, goat cheese sprinkled with pistachios, melba toast, hummus, and lots and lots of grapes. Jessie had suggested they also get fixings for s'mores but Kirby shot that idea down. There were no s'mores in Northern Africa.

Well, there were no kegs of Schlitz either, Jessie thinks, and yet that's what they're drinking at this oasis. The keg is in the back of Mr. Crimmins's pickup, which he's letting them borrow, though he isn't coming to the bonfire.

"You young people have fun," he said. "And tomorrow, come over to the house. Your grandmother left a list of things she wanted you to have."

Things she wanted you to have. Exalta's considerable collection of whirligigs and whimmy-diddles will be divided up among the four grandchildren. Exalta's jewelry—the rings she kept in exquisite porcelain boxes and the bracelets and necklaces that lived in a locked case—will be passed to Kate, Jessie, Blair, Kirby, and Magee. Even one-quarter or one-fifth of these possessions will be worth quite a lot, Jessie knows, but only if she sells them. She may, in fact, sell some of the jewelry to ease her third year of law school—maybe buy a new desk lamp or an interview suit—but the whirligigs and whimmy-diddles are so inexorably *Exalta's* that Jessie could never let them go. She will be their steward until she dies, and every time she sets eyes on them, she will think of her grandmother.

People start arriving the second it gets dark. Blair has left the twins back at the house; she hitches a ride to the beach with Tiger and Magee. The Dunscombe twins show up with their husbands. Joey Whalen pulls up in his Porsche, and Larry Winter is driving his grandmother's ancient Jeep Cherokee. There are a bunch of friends of Kirby's from her Madequecham days as well as people that Blair, Kirby, and Tiger knew from sailing at the Field and Oar.

Kirby has a boom box and Tiger brought serious speakers. As soon as the fire is lit, there's music: Led Zeppelin's "Kashmir" sets the mood, followed by Earth, Wind, and Fire, the Doobie Brothers, Bob Seger, Rod Stewart. Jessie stands at the food table and tries an olive, though she isn't hungry. She's not sure whom to hang out with. Kirby is surrounded by her old friends, all of them smoking clove cigarettes. Tiger and Magee are talking to the Dunscombe twins about whatever it is that's important to married people—mortgages? casseroles?—and Blair is the bologna in a Larry Winter–and–Joey Whalen sandwich.

Blair tries to lasso Jessie. "You remember Larry Winter, don't you, Jessie? He lives in Florida now."

Blair obviously wants to do the sorority bump-and-roll, passing off Larry to Jessie, but nope, sorry, Jessie isn't *that* desperate for company. Larry Winter is a hundred years old, or thirty-five, and he has a mustache like Rollie Fingers.

"Hitting the keg," Jessie says.

She does hit the keg, filling two plastic cups with cold Schlitz, then she strolls past the firepit to the water's edge. She feels like a stranger in her own family, but there's nothing new about that. She fingers the gold knot at her neck and runs it along the chain. The necklace was originally a gift to Exalta from Jessie's grandfather on the occasion of their first wedding anniversary. It's priceless, and Exalta chose to give it to Jessie.

Jessie guzzles down one beer, feels a little better, reminds herself that, as soon as she wants to, she can rejoin the party and talk to Heather and Helen Dunscombe. They went through the predictable trajectory of being friends, then hating each other, then being friends again after it turned out that both Jessie and Helen Dunscombe had been molested by their tennis instructor, Garrison. But Jessie's afraid they'll have nothing in common now. Jessie is in law school and lives in Greenwich Village. She's single. The twins are married and live in the suburbs. Jessie takes the subway; the twins drive station wagons. This time next year, Jessie will be studying for the bar exam. This time next year, one or both of the Dunscombe twins will be pregnant.

Will Jessie still be single this time next year? She can't believe it's 1979 and yet the first thing a person wants to know about a woman is if she has managed to catch a man. The song changes to Donna Summer's "Heaven Knows." *Heaven knows it's not the way it should be.* Do people care if Donna Summer is married or single? They do not; she is fabulous either way. So there's hope.

Jessie has nearly finished her second beer when someone plops in the sand next to her.

"Jessie Levin," a voice says. "Surprise."

Jessie turns. Male person, her age or maybe a little older. Shorn head, so what Jessie thinks at first is that Tiger saw her sitting by herself, felt sorry for her, and sent over one of his army buddies.

"Surprise?" she says.

"It's me," he says. "Pick."

6. PARADISE BY THE DASHBOARD LIGHT

Blair is desperate to get rid of Larry Winter. How had she entertained the thought even for a second that there might still be something between them? He came to the church in a tan leisure suit with a wide-collared paisley shirt underneath, and although he was kind and solicitous with his grandmother, Blair had to close her eyes against the sight of him. Then at the reception, he'd been stuck to her like flypaper. She was unable to talk to anyone else, meaning she couldn't have a proper, private conversation with Joey Whalen.

Well, that's not exactly true, is it? There were the stolen moments the night before.

After the twins went to the guest cottage to watch *Mork and Mindy* before bed, Blair slipped out to Joey's Porsche under the pretext of saying good night.

"I can't believe you came," Blair said.

"Family," Joey said.

"Yes, well," Blair said, meaning *Your brother didn't think it was worth flying up from Houston for.* But Angus must have called Joey, because how else would he have heard about Exalta? Maybe Angus suggested Joey appear on Nantucket in his place. Maybe — is Blair reaching here? — Angus realized that long ago, he thwarted the romance between Blair and Joey. Because Blair and Joey had been a couple first! "I'm grateful you're here. And the kids..." The kids had been ecstatic when they saw their uncle, all thoughts of experiments and puzzles abandoned. They had launched themselves into Joey's arms like little rockets. Joey was God, Santa Claus, and Jim Rice rolled into one.

"I love those kids like they're my own," Joey said.

And me? Blair wanted to ask. *Do you love me like I'm your own?* Joey is still a bachelor, still working in advertising. He's the head of the national campaign for Stouffer's, so he travels the country and eats a lot of French bread pizza. The pay is good and he has no one to support but himself, hence the Porsche and a summer place in Newport.

"Well, Blair," Joey said, sliding down into the leather bucket seat of the Porsche. "I guess I'll see you tomorrow."

Tomorrow meant church, family, obligation. It seemed like Joey was going to leave without so much as a goodnight kiss. Was Blair going to let that happen?

Blair ran a finger along the racing stripe. "This car is foxy," she said. "How fast does it go?"

Joey hadn't hesitated for even a second. "Get in," he said. "I'll show you."

They'd ended up zipping down the Madaket Road, then careening along Cliff before they stopped to make out at the end of Hinckley Lane. It might have gone even further; Blair might have let Joey have her across the hood or she might have followed him back to his room at the Jared Coffin House, but at the last minute, she suffered a crisis of conscience and stopped him.

"My brother wins again, I see," Joey said.

"Just think how it will *look!*" Blair says. "It'll look scandalous…*incestuous,* even."

This made Joey laugh. "*We* aren't related," he said.

"I know…"

"But you care what people think," Joey said. "Because you're just like your mother and your grandmother."

"I am not," Blair insisted. "I'm my own woman."

"If you want to know how it will look, I'll tell you," Joey said. "It'll look like I've been crazy for you since the day I met you. It'll *look* like I've been biding my time until the inevitable happened and you and Angus split. And even then, I've let a proper amount of time pass. But now I'm here and I want to make this work."

Wasn't that what Blair wanted too? She had thought of Joey every day since returning to Boston, but she'd been too timid—and, yes, too conventional—to consider calling him. Plus, he was impossible to pin down; the only person she could have asked about his whereabouts was...Angus. So his appearing on Nantucket was both a surprise and an answer to a longing that Blair was hesitant to admit she'd been holding in her heart.

"Drive me home, please," Blair said. "I need to think about it."

Now here it is, a full twenty-four hours later, and Blair has reached a decision. She wants to be with Joey Whalen. Maybe it's outrageous—dating her ex-husband's brother—or maybe it happens all the time. Angus won't be at all surprised and neither will Blair's family. The children, though—how will Gennie and George feel about their mother dating their *uncle?* And their uncle possibly becoming their stepfather?

Well, they'll be either thrilled or disgusted. Or, more likely, thrilled one day and disgusted the next. But Blair won't sacrifice her own happiness for the sake of the children. She reasons that if she's happy, the children will be happy. This is a modern attitude—her neighbors will say she's been reading too much *Redbook*—but come on, it's 1979, and in six months, it will be 1980!

Blair is going to tell Joey Whalen yes. Yes, she wants to be with him. She doesn't care that he lives out of a suitcase. He can spend time at her house in Chestnut Hill; she can take the twins to Newport. It'll be exciting. Blair will have a family situation that is just as wacky as everyone else's at Radcliffe.

Her only problem now is a small one. She has to get rid of Larry. But how? He can't take a hint!

Kirby approaches out of the darkness. "Anyone here want to smoke some weed?"

Blair says, "I bet Larry does."

Both Joey and Larry laugh, then Larry clears his throat. "Actually, I'd love to."

"Dynamite," Kirby says. She's wearing an ivory caftan that in this moment makes her seem like an angel of mercy. "Come on, Larry. Let's go for a walk."

Kirby links her arm through Larry's and they wander away. Blair reaches for Joey's hand.

"Drive?" he says.

"You must read minds," she says. "Let's go."

7. LIFE IN THE FAST LANE

The weed is schwag—Kirby got it from her Spring Street dealer, Pope, whose product is inconsistent—but it hardly matters because Kirby is with Larry Winter! Kirby stole him right out from under Blair's nose!

It's a triumph worthy of its own *Cosmo* column: "When Dreams Come True: Hooking Up with Your Teenage Crush as a Grown Woman."

Seventeen years earlier, in 1962, back when Kennedy was president, Kirby harbored an excruciating crush on Larry Winter, but he had been in love with Blair. Kirby used to babysit Larry's pain-in-the-ass little sisters, and Larry would be saddled with the task of driving Kirby home at the end of the afternoon. Kirby was only fourteen; she wore braces and had acne across her forehead and was every bit the ugly duckling. Larry, meanwhile, was a man—seventeen, eighteen—headed to Georgetown to major in political science. He wanted to run for president.

Later reports from Mrs. Winter that were relayed to Kirby from Exalta indicated he'd gone in a different direction. After college, Larry worked as the food and beverage manager at a private club in Vero Beach, Florida.

Kirby won't lie: it was disappointing to hear this.

But then, recently, Exalta made a point of mentioning that one of the wealthy members of the Vero Beach

Club had given Larry seed money and he was opening a nightclub in Key Largo.

A nightclub! That was something Kirby could get behind.

She isn't at all surprised that Larry accepted her offer of a toke because everyone in the nightclub world partook of a little something—usually more than a little and occasionally more than one thing. She also isn't surprised when Larry exhales, winces, and says as he passes the joint back to Kirby, "This shit is terrible."

"I know," Kirby says. "Sorry. I do have some powder if you want to snort a line."

"What?" Larry says. "You mean...*cocaine?*" He sounds completely scandalized and Kirby rolls her eyes, but it's dark so he doesn't see. *You own a* nightclub? she thinks. *In the Florida* Keys? *Just south of Miami, which might as well be named* Cocaine City?

"Yes," Kirby says. "I mean cocaine." She has a glass vial hanging from a chain around her neck; she pulls it over her head, taps out a tiny amount onto the back of her thumb, and snorts it up. "Want a line?"

"No, I don't want a *line!*" Larry says. "You should be ashamed of yourself. You just did cocaine right in front of me."

"Are you stuck in the Stone Age?" Kirby asks. "Because you sound like Fred Flintstone. I wouldn't have pegged you as being so...square."

Even in the dark, she can see Larry grin. His teeth

are so white, she wonders if they're fake. "I'm not square," he says. "I was putting you on. Of course I want a line."

Ha! Oh, boy, Kirby is relieved. She had a vision of Larry tattling on her to Mrs. Winter or, worse, Kate, and then it would be straight to rehab for Kirby. She had thought twice about bringing the cocaine to Nantucket because no one on the island partied this way, but her gamble paid off. She is going to fly high with her teenage crush Larry Winter.

She taps out a bump for Larry and he hoovers it right up, then sniffs, waiting for the rush to hit.

"God*damn!*" he cries out at the ocean. He turns back to Kirby, who has capped the vial and tucked it back down her dress. "Is it all right if I kiss you?"

Hell yes! Kirby thinks—and a second later, she and Larry Winter are making out. But something is wrong. Larry's mouth is open too wide; it feels like he's trying to swallow her. Maybe it's the drugs, or maybe he's just completely inept. Their teeth clash, making a plasticky sound, and Kirby thinks, *Definitely false teeth.*

She pulls away. "Easy there, cowboy." She can feel Larry's erection through his tight polyester pants. The *Cosmo* girl in her is mildly intrigued; it's bigger than she imagined—but Kirby can't decide how far she wants this to go. She finds herself in this position all the time when she's out. She'll be dancing with some guy and he'll want more, and if he's cute or ugly but confident, she'll lead him to her secret alcove and kiss him. But she always remains in control of the situation. Occasionally this leads to sex in Kirby's loft; she never goes home with anyone and she never, ever has sex in the club. Part of being a liberated woman, she tells the girls at the magazine — they hang on Kirby's every word — is remaining free to walk away at any moment.

Larry grabs the back of Kirby's head and puts his sloppy mouth on hers like she's a Big Mac. She pushes him off again. "Whoa, buddy, let's slow things down a little." In an attempt to be tender, she reaches up to touch his long feathered hair. It's soft and silky between her fingers. Larry Winter has good hair, like David Cassidy's, and hasn't Kirby always wanted to have sex with David Cassidy? She moves her hands so that she's stroking Larry's long mustache. He used to be so clean-cut — he was an Exeter squash player when he dated Goody Two-shoes Blair — and Kirby can't help but be delighted by his transformation into a modern man. He isn't living back in the Eisenhower administration like everyone else on this land-that-time-forgot island.

They start kissing again but it isn't any better and Larry's hands are sliding down her back toward her...

She pulls away. "Larry."

He says, "You are so...*cool*, Kirby. You give off this incredible vibe — sexy, fun, *fascinating*. I can't believe I spent so many summers mooning over Blair. I should have been with you."

The music from the bonfire floats down the beach. "Rebel, Rebel" by David Bowie. This is Kirby's song.

You've torn your dress... Your face is a mess. Who is Kirby if not the rebel of her family? She was the one who protested the war, swore at the cops, got arrested, got pregnant out of wedlock, and dated a rainbow of men, including the "one who got away," Darren Frazier. Darren ended up marrying Kirby's best friend, Rajani, and they now have four beautiful children, which was what motivated Kirby to leave Boston and move to New York, where she has managed to push herself even closer to the edge. Misbehaving is the only way Kirby has ever been able to steal the spotlight from perfect achiever Blair, golden only son Tiger, and precious baby Jessie.

But now, here is Larry Winter telling Kirby that he prefers her to her older sister. All the longing and jealousy that fourteen-year-old Kirby, with her braces and her acne, felt vanishes—*poof!*—in that moment. Her attraction to Larry Winter was never about Larry Winter, she realizes. It was about how she felt about herself. The satisfaction of being acknowledged as a sexy, fun, *fascinating* (this adjective gives Kirby a particular thrill) woman is more powerful than any drug.

"Hey, thanks, Larry," she says. "Now, if you'll excuse me, it's time I got back to the party."

8. Looks Like We Made It

Tiger can't believe it when Magee asks him to bring her some beer from the keg, and he's even more surprised when she chugs the entire thing without stopping. Who is this woman and what has she done with his wife?

She emits a ladylike burp and hands him the empty plastic cup. "Another."

"Another?" Tiger says. "Seriously?"

"Please?" she says. "I want to get drunk."

"You..." Tiger can't believe this. "Are you sure?"

"Your grandmother is dead," Magee says. "And do you know what advice she gave me?"

Tiger is afraid to ask. "What?"

"She said, 'When you don't know what else to do, have a good, stiff drink.'"

Yes, Tiger thinks, *that does sound like Exalta.*

"And I don't know what else to do," Magee says. "We've tried everything."

"But you've been so careful with your health—"

"It's not working!" Magee says. "So I'm going to try the opposite."

"Okay," Tiger says. He's skeptical but he fetches Magee another cold beer and, when she finishes that, another. That's three beers, but Magee isn't done. She wants something more, something stronger.

"Something *stronger?*" Tiger says. "There isn't anything stronger at this party."

"The flask," she says. "In your glove compartment."

"Ha!" Tiger says. Guess he should have known he couldn't keep a secret from his wife. There's a flask of

Wild Turkey that Tiger keeps in the glove box of the Trans Am. Tiger offers the flask to any Vietnam vet he happens to meet.

Magee is a veteran of sorts, he supposes. She put in all those hours of service to Exalta.

"All right," Tiger says. "I'll get the flask." He grabs it from the car, and he and Magee both take a pull. Magee doesn't cough or sputter; she doesn't even grimace. She is tougher than half the guys in the Fourth Infantry.

Later, Tiger and Magee dance in the sand. The song is by the Bee Gees, "Tragedy." But instead of a tragedy, the night feels like a miracle. Magee is joyfully, ecstatically blotto. She raises her hands in the air; she twirls around, sings along. It takes no convincing for Tiger to lead Magee down the beach with one of the kilim rugs rolled under his arm. They lay the rug out in a secluded spot in the dunes and they make love in a way that they never have before. Magee is uninhibited, carefree, wild. She leaves scratch marks down his back, bites his ear, thrusts right along with him until she screams. Screams!

Tiger falls back on the rug, breathless.

Best of my life, he thinks. "Did that feel . . . different to you?" he asks.

"Oh, yes," she says. She props herself up on her elbow and grins at him. "Mark my words, Tiger Foley: nine months from now, you're going to be a father."

9. REUNITED

Jessie didn't learn what she knows about love from being with Theo Feigelbaum. No—Jessie's first teacher in lessons of the heart is the man with the shorn head who is now sitting next to her: Pickford Crimmins. Pick.

Jessie jumps to her feet. "Pick?" she says. "I thought you were in…Africa?"

"I was," Pick says. "I got home to Cali last week. And then I called Bill and he told me about Exalta, so I hitched a ride with a buddy who was going to Philadelphia and I took a bus the rest of the way."

"I can't…I don't…wow." Jessie needs to get a grip. "So, how was the Peace Corps? You were in…"

"Kenya," he says. "I worked in Nairobi for a while digging wells. Then I was sent out to the Mara, the Kenyan savanna. It was incredible, Jess. It was like an episode of *Wild Kingdom* every day. We saw a giraffe give birth, a cheetah kill, prides of lions, baby elephants, the black rhino. For six weeks, I lived with the Maasai villagers. I learned how to shoot a bow and arrow. I drank cow's blood. I learned the tribal dances."

Jessie nods dumbly. She'd thought it was amazing that she got an A in her torts class and managed to successfully transport two corned-beef sandwiches on the subway.

"I'm sorry I didn't have any time to write letters

home," Pick says. "I'm sure Bill thought I dropped off the face of the earth."

"He's proud of you," Jessie says, which she's sure is true, though Mr. Crimmins never says much about his own family, probably because his daughter, Lorraine, who lives on a commune in California, has caused so much anxiety and confusion for the Foley-Levins. Jessie knew Pick went to Africa with the Peace Corps, and she'd been glad, hadn't she? Partly because she liked knowing that Pick was contributing in a positive way to the world and partly because Africa was so remote that Jessie's lingering feelings for him became a moot point.

Pick settles back into the sand and Jessie follows suit. The party rages behind them but Jessie doesn't care. Pick is here.

"So," he says. "Tell me about everyone. Actually, forget everyone. Tell me about you."

"I live in Greenwich Village," Jessie says. "I'm a second-year law student at NYU."

"Law school," Pick says. "Like your dad."

"I guess," Jessie says. The law that David practices — corporate litigation — is last on Jessie's list of interests. "I want to practice immigration law. Or maybe work for the ACLU. I want to help people."

"That's my girl," Pick says.

Jessie wonders if she's trying to make herself sound altruistic in order to impress Pick. She has never before mentioned immigration or civil rights law. If she'd said this to Theo, he would have gone on a diatribe about Jessie's "privilege." She could *afford* to practice immigration law; hell, she could become a public *defender*—because she had a trust fund. But as for Theo, he was looking at a big-firm, big-money future. He wanted to be in-house counsel at a Wall Street bank.

"I made Bill promise to tell me if you got married," Pick says, "so I could come home and disrupt the wedding like Benjamin in *The Graduate*."

Jessie smiles. "You did not."

"I did."

"Well, I'm not married."

"Boyfriend?"

"Theo," she says, and even though Pick is sitting a foot away from her, she can feel him tense up. "But we broke up. He cheated on me."

"What an idiot," Pick says.

Jessie nudges him with her elbow. "You're one to talk."

"What?"

"That summer you lived with us, you left me in the dust for Sabrina."

"Sabrina who?"

"Sabrina was... the girl you worked with at the North Shore restaurant. You started dating her."

"Oh," Pick says. "I don't remember Sabrina."

"You *don't?*" Jessie says. She finds this unfair. Jessie had been crushed when Pick introduced her to Sabrina one fateful day at Surfside Beach; it was a moment that has both haunted her and served as a cautionary tale. When you fall in love, your heart opens in a burst of flower petals and gossamer streamers. But beware, because that same heart can just as quickly be cored like an apple, the most tender piece of you extracted and thrown onto the compost pile of the unrequited. For the past ten years, Sabrina—not the girl herself but the specter of someone prettier and more desirable— has haunted Jessie, inspired her even.

"You kissed me," Jessie says. "Twice. You really kissed me."

"Yes," Pick says. "That I do remember. Upstairs in the cottage."

"And then a couple of days later, you were dating Sabrina."

"*I'm* the idiot, then," Pick says. "All I remember is that you were young—too young. I thought I'd get in trouble if anything else happened. The dynamic between me and your family was weird. I didn't know why at the time, but I know now. And I'm assuming you know?"

"That Wilder Foley was your father?" Jessie says. "Yes." Wilder Foley was Kate's first husband, the father of Blair, Kirby, and Tiger; he'd had an affair with Lorraine Crimmins and gotten her pregnant. So Pick is a half sibling to Blair, Kirby, and Tiger, just like Jessie.

"When my mother and I left Woodstock that summer, I told her I wanted to go back to Nantucket to live with my grandfather. And she said we had burned that bridge forever."

Jessie takes a breath. Conversations like this happen all the time at funerals and weddings and baptisms, she knows. Secrets are revealed; there are reckonings.

"How *is* your mother?" Jessie asks, desperate to change the subject.

"Oh, fine," Pick says. "Busy with her organic farming, which is actually starting to make her some money. She fully believes organic produce is the future."

Jessie hasn't the foggiest idea what "organic" produce is, but she doesn't admit that.

"Now tell me about everyone else," Pick says. "Blair, Kirby, Tiger." He laughs. "Our siblings."

The phrase is so surreal that Jessie is stymied for a moment. But then she laughs along and starts to talk: *Blair and Angus divorced...Angus in Houston, Blair and the twins in a suburb of Boston...Kirby writes for* Cosmo; *if you pick up any issue at the grocery-store checkout, you'll see her byline, she lives in SoHo, housesitting for this famous artist, Willie Eight, yeah, I'd never heard of him either, the only artists I know are dead except for Andy Warhol, who Kirby has met, she has a Polaroid of them together, she hangs out at Studio 54 and Limelight, dancing the night away...Tiger is married to Magee, they don't have kids yet, Tiger owns five bowling alleys and he drives that Trans Am you probably saw...He's a good person, my brother, I just want him to be happy.* Jessie finds her eyes are burning with tears as she says this. *I want them all to be happy, and if I had a magic wand, that would be my first and only wish—for Blair, Kirby, and Tiger to be happy.*

"What about you?" Pick says. "Don't you want to be happy?"

Jessie isn't sure how to explain it. She knows, somehow, that she is stronger than her three siblings. This is a bold statement because the three of them are big personalities; her sisters are beautiful and smart, and her brother is a war hero. But Jessie worries about them in a way that she doesn't worry about herself.

"I am happy," she says. "Though I could use another beer. And you should mingle. I don't want to monopolize you."

"I have to tell you something," Pick says. He gets to his feet and offers Jessie a hand to pull her up. "I'm moving to New York."

"You are?" Jessie says.

"I was offered a job with the Economic and Social Council at the UN," Pick says. "Which probably sounds fancier than it is. The pay is peanuts. I'm going to have to live in Brooklyn."

Brooklyn? Jessie tries not to cringe. "That's great!" she says. "We'll be neighbors."

Pick is still holding on to Jessie's hand. "Hopefully more than just neighbors," he says. "You know, when I was in Kenya, I had this recurring fantasy." He pauses. "Want to hear it?"

Fantasy? Jessie panics, thinking of the one awkward evening when Theo insisted on reading *Penthouse* Forum letters aloud to her. "Sure?" she says.

"My buddy Tremaine, who I shared a tent with out

in the Mara, had this tape recorder and three cassette tapes, one of which was *The Stranger* by Billy Joel. He played it *all* the time, and do you know that song 'Scenes from an Italian Restaurant'?"

"Bottle of red," Jessie sings.

"Bottle of white!" Pick cries out. "Yes! So I always thought of you when I heard that song and I dreamed about meeting you in New York City at a restaurant like that. Red-checkered tablecloths, a single candle dripping down the Chianti bottle, the whole deal." He shrugs. "I thought it would be romantic."

Me, Jessie thinks. *He dreamed about meeting me.*

"So when I get to New York, can we do that?" Pick asks. "Can we meet at a place like that?"

"Of course," Jessie says. She doesn't eat out at restaurants; she has no money. But the instant she gets back to the city, she's going to find the best Italian place in *all* of New York. Oh, man, you'd better believe it.

10. WE ARE FAMILY

The kids are all at the bonfire, which leaves Kate and David at home alone. They watch the sunset and David opens a bottle of Pol Roger champagne. When Kate raises an eyebrow at the significance—Is David *celebrating* Exalta's death? They did always have an uneasy relationship—he says, "Something to cheer you up."

He's right, as always; the bubbles cheer her up. It's an unusually warm evening, so they drink with their feet dangling in the pool, the bottle in an ice bucket between them.

Kate's thoughts wander. Where is Exalta now? Anywhere? It seems impossible that she's gone, and yet that's what happens to all of us, eventually. It's a reminder to live while we can and take care with the legacy we're leaving behind. Kate feels proud of this house, this property, the decision she made ten years ago to move out here to the wilds of Madaket and build a summer retreat where she can shelter her entire family. It had seemed radical at the time, Kate remembers.

"Do you want to go out to dinner?" David asks. "The Mad Hatter? DeMarco's?"

"It's too late," Kate says. "Everyone stops serving at nine."

"We could still order a pizza from Vincent's," David says. "Or skip dinner and get ice cream."

Kate says, "Let's do something crazy."

She can tell from the way his face brightens that he thinks she means sex there in the pool or scouring Kirby's bedroom for a joint to smoke.

"I'm game," he says.

"Let's crash the party," Kate says. "We'll pick up Bill and take him with us."

It feels like a joy ride, even in David's staid lawyer car, the Cadillac. They have the windows down, Elvis on the radio, and Bill Crimmins—who Kate thought might be hesitant to join them—lounging across the back seat, enjoying the fine leather.

"I'm so glad you called," Bill says. "The house feels too big now that she's gone."

"But Pick is staying with you," Kate says. She's relieved that Pick has shown up—as long as Lorraine is safely on the West Coast—so that there's someone to keep an eye on Bill.

They rumble down Barrett Farm Road through the open landscape until they come upon a line of parked cars, and Kate hears music. She climbs out of the Cadillac in her bare feet. She's wearing a paisley beach cover-up, which is the only thing in her closet that looks even vaguely exotic. If Kate travels back a hundred years—okay, forty—she's a teenager being naughty, sneaking out of All's Fair while her parents sleep and hopping in the back of Trip Belknap's Studebaker, heading to a fire just like this one, populated with boys who do not yet know they'll soon be heading off to war.

Tonight, instead of defying her parents, Kate is defying her children.

Young people only. Bah!

Kate is nearly to the beach when she sees a young couple huddled together, obviously trying to make a clandestine escape.

"Blair?" Kate says. Blair is with . . . Joey Whalen. Surprise, surprise.

"Mom?" Blair says. Her face has always been easy to read and her expression now is one of sheer horror. She's been caught. With Joey.

Joey doesn't look caught, however. Joey is too smooth to ever look caught. "Hey, Mrs. Levin, Mr. Levin, Mr. Crimmins," he says. He spins around and flings his arm open like a game-show host, as though the beach and the fire and the assembled crowd and even the ocean beyond are their grand prize. "Welcome!"

Blair and Joey together — is that such a bad thing? Kate wonders. Joey Whalen is much better suited to Blair's temperament than Angus ever was.

Joey and Blair dutifully escort the old people with their brittle bones down to the sand.

Blair takes Kate's elbow. "What are you doing here, Mom?"

Kate wants to say, *You are hardly one to be asking questions.* But instead, she smiles. "I came to party," she says, and this sounds so absurd, they both laugh. "Would you fetch me a drink, please, dear, and let your brother and sisters know I'm here."

"There's nothing to drink except keg beer," Blair says.

"That's fine," Kate says. "I'll have a beer."

"You will?"

"I will."

Blair returns with a foamy beer in a plastic cup, and clearly she has also made the announcement because soon Kate is surrounded by her children — Tiger, along with Magee, both of whom look happier and more relaxed than Kate has seen them in years; Kirby, who Kate expected to be angry but who instead throws her arms around her mother in what appears to be glee; and Jessie, who's with an incredibly handsome, upright young man whom Kate recognizes as Pick Crimmins.

The song changes and a cry goes up. The kids form a circle and start dancing. This, Kate knows, is her cue to exit, but suddenly David is on one side of her and Bill Crimmins is on the other and they, too, are part of the circle.

The lyrics announce the obvious: *We are family!*

Kirby dances in the middle of the circle and everyone cheers her on. She is replaced by Jessie, and Jessie is replaced by Magee.

Magee can really dance. How did Kate not know this?

Magee heads straight for Kate with her arms outstretched.

"Your turn, darling," David says, placing an encouraging hand on Kate's back.

My turn? Kate thinks. Surely not. Exalta would never in a million years have been caught in the middle of a circle dancing to a disco song.

It takes only a second for Kate to realize that she isn't Exalta. She is Kate Nichols Foley Levin, the new matriarch of this gathered family. She is in charge now and she will make her own decisions.

Kate passes her cup to David and dances through the sand to the center of the circle. Her family cheers.

That's right, she thinks. She may be old, but she still has some surprises left.

Summer of '89

(Read with *Summer of '69* and "Summer of '79")

This novella has never been published!

As soon as I published "Summer of '79," the requests flooded in: *Please write "Summer of '89."* I was happy to oblige, because the 1980s were "my" decade, though I do feel like the "true" '80s were 1981 to 1987, my junior-high and high-school years. My sister and I would get dropped at the roller-skating rink; I raced home from the bus every afternoon to watch *General Hospital* (especially the week that Luke and Laura got married). I mourned the loss of my father in a plane crash in November of 1985; I fell in love for the first time; I played clarinet in the marching band; I was inducted into the National Honor Society, then got in big trouble on a class trip. I worked in Men's Accessories at Gimbels at the King of Prussia mall and drove to and from work in a 1976 Buick Skylark that I shared with my twin brother. I was voted Most Likely to

Succeed. I decided to attend Johns Hopkins and major in creative writing—and while all this was happening, I was listening to the radio, specifically 93.3 WMMR out of Philadelphia. In 1982, I loved Rick Springfield. In 1985, I discovered Bruce Springsteen, thanks to a babysitting job. In 1987, I loved Billy Joel (I spent all night waiting for tickets outside the mall) and Cat Stevens and Elton John.

In the summer of 1989, between my sophomore and junior years at Johns Hopkins (also immortalized as the summer of the Indigo Girls), I lived outside Boston with my aunt and uncle, and I would drive to my family's house on the Cape on the weekends. I worked at a summer-enrichment program at UMass Boston, where I tutored gifted middle-school students from underserved public schools. What I remember best about that summer is that it rained every single weekend—but in this novella, the sun is shining!

1. She Drives Me Crazy

Jessica Levin (rhymes with *heaven*) endures "planes, trains, and automobiles"—the subway from her Midtown law office to JFK, a flight from New York to Boston, a bus from Boston to Cape Cod—and reaches the ferry to Nantucket with five minutes to spare.

Phew! When the bus got stuck in traffic going over the Sagamore Bridge, Jessie became convinced she was going to miss her boat, and the next forty-five minutes played out like a thriller—would she make it or wouldn't she?

She would! She's here! The adrenaline coursing through Jessie propels her all the way to the top deck, where she liked to sit when she was a kid.

She collapses in a molded plastic chair in the midst of what feels like a wild Friday night at the Odeon; she has unwittingly joined party *central*. Leaning against the railing is some guy in Nantucket Reds, an alligator shirt, and a navy blazer with a can of Meister Bräu in each hand, a boom box wedged between his L. L. Bean moccasins, and a Brat Pack snarl on his face. Jessie overhears a girl in a snug neon-pink minidress call him "Blowman" — no surprise there.

Blowman appears to be a few years older than Jessie; he's probably a bond trader at Drexel Burnham, where all the criminals work. While she's assessing him, he catches her eye and offers her one of the beers in his hand.

"You look like you could use an attitude adjustment," he says.

Jessie glares at him over the tops of her Wayfarers. "No, thank you."

Blowman recoils like Jessie has tried to bite his nose and she nearly laughs. She loathes all Wall Street types and has made it her job to hold them accountable. She would love to tell Blowman that she has just represented three women in a sexual-harassment case against the investment bank behemoth Arnolds and Major and only the day before won her clients a million-dollar decision.

One million dollars! The decision had been called "landmark" that very morning in the *Post*. Suddenly, it seems not impossible that Jessie will be made a senior partner before she turns thirty-five. The only thing better than the win is that the opposing counsel was Theo Feigelbaum, Jessie's boyfriend during her first and second years at law school. The reason Jessie took the case for the three plaintiffs (other than wanting to help out womankind) was that she knew Theo was Arnolds and Major's in-house counsel and she couldn't resist going head-to-head with him.

The boom box between Blowman's feet plays a halfway decent mixtape—Billy Joel, Dire Straits, the Cure. Jessie *does* need an attitude adjustment, because despite the million-dollar decision and despite slicing Theo as thin as the corned beef he used to love so much, Jessie is filled with leaden dread about the weekend ahead. She's heading to the island to celebrate her niece's and nephew's twentieth birthday; Jessie has been dreaming about the beach, about floating in her mother's swimming pool and playing tennis against her nephew George at the Field and Oar Club. But the night before, Jessie's longtime boyfriend, Pick Crimmins, received a phone call with some unsettling news. Now Jessie suspects her weekend will be spent trying to keep her mother, Kate, from committing murder.

And Pick isn't there to help her. He left that morning for West Berlin, where he's representing the UN's Economic and Social Council; he thinks it will be only a matter of months, maybe weeks, until the Berlin Wall comes down.

Jessie sighs. She misses him already. The conflict between East and West Germany might be easier to sort out than what Jessie is facing on Nantucket.

After disembarking, Jessie watches as her fellow passengers are picked up by friends in beat-up Jeeps or frosted-haired matrons in woody wagons or—in the case of Blowman—by a shiny beige Humvee with tinted windows that very clearly has never seen a day of combat. Soon Jessie is the only one left waiting, her weekend bag and her bulging briefcase at her feet. She looks toward the terminal, wondering if she'll have to go in and use the pay phone. She called her mother immediately after Pick shared his news the night before. But it was late and Kate had just gotten home from an evening out with her friend Bitsy Dunscombe. They had gone for a "Madaket mystery or two" at the Westender, and because Jessie wanted to deliver Pick's news when Kate was sober, she ended up telling her mother only that she would be arriving the next day on the five o'clock ferry.

Kate might have had three or four Madaket mysteries, Jessie thinks, because it seems she's forgotten all about her promise that "someone" would drive "all the way to town" to pick Jessie up.

Jessie's father, David, had died of prostate cancer in January, and Jessie is, frankly, alarmed at how tidily Kate has dealt with her grief. She is having a far easier time of it than Jessie, who still cries several times a week in a stall of the firm's ladies' room. Kate, meanwhile, seems lighter, sprightlier, possibly even *happier* than she's ever been.

That happiness will be dampened once Jessie talks to her.

Jessie wanted to call one of her siblings to share the

burden of what Pick had learned, but Blair is in Paris doing research for her dissertation on Edith Wharton and Tiger and Magee have four little boys ages nine to three, which is the definition of "having their hands full." So Jessie set aside a months-long grudge and called Kirby out in Los Angeles, where it was still a reasonable hour—but she got Kirby's answering machine. Despite Jessie's vow not to speak to Kirby until she issued an apology for what she'd done, Jessie left a desperate message. "Kirby, it's Jessie, I really need to talk to you. Really, Kirby, so please call me back, no matter how late."

Kirby had made no secret of the fact that she moved to California to escape her family. How she described them to the fabulous Hollywood people she met wasn't something Jessie liked to dwell on. She probably claimed she was an orphan.

Was that harsh? Maybe—but Jessie lay in bed awake half the night and Kirby didn't call back.

Kate has been billing this coming weekend as a "family reunion." (*Do two more troublesome words exist?* Jessie wonders.) While it's true that Tiger and Magee and the boys will be arriving tomorrow, and that George, who is interning for Massachusetts congressman Bill Welby, is bringing his "new girlfriend," and that Genevieve is spending the entire summer living on Nantucket with Kate, it can't properly be called a family reunion when neither Blair nor Kirby will be there.

Jessie will be the only one of her mother's daughters present. This feels like a setup.

Just as Jessie is starting to regret not taking Blowman up on his offer of a beer, the family's rattletrap car pulls into the parking lot—a 1967 International Scout that still somehow runs.

Behind the wheel is... it takes Jessie a second to realize that the person with the hot-pink flattop crew cut, a left ear pierced with safety pins, and a tattoo of a toadstool on her forearm is her niece, Genevieve Foley Whalen.

Things are even worse than Jessie thought.

"Genevieve, hey!" Jessie says, her mind reeling. The hair, the piercings, the tattoo—it's a lot to take in. What does Blair think about this? Jessie wonders. What does *Kate* think about it? And why didn't anyone warn Jessie that Genevieve looks like someone pulled from the bottom of a mosh pit? Jessie has tried to be a good aunt, monitoring the twins' interests and styles over the years. In middle school, Genevieve was into the *Preppy Handbook;* she wore Fair Isle sweaters, a grosgrain-ribbon headband, pearl earrings. Then Genevieve fell prey to Madonna fashion—lace hair bows and fifty rubber bracelets. When Jessie saw Genevieve two summers ago, before she started at Brown, she had been wearing acid-washed jeans shorts and a banana clip in her unfortunately permed hair.

"Hey." Genevieve stares straight ahead, her black-lipsticked mouth in an impatient line.

Jessie is tempted to make a comment about Genevieve's appearance, but she practices her lawyering skills and considers Genevieve's motives. Why the piercings? Why the tattoo? Is it just teenage rebellion, which Kirby perfected a generation earlier? Or is it self-loathing?

The twins have experienced their share of upheaval. Blair and Angus split when the kids were in fourth grade and then Blair married Angus's brother, Joey Whalen. Blair had tried to normalize this—Joey was the brother she *should* have been with all along, she claimed. He was the charming, outgoing one, whereas Angus was strange, antisocial, and too smart for his own good. This may have been so, but the arrangement left her children with a stepfather who was also their uncle. It had a whiff of incest about it until it was explained to people. (Of course, the same might be said about Jessie and Pick's relationship, since they are both the half siblings of Blair, Kirby, and Tiger, albeit on different sides.)

An anthropologist would have a field day at their family reunion.

Angus cut all ties with his brother, communicated with Blair only through their attorneys, and refused to ever travel back to Massachusetts. For a while, George and Genevieve flew to Houston on their vacations, but George stopped going his freshman year in high school, saying he'd rather stay home and hang out with his friends. Genevieve, who was proving to be a formidable intellect herself, continued to travel to Houston, where Angus would bring her to work with him at NASA headquarters. He was the space shuttle program's manager on the *Challenger* mission that was scheduled to launch in January 1986. Genevieve had gotten special permission to take a week off from school so she could meet Angus in Cape Canaveral and watch the launch in person—from the control tower, no less!

Jessie remembers the whole country's excitement about the *Challenger* launch; Christa McAuliffe, a civilian teacher, would be aboard. Jessie was disappointed when they delayed the time of the launch, because she had court at eleven and wouldn't be able to watch like she'd planned. When her case adjourned and Jessie stepped out into the courthouse hallway, she sensed something wrong. People everywhere were huddled together, crying. A bailiff she'd become friendly with named Moses took Jessie's arm and said, "Have you heard?"

The *Challenger* had exploded. All seven crew members were dead.

Jessie hailed a cab and took it back to her Midtown office. She tried to call Blair at home, but the line was busy. Jessie had to remind herself that Genevieve and Angus were physically safe—but what about mentally? Could you watch that kind of epic tragedy *in person* and survive with your psyche intact?

Apparently, Angus had expressed repeated concerns about launching the shuttle in such cold weather; the temperatures in Cape Canaveral that day had been just above freezing, the delays due to ice. Angus was specifically worried about the rubber O-rings in the solid rocket booster not forming a seal in such low temperatures. But Angus had a reputation for being a nervous Nellie and his superiors at NASA were receiving political pressure to *just launch the damn thing, already.*

Immediately following the disaster, Angus took a leave of absence from NASA; the following September, he taught classes at Rice University but made it only halfway through the semester before he had a nervous breakdown.

Genevieve, meanwhile, returned home to Boston with a certain macabre celebrity, and she embraced it. Her college essay took the form of a letter from the *Challenger* project manager to NASA administrators explaining all the reasons why the launch should have been delayed. That essay got Genevieve into Harvard, Stanford, Duke, Princeton, and Brown.

It was at the start of Genevieve's freshman year at Brown — and George's at Babson — that Blair discovered Joey Whalen had a mistress up in Montreal. By the time the twins came home for Thanksgiving, Blair had kicked Joey out and filed for divorce.

George handled this news with the same equanimity he'd displayed his entire life. Some people were just like that, Jessie had learned; they sat in the middle of the seesaw and were unbothered when it tipped one way or the other.

Genevieve, however, slid right off the end and into

a figurative mud puddle. She started dating the drummer in a band called Fungus that played the underground punk clubs in Providence and Pawtucket.

"She told me she's done something to her hair that I'm not going to like," Blair reported to Jessie over the phone.

"Something like another perm?" Jessie said. She, too, had broken down and gotten a perm and now she looked like Gilda Radner if Gilda had stuck her finger in a socket. "Or crazy like a mohawk?" The phrase *underground punk clubs* was not encouraging.

"She didn't elaborate."

Blair had sounded pretty sanguine as she relayed this news. Jessie said, "Do you think you should go down there overnight, maybe take her to dinner?"

Blair laughed. "She won't have dinner with me, Jessie. She says *I'm* the reason she's so messed up." Blair sighed. "Boys are so much easier."

Jessie had wanted to reply that not only was this answer a cop-out, it also sounded disturbingly like something their own mother might say.

Jessie had considered taking the train to Providence to lay eyes on Genevieve herself but she was busy with work and she didn't want to overstep her bounds, and she came up with any number of other excuses for not making time to see her niece, so this state Genevieve is now in may be partially Jessie's fault.

"How's your summer been?" Jessie asks. "Are you working?"

"Why, yes!" Genevieve says in a surprisingly bright tone. "I'm the floor manager in women's fashion at Murray's Toggery. I won employee of the week for selling the most Pappagallo."

Jessica blinks. "So you're not working?"

"Grammy set me up with two interviews, one at the needlepoint shop and one at the watercolor gallery," Genevieve says. She arches an eyebrow, also pierced. "I'm not working."

"What about your boyfriend?" Jessie says. "Are you still with the drummer?"

They're at the top of Main Street, and the Scout judders over the cobblestones in a way that feels violent.

"Mouth?" Genevieve says. "I'm not sure."

Jessie clenches her jaw until they reach the smoother terrain of Madaket Road. A drummer named Mouth in a band called Fungus. It dawns on her that this is probably the meaning behind the toadstool tattoo. "What does that mean, you're not sure?"

"Well," Genevieve says. "He has a wife."

Jessie waits a beat to see if Genevieve is joking about this the way she was joking about selling Pappagallo, but then Jessie notices Genevieve's eyes filling with tears, and the Scout swerves over the center line. When Jessie instinctively reaches for the wheel, Genevieve yanks it away like it's a toy Jessie is trying to steal. "Why don't you pull over?" Jessie says. "I can drive." Madaket Road famously has twenty-seven curves and they're only at number one.

"I can drive!" Genevieve says, though mascara-darkened tears are streaking her whitish foundation.

"Gennie, please," Jessie says. She points to the parking lot at Sanford Farm up ahead. With a huff, Genevieve smacks her hand down on the turn signal and whips them in.

After they switch places, Genevieve releases great, hiccupy sobs and Jessie reaches over to rub her niece's shoulder. Jessie's only thirteen years older than Genevieve, so she feels like she's in a unique position to impart some wisdom. She has experienced her own heartbreak; the first time was with Pick the summer that Genevieve and George were born. Jessie fell for Pick the instant she laid eyes on him — he was making a BLT in their guest cottage, Little Fair — and later that summer, he had been her first kiss. But then Pick started dating a girl he worked with at the North Shore restaurant. Even now, after Jessie and Pick have been together for ten years — three dating, seven living together — Jessie can still recall the specific nature of that pain, so fresh and intense it was nearly beautiful.

Then, years later, as a student at NYU's law school, Jessie had suffered through a breakup with Theo Feigelbaum, which left her more angry than sad.

"I know how you feel," Jessie says.

Genevieve's laugh is a single, startling gunshot. "You don't."

"Fair enough," Jessie says. "But I can promise you, you won't always feel this bad. You'll meet someone else —"

"I don't *want* anyone else!"

Jessie nods—she's doing a terrible job here, throwing gasoline on the smoldering fire of Genevieve's emotions with every word that comes out of her mouth. *Let it go,* she thinks. She doesn't need to take on Genevieve's drama; she'll have enough on her hands when she tells her mother the news. But when Jessie turns the key in the ignition, she hears faint, familiar strains of a song she loves, and she turns it up. Then, as a symbolic gesture, she releases her hair from its tight professional bun and pulls out onto Madaket Road. She wants to create a cinematic moment—two young women driving along a curvy island road, wind in their hair, singing at the top of their lungs: *She drives me crazy! And I can't help myself!*

But Jessie's fantasy fizzles when Genevieve switches the radio off.

"I hate that song."

Jessie tries not to take offense. Genevieve probably listens to bands Jessie has never heard of; she has a sense that in the world of punk, to be authentic is to be obscure. But in Genevieve's determination to be disagreeable, Jessie hears a cry for help, and Jessie decides that, no matter what it takes, she will find a way to bond with her niece. She will forge a real connection this weekend. She will become Genevieve's trusted person, a mentor, a life raft.

Genevieve says something Jessie doesn't hear. "What's that?" Jessie says. She slows the car a bit.

"I said, I wish Aunt Kirby had come. She's so cool."

Jessie blinks. Kirby, whom none of them have heard from in months and who didn't bother returning the urgent message Jessie left on her answering machine, is cool?

Jessie takes the next curve so fast that Genevieve grabs the dashboard and Jessie thinks, *Who's cool now?*

"Dude!" Genevieve cries out.

"There are still twenty-five curves left before home," Jessie says. "Better buckle up." Then she comes to her senses and eases off the gas. It's amazing how quickly being with her family has turned Jessie back into a child.

2. LOVE SHACK

It's nearly midnight when George and Sallie reach All's Fair. The street is poorly lit, the neighbors' windows are all dark, and when George lifts the welcome mat, he can't find the key. His kingdom for a flashlight. The key must be there somewhere, but when George gets down on his knees and runs his hands over the damp wooden deck boards beneath the mat, he feels nothing but pill bugs, which make him snap back in a way that is seriously uncool, and he mustn't appear uncool in any way in front of Sallie.

"I'm not sure what's happening," George says. "The key is always there. It's been there for the past forty years."

Sallie shifts the bag from Savenor's in her arms — she insisted on bringing sun-dried tomatoes and the Iberian ham that she likes — and says, "Is there another way in?"

George now regrets stopping at the Club Car for martinis on their way from the ferry. He had three drinks to Sallie's one, using the Kentucky driver's license of an older clerk in Welby's office. (The bartender had frowned at it and said, "Is this thing real?," to which George responded in what he believed to be a convincing bourbon-and-racehorse drawl, "What do y'all think?") When he ordered the third martini, Sallie put a maternal hand on his back and asked if he was nervous and he said, "Why would I be?" It had become a strategy of his to answer questions with questions; it threw people off, put them on the defensive, or so he liked to believe.

"You're an adult, George," Sallie said. She held up her empty glass to him. "Almost twenty years old." Her eyes flicked to the bartender. "I mean, twenty-two, plenty old enough to bring a woman home for your family to meet."

Plenty old enough has been a favorite phrase of Sallie's since they secretly started seeing each other six weeks ago. George was interning for Congressman Welby in the offices on Sudbury Street. George's buddy Raymond (whose ID George was using) had set him up on a blind date with his cousin Dana, an assistant to Governor Dukakis. George wasn't sure how he felt about dating a Democrat, but in the snapshot Raymond showed him, Cousin Dana looked a little bit like Phoebe Cates, so George agreed to meet her at a bar behind the statehouse called the Twenty-First Amendment.

When George walked into the bar—not as confidently as he might have because it was his first time using the ID—he heard someone call his name.

"Is that George Whalen?"

The bar was crowded, dark, and smoky, and the clientele were dressed in a style George thought of as "state government," which wasn't as upscale as "federal government." (George was the only person in the place wearing a bow tie and suspenders.) He glanced around, thinking the voice must belong to Cousin Dana, but his eyes landed on a very attractive redhead smoking a cigarette and drinking a martini.

George blinked. It was not just any attractive redhead, he realized. It was his mother's best friend, Sallie Forrester—and George's first instinct was to walk right out, because Sallie was only too aware that George was underage. Sallie must have read his mind, because she beckoned him forward with an elegantly manicured finger, and when he was within reach, she yanked one of his suspenders and murmured in his ear, "Don't worry, Georgie, I won't tell." Instantly, George got an erection. This was Sallie, whom George had fantasized about all through puberty. He used to stroke himself upstairs as Sallie and his mother and Joey Whalen and whatever thug Sallie was dating—she had a penchant for thugs—sat downstairs drinking martinis and smoking. George used to imagine Sallie excusing herself for the ladies' room, sneaking upstairs to George's room, ducking her head under his covers, and pleasuring him with her mouth.

It was powerful stuff, and George found himself captive to his old horniness now. He should say goodbye and go find Cousin Dana. Better Phoebe Cates than Anne Bancroft.

"Sit down, George, you cutie," Sallie said. "Let's get you a drink."

When George ordered a Sam Adams, his voice cracked—he had unwittingly reverted right back to his fifteen-year-old self—but the bartender didn't notice or didn't care. He probably thought Sallie was George's mother or aunt. He set a sweating bottle of beer in front of George and said, "Buck fifty."

"Put it on my tab, Matthew," Sallie said. "And bring him something stronger. Shot of Wild Turkey."

It had been the most transformative night of George's life. At first, George figured Sallie was plying him with alcohol so that he would talk about his family. She asked him what he "really" thought of Joey Whalen. (Sallie thought he was a snake. "He made a habit of pinching my behind when Blair wasn't looking. It came as no surprise he was keeping a piece of French toast up in Montreal.") The shot of whiskey had loosened George; if Sallie wanted confidences, he was happy to oblige.

There was a way, George told her, in which Joey's presence in their lives had always felt temporary. He traveled a lot for work in his position with Nestlé—he had done such a good job with Stouffer's that they'd put him in charge of the national accounts for Hot Pockets, hoping he would work the same magic—so Joey's presence at home always felt like a special occasion. Joey took George to car shows, where he routinely chatted up the foxy women showcasing the Shelby Cobras, and Patriots games, where he "rated" the cheerleaders. George understood all this as part of Joey's persona—that he was more than a salesman; he was a connoisseur of the finer things.

George had no lasting beef with his uncle (he could never quite bring himself to use the term *stepfather*). Besides, Blair had changed in the years since she'd been married to Joey—hadn't Sallie noticed? She'd become "career-driven." She was determined to get her doctorate, to publish papers, to get tenure!

"Yes," Sallie said, exhaling a stream of smoke sideways from her strawberry-red lips. "I've been a good influence on her."

Right—Sallie was a Working Girl. She was a vice president at Fidelity and had her own secretary, a man. She'd conceived her son, Michael, by using a sperm donor, and she was raising him alone; he was now freshman-class president and captain of the JV basketball team at Buckingham Browne and Nichols. Sallie had courtside Celtics tickets—she handled investments for Larry Bird—and she drove an Aston Martin that had a *phone* in it.

Next, Sallie asked George about Genevieve. "What is going *on* with her, exactly? Please don't mince words."

Don't mince words? George thought. *Okay, she's a screwup.* Their mother liked to say that the *Challenger* explosion had messed with Genevieve's head, but really, George knew, the problem lay deeper than that. Their parents' divorce, their brief move to Houston—where the fourth-grade girls had teased Genevieve mercilessly about her "accent" and then crucified her further when she tried to speak like them—and their mother's marriage to their uncle had all taken a bite out of Genevieve's self-esteem, and now it resembled a moth-eaten rag. She was far smarter than George—he was the first to admit that—but she was fragile, whereas George was sturdy. If he'd been bitter about not being admitted to a single Ivy, while Genevieve was accepted at three, this feeling quickly dissipated when he realized that, although he might not have as much elite intelligence, he had the people skills he needed to be successful.

But was he charming enough to seduce his mother's best friend?

Apparently so. The evening at the Twenty-First Amendment ended with Sallie inviting George back to her apartment on Stuart Street for a nightcap (Michael was sleeping at a friend's house out in Sherborn). As soon as they walked in the door, Sallie removed George's jacket, slipped off his suspenders...and the rest of the night was plucked straight from his fifteen-year-old self's fantasies. When he woke up the next morning, Sallie was wearing only his bow tie.

Their union was scandalous. They acknowledged this fact the next morning over tiny cups of espresso Sallie made in an Italian machine that sounded like a Lamborghini. Their hookup would have been outrageous even if Sallie *hadn't* been Blair's best friend. George was only nineteen! He was only six years older than Sallie's son!

"But *men* do this," Sallie said. "All the time. A forty-three-year-old dude and a nineteen-year-old chick—does anyone bat an eye?"

"You're right," George said. He'd assumed this was a crazy one-night stand, but what Sallie seemed to be indicating was that it could be something more. George wanted it to be *so* much more! He was gobsmacked not only by Sallie's beauty but by her sophistication, her wit, her intellect, her success, her self-confidence. Girls like Cousin Dana were...well, *girls*. Sallie was a paragon of womanhood. She could easily grace the cover of *Redbook*.

Before George left Sallie's apartment, she kissed him and said, "Let's see what happens, shall we? But for now, not a word to anyone."

Not a word to anyone. Let's see what happens. George's elation quickly fermented. He understood he couldn't contact Sallie first; he would have to wait for her to reach out. One day passed, two days, three days. Had the night even happened? Raymond was pissed that George stood up Cousin Dana and demanded his license back, forcing George to lie and say he'd lost it (because what if Sallie did call and George needed to meet her at a bar?). Day four passed—the image of George's mouth on Sallie's milky-white breast was fading, and doubt crept in. Had his lovemaking been subpar? (He'd had sex with only two other girls: his high-school sweetheart, Bethany, and some chick from Pine Manor named Caroline when they were both very drunk.) Sallie had dated all kinds of men, and the ones George remembered were giants—tall, broad, muscle-bound (and, he assumed, well-endowed). How could George compare?

Day five. A call came into George's work phone just as George was about to leave for the day and take his frustrations out by playing rugby against some of the Harvard guys who worked for Tip O'Neill. It was Sallie, calling from her car. Michael had successfully finished his year at BB&N and she'd just put him on a bus to Camp Winona in Bridgton, Maine, for the summer.

"I'm a free woman," Sallie said. "Want to get a pizza?"

In the six weeks that followed, there was pizza, sex, drinks at the Copley Plaza, a Red Sox game, sex, a matinée of *Dead Poets Society* sneaked in during lunchtime on a workday, sex, canoeing on Walden Pond, a tour of Louisa May Alcott's house, sex, a trip to the top of the Pru, sex, a wine-soaked dinner at Biba, sex, the Degas exhibit at the MFA, a ride on the Swan Boats in the Public Garden, sex—and a (by then) nostalgic visit to the Twenty-First Amendment, where George told Sallie he would be celebrating his twentieth birthday on Nantucket with his family.

"But not your mother," Sallie said. "She's in Paris."

"Right. It'll be my sister, Aunt Jessie, Uncle Tiger and Aunt Magee and their kids, and my grandmother."

"Your grandmother has always liked me," Sallie said. She eased an olive off the toothpick with her lips in a mesmerizing way. "I should come with you."

George thought she was kidding. Their affair was completely secret, and now Sallie was talking about telling his *family?* Preposterous. But she brought it up again that night in bed, saying that it was the perfect opportunity to bring the relationship out into the light.

"It'll be better without Blair around," Sallie said. "Better for her to hear about it after the rest of your family has accepted it."

George laughed. The rest of his family wasn't going to accept it. His aunt and uncle might be okay with it, but his sister, no. His grandmother, no.

"I'm not sure it's a good idea," George said.

"Of course it's a good idea," Sallie said in a way that let George know the decision had been made. "You're plenty old enough."

Is there another way into All's Fair? George wonders now.

"I'll try the back door," he says with more confidence than he feels. He can't believe the key isn't under the mat; in his mind, that key was as constant and unmovable as the Civil War monument at the top of Main Street. "You stay here." He heads down the block and around the corner, past the guest cottage, Little Fair, and through the gate into the backyard. This would be so much easier with a flashlight. He presses the button on his digital watch and the face glows a ghostly green that provides just enough light to lead him first to the front door of Little Fair (locked) and then across the lawn and brick patio to the back door of All's Fair (also locked).

George wants to scream. This is so humiliating! He can't get into his own house!

Well, it's not exactly "his" house, nor is it the house where he's expected. He's expected at a house six miles west on Red Barn Road. All's Fair is the family's "in-town residence," and ever since the caretaker, Mr. Crimmins, died a few years earlier, it has been used for overflow family, which normally meant Blair, Joey Whalen, and the twins. (George's grandmother Kate didn't quite approve of Blair's marriage to Joey, and sticking her in the fusty old Fair Street house was one way of showing it.)

George knows that his grandmother has made up a room for him at the big beach house, but he made a decision on the ferry to stay at All's Fair instead. He told his grandmother only that he's bringing "a new girlfriend." She has no idea it's Sallie Forrester.

Every time he tries to imagine how his family will react—with abject horror, disgust, anger, or, worst of all, mirth—he wants to put Sallie on the ferry back to the mainland. They should keep their union a delicious secret. How did he let her convince him that bringing her along was a reasonable idea?

Part of him wonders if he's overreacting. Maybe it's no big deal that he's dating a forty-three-year-old woman. After all, everyone in the family likes Sallie. George is proud to be worthy of her desire and affection (he won't presume love, though he feels they're moving in that direction), and doesn't he want to show it off?

Every second he's back here massaging this quandary, he's leaving Sallie out front by herself in the dark. George gropes around the patio for a loose brick, pries it free, then smashes the lower quarter pane of the back door's window and reaches through to unlock it.

In his haste, he slices his hand on a jagged shard of glass, a nasty gash in the meaty part of his palm, just below his thumb. Even in the near dark, he can see a line of blood rising up in his white flesh. After he opens the door and steps into the kitchen, he grabs a dish towel hanging over the lip of the sink. He feels right away that it's crusted with something— dried ketchup or a smear of melted Velveeta cheese. He'll probably end up with gangrene but at least he's inside—a triumph!—and with the towel pressed to his wound, he gallantly welcomes Sallie to his ancestral summer home.

*   *   *

He gives Sallie a quick tour of the house's charms—the mural on the dining-room walls, the "buttery" hidden under the stairs, his great-grandmother's collection of whirligigs and whimmy-diddles. Nothing in this house has changed in decades except for the key—where is the goddamn key? Now George is going to have to explain the broken window, but that will wait until tomorrow.

He lets Sallie pick which bedroom she wants, and she chooses George's great-grandmother's room, the one with a bed so high it requires a footstool. This is the last room George would have picked. Exalta *died* in this room and all George can think is that her spirit is hovering around in the cobwebbed corners or hiding in her cedar closet. Exalta had a reputation for being an imperious grande dame who could bust a grown man's balls with one withering look, but George remembers a kind old lady who kept a stash of cherry Charms lollipops hidden in a drawer of the dining-room buffet. She would give one to George and one to Genevieve every afternoon, even though their mother forbade sweets before dinner. Exalta used to pinch George's cheeks and tell him he looked just like her late husband, Pennington Nichols, "the finest man I've ever known."

"Are you sure you don't want to stay down the hall?" George asks, but Sallie pushes him back against the bed and undoes his belt, and George hopes Exalta's ghost is averting her eyes.

He's a fool for love.

*　　*　　*

He wakes up to birdsong and gentle light nosing in around the window shades. He gazes first at the white curve of Sallie's ass; this is a lovely distraction from the angry, throbbing wound on his hand. He peels back the dish towel but his blood has acted as an adhesive, so the process is painful (and gross—the towel, he now sees, is stained with egg yolk).

He probably needs stitches; the wound is a deep black mess, though it might be too late for that. In the bathroom medicine cabinet, George finds a bottle of hydrogen peroxide that's likely older than he is and a roll of white medical tape. He fixes up the wound as best he can, longing for a bottle of Tylenol, even expired Tylenol. His head is pounding from the three martinis. He descends to the kitchen, hoping for bread so he can make toast, and sees the broken glass glittering on the floor. He grabs a broom, thinking he'll need to call someone to fix the window, but who? Mr. Crimmins is dead. Have they hired anyone to replace him?

In the refrigerator, George finds only one thing: a bottle of Moët et Chandon champagne, Sallie's favorite. *Aha!* he thinks. What incredible luck! He checks the pocket of his khakis and finds one soft, wrinkled five-dollar bill. (He paid for the martinis the night before in an attempt to be a magnanimous host, but there's a reason Sallie pays for everything, which is that she has money and he doesn't.) He heads out the back door.

George's first stop is the A&P down by the ferry

dock, where he buys a carton of orange juice. He wants flowers as well but the only bouquets in the produce section are carnations (George once bought Sallie a bouquet of carnations and he noted the look on her face. Never again). He decides instead to cut a hydrangea blossom off the bush in front of All's Fair.

With this mission in mind, he heads back up Main Street. He'll find a tray and bring Sallie the champagne in an ice bucket, the juice in a glass pitcher, the hydrangea in a bud vase. He strolls past an open-bed farm truck parked in front of the Camera Shop and slows to check out the cartons of fresh-picked strawberries that a woman is setting out. He wonders what she's charging for them; he has three dollars and eighty-five cents left.

The woman turns and her eyes meet George's. Does she look familiar? She's older, probably close to his grandmother's age, with long, hippieish gray-blond hair; she's wearing a shapeless chambray dress and Birkenstocks.

"Good morning," George says. "How much for a quart of berries?"

The woman studies his face for so long that George grows uncomfortable. The plastic bag with the juice is biting into his bad hand.

"Do you belong to the Nichols family, by any chance?" she says. "You're a dead ringer for a man I used to know named Penn Nichols. He lived on Fair Street."

"My great-grandfather," George says, offering the woman his good hand. "I'm George Whalen, Blair's son?"

The woman takes his hand and holds it between the two of hers. "Blair's son, I can't believe it. I've known your mom since she was born." The woman laughs. "Though I haven't seen her in thirty-five years."

"She's in Paris right now," George says, gently but firmly reclaiming his hand. "Working on her doctorate."

The woman shakes her head in amazement. "She was always so smart, reading her little books…"

George says, "Yes, that sounds like my mom. Well, it was nice to meet you." He glances up the street, desperate now to get away. "I have to be—"

"Here," the woman says, handing him a carton of berries. "Take these, a gift from me. They're organic, picked early this morning from a farm I'm working on by the artist colony on Polpis Road." She pauses. "Tell your mom I said hello, and your grandmother too, for that matter. My name is Rain."

Rain? George thinks as he heads up the street. He has a hard time believing that either his mother or grandmother knows an aging hippie named Rain—but he is psyched about the free berries.

George bursts into the kitchen through the back door, excited to tell Sallie that the berries are organic (whatever that means) and even more excited to set down the bag with the juice. His hand is killing him, and when George looks, he sees he's bled right through the white medical tape. As he moves to the sink, he hears a thunder of footsteps and then voices.

What?

George's nine-year-old cousin, Frog, runs into the kitchen. "George is here!" Frog shouts, wrapping his arms around George's middle.

No! George thinks. *No, this isn't happening!* Two seconds later, he hears a shriek come from upstairs. That would be Aunt Magee, discovering a naked woman in Exalta's bed.

Tiger and Magee and the kids are staying *here?* How did George not know this? They always stay at the beach house! George's head starts spinning; his vision splotches black and yellow before narrowing to a pinpoint. He crumples to the floor.

3. NEW SENSATION

Kate tiptoes past the room where Jessie is sleeping, then creeps down the stairs, where she presses the button on the Mr. Coffee and prays that neither the gurgling sound nor the smell of Folger's dark roast will wake her daughter up. Once her coffee is brewed and she has added two Sweet'n Lows to her mug, being oh so careful not to chime her spoon against the side, Kate slips onto the sunporch and eases the glass doors closed behind her. She picks up the phone and dials Bitsy.

The phone rings six times, then Bitsy breathlessly answers. "Hel-*lo?*"

"Bits," Kate says. "It's me."

"Hold on," Bitsy says. "I have to pause the tape." In the background, Kate hears the drill-sergeant voice of Jane Fonda directing the viewer to lift her leg like a dog at a fire hydrant. Kate can just picture Bitsy on all fours in her leotard and leg warmers on the carpeting in front of the TV in the family room. She does the Jane Fonda tapes every morning because she wants to lose the twenty pounds she gained when she divorced Arturo. *Unlike you,* Bitsy said, *I hope to have a man look at me again.*

When Bitsy returns to the phone, she says, "You do realize what time it is? Why are you awake?"

"I need you to come pick me up," Kate whispers. "Now."

"Now?" Bitsy says. "I'm not finished with my workout."

"Yes, you are," Kate says. "It's an emergency. I need you to save me."

Kate hangs up and gazes out the screen toward the beach. The sun is just high enough to make the ocean sparkle.

Kate's house is filling up for the twins' twentieth-birthday celebration, and although this is exactly the kind of gathering Kate and David dreamed about when they bought this house, Kate can't help but feel... invaded. Just look at her: She's sneaking out to avoid her own daughter!

The evening before, Jessie arrived in the foulest of

moods. She was bent out of shape because Genevieve had shown up ten minutes late (that Genevieve had deigned to show up at all was a minor miracle, Kate thought. Genevieve didn't do well with "being told what to do"). Then, when Jessie learned that Kate was going out with Bitsy to hear David Halberstam speak at the Atheneum and then to dinner at 21 Federal, she had what amounted to a toddler's meltdown. Kate might have expected such theatrics from Kirby and, on a bad day, from Blair, but not from Jessie.

"I'm sorry I made plans, darling," Kate said. "George and his new girlfriend aren't getting in until late tonight, and Tiger and Magee arrive first thing tomorrow, so I didn't anticipate having to entertain anyone this evening."

"Because I don't matter," Jessie said.

"If you remember correctly, darling," Kate said, "you were supposed to be coming with Pick. I thought the two of you would be having dinner at the Second Story like you usually do the night you arrive."

"Pick is in Berlin, Mother."

"I'm aware. But when we made the plans..." She waves a hand. "I don't want to quarrel. I'm going out with Bitsy."

"You've been out with Bitsy every night this summer, from what I understand!" Jessie said.

What of it? Kate thought. "If I had another ticket, I would offer it to you, darling."

"That's not the point!" Jessie said.

Well, then, what is the point? Kate thought. "I'm leaving you the car. You and Genevieve can go to the Mad Hatter if you want. Or call Bitsy's girls. Helen is single now too, you know... such a bizarre and upsetting story. It would be good for her to get out. Maybe she'd like to go to Thirty Acres."

"I can fend for myself, Mother." Jessie took a breath and seemed to soften. "You and I need to have a talk, and we should do it before everyone else arrives."

Immediately, Kate's hackles went up. "Of course, darling."

"Tomorrow morning?" Jessie said. "Early?"

Kate gave Jessie a thumbs-up, but she had absolutely no intention of being around for any kind of talk.

Kate quickly downs her coffee, grabs her round Jackie O. sunglasses, and goes out to wait for Bitsy on the porch.

Hurry up, Bitsy! Kate thinks.

She spies a billow of dust and sand in the distance, and a few seconds later, Bitsy's red Miata comes to a screeching halt at Kate's front door. Wasting no time, Kate hops in. "Go!" she says.

"I feel like we're on the lam," Bitsy says, cackling. "What are we running away from? I thought Jessie got in last night."

"She did," Kate said. "That's the problem. She told me we needed to talk. Alone."

"About what?" Bitsy says.

"I haven't the foggiest, but from her tone of voice, I could tell it was something I wanted to avoid. It's like she's the parent now and I'm the child. She's so...*judgy*. And not cute like Judge Wapner."

"He *is* cute," Bitsy agrees. "I wonder if he's single."

Kate leans back in the seat, her whole body relaxing now that they've made a clean getaway. She fears that Jessie wants to "talk" about Kate's lifestyle—namely, her drinking and gallivanting about with Bitsy. Jessie may suggest, encourage, or demand that Kate "tone it down." Kate is, after all, a widow.

But that's just the thing.

Kate's second husband, David Levin, died in January, and before he passed, he made it eminently clear that he wanted Kate to keep on living. "We had thirty-five beautiful years together," he said. "How lucky are we? If you cry, let the tears be ones of gratitude. And then go out and enjoy your freedom."

Kate had shushed him; what he was saying was absurd. She was losing her husband, her best friend and beloved. People didn't just bounce back from that.

But Kate discovered that David was right. After a few months of wallowing around in sorrow and misery and loneliness and the pragmatic reality of being in charge of everything (property taxes, insurance policies, oil changes in their cars), Kate woke up one day and felt...lighter. She had been a wife since she was twenty-two years old—first the wife of Wilder Foley and then, a scant year after Wilder killed himself, the wife of David Levin. Kate realized there was a flip side to loneliness—liberation. Kate didn't have to worry about anyone but herself; her whims and wants were the only ones she needed to consider.

She bought pretty flowered sheets for her bed. She stocked the fridge with Ballpark franks and the cabinets with bags of Fritos. She watched *Thirtysomething* every Tuesday night on the new TV she'd had installed in her bedroom, often with a bowl of rocky road ice cream on her lap, and she left the dirty dish on her nightstand until morning. She went days without applying lipstick; she stopped coloring her hair but then felt that being gray made her look too much like her mother, so she went platinum blond.

When Kate arrived on Nantucket, she reconnected with her lifelong friend Bitsy Dunscombe. Kate and Bitsy's relationship had been something of a roller-coaster ride; there was a summer, twenty years earlier, when they'd had a screaming match in the middle of the Opera House restaurant. But beneath the petty jealousies and the score-keeping lay genuine affection. Kate and Bitsy were both older now—a stone's throw away from seventy!—and Bitsy found herself single as well. She and Arturo had amicably parted ways after nineteen years of marriage, and Bitsy, who was on the hunt for husband number three, was only too happy to serve as Kate's partner in crime. The two ladies were as inseparable this summer as they had been as teenagers—and they were having even more fun. They used to spend every waking moment at the Field and Oar Club but Bitsy had soured on the place. *It's so uptight! There are so many antiquated rules!* There was a whole social scene that they had previously largely ignored waiting for them outside the club.

They went for brunch at the White Elephant and for drinks at the Atlantic Café. They had Italian food at DeMarco's and a delicious cocktail called the Elbow Bender at the Lobster Trap. They lounged by the Summer House pool and even ventured once to the Muse to hear live music. They went to plays at Bennett Hall and to lectures at the Atheneum. Every Friday night, they strolled the galleries of Old South Wharf, holding little plastic cups of bad white wine, then headed over to the Rope Walk for lobsters. On sunny days, they would drive Kate's Scout out to Smith's Point and sit in upright chairs doing their needlepoint. Kate was making a belt for Tiger, and Bitsy was working on a pillow that read: *Lord, lead me not into temptation. I can find it well enough on my own.*

Kate couldn't remember ever having so much fun. The last thing she wanted to hear was that Jessie didn't approve.

Of course, it was also possible that Jessie wanted to talk to Kate about Genevieve — and Kate relished this idea even less. It's true that Genevieve is having a difficult time. At first, Kate was not only appalled but *frightened* by her only granddaughter's appearance. She wore black from head to toe, even black lipstick. She was pierced like a human pincushion and she'd gotten a *tattoo* on her *forearm*, where everyone could *see* it. She had shaved off her lovely blond hair and dyed the resulting crew cut flamingo pink. She wore a leather jacket that smelled like a rotting animal, apparently a gift from the oh so inappropriate punk-rocker boyfriend who lived somewhere in Rhode Island.

What had happened to the sweet, smart girl Genevieve used to be? Kate wondered back in June when Genevieve set foot in the house on Red Barn Road with an army-green rucksack at her feet. (Where was the cute quilted duffel from Pierre Deux on Newbury Street that Kate had given her for Christmas?) Was this *Invasion of the Body Snatchers*?

Kate realized she had two choices: Freak out, as the kids liked to say, or pretend everything was fine. She chose the latter. She told Genevieve that she'd spoken to Erica Wilson at the needlepoint shop and to Reggie at the watercolor gallery about hiring Genevieve for the summer. Genevieve had laughed and said, "Uh… no and no." Kate was almost relieved; she couldn't imagine someone who looked like Genevieve selling embroidery thread or landscapes of Nantucket harbor. Kate couldn't even bring Genevieve to the Field and Oar Club; she didn't begin to meet the dress code.

Somehow, Kate managed to keep her composure as she got Genevieve settled in the guesthouse and reminded her about using only the outdoor shower. "I bet you've missed the pool," Kate said. "And the ocean!"

Genevieve shrugged. "I didn't pack a bathing suit."

Kate clapped a hand over her mouth. Her granddaughter had come to Nantucket for the summer without a bathing suit? This was no longer the little girl in the pink ruffled one-piece and plastic goggles that Kate had to bribe with a tin of Charlie's Chips to get out of the water. This was a young woman who was wearing what looked like...combat boots.

Kate had let Genevieve "settle in," then she hurried back to the house, where she called Bitsy and cried.

Bitsy had lots of experience with family drama. Just look at what had recently happened to Helen. "I'd advise you to meet Genevieve where she is," Bitsy said. "She's a kid, trying to find herself. You remember Kirby at that age."

Oh, dear, yes, Kate thought. Kirby had been arrested twice for protesting the Vietnam War. And now she was out in Hollywood "producing," whatever that meant, and they never saw her.

Although it was nearly physically painful, Kate let Genevieve be Genevieve. And, surprise, surprise, the two of them had gotten along quite well all summer. Genevieve woke up around noon, whereupon she drank a cup of black coffee and ate a bowl of Cap'n Crunch. She spent her afternoons watching talk shows on television, each one worse than the last—Maury Povich, Jerry Springer, Morton Downey Jr.—and Kate would occasionally join her on the sofa in the name of bonding. Wouldn't you know, Kate always got sucked into the ridiculous or pathetic plights of the guests on the show, and together, Kate and Genevieve would heckle, hiss, boo, or howl with laughter.

In an attempt to lure Genevieve outdoors (she was as pale as a vampire), Kate served her lunch on the patio by the pool—Genevieve was partial to home-made English muffin pizzas—and one day, Kate asked Genevieve if she wanted to play cards. They started with crazy eights, then moved on to hearts, spades, and gin rummy.

Genevieve, Kate found, could be bargained with. Genevieve agreed to go to Murray's to buy a bathing suit (black, of course) and accompany Kate to the beach, but in exchange, Genevieve asked Kate to listen to an entire Ramones album on Genevieve's Walkman. Genevieve would drive Kate and Bitsy into town so they could drink as many Moscow mules as they wanted at the Brotherhood in exchange for permission to make long-distance calls from the house phone. (Who was she calling? Kate assumed it was the punk-rocker boy-friend. The first phone bill showed repeated calls to a number in Rhode Island, but none of the calls lasted longer than a minute.)

When Kate caught Genevieve smoking behind the guest cottage, she at first thought to punish her, but grounding wouldn't work, as she never went anywhere, and making her eat the cigarette seemed cruel. So instead, she asked Genevieve for a cigarette and then a light. Kate hadn't smoked in years—David didn't tolerate it—but David was gone. It did feel a little unwholesome, smoking with her grandchild—what would Nancy Reagan think?—and so with her first, delicious exhale, Kate said, "This is a filthy habit."

Genevieve leaned back against the shingles of the house and watched Kate smoke with a bemused expression on her face that morphed into something resembling an actual smile. "You're cool, Grammy," she said.

Kate winked at her pierced, tattooed, flamingo-haired granddaughter, trying not to let on how much this comment pleased her.

From that moment on, things had changed between Kate and Genevieve. There was a respect between them, an understanding, a kind of (dared Kate use the word?) friendship.

But Jessie's arrival threatened to disrupt their delicate balance.

"Where shall we go?" Bitsy asks as they pull out onto Madaket Road.

"Is it too early to get a drink?" Kate says.

"Let's go to town," Bitsy says. "I've heard there's some kind of farm truck with strawberries for sale."

Kate nods, though she hoped to avoid Main Street. Tiger and Magee are due to arrive with the boys and they've opted to stay at All's Fair because it's closer to the ice cream shops and the movie theater. Kate knows the first thing Tiger will do is march the boys over to Congdon's Pharmacy for breakfast at the counter, and she can't risk having them see her. She's not sure what's *wrong* with her — it's her beloved son and her grandchildren — and all she can say is she's not quite ready. Tiger and Magee will bring the boys over at lunchtime to hang out at the beach and that's fine. Kate will be able to embrace the chaos in a few hours — just not right now.

When Bitsy parks, Kate says, "You go. I'll stay in the car."

"You sure you don't want to come?" Bitsy says. "The strawberries are organic. They're from the hippie farm on Polpis Road."

"Isn't all produce organic?" Kate asks.

Bitsy laughs like Kate has made a joke and gets out of the car. Kate adjusts her Jackie O. sunglasses, sinks down in her seat, and closes her eyes. It's only a weekend, she thinks. Tonight they're having a family barbecue and tomorrow night is the clambake on the beach for the twins' birthday. Magee called to order a cake from the Bake Shop; they'll have champagne, and Tiger is bringing fireworks.

Kate looks up the street toward Fair. Twenty years earlier, Blair's water broke in Buttner's department store, and poor Jessie came running into the house, screaming her head off. Kate had been at the cutting board in the kitchen slicing cucumbers — she would put them in a bowl of tarragon vinegar and chill them in the fridge for the simplest summer salad — but when she heard Jessie yelling, "It's happening, Mom, the babies are coming!" she snatched up the keys to the Scout and was out the door in seconds. She hadn't anticipated Blair's reluctance to drive over the cobblestones, but they were lucky—it was the middle of the day, and Fair Street was quiet. Kate had thrown the car in reverse and backed down Fair, a decision that became family legend.

Kate is so lost in thought—she can't think about the twins' birth without growing a little misty-eyed—that when Bitsy opens the car door, she startles.

"Where are the strawberries?" Kate asks, because Bitsy is empty-handed.

Bitsy gives Kate a look that can only be described as panicked. "I decided not to get any after all," she says. "They were moldy and gnats were swarming."

"Oh, heavens," Kate says. "So much for organic."

Bitsy throws the Miata in reverse and hits the gas in a way that is incompatible with the cobblestones of Main Street. Kate's teeth rattle. "What is *wrong* with you? You seem spooked. Did something happen? Did you see Tiger and the kids?"

"No," Bitsy says. "But I'm taking you home. I think you'd better talk to Jessie after all."

Kate sighs. She knows not to engage with Bitsy when she's acting flighty like this. Besides, Bitsy is right; Kate can't avoid Jessie forever. She might as well get the little talk over with so she can enjoy her weekend.

When Bitsy pulls up in front of Kate's house, Kate leans over to kiss her friend's cheek. "You're the best

friend I could ask for. Come tonight at six for the barbecue, and tomorrow night is the twins' party. Please
bring Helen."

"I'll be there," Bitsy says. "But I can't promise about
Helen; she's still avoiding people."

Kate waves a hand. "Tell her she doesn't need to be
ashamed. I have a whole houseful of issues right here.
She'll fit right in!"

Bitsy drives off with a toot of the horn and Kate
smiles, thinking maybe she'll get a little sports car too.
Why not?

She walks into the kitchen to find Jessie shouting
into the phone. "You have got to be *kidding* me!" When
Jessie notices Kate, she lowers her voice and says, "Mom's
here, I'll call you back." She hangs up.

What now? Kate thinks. "Was that Tiger?" she asks.
"He's here?" There must be a problem at All's Fair —
mice, or maybe someone left the front door unlocked.
Things haven't been the same with that house since
Bill Crimmins died.

"Yes," Jessie says. "Guess who Tiger and Magee found
sleeping in Nonny's bedroom at All's Fair?"

Kate shakes her head. She can't begin to guess.

4. Free Fallin'

The phone next to Genevieve's head rings and Genevieve snatches it up, thinking it's Mouth, calling to

retract all the things he'd said the night before (she knew they were too good to be true), but before Genevieve can speak, she hears her aunt Jessie pick up an extension in the big house with a groggy hello. A split second later, Genevieve hears her uncle Tiger say, "Jess, are you sitting down?" Genevieve hangs up before either of them realizes she's on the line and falls back to sleep.

When she wakes up again, it's quarter past ten, still a little early for her, but she bounces out of bed like a freakin' cheerleader. The night before, while her grandmother was out with Bitsy and her aunt was taking a long walk on the beach by herself, Genevieve called the Grease Monkey garage in Central Falls—Mouth was a mechanic there and it was also where his band, Fungus, practiced—and for the first time, Genevieve didn't have to hang up, because for the first time, Mouth himself answered instead of his wife, Danielle, who was the garage manager.

"Baby, it's me," Genevieve said.

She heard Mouth exhale. "Thank God you finally called," he said. "I've been dying without you."

Genevieve didn't tell him that she'd called every day since she'd been on Nantucket—her grandmother was going to *have a baby* when she got the phone bill. Instead, she'd played it cool and said, "I was just listening to some Mudhoney and it made me think of you."

"I told Danielle about the two of us last night," Mouth said.

Genevieve gasped. "You did not."

"Well, Pierre let something slip, the dumbass, but it's fine. She was going to find out sooner or later."

Was she? Genevieve wondered. Mouth always claimed he was hamstrung where his wife, Danielle, was concerned because her parents owned the garage and they were also bankrolling the band, so Mouth needed to keep Danielle happy, which meant he could never leave her and she could never, ever find out about Genevieve. Genevieve's relationship with Mouth had meant months of living in the shadows; the good news was Danielle rarely came to Mouth's shows because she found them "too wild." The one time Danielle did appear, Genevieve blended into the crowd and scrutinized her rival. Danielle wore a boatneck cotton sweater and a pair of slacks and flats; she looked like a secretary. Plus, she was *old,* maybe thirty. Genevieve had actually been disappointed that Mouth's wife was so uncool; she'd nodded along to the music in places but she didn't try to dance, and as soon as the crowd started to bounce and pogo — which Genevieve did with extra enthusiasm — she left.

"Did she move *out?*" Genevieve said.

"She told me to move out," Mouth said. "I'm just here at the garage grabbing my tools."

"Grabbing your tools?" Genevieve said. "Where will you go?"

"It's like we always talked about," Mouth said. "I'm coming to be with you."

* * *

I'm coming to be with you. Here were the words Gene-vieve had been longing for since the night she attended her first Fungus show, when the bouncer at the Decline invited her backstage afterward, saying, "The drummer, Mouth, saw you in the crowd. He asked me to find you."

"He *did?*" Genevieve said. This statement seemed nothing short of miraculous. Genevieve had, at that point, only dipped her toe into the pond of punk—she'd worn her Rocky Horror T-shirt, a studded dog collar, and heavy black eyeliner. She let the bouncer lead her down to the damp, smelly basement room where the band hung out, and she tried to recall which guy was the drummer. (Like everyone else at the show, she'd been mesmerized by Rancid Pierre, the lead singer, who wore silver contact lenses.) It turned out the drummer was a thick-necked guy with a shaved head and a zip-per tattoo running down the center of his cranium to his neck. He introduced himself as Andrew but said most people used his stage name, Mouth.

"Why Mouth?" Genevieve asked.

Mouth brought Genevieve's hand to his lips and then sucked the length of her middle finger. Her first instinct was to yank back—the women at Brown were all about consent, *no means no,* et cetera—but Genevieve found herself aroused. A few minutes later, once she had been offered a cold Coors Light (which she accepted) and a line of cocaine (which she didn't), she and Mouth found a moldy chair in a corner of the room and made out.

For a long while, Genevieve saw Mouth only at shows, all of which started at midnight and ended at two or three in the morning. They would drink a beer or two in the gross basement, talking with the rest of the band about how the show had gone, what their take at the door had been, how they could attract more fans, whether their so-called manager, Ernie, was doing them dirty, whether the cover art of their EP—a standard-issue red-and-white toadstool—was too predictable. Then they would head out to Genevieve's black Integra, which had been a high-school graduation present from Joey Whalen (Joey was known for extravagant gifts), and have sex in the back seat.

This routine stayed the same, but Genevieve changed. One night, she drank Jim Beam with a wiccan in her dorm named Esther and she let Esther pierce her left ear with a row of safety pins. Next came the vintage leather jacket that Genevieve found in a thrift shop on Orchard Avenue. She told everyone it was a gift from Mouth, not quite a lie because when Mouth saw it, he said it was exactly the jacket he would have bought for her if he could, but he couldn't because jackets like that were expensive and in his real life, Mouth (Andrew) was a mechanic and his wife kept very strict control over his finances.

Yes, Genevieve knew Mouth had a wife. She'd asked him about it the first night because he was wearing a dark, flat ring.

Ball and chain, he said, then he jammed his tongue down Genevieve's throat.

Initially, Genevieve cared very little about the wife. She was as incomprehensible to Genevieve as Genevieve's differential equations course was to Mouth. He was a mechanic; she was an engineering major at Brown. Their Venn diagram overlapped only at the Decline, in the wee hours of the night.

But as the weeks and months passed, the things that didn't bother Genevieve suddenly did. She kept trying to find new ways to prove her devotion. She got the toadstool from Fungus's album cover tattooed on her forearm. ("You realize you'll have that thing when you're eighty?" Genevieve's roommate, Melanie, said. "You'll be buried with it.") Then Genevieve shaved off most of her hair and dyed her buzz cut pink. (She'd considered a mohawk but that seemed too obvious.)

Genevieve and Mouth started talking about "being together." When was Mouth going to leave his wife? He repeated the same litany about the garage, Danielle's parents; they'd invested in the band, his Zildjian cymbals were expensive! Genevieve's devotion to Mouth became an obsession that bordered on insane. And why? He wasn't handsome; he wasn't particularly successful. But he was exotic, especially in the context of Genevieve's collegiate life. She was dating a *real person,* not some privileged Ivy League elite who popped in a Steve Miller cassette and turned on his lava lamp when he wanted to seduce a girl.

When the school year ended, Genevieve talked about subletting an apartment on Prospect Street. She dreamed of cooking for Mouth, of having sex with him in a real bed, of having a shared life, but when she finally summoned the courage to mention this, Mouth blanched. "Shouldn't you spend the summer with your family?" he asked. "I'm sure they miss you."

There were a lot of words to describe Genevieve, but *stupid* wasn't one of them. She didn't bother telling Mouth that her mother was spending the summer in Paris or that her twin brother, George—*who was working for a Republican*—would be only too happy to have their family home in Wellesley to himself. She knew Mouth was trying to get rid of her. He would spend the summer underneath broken-down Dodge pickups while his wife in her slacks complained about the price of pork chops at the Finast.

Fine, Genevieve thought. She'd seen *St. Elmo's Fire* three times her junior year in high school, so she knew the best way to get someone to love you was to ignore them. "You're right," Genevieve said. "I'm going to spend the summer on Nantucket with my aunt Kirby. She's a Hollywood producer." Genevieve kissed Mouth and patted his cheek with as much derision as she could muster. "See you around." Genevieve then climbed into her Integra and drove away before Mouth could see her cry.

Now, it seems, her bluff has worked. Mouth wants to be together. Starting this weekend, he said.

"This weekend?" Genevieve said.

"It's your birthday," Mouth said. "Of course I'm coming."

"My whole family will be here," Genevieve said. "Could you maybe get a hotel room?"

"Baby, you know I don't have that kind of money. Plus, I just lost my job. Don't you want me to stay with you?"

"No, I definitely do," Genevieve said. "But my grandmother will be here and my aunts and uncle, and they're pretty conservative. I'll have to introduce you as Andrew."

"That's my name," Mouth said.

"And you should probably bring a collared shirt."

"A collared shirt?" Mouth said. "Are you kidding?"

Was she kidding? It felt a little bit like lipstick on a pig because a collared shirt wasn't going to cover the zipper tattoo across Mouth's skull. Genevieve's grandmother had proved to be incredibly cool, but Genevieve sensed that introducing Mouth to Kate would be pushing it.

"Do you not own a collared shirt?" she asked. She wondered what kind of man *didn't own a collared shirt.* "Couldn't you go to the Gap?"

As Genevieve gets dressed for the day—as a concession to the family reunion, she pulls on a black jersey sundress and scrubs her face of her usual Goth makeup— she realizes that her feelings about Mouth's arrival aren't what she expected them to be. This makes no sense. For the past four weeks, all Genevieve has wanted was for Mouth to leave his wife, for him to pick *her*. But now that this has actually happened—Mouth claims he's coming to Nantucket *today*—Genevieve is experiencing what can only be described as second thoughts.

She hopes to talk to her grandmother alone, ask if maybe Andrew can sleep on the sofa on the sunporch, but when Genevieve enters the kitchen, she finds Kate, her aunt Jessie, and her aunt Magee deep in conversation. They're discussing something private—Genevieve can tell by their tone and by the way they clam up the second she sets foot in the kitchen.

"Hi," Genevieve says. "What's going on?"

Aunt Magee, whom Genevieve's mother describes as "very high-strung," glowers at Genevieve. "We found out about George's girlfriend."

"Found out what?" Genevieve asks. She vaguely recalls hearing that George was bringing a girlfriend to Nantucket for the weekend, but Genevieve hasn't given one second's thought to what the girl would be like, because she figured she already knew. The girl would be named Molly or Cassie and be blond and perky and wearing a madras shift dress and Tretorns. But now Genevieve's mind wanders from this stereotype. Is George, too, dating someone "inappropriate"? Someone with a thick Southie accent, someone without a college diploma, without a *high-school* diploma, or a neo-hippie who doesn't wash her hair or shave her armpits, or a punk like Genevieve? Or maybe—this is too juicy to even contemplate — George got Molly/Cassie pregnant!

"It's Sallie," Jessie says. "George is dating Sallie Forrester."

When Genevieve returned to Boston from Cape Canaveral, people asked what it had been like, watching the space shuttle explode before her very eyes. Genevieve's honest answer — which most of her friends and acquaintances found disappointing — was that she didn't understand what was happening. She saw the shuttle burst into flames and she heard her father shouting, but there were long, suspended seconds where she just didn't *get* it.

George is dating Sallie Forrester. Their *mother's* Sallie Forrester? *Their* Sallie Forrester?

That's absurd, Genevieve thinks. It's impossible. "No, he isn't," she says.

"She's here with him," Magee says. "They're together. They've been seeing each other for weeks."

Genevieve breaks out into a light sweat as she tries to keep herself from imagining her brother George, who is nineteen — a freaking teenager — sleeping with Sallie Forrester, their mother's best friend.

Ew, she thinks. *Ew, ew, ew!*

Genevieve has always looked up to Sallie, worshipped her, even. Sallie is so...cool; she's always *been* cool. And the coolest thing about their mother is that she has a best friend like Sallie. Genevieve wobbles; she feels like her feet aren't touching the ground. She's come unmoored.

"Here, sit down," Jessie says. "Can I bring you a coffee?"

"Yes, please." Genevieve sits and stares at the table until the mug lands in front of her; she's afraid to look up. Her grandmother and her aunts are clearly gauging her reaction, but what *is* her reaction? It feels like her emotions are wedges on a spinning game-show wheel. Where will she land: amused, disgusted, betrayed, unconcerned? She herself has no idea. "How did this happen?"

"They bumped into each other at a bar," Jessie says. "George went to meet a blind date and Sallie was there."

"She preyed on him!" Magee says. "It's appalling."

Genevieve is quiet for a moment; she sips her coffee. "Well," she says. "He's always had a crush on her." She only realizes the truth in these words as they pass her lips. She isn't even sure how she knows this; George certainly never admitted to anything of the sort. But Genevieve now remembers the puppy-dog look in his eyes whenever Sallie was around and the mean nicknames he would invent for Sallie's boyfriends and the way he would offer to play with Sallie's son, Michael, the world's most annoying child, turning down Sallie's offer of babysitting money. Genevieve doesn't believe all the hooey about twins having a secret channel of communication, but in this instance, she would say that what might have been invisible to everyone else was obvious to Genevieve.

Genevieve can easily picture the scene when George ran into her at a bar. He was going on a blind date, probably dressed in his young Republican getup of bow tie and suspenders (like a circus clown!), and he'd obviously procured a fake ID (as Genevieve had from a guy at Brown who started a cottage industry supplying underclassmen with Louisiana driver's licenses for fifty bucks a pop). What had George thought when he saw Sallie? Probably he'd tried to duck her, because who wants to see a friend of your parents when you're out at a bar underage? Genevieve imagines Sallie tapping George on the shoulder as he chats up Molly/Cassie and then Sallie, for whatever reason, deciding it would be fun to steal George's attention away, which she does easily because she, too, has always known about George's crush. Then they proceed to drink together—martinis or champagne, though in this case, Genevieve guesses martinis—and after two or three or four, Sallie begins to wonder if she's too old to be attractive to George and decides she'll find out.

But that leads Genevieve only to a one-night stand. How did Sallie not wake up the next morning and shrivel at her own poor decision-making? Sleeping with a child who is like a nephew to her? Well, either Sallie is more insecure than Genevieve would have guessed and is using George to prove her own ageless desirability...or they've fallen in love.

What had their mother, Blair, told them when she announced she was marrying their uncle? *The heart wants what it wants.* Genevieve has learned that only too well in the past year, and apparently, George is learning it too.

Genevieve realizes her grandmother has been awfully quiet. "What do you think about it, Grammy?"

Kate sighs. "Is it really the end of the world? George is turning twenty tomorrow. Tiger went to war at nineteen. My parents were married at twenty-one, and I was married at twenty-two. There have been May-December romances since the beginning of time. This will end for its own reasons, probably sooner rather than later. We don't need to get involved. Nobody has died."

Right, Genevieve thinks. When she closes her eyes, she sees the fiery ball of the *Challenger* in the sky. For a split second, it had looked like a shooting star. *Nobody has died.*

"That's very liberal of you, Kate," Magee says.

"Yes, Mom," Jessie says. "You sound like a modern woman."

"Who knows," Kate says, winking at Genevieve. "Maybe I'll take a younger lover myself."

5. YOUR LOVE

Sallie insists on taking George to the Nantucket Cottage Hospital's emergency room so that a doctor—"preferably a surgeon"—can look at the cut on his hand. Initially, George protests. Yes, he fainted in the kitchen, but part of that was due to his hangover and his shock at finding his uncle's family at the house, and he probably shouldn't have made that trip to the store, it was a hot morning already and All's Fair didn't have air-conditioning. He's babbling, he realizes, and his hand is throbbing and he's bleeding through the towel someone brought him. He hears Sallie telling Tiger that they need a ride in the minivan.

Tiger drops them off at the emergency room with a terse "Good luck." He's angry or upset—maybe because George broke into the house like a common burglar (the cut is what he deserves) or maybe because George and Sallie are together or maybe because Sallie demanded a ride rather than asked for one.

"Thank you," George says meekly.

It's not yet nine in the morning on a Saturday but the emergency room is busy. The two people who George makes eye contact with are an exhausted-looking woman holding a whimpering toddler and a girl about George's age who has road rash down the length of one bare leg. Sallie marches to the triage desk while barking, "Hold your hand over your head, George, how many times do I have to tell you?"

Obediently, George raises his hand wrapped in the towel. He really, really wants to lie down but instead he hides behind Sallie as she berates the poor nurse, an older woman with hair dyed coal black, rimless glasses, and an underbite. Her name tag says MARCIA.

"George needs to be seen *right* away," Sallie says. "Look at the blood!"

"It's head trauma?" Marcia asks, because in his exhaustion, George has rested his bad hand on top of his head.

"It's his hand," Sallie snaps. "He's cut his hand and he needs a surgeon!"

George has never heard Sallie sound anything but charming and sassy; this abrasive, nearly rude side of her is new to him, and he's afraid the nurse will take offense, but Marcia just chuckles. "The only surgeons on Nantucket today are on the golf course." She hands Sallie a clipboard. "You and your son can have a seat. Fill this form out and return it to me when you've finished."

Sallie mutters under her breath, "He's not my son," and George feels the same mortification he always feels when people assume Sallie is his mother, but it's worse now because of what happened back at All's Fair. Tiger and Magee handled the surprise of Sallie...badly. Magee was kneeling over George when he regained consciousness, and right after she realized he was okay, she whispered, "You should be ashamed of yourself, George. What will my boys think? They look up to you."

George tries to take the clipboard but Sallie won't relinquish it. "I'll fill it out," she says. "I've known you since you were born."

Marcia calls out, "Lopez," and the woman with the

toddler stands. George rests his head against the back of the chair and closes his eyes.

"What's your Social Security number?" Sallie asks. As George is mumbling the digits—the last four are either 6304 or 6403, he can't seem to remember which— Marcia says, "Dewberry!" George snaps to attention, confused. Dewberry is Raymond's last name and therefore the last name on George's fake ID and he's trained himself to respond to it. The girl with road rash pushes herself out of her chair and limps after Marcia.

Sallie calls out, "We'd better be next!"

They are not next. A man cradling his arm goes in, followed by a kid with a beesting who is blowing up like the Stay Puft Marshmallow Man.

Sallie huffs out a stream of frustrated air and falls into her chair. "I don't understand what your family's problem is. You're an *adult*. You're plenty old enough. You're turning twenty tomorrow."

George can barely nod. His arm is falling asleep from holding his hand over his head.

"I'm sure they want me to leave," Sallie says. "But I'm not going anywhere. They'll just have to deal with me. With *us,* as a *couple*."

George isn't sure what Sallie expected. Did she really believe his family was going to embrace the idea of George dating a woman twenty-three years his senior? It didn't matter that Sallie was Blair's friend and they'd all known her for decades—that made it worse! George groans as he wonders if anyone has called his mother in Paris. Why had he let Sallie talk him into bringing her here? Why hadn't she been content to leave it a secret? Things had been so perfect.

"Whalen?" Marcia calls out.

Sallie rises and helps George to his feet. "You could have told me you didn't have a key," she says. "I would have paid for a locksmith or we could have gotten a hotel. At the very least, you could have told me last night that you cut your hand. You need to work on your decision-making, George. There are times you act like a child."

Marcia clears her throat impatiently as George and Sallie make their way toward her. "Parents of adult children need to stay in the waiting room," she says to Sallie.

"I'm *not* his mother!" Sallie says.

"Well, then, you really need to stay in the waiting room," Marcia says, and she takes George by the arm.

In the exam room, George climbs up onto the table and promptly lies down. The towel around his hand is a soggy red mess but he's happy to be alone. This isn't how the weekend was supposed to go, he thinks. He and Sallie should be up in bed, drinking champagne, eating organic strawberries.

But who was he kidding? That was never going to happen. It's a family reunion.

*   *   *

"I'm here for a family reunion," George says to the girl with road rash. Road Rash and George have both been treated and are waiting in a room to be billed and released. George is, finally, feeling no pain. They gave him a local anesthetic when they cleaned up his hand as well as a Vicodin. Road Rash had her leg cleaned up, the gravel embedded in her skin removed (their exam rooms had been separated by just a curtain, so George heard her yipping with pain and the physician assistant urging her to keep still), and her wound dressed. She might have been given pain meds as well because she seems pretty chipper for someone who fell off a moped. "My grandmother owns a house in town and one out at the beach and tomorrow is my twin sister's and my birthday, so basically my whole family is showing up. Well, I mean, except for our mother."

Road Rash draws back. "Isn't the woman with you in the waiting room your mother?"

"No," George says. "That's my lady friend."

Road Rash, who is sitting in a vinyl chair across from George, gives another yip and then a big, silly smile crosses her face. Here, then, is the mirth George has been dreading. She sings out, *"You know I like my girls a little bit older."*

George and the Vicodin laugh. "I'm George," he says. "George Whalen."

Road Rash gasps. "No, you are *not!*"

"Yes, I am *so!*" he says.

"You work for Congressman Welby, right?" she says. "You're the one who stood me up?"

George hasn't really taken a good look at Road Rash's face, but when he does, he realizes she does look sort of familiar, but what does she mean, he stood her up?

"I'm Dana Dewberry," she says. "Raymond's cousin."

Cousin Dana! he thinks. Ha-ha-ha-ha! What are the chances? She does look a little like Phoebe Cates. Maybe even prettier.

Marcia the nurse pokes her head in with yet another clipboard, which she hands to Cousin Dana. "Sign here and you're free to go." She shakes her head at George. "Your aunt needs to learn some manners."

"It's not his aunt," Dana says. "It's his *lady friend.*"

"And I'm Barbara Bush," Marcia says.

Dana limps over to George and writes something in the palm of his good hand. It's her phone number. "When you and Auntie break up," she says, "you owe me a drink."

6. IN THE AIR TONIGHT

Has Magee always been this annoying? Jessie wonders.

It's four in the afternoon on Saturday, the barbecue starts at six, and Jessie has somehow been cast in the role of Magee's assistant. When Kate first informed Jessie that Saturday would be a family barbecue, a less formal gathering than Sunday's birthday clambake, Jessie thought it would be burgers and dogs, a tub of potato salad from the deli, and maybe, if they had the energy, some kind of tiki cocktail for the adults. (Jessie's father, David, had adored a good mai tai and daiquiri.)

But Magee has taken charge of the family barbecue using a cookbook called *Entertaining,* by Martha Stewart, that has gained a cult following in the wealthy suburbs of Connecticut and Massachusetts, and it has become a real production. There are lists detailing the menu, the timetable, and the "provisioning." While Jessie reviews the details of her next corporate sexual-harassment case, Magee buzzes around her, chopping, slicing, shredding, whisking, and using up, one heaping spoonful at a time, an entire jar of mayonnaise.

"Are you busy?" Magee asks. "Because I could use some help."

Jessie looks up. Is it not obvious that she's busy? Where is everyone else? Well, Tiger has the boys at the beach because Magee wanted them "out of her hair" (Magee wears her hair in a dramatic wedge cut with gelled bangs). Kate is on the patio, napping in a chaise. Genevieve retreated to her bedroom in the guesthouse after dropping the bombshell that her boyfriend is coming. (But how could any of them protest after George showed up with Sallie? Jessie might have mentioned that, as of yesterday, the boyfriend was married, but she kept her mouth shut because the last thing they needed was more drama.) George and Sallie were at the hospital because George had cut his hand while breaking into All's Fair.

Jessie's eyes linger on the reclining figure of her mother. It's amazing she can sleep.

"I'm out of mayonnaise," Magee says. "And I forgot seltzer for the kids' sparkling lemonade."

"Can't they just have regular lemonade?" Jessie asks. She had watched Magee juice the lemons, add "extra-fine" sugar (a variation Martha suggests) and cold water and muddled leaves of fresh mint.

"It's a party, so the kids will want 'soda.'" Magee uses air quotes. "But they'll settle for fizzy lemonade. And we need mayonnaise anyway. It would be such a huge help if you could run to the Finast."

Jessie can't help huffing as she stands up. *Some of us have actual work to do!* she wants to say. It's not her fault that Magee has jumped off the entertaining deep end.

To start, Magee has assembled a seafood tower of jumbo shrimp, poached scallops, and cracked lobster claws that will be served with some kind of herbed mayonnaise sauce. For their main course, it will be grilled swordfish (slathered with mayonnaise; it helps keep the fish moist), pork spare ribs for those who don't like fish, and rainbow veggie kebabs for those who don't eat fish or pork. There's potato salad, creamy coleslaw, and mac-aroni salad. There are deviled eggs. There's a hollowed-out watermelon filled with fresh fruit salad; Magee complained that the melon baller gave her a callus. There are cherry tomatoes stuffed with guacamole. And for dessert, there's a chocolate caramel tart. (Magee apologized to the people who cared—which was no one— that she'd used a Pillsbury crust instead of making her own.)

It's too much, Jessie thinks. *She's showing off.* "Sure," Jessie says with manufactured equanimity. "I'd be happy to go to the store."

It does, in fact, feel good getting out of the house. Jessie has been in a sour mood since she arrived on Nantucket, although she should be not only relaxed but jubilant about her landmark case and seven-figure decision. But there hasn't been time or space to tell anyone about it and nobody has asked, not even a perfunctory "How's work?"

Jessie is also still weighted down by the news Pick shared because she hasn't had a chance to talk to her mother. Jessie is tempted to just keep her mouth shut and let Kate find out on her own—but no, Jessie can't do that.

She's irked that Blair is in Paris when she should be here, dealing with her children.

She's more than irked that Kirby is in Los Angeles acting like the rest of them don't exist.

The chilled air of the supermarket is soothing, and Jessie wanders through the produce section, admiring the neat pyramids of plums and peaches. Her fellow shoppers are smiling and sunburned, the backs of their legs breaded with sand, as they pluck boxes of Popsicles from the freezer. Jessie clutches a jar of Hellmann's in one hand and a bottle of club soda in the other. She walks, very slowly, to the checkout line, wishing there were more things on her list, wishing she could stay just a little while longer.

When Jessie pulls onto Red Barn Road, she sees a taxi up ahead bouncing over the potholes and ridges in the dirt road, kicking up dust. Jessie shakes her head; the Nantucket taxi drivers, most of them college students, think they're Mario Andretti.

Jessie takes a deep breath as she watches the taxi whip into their driveway. She grabs the grocery bag and moves her sunglasses to the top of her head.

A man gets out of the taxi, hands some money through the window, then turns to face the house as the taxi drives off. He looks hesitant to approach and Jessie can't blame him. This, she supposes, is the boyfriend.

"Hello!" she calls out. She strides over, hand extended. "Are you..." She can't remember what Genevieve said his name was. Mouse?

"Andrew Flanagan," he says, taking her hand and offering a tentative smile. "Friend of Genevieve's."

"I'm Jessie Levin," she says. "Genevieve's aunt. Nice to meet you." Jessie finds herself slightly disappointed that Andrew is so normal-looking. He's short with pale, scrawny legs sticking out of ill-fitting khaki shorts. He's wearing a white Izod shirt and a baseball hat over his shaved head. He looks to be about twenty-five or twenty-six. Only yesterday, Jessie would have said he was too old for Genevieve, but now, of course, the family metrics have changed.

"Welcome to Nantucket, Andrew Flanagan," Jessie says. She's tempted to add, *Where's your wife?* But she wants to establish herself as the cool aunt, though this will become obvious once Andrew meets Magee.

Andrew takes off his Red Sox cap and Jessie stifles a gasp. Andrew has a zipper tattoo that starts at his forehead and crosses his skull like someone could pull back the tab and reveal his brains. Here, then, is the punk she's been promised.

"Let's go find Genevieve," Jessie says, trying to keep a straight face. "And I must introduce you to my mother."

An hour later, Jessie decides that Magee isn't annoying — she's amazing! She has transformed the simple wrought-iron table on the pool patio into something worthy of a magazine spread. The table has been covered with a periwinkle-blue Provençal-print tablecloth and topped with lavish bouquets of hydrangeas. At one end sits a large glass vessel filled with the most delicious rum punch Jessie has ever tasted. (The secret, Magee told her, is almond extract.)

The secret, Jessie thinks, is that it's strong. It takes only one glass for Jessie to achieve the "attitude adjustment" she has needed since she arrived. The punch is so sublime that suddenly everything happening in the house seems amusing, nearly whimsical.

Take, for example, the moment that George and Sallie make their entrance.

The kitchen is crowded. Tiger and Magee's boys—Frog (Richard, age nine), Puppy (John Wilder, age seven), Penn, age five, and Nichols, age three—are all fresh from the outdoor shower with their hair combed, wearing matching outfits of blue polo shirts and blue seersucker shorts. Tiger makes them line up by age as they wait for Magee to pour them cups of lemon "soda." They're so cute that Jessie regrets not bringing a camera.

"You should take a picture for your Christmas card," Jessie says.

Magee hands Nichols a sippy cup. "We have a professional photographer for that back home."

Of course you do, Jessie thinks. But the punch has put her in such a generous frame of mind that she just kisses Puppy on the cheek and says, "They can be the picture for my Christmas card." What else would she use? she wonders. A picture of her sitting behind the mountains of files on her desk? She and Pick on the sofa with Chinese takeout and the TV on in the background?

Puppy squirms from her grasp, crying out, "George is here!" All the boys race to the door as George and Sallie step inside.

"Hey, guys!" George says in an ebullient, nothing-is-wrong-here voice as he waves around his bandaged hand. The boys grab George around the legs, and Frog asks if they can go outside to throw the football.

"That's a great idea," Tiger says. "Let's get out of Mom and Aunt Jessie's way and see if George can catch the football one-handed."

Coward, Jessie thinks as Tiger slips past Sallie and out the door, the boys and George trailing him, leaving Jessie, Magee, and Sallie behind.

"Jessie, hi!" Sallie says in the same unembarrassed, unconcerned tone that George used. They must have decided in the car to *just act natural.* "You're as thin as a rail, I'm jealous. Have you been working like crazy?"

Jessie regards her eldest sister's best friend for a moment. She has always liked Sallie, *loved* Sallie—and it's not lost on her that Sallie is the first person to ask a single question about how she's been doing. But under the circumstances, it's hard not to think of Sallie as a predator. She's looking aggressively elegant in a kelly-green shift dress with matching green mules and there are emerald studs in her ears (real, Jessie is certain). She looks pretty and, yes, youthful, as though dating George has reverse-aged her. But George *should* be with someone wearing a jean skirt and Jellies, someone who listens to Belinda Carlisle. *What are you thinking?* Jessie wants to ask Sallie. *He's a teenager. He can't even buy a beer legally.* And beyond that, he's Blair's child. It's very likely Sallie held George as a baby, maybe even changed his diaper. Jessie has learned enough about sexual power dynamics to know that Sallie holds all the cards in their relationship — she probably pays for everything and makes all the decisions, including the decision to come to Nantucket this weekend. She will decide when the relationship ends, and George will be left heartbroken.

But then, suddenly, Kate's words ring in her ears: *Is it really the end of the world?*

Jessie opens her arms. "Hi, Sallie," she says. "Welcome." She gives George's new girlfriend a squeeze.

When they separate, Sallie's eyes are shining with gratitude. She holds out a white paper bag. "I brought Iberian ham from Savenor's sliced paper thin and a jar of sun-dried tomatoes. I thought we could put them out as hors d'oeuvres."

"No," Magee says. "Absolutely not. We have enough hors d'oeuvres."

"Don't be silly," Sallie says. "There's no such thing as enough hors d'oeuvres."

"Actually," Magee says, "there is." She opens the fridge and removes the seafood tower, arranged on a three-tiered silver tray that she must have brought from Wellesley because serving pieces like this don't live here at Red Barn Road. It's impressive, Jessie has to admit, the decadent amount of plump, pale pink jumbo shrimp, poached scallops, and rosy lobster claws on crushed ice, all garnished with wedges of lemon and a sprinkle of fresh parsley — like something plucked straight out of La Coupole in Paris. Next, Magee pulls a tray of mini-quiches from the oven and moves them with tongs, one by golden fragrant one, onto a pristine white platter. Finally, she fills a cut-glass bowl with pecans that she has toasted with rosemary and bits of bacon. Jessie had watched her making these nuts earlier that morning—they smelled *divine*—but hadn't been brave enough to ask to try one.

Undeterred, Sallie moves to the cabinet and brings down one of their everyday dinner plates; she unwraps the ham and lays out slices in a messy circle. Magee watches her, and when Sallie reaches for the jar of tomatoes, Magee snatches it up first. "No," she says. "You'll ruin my aesthetic."

"Ruin your *aesthetic?*" Sallie says. She laughs. "That's the most pathetic thing I've ever heard."

"Do you know what *I* think is pathetic?" Magee says. "You dating a child. It's beyond pathetic. It's criminal."

"Magee," Jessie says.

"George is *not* a child," Sallie says. "He's plenty old enough to make decisions about who he wants to spend time with."

Jessie can see where this is going, and the last thing she wants to do is stay and referee. She picks up the bowl of nuts and heads outside. She needs another drink anyway.

But getting another drink comes at a cost because next to the rum punch, Kate is talking to Andrew Flanagan.

"Tell me what you do for a living," Kate says. "I'm assuming your drumming doesn't pay the bills?"

"I'm an auto mechanic, ma'am," Andrew says.

"Wonderful!" Kate says with such over-the-top enthusiasm that one would think she had spent all day searching for an auto mechanic. "You know, we Nichols women have a penchant for blue-collar men. My mother, God rest her soul, spent over a decade in a relationship with our property's caretaker. Lovely man, Bill. It never mattered to Mother that he worked with his hands." She pauses. "Of course, Genevieve attends what's known as an Ivy League school—"

"He knows what an Ivy League school is, Grammy," Genevieve says. "Everyone does."

"So you two *are* a bit of a mismatch from that perspective. Genevieve is *quite* bright. Her father is a *rocket scientist,* has she told you that? We don't talk about Angus often around here, but I think this family agrees that there's such a thing as *too* smart." She pauses and Jessie fills her glass to the top. "Do you have any college, Andrew?"

"Not a day," Andrew says, and a mortifying silence follows that is blessedly broken when Bitsy Dunscombe and her daughter Helen walk in.

Their arrival coincides with Magee presenting the seafood tower with a "Ta-da!" But everyone is too distracted by the Dunscombes' arrival to notice. Magee appears at Jessie's elbow and says, "I thought this was a *family* barbecue. I'm not sure there's enough food for extra guests. Why didn't anyone tell me?"

Jessie plucks a shrimp off the top tier and drags it through the herbed mayonnaise sauce. "You have enough to feed the entire island here, Magee. It'll be fine, please relax."

"I'll relax when that hussy leaves," Magee says, and she storms back to the kitchen, giving Sallie a wide berth. Sallie is holding the plate of Iberian ham with a sad hill of sun-dried tomatoes dumped in the middle, glistening with orange oil. It does sort of ruin the aesthetic, Jessie thinks, but Sallie sets the plate down with triumph on her face.

Jessie fills a glass with punch for her childhood friend Helen and says, "Let's go to the beach. You'll thank me later."

"I'll thank you now," Helen says. "My mother dragged me here even though I told her I couldn't stand to be around a happy family at the moment."

Ha-ha-ha-ha! Jessie thinks, and she leads Helen to the beach path.

"I forgot how beautiful it is out here," Helen says. "We're stuck on Main Street. The only water I see is the harbor. This is so … wild."

Wild is a good word for it. The beach at Red Barn Road is a curve of wide golden sand backed by dunes and eelgrass. At this time of the evening, the only person visible in either direction is a lone surf caster to the west, silhouetted by the setting sun.

Jessie is eager to disabuse Helen of the notion that they're a happy family, but before she launches into describing the Byzantine twists and turns of the weekend, she says, "How are you doing?"

Helen kicks off her Pappagallo flats—she's been through hell but still looks like a catalog model—and plunks herself at the base of a sand dune. "How much do you know?"

Jessie knows what Kate has told her, which is some version of what Bitsy told Kate. "I know that Colin died."

"Of AIDS," Helen says.

"Yes, I'm so sorry," Jessie says. She'd sent a card as soon as she'd heard; the service had been private.

"He was gay," Helen says. She takes a healthy slug of her drink. "My husband was gay and I had no idea. He told me he had late rounds at the hospital; I believed him. For years I believed him, and he was visiting those bathhouses, going to raves in Alphabet City, stripping down and dancing in black light." Helen looks at Jessie. "One day I found fluorescent paint on one of his good white dress shirts and when I asked him about it, he said he'd done arts and crafts in the pediatric cancer wing."

"Oh, Helen."

"We never had sex," Helen says. "I mean, a few times when we were dating and then once on our honeymoon, and that was it. And I was *happy* about it. I was thrilled that Colin wasn't all over me the way that Robert was with Heather..."

Yes, Jessie thinks. Helen's twin sister, Heather, had

given birth to three children in three years and then, according to Bitsy, had her tubes tied.

"Because honestly, Jess? I think I'm frigid."

"You do?" Jessie says. She buries her feet in the sand and takes a sip of her drink. She doesn't have a lot of women friends and isn't used to talking about sex with anyone except Blair and Kirby—and those conversations are well in the past.

"I think it was all that shit with Garrison," Helen says. "It scarred me."

Jessie nods. Garrison was the tennis instructor at the Field and Oar Club the summer Jessie and Helen were thirteen, and he had abused them both. It happened to Jessie only once; Garrison pressed his erection into Jessie's buttocks while he was showing her how to swing a backhand. Jessie hadn't had the words to tell anyone what happened, though she'd immediately asked her grandmother to switch her instructor. Jessie wasn't frigid, but she still refused to get on a crowded subway car and she was intent on making a name for herself by nailing the jerks who took liberties with their female colleagues in the office. Oh, was she!

Helen, she gathered, had suffered with Garrison much worse. Jessie had once seen Helen crying in the ladies' room at the Field and Oar Club, and she somehow knew it was because of Garrison. That was the moment Jessie and Helen had become real friends.

"I get it." Jessie reaches for Helen's hand, and Helen starts to quietly weep.

"You're practically the only person who's not afraid to touch me," Helen says. "Even my own mother is afraid. She's set aside a mug and a drinking glass and a set of utensils just for me. She thinks I *have* it. Everyone thinks I have it. Heather won't bring the kids over." She bows her head between her knees like someone in a plane that's about to crash. "Colin had a lover, a boyfriend, named Trey. Trey was also a doctor — he worked at St. Vincent's, where all those men were dying. Trey died in February — it was on Valentine's Day. Colin didn't come home at all that night. And then, right after Easter, Colin told me he was infected. At first he claimed he'd gotten it from treating a patient, but as he got sicker, he told me the truth."

Jessie releases a breath. In front of them, the ocean encroaches and recedes with indifference to any human drama unfolding on the shore. "Did it make you feel any better?" Jessie asks. "Learning the truth?" She doesn't tell Helen, but she bumped into Colin on Dominick Street the previous Christmas. Jessie had been haunting record shops in search of a bootleg recording of Woodstock as a present for Pick and she'd seen Colin through the window of Alison's. He'd been at a table for two with another man, and they were deep in conversation; something about it seemed odd to Jessie but she thought she'd pop in anyway to say hello. Then she noticed Colin and the other man were holding hands across the table. She had also noticed that the other

man was gaunt and ghostly pale with a dark spot at his
jaw.

"No," Helen says. "Not really." She mops her tears
with her cocktail napkin. "I just really loved him as
a person, as a friend, and I hated seeing him suffer.
All those men dying...thousands and thousands of
them." She sniffs. "Enough of my maudlin story. Tell
me what's going on with you guys. How's the family
reunion–ing?"

Jessie waves a hand. "Oh, fine," she says. "I mean,
there's stuff going on, but it's not the end of the world."

It's not *the end of the world,* Jessie thinks. Her family is
downright lucky; their problems are surface wounds.

When she and Helen return, they find people eating in small groups. Kate and Bitsy are inside at the
kitchen table. Tiger, Magee, and the kids have com-
mandeered one end of the outdoor table, and the twins
and their respective dates are eating on chaises by the
pool—George and Sallie are sitting sideways on one,
facing Genevieve and Andrew on the other. Sallie and
Andrew are having a heated conversation about the punk
scene in Boston. Andrew says there isn't one and Sallie
disagrees, citing the Middle East in Cambridge and
edgier underground places in the South End.

Helen takes a single vegetable kebab and heads inside,
but Jessie can't handle Kate and Bitsy right now, nor
does she want to crash Tiger and Magee's family meal

or be a fifth wheel with the twins. She ends up pouring herself another glass of punch, piling a plate with swordfish and macaroni salad, and settling on the side of the pool, her feet dangling in the water. She has always told Pick that she never quite felt she belonged in her family. Tonight is the perfect example.

After Tiger and Magee take the children back to All's Fair and after George and Sallie check into their suite at the White Elephant ("It's a surprise for my birthday," George said, though they all knew there was no way George and Sallie could return to All's Fair) and after Genevieve and Andrew head out to "hear some music" (on the car radio, Jessie thinks, while they have sex in the back of the Scout on some dead end off Red Barn Road) and after Helen has dragged Bitsy to the red Miata, Jessie finds herself alone in the kitchen with her mother. This is unexpected and unplanned. It's so late, and Jessie and Kate have both had so much to drink that Jessie nearly decides to call it a night and go up to bed. Then again, it's so late and they've both had so much to drink that Jessie thinks, *What the hell.* And, *It's now or never.* This is her chance.

"Mom," Jessie says. "There's something I have to tell you."

"Is it about Bitsy?" Kate says. "Or Genevieve? Or, hell, George and Sallie? Because I don't want to hear it."

"Lorraine is on Nantucket this summer, Mom," Jessie says. She takes a beat, waiting for this information to sink in. "Lorraine Crimmins. She's working at an organic farm on Polpis Road, apparently. She's telling people to call her Rain. She's been selling strawberries on Main Street."

Kate turns to Jessie with wide eyes. "She's selling strawberries on Main Street?"

Jessie nods. "Yes." Does Kate *get* it? Does she *understand?* She's talking about Lorraine Crimmins, daughter of their beloved caretaker Bill Crimmins and mother of Jessie's boyfriend, Pick. She's talking about Lorraine Crimmins, who served as housekeeper, cook, and nanny to Blair, Kirby, and Tiger but who then had an affair with Kate's first husband, Wilder Foley, and became pregnant with his child, causing the downfall of the Foley family.

She's talking about Lorraine Crimmins, Kate's sworn enemy.

Kate doesn't yell; she doesn't break down and cry; she doesn't spit out that Lorraine Crimmins knows better than to set foot on this island: *It's my island, she gave up her right to it when she slept with my husband, when she caused his death!*

Kate does none of these things. Instead, Kate chuckles. "That's why Bitsy came back without any strawberries. She said it was gnats, but really, she's just a good friend. The best I've ever had." When Kate looks at Jessie, her eyes are shining with tears. For all her youthful hijinks this summer, Jessie thinks, her mother in this moment looks every one of her sixty-eight years.

And she looks so much like her own mother, Exalta, that Jessie is spooked.

"Let's get you up to bed, Mom," she says.

Kate allows Jessie to help her to her feet. "Yes," she says. "I'm tired."

7. WELCOME TO THE JUNGLE

She hasn't slept in twenty-seven hours—Kirby's last-minute decision to fly east landed her in the middle seat of the back row of the plane, where she could enjoy the smell of the chemical toilet—so when she finally boards the ferry at the fresh hour of eight a.m., she buys herself a Bloody Mary and tells herself she's earned it. What's that saying? Fifty percent of life is *just showing up*.

Here I am, Kirby thinks when the ferry docks in Nantucket. The prodigal aunt.

She goes into the terminal to use the pay phone, stopping at the ladies' room first. Kirby flew without bags, but one look in the smudged mirror tells her they're under her eyes. (Ha-ha.) Her skin is blotchy and dull, her hair, which she cut into a bob and permed in an attempt to look younger (her long, straight hair *screamed* sixties flower child), is crispy with product (so much mousse, too much). But the vodka on the boat has given her a little spark—just enough, she hopes, to get her to Red Barn Road, where she will experience the "authentic high" (she's using rehab-speak here) of taking her family *completely by surprise.*

She has to hurry; the buzz feels like a lit match burning to its end.

She calls the house and a voice says, "Good morning, Levin residence."

It's not Kirby's mother, which would have been Kirby's first choice, or Genevieve, which would have been her second. It is, in fact, her last choice.

"Jessie?" Kirby says. "It's me." She pauses. "Kirby."

Jessie hangs up.

Fair enough, Kirby thinks. She deserved that. She calls back. The phone rings five times, then it's picked up and slammed down. It's like they're children again. Kirby searches through her Gucci change purse that she bought on Rodeo Drive in more prosperous times, but she can't find another quarter so she slides in three dimes. She's so broke that wasting that extra nickel pains her.

Jessie picks up on the first ring. "No one wants to talk to you."

"But I'm—"

Jessie hangs up.

"Here," Kirby says.

Fine, Kirby thinks. She'll walk. She has only her purse and a loden suede weekend duffel that she bought at Joan and David, also in more prosperous times. She's wearing Capezio ballet flats, black leggings, an oversize white button-down. She puts on Ray-Ban aviators, hoping she evokes Kelly McGillis in *Top Gun,* and off she sets.

Her spirits start to sing as she passes all of the familiar landmarks in town. There's Steamboat Pizza, the Whaling Museum, and the Sunken Ship, where she and Blair and Tiger used to buy new rope bracelets at the start of every summer. Kirby knows that if she goes inside, there will be, next to the register, a glass jar of pristine new bracelets, white as bone. Is she too old to wear one? Yes, she thinks. She's forty-freaking-one! She keeps going.

She passes Hardy's General Store, with its familiar smell of sawdust and paint, then takes a right on Main. The sun is already hot; she's sweating in her tight black leggings. How will she make it all the way to Red Barn Road?

She passes a farm truck parked in front of the Camera Shop. A woman who really does look like a sixties flower child is selling quarts of organic strawberries for six bucks. Ha! Kirby thinks. She thought that calling something organic and selling it for twice as much as normal was only a California thing.

She heads up to Mitchell's Book Corner and stops for a minute to check out the titles in the window: John le Carré, Mary Higgins Clark, Salman Rushdie. As Tyesha always says, *Reading is a great place to find your next movie,* and it's not always the bestsellers that are hits. Right, Kirby thinks. What she needs is a sleeper.

She wants to pluck a book out of obscurity, pitch it, make it a blockbuster, and save her reputation—if it's not beyond saving. There's a book called *A Time to Kill* by John Grisham. Kirby has never heard of him, but it looks like a legal thriller and Scott Turow already has that territory covered. There's a novel by someone named Kazuo Ishiguro called *The Remains of the Day*—definitely obscure, probably too obscure to be made into a film.

Kirby continues up Main Street and rounds the corner onto Fair. She needs to make a pit stop. When she reaches All's Fair, she rounds the corner onto Plumb Lane, unlatches the gate, and steps into the backyard, just in case someone else in her family is in residence. She sees that the glass in the back door has been papered over. Vandalism, here on Fair Street? Burglary? Kirby eases the door open—someone must be staying here— and tiptoes into the kitchen, where she sets her bag down for one blessed second. She opens the fridge to find a carton of juice, a quart of strawberries that she's betting came from the hippie on Main Street, a gallon of milk that's three-quarters gone, eggs, a pound of bacon, a bowl of plump green grapes, a jar of apricot preserves, and—Kirby can hardly believe her eyes—a bottle of Moët et Chandon champagne.

It's the answer to her prayers.

She hears what sounds like a herd of cattle upstairs, then little-person voices, and she swears under her breath—Tiger and the kids are here. While Kirby would love nothing more than to sit in the backyard with her brother and a couple of mimosas, she can't handle Magee for even one second. Kirby grabs the bottle of champagne and slips out the back door.

She waits until she's halfway down Lucretia Mott Lane before she pops the cork. It flies into someone's rosebushes, and Kirby brings the bottle to her lips. She lets the bubbles run down her chin and all over her white shirt. It's official, she thinks. She's a lush, a derelict, a poseur, and a grifter. If Tyesha Bradford, Kirby's girlfriend of the past two years, could see her now, walking down the charming, leafy Nantucket streets drinking Moët straight from the bottle at nine thirty in the morning, she would think...what? That she'd wasted eight grand sending Kirby to rehab at Clarity Farms? That she was justified in firing Kirby from her production company, Silver Dollar? That she was even more justified in breaking things off with her?

Kirby takes another slug off the bottle as cars pass— the usual Jeep Wagoneers and woody wagons. Kirby is relieved that she hasn't seen anyone she knows, but as she reaches Caton Circle and starts out the Madaket Road bike path, she becomes annoyed. She could really use a ride. How *dare* Jessie hang up on her!

She should have returned the message that Jessie left on her machine a few days ago. But she had done one better—she had come in person. And she was staying. (*What does that mean, staying?* she wonders. Would she move into the house on Red Barn Road for the remainder of the summer and into the fall? Would she do the unthinkable and stay on Nantucket *through the winter?* There was, at this point, nothing left for her in LA.)

The more Kirby thinks about this, the more she dreads what lies ahead.

Namely: explaining herself.

As far as her family knows, she's a success. When she moved to LA, she immediately got a job as the fifth assistant to the director John Hughes. (Basically, she made coffee and dinner reservations for the first four assistants.) But even so, she had worked on the movies that defined a generation: *Sixteen Candles. The Breakfast Club. Ferris Bueller's Day Off.* She befriended the second assistant, Tyesha Bradford—and then, one night at a party in Malibu, they became more than friends.

What a surprise *that* had been! Kirby had dated only men up to that point but her chemistry with Tyesha was undeniable. Tyesha had been born and raised in LA; her family was in real estate. She was smarter than Kirby, better educated, sexier, savvier, more seasoned. She had that elusive thing called class. Kirby could see it in the way Tyesha layered her thin gold necklaces and wore her Stanford class ring on her index finger. She had buttery leather accessories—bags with the right-length straps, the perfect compartments for keys and wallet, boots with the right heel, the most stylish silhouette. She could order wine, speak Spanish with her doorman, discuss the latest work of Alice Walker, of Walker Percy.

The summer before, Tyesha started her own production company, and Kirby went with her. Kirby was technically a production assistant, but Tyesha treated her like a partner. When they produced an independent film called *The Drum Major,* Tyesha was launched into the spotlight, and she grabbed Kirby's hand and pulled her into the bright circle right beside her. For a few golden months, they were courted by studios, invited to glamorous parties.

They needed a follow-up. Kirby suggested pitching their own story, a movie about a girl from Boston who moves to LA to escape her emotionally stunted family and meets a stylish, ambitious African American woman. They fall in love.

"You haven't given me any conflict," Tyesha said. "I'm falling asleep."

"How about if the chick from Boston is a bad girl," Kirby said. "What if she has a secret cocaine habit and sleeps with men behind her lover's back?"

Even now, Kirby can feel the tension that had filled Tyesha's apartment in Silver Lake.

"Do you have a secret cocaine habit?" Tyesha asked. "Are you sleeping with men behind my back?"

The answers were yes and yes. In fact, Kirby had been high the moment she said it. It was a testament to how screwed up she was that she hadn't even meant to confess; the truth had just popped out.

Kirby scoffed. "Of course not."

But smart, savvy Tyesha had gleaned the truth in the slight pause that preceded these words, and when she pressed, Kirby folded. Her lame defense: She had been using cocaine long before she even moved to LA (does Tyesha not remember her talking about her Studio 54 days with Warhol?); she'd thought Tyesha was fully aware and turning a blind eye. But Kirby had her habit under control. She only called her dealer, Brody, once a week and occasionally she scored at a party. When she did a line or two at a party, she sometimes found herself making out with some lighting guy or second grip named Scott or Dean, which led to having forgettable sex in the host's closet while Tyesha was out at the party chatting up the most influential person in the room (one night it was Brigitte Nielsen, another night, Danny Glover).

"I know Glover is a legitimate big deal," Kirby said. "But when I asked you to introduce me, you swatted me away."

"Are you listening to yourself?" Tyesha asked.

With infinite graciousness, Tyesha had paid for Kirby to go to rehab and promised that when she got out, she would still have a job. In the four weeks that Kirby was at Clarity Farms, Tyesha landed not one but two movies with major studios and hired a new partner, a woman named Alicia who had formerly produced movies with both Brigitte Nielsen and Danny Glover. Kirby still had a job but she no longer had any influence. The people who made the decisions now were Tyesha and Alicia.

"So many vowels," Kirby joked, but Tyesha didn't find it funny.

The dramatic end came when Kirby went to pitch a film called *The Secret Pasture.* It was a girl-and-her-horse screenplay set in Canada. Kirby knew the pitch was a throwaway and wouldn't get picked up anywhere, and in her resentment about this (and, face it, about Alicia), Kirby called her dealer, Brody, and did a couple lines right before taking the meeting. Then, instead of pitching *The Secret Pasture,* she pitched a made-up movie called *The Porn Star's Girlfriend.*

"It was just a variation on a girl-and-her-horse," Kirby deadpanned. But Tyesha didn't find it funny. Tyesha fired her *and* broke up with her. In response, Kirby jumped on a plane, and now here she is, drunk in the sun, trying to get home.

She's crossing Millbrook Road when a shiny Humvee pulls over. Kirby knows that men who drive cars like this are compensating for something, but the dude who pokes his head out the window asking, "Want a ride?" is as handsome to her in that moment as Richard Gere in his naval officer uniform. She feels the searing heat of the pavement through the soles of her Capezios; she doesn't care if it's Freddy Krueger behind the wheel, she's getting in.

"Hell yes," she says. She hoists herself up into the

passenger seat and offers the driver the last of the champagne, which he sucks down as he hits the gas.

Kirby has found a soul mate!

"I'm Kirby Foley," she says. "Thank you for stopping. I live out on Red Barn Road but I'll ride as far as you're going."

"I'm going where you're going," her new soul mate says.

Kirby narrows her eyes at him. He's younger than her, maybe closer to Jessie's age. He's a bit rumpled-looking. If Kirby had to guess, she would say he'd stayed out all night and was only now heading home. "My name's Charlie," he says. "But everyone calls me Blowman."

Kirby hoots. "Oh, yeah?"

"Yeah," he says. "You want to party?"

"What, you mean now?"

"Of course now," Blowman says, tossing the empty champagne bottle into the back seat. "Seems like you started without me."

"I should get home," Kirby says. The turn for Red Barn Road is up ahead. "Take a left here."

"How about we do a line before I drop you off?" Blowman asks.

Kirby takes a deep breath. Tyesha was all about breathing, centering herself, flow, yoga, fruit smoothies, vegetables in the juicer, fresh air, karma, mantras, chakras—the whole California cliché. Tyesha would forbid Kirby to do a line with this young, handsome stranger. *Go home!* she'd say. *You're already drunk!*

That's correct, Kirby is already drunk. A little cocaine might straighten her out.

"Sure," she says.

That's all Blowman needs to hear. He pulls off into the low brush alongside Red Barn Road, takes a mirror and a vial out of the Humvee's console, and cuts two lines with his Discover card. Kirby would have pegged Blowman for the kind of guy who snorted through a rolled-up hundred, but no, he has a little straw. Fine. Kirby hoovers up a line, then she wipes under her nose and rubs her finger across her gums. Derelict. She stares out at the landscape before her—the ribbon of ocean and her mother's house in the distance. She would never have made it by herself, walking. She would have dropped long ago and become breakfast for birds of prey.

Birds of Prey sounds like a movie title. Maybe Blowman can star in it.

She can't believe how utterly hopeless she is.

Blowman pulls into the driveway, pestering Kirby for her phone number, but she's finished with him. As she's climbing out of the Hummer, the front door opens and Jessie steps out, glaring.

"Oh my God," Blowman says. "Not her again."

"That's my sister," Kirby says. "You know her?"

Blowman throws the Humvee in reverse and screeches out of the driveway. Kirby looks after him with something like longing before turning to face her reckoning.

"Surprise," she says to her sister. "It's me."

8. Total Eclipse of the Heart

Kate wakes with the dawn, although *wakes* isn't quite accurate because she never managed to fall asleep. Whatever she'd thought Jessie wanted to talk about, it never occurred to her that it would be Lorraine Crimmins. Lorraine is back on Nantucket. Living here. *Growing* things.

This is ironic, since in Kate's experience, Lorraine has only been successful at destroying things.

Lorraine Crimmins—back in the sixties, she changed her name to Lavender, and now apparently she's Rain. While Lorraine was working for their family as a housekeeper, cook, and nanny back in the 1950s, she and Wilder had an affair and she became pregnant. Kate had left Wilder, but he came crawling back. And then, when Kate announced that she was divorcing him, he shot himself.

Afterward, Lorraine moved to California and raised her son, Pickford, in a commune. She abandoned Pick in 1969 when she wanted to do some "traveling." Bill Crimmins had driven out to the West Coast to pick the boy up and bring him back to Nantucket.

The last time Kate had seen Lorraine was in August of 1969, when she showed up — barefoot, grungy, and probably high on all kinds of drugs — to take Pick back to California. By way of Woodstock. (Kate rolls her eyes every time she thinks about this. What kind of mother takes her child to Woodstock!)

Kate had been crystal clear — with Lorraine, with Bill, with Pick. She never wanted to see Lorraine again. Kate didn't own Nantucket, of course, but she'd thought it was understood that Lorraine had forfeited her right to be here. This was Kate's turf!

She sounds hopelessly old-fashioned; they aren't the Sharks and the Jets. Two decades have passed since Kate last saw Lorraine. Maybe Lorraine thought that was enough time.

When the clock strikes seven, Kate calls Bitsy. "Will you come get me, please?"

"Again?" Bitsy's voice is groggy; it's too early even for Jane Fonda.

"I need strawberries," Kate says.

There's a pause. "Kate."

"Bitsy," Kate says. "I need strawberries."

Bitsy shows up fifteen minutes later and for once in her life, she seems to be at a loss for words. This is just as well; Kate needs to think. How can she persuade Lorraine to leave? Kate has no idea, but she knows one thing: The island isn't big enough for both of them.

She can't be bumping into Lorraine Crimmins at the Finast or the post office.

The Miata rumbles up the cobblestones of Main Street and Bitsy snags the first available parking space. "The farm truck is in front of the Camera Shop," Bitsy says. "I'll wait here. Whistle if you need backup."

Kate wants to laugh but she's too anxious. "You make it sound like I'm going to a rumble."

"Aren't you?" Bitsy says, and Kate climbs out of the car.

Thirty years ago, twenty, even ten, Kate would have cared about how she looked when she faced her husband's mistress, but Kate doesn't care anymore. This morning she's wearing a plain navy T-shirt and capri pants, white Keds, and she didn't bother with makeup; she can't remember if she ran a brush through her hair. She's beyond thinking that Wilder slept with Lorraine because Lorraine was prettier or more desirable. Wilder slept with Lorraine because he was unstable and wanted to act out.

Kate marches up to the farm truck and sees the back of a woman with very long gray hair. Could *this* be Lorraine, looking so...old? Lorraine is four years younger than Kate, so sixty-four. And she's always had long hair. *Yes,* Kate thinks.

When Lorraine turns around and sees Kate, she reels back, stumbling in her Birkenstocks. Things have improved a bit for Lorraine, Kate thinks. She's wearing shoes.

"Katie?" Lorraine whispers.

Kate shakes her head. No one has called her Katie since…well, since David died, but David's "Katie" was sweet and tender, whereas Lorraine's "Katie" hearkens back to their long-ago past. Lorraine came to work at All's Fair when she was sixteen and Kate only twenty. The war had been raging in Europe, but the Japanese had not yet bombed Pearl Harbor.

"Good morning, Lorraine," Kate says.

"I go by Rain now," Lorraine says.

Yes, that's what Jessie said. When Lorraine showed up at All's Fair twenty years earlier, she'd called herself Lavender. Lorraine Crimmins is the kind of troubled soul who sheds identities—and names—like a snake sheds its skin.

"I heard you were selling strawberries." Kate eyes the rows of green cardboard containers filled to the brim with fat, bright red berries. There are no gnats, no mold; these are the nicest-looking strawberries Kate has ever seen. The hand-printed sign says they're ORGANIC, from the POLPIS FARM COOPERATIVE, and that they cost six dollars a quart. Highway robbery. "You must have known I would find out you were here eventually." She sweeps her arm like one of the gals on *The Price Is Right*. "You're on Main Street."

Lorraine picks up a quart of berries and shoves it at Kate. "Take these, free of charge," she says. "Just please leave me alone."

"You know what's funny?" Kate says. "I'm here to ask *you* to leave *me* alone. You don't belong on this island and you know it."

At this, Lorraine sets her shoulders back and juts out her chin. "I was born and raised here. And my father before me. I'm a native islander, not some summer person from the big city who shows up every summer to take the best bite from the apple and then leave."

Kate nods. Since she was a child she has understood the resentment that locals have for the summer people. "I thought we had an understanding." Kate lowers her voice but inches closer to Lorraine, so close that she can smell Lorraine's musky odor, her unwashed hair. She won't make a scene, she tells herself. But she will get her point across.

"Such an interesting choice of words," Lorraine says. "*Understanding.* What I remember is that your parents told my father that I had to go. They gave him a hundred and fifty dollars. He bought me a bus ticket to California and made it eminently clear that I was not to show my face back on the island again." She grimaces. "My own father."

"And yet here you are," Kate says.

"My father is dead," Lorraine says, and the quart of strawberries that she holds in her hands starts to quiver. "Pick didn't even bother to call when it happened. Instead, he sent me a letter telling me you all had decided against a service, that my father's ashes would be buried in a small plot next to Exalta's and Penn's."

Lorraine narrows her eyes, which are still a lovely frosted-glass blue. "My own son asked me not to come back east to pay my respects because he didn't want to upset *you*."

Kate absorbs this. It's true; they didn't have a service for Bill. Part of this decision was because Bill had outlived all of his contemporaries. But part of it, Kate admits, was that she didn't want to see Lorraine. "Well," Kate says, but then she stops because she's at a loss for words.

"I loved Wilder, Katie."

Lorraine could have dumped the berries she's holding all over Kate's head and she wouldn't have been more surprised. "What?"

"I loved him," Lorraine says. "Or at least I thought I did at the time. In the commune, we held group-therapy sessions, sitting in a circle around the fire, drinking homemade wine. My community helped me understand that it wasn't Wilder I was in love with. It was Wilder and you—and Blair and Kirby and Tiger. I envied your family so much, all I wanted was to be a part of it. So when Wilder showed an interest in me—even though I knew it was fueled by alcohol and pills—I said yes." Her hands are shaking so badly now that she sets the strawberries down. "When I found out I was pregnant, I was ecstatic. I'd been hoping I'd get pregnant."

Kate flexes her hand. She wants to strike Lorraine— even all these years later, she wants to slap her silly. *He was my husband, not yours!* Kate and Wilder had three young children! Didn't Lorraine see how destructive her behavior was? How *selfish?*

Only now do Lorraine's eyes fill with tears. "When I heard Wilder died, I wanted to believe he'd killed himself because we couldn't be together. I wanted it to be your fault. But that was just a fantasy. He killed himself because I ruined his life. His death was my fault and I've carried it with me every day for thirty-five years." She wipes away her tears. "I came back to Nantucket because I heard about this farm cooperative and I've become something of an expert in the field of organic produce. But I also came back to Nantucket because I knew I'd see you eventually. I *wanted* to see you, Katie—so I could apologize. I'm sorry for all the pain I've caused you." She reaches out with one of her farm-grimy hands to clench Kate's arm. "I'm sorry, Katie."

Suddenly the decades melt away; Kate is a young mother and Lorraine a teenager, desperate to please her new employers. It's a beastly hot day; Kate and Wilder have just returned from the beach with Blair, who is six months old. When they walk in the back door into the kitchen, they find Lorraine waxing the kitchen floor. She has also cleaned the oven, scrubbed the range, reorganized the dry goods in the pantry. She takes the fussy baby from Kate's arms and says, "Let's get you a cool bath and some powder and then I'll put you down for a nice nap." Kate is dizzy with relief and also impressed with Lorraine's easy confidence and intuition where the baby is concerned, especially since Lorraine doesn't have a mother herself. Before Lorraine whisks Blair from the spotless kitchen, she turns to Kate and Wilder and says, "I made a pitcher of iced tea. It's in the icebox. There's a platter of cheese and crackers in there as well, and that chutney you like, Katie." Young Lorraine wants only to help, to make their lives easier. And hadn't Kate felt God's grace in being relieved of the baby for an hour, in the first sip of minty tea?

Now Kate sighs. Her anger is heavy. What if she just set it down? What if she accepts Lorraine's apology for this ancient wrong and is done with it?

"We're having a party tonight," Kate says. "At my beach house on Red Barn Road. Why don't you come?"

Lorraine's eyes flood over and she reaches out to hug Kate, who reluctantly finds herself patting Lorraine's back. She's sure everyone walking by is wondering what on earth is causing two old ladies such emotions.

It's a long, long story.

Kate and Lorraine pull apart. Kate says, "I'll take a quart of those strawberries after all."

Kate pops one of the berries in her mouth on the way to the car; it's even sweeter and juicier than she imagined. When Kate opens the Miata's passenger door, Bitsy lowers her sunglasses and peers at Kate over the top.

"I was just about to come save you," she says. "What happened?"

Kate eats another berry, then hands the box to Bitsy.

"It would have made a fine episode of *Maury Povich*," she says.

"What is that supposed to mean?" Bitsy says.

"I think I'm finally growing up," Kate says.

9. LIVIN' ON A PRAYER

The clambake was her aunt Magee's idea.

"Look at all those lobsters!" Mouth says. He has dragged Genevieve down to the beach so they can watch the caterers dig a coffin-size hole in the sand, start the fire, and lay down the stones and then the seaweed. "Aren't you excited?"

Not really, Genevieve thinks. Nobody asked what she wanted for her birthday because, in her family's mind, she's still a child, and the deciding is done by the adults.

Mouth — or Andrew, as everyone is now calling him — is all dialed up about the clambake. The little-necks, the mussels, the linguica and small red potatoes, and thirty ears of Bartlett's Farm corn will be steamed in the sand. They're eating on the beach, at a long table with folding banquet chairs.

"Do you think I'm dressed okay?" Mouth asks.

"I mean, yeah?" Genevieve says. "Andrew" has taken a shine to Nantucket — maybe too much of a shine. He loves the house. He loves the in-ground pool, the path to the beach, the separate cottage just for guests, the sunporch (where he's sleeping), and the circular driveway paved with white shells. It's like something out of a movie, he says. "Why didn't you tell me, babe?" He went crazy over the outdoor shower, even though it's rudimentary and affords very little privacy. (Genevieve would choose to shower indoors if she were allowed, which she is not.) He loves the Scout — he's a mechanic and a vehicle like that is catnip — but he doesn't seem to realize that it's a bitch to drive. The steering column is stiff, the gearshift sticks, the thing rattles so badly that Genevieve always fears it's going to lose a quarter panel.

Genevieve feels three unexpected ways about Mouth's presence here on Nantucket.

A) Let down. Her family's reaction was one of benign acceptance because George stole all her thunder in the inappropriate-partner department. She had been anticipating — and maybe even hoping for — more of a disruption.

B) Annoyed. Mouth is suddenly obsessed with "fitting in" and "looking the part." That morning, he'd asked Genevieve if they could ride into town so he could buy a new outfit at Murray's. Genevieve indulged him, even though it was *her* birthday and the very last place she wanted to spend even an hour of it was the bastion of prep that was Murray's Toggery. Mouth bought a pink polo shirt — a real one, with the little horse — and a pair of madras shorts that the saleswoman told him would fade with every washing. A look of concern crossed his face until Genevieve explained that *faded* madras was far more authentic than bright, crisply colored madras. "The rules here are completely backward," she said.

C) Creepings of the Ick. "The Ick" is what a girl feels when it's time to break up with someone because everything he says and does makes her skin crawl.

Genevieve doesn't understand how only yesterday she could have been *so in love* with Mouth and yet now that he's here, she feels only a gross disdain. She was so happy to hear he left Danielle — Genevieve had won! — but this elation quickly changed to panic. Two of the three things that she finds the most attractive about him — his unavailability and his status as a person in the world with a "real job" — are gone. All that's left is his "punk-ness," but as Genevieve regards his new outfit (he also bought a webbed belt and a pair of Reef flip-flops), the only vestige of the Mouth she became so obsessed with is his head tattoo, and he keeps that covered with a Red Sox cap at every opportunity.

"I really like your family," Mouth says, putting an arm around Genevieve, squeezing her closer, pressing his hot, wet mouth to her neck in a way that makes her pull away just a little. "Your aunts and uncle are so cool. Your uncle basically offered me a job."

"He said he'd see what he could do." That afternoon, Mouth and Genevieve had joined her family on the beach. Mouth hung out with Tiger and the boys, who were bodysurfing, which left Genevieve with her grandmother and her aunts. Magee was needlepointing under an umbrella, and next to her, Grammy read a Dominick Dunne novel. Aunt Jessie and Aunt Kirby were on either side of the umbrella, so far apart it didn't look like they were part of the family.

Genevieve set up a chair next to Aunt Kirby. She was honored that her aunt had made the effort to get to their birthday—what a surprise!—but Genevieve quickly surmised that things with her cool aunt were not that cool.

Kirby showed up drunk, for starters, so drunk that she slurred her words, and when she hugged Genevieve, she started to cry, confessing that she was an absolute wreck. She'd lost her fancy Hollywood job, and her girlfriend broke up with her. Genevieve had tried to conceal her surprise—she didn't know Aunt Kirby was gay! Yes, apparently Kirby's girlfriend, Tyesha Bradford, had both fired her and ditched her. So Kirby wasn't really here for Genevieve and George's birthday; she was here because she'd run out of options.

This was disappointing. Genevieve had placed her aunt on a pedestal, and that pedestal was crumbling.

"Hey," Genevieve said when she settled in her chair. Kirby was wearing a shocking excuse for a bikini— the bottom was just a string that ran up her ass crack—and she was skeletally thin. Genevieve had always admired Kirby's long golden-brown hair, but Kirby had cut and permed it. Kirby's skin was even pastier than Genevieve's, though her shoulders and ass cheeks were turning rosy. "You should probably get out of the sun. It looks like you're burning."

Kirby mumbled something unintelligible. She was half asleep.

Genevieve wandered over to where Mouth and Tiger were standing and watching the boys ride the waves. She overheard Mouth asking if there was any room for him at Tiger Lanes. "I'm an auto mechanic," Mouth said. "But I'm sure I could run a bowling alley. You own a bunch of them, right?"

Tiger yelled for Puppy to come in closer to shore. "We have thirty-two locations," Tiger said. He gave Mouth an appraising look, and Genevieve wanted to sink into the sand. Tiger Lanes ran popular TV commercials that used the slogan "Wholesome Family Fun." The *wholesome* had been Magee's idea, as were banning heavy metal and punk music from the jukeboxes. (She was a regular Tipper Gore.) But the slogan had been successful. Everyone who bowled, bowled at Tiger Lanes. Tiger was a millionaire. "Give me your number before you leave tomorrow. I'll see what I can do."

Once the lobsters and potatoes and corn are covered with more seaweed, then a damp tarp, then sand, Genevieve wants to go back to the house to see if George has arrived.

She hasn't seen him all day or had a chance to wish him a happy birthday. She and her brother have nothing in common—people have always referred to them as "cheese and chalk"—but there are certain things only he understands, such as the fact that every time they have an important birthday, the newspapers write about the tenth or fifteenth or twentieth anniversary of the moon launch (their actual birthday) and of Teddy Kennedy sinking the car on Chappaquiddick (the day after their birthday). Genevieve (and George, she knows) has always felt defined by the launching and the sinking.

"I'm going back to the house," Genevieve tells Mouth.

"You sound angry," Mouth says. "Is it because I didn't buy you a present? I'm sorry, babe. I just didn't have the money for something nice."

But you had it for a new shirt and shorts, she thinks. *A webbed belt and flip-flops.* Genevieve shrugs. "Presents don't matter."

"I'll make it up to you once I get a job running one of your uncle's bowling alleys," Mouth says. "I'll pay all our rent, our utilities, our groceries, and I'll buy you something nice every week."

Genevieve blinks. *Ick,* she thinks. She hurries down the path toward the house. *Let George be there,* she thinks. *Please.*

It's six o'clock, and the clambake is supposed to start at six thirty, but Sallie hasn't even showered yet, and getting ready takes her an hour...when she hurries.

"Sal," George says. Sallie is tucked under the sheets and fluffy duvet of the hotel bed, smoking a cigarette, reading the Nantucket Chamber of Commerce guide. "We're going to be late. We're supposed to be there in half an hour."

"Looks like we missed a gallery down on Easy Street," Sallie says. "William Welch."

George pulls his bow tie out of his suitcase and stands in front of the mirror. He *hates* being late. Even being on time feels sloppy; he likes, always, to be early. Sallie is intentionally sabotaging his birthday dinner, right? She doesn't want to go — and he has become only too aware that Sallie sets the agenda. They spent the afternoon shopping in town. It's true that Sallie bought George a pair of vintage cuff links at Tonkin's, but the rest of the day, they'd shopped only for Sallie. First it was clothes at Eye of the Needle and Vis-à-Vis, then it was off to the galleries. George actually can't believe there's one they missed. They must have gone into a dozen, with Sallie leading the way and George following like a dog on a leash.

She had, mercifully, agreed to stop for lunch at the Nantucket Pharmacy sandwich counter. George ordered ham-and-pickle salad on rye and Sallie a turkey club, and they shared a chocolate frappe in honor of his birthday. But then something happened. The bell on the door jingled and George turned to see Cousin Dana walk in.

When Dana saw him sitting with Sallie, she beelined over.

"Hi, I'm Dana Dewberry," she said, offering Sallie her hand. "A dear friend of George's."

George flushed. He and Dana were hardly "dear friends." "I met Dana yesterday at the hospital," he said. He gave her a weak smile. "How's your leg?"

"Better, thanks for asking." Dana winked at Sallie. "You have quite a catch there. You're one lucky lady!"

"Aren't I just," Sallie said, giving Dana an assessing look. She plunked a twenty down on the counter. "Well, Dana Dewberry, dear friend of George's, you'll have to excuse us. We have some more shopping to do."

"We can go to the William Welch gallery tomorrow before our ferry," George says to Sallie now. "Would you please get ready?"

"No," Sallie says, slapping the chamber of commerce guide down on the bed.

"What do you mean, no?" George says. He sits down beside her. "Believe me, I'd rather order room service and lie around naked too, but it's my birthday party. My family went to a lot of trouble."

"Ha!" Sallie says. "Magee called a caterer."

"Even so, it's my birthday."

Sallie reaches for his hand, the one not bandaged, the one that has Dana's phone number still faintly visible across the palm. "While you were napping, I took the liberty of copying down this number and I called it."

George feels like his bow tie is choking him. "That's nothing, it's just—"

"The answering machine told me it was the phone number of someone named Dana." Sallie turns George's chin so he has no choice but to look her in the eye. "The number of the girl who introduced herself at the pharmacy."

"Yes, but—"

"But what?"

"It's not what you think."

"What do I think?"

"She wrote it there, not me."

"Obviously, George. You only have one working hand."

"I'm not even sure why she wrote it," he says. "I didn't *ask* her to. I barely know her."

"She wrote it because she wants you to call her."

"Well, I don't *want* to call her." He swallows. "I love you."

Sallie shakes her head. "Don't," she says, "confuse lust with love."

"I'm not, I'm—"

Sallie grasps George's good hand, which is now his bad hand because of Dana's phone number. "You *should* be going out with girls like Dana. She was cute. She looked like Phoebe Cates. You're twenty years old, George. You should be dating girls your own age, not dried-up husks like me."

"Sallie," George says, finally finding his voice. "You are the most beautiful, most intelligent, most colorful, vivacious, fun-loving, and interesting woman I've ever met. Every other woman pales in comparison to you."

"We're going to end things while you still feel that way," Sallie says. She touches his face. "My dear, sweet George."

"*End* things?"

Sallie sighs. "Yes, I'm breaking up with you. Now pack your things and go to your party." She lights a new cigarette and exhales a plume of smoke. "Please give your family my sincere regrets."

10. DON'T WORRY, BE HAPPY

Magee couldn't have ordered up a more perfect evening. The sun sets in wisps of gold and pink just as the caterers set a scarlet lobster on everyone's plate. Bowls of mussels, potatoes, corn, and lemon wedges make the rounds. Every guest has his or her own butter warmer. With a dinner like this, Magee happens to believe, there can't *be* enough butter.

Thank heavens the caterers didn't balk when Magee told them there would be extra guests. Genevieve's boyfriend, Andrew (Magee privately thinks of him as "Mr. Zipperhead"), was a surprise, and then Kirby appeared, drunk as a street hobo, but everyone in the family (except Jessie and, of course, Magee) looked the other way and exclaimed how happy they were to see her. (She has always, *always* gotten away with murder.) Five minutes before they were supposed to sit down, a woman with a long gray braid wearing white overalls cuffed over

Birkenstocks walked into the party holding a strawberry shortcake. Magee gasped because at that second,
she realized she had forgotten to send Tiger to the Nantucket Bake Shop to pick up the twins' cake!

Magee had intercepted the woman and relieved her
of the shortcake. "How much do we owe you?" she
said. "And who did you speak to about ordering this?"

"I'm here for the party," the woman said. "Kate invited
me." Then she looked at Magee as though *Magee* were
the interloper and said, "Who are *you?*"

"Magee," she said. "Tiger's wife."

"Aha!" the woman said. "I'm Rain. I sell strawberries on Main Street and I made this shortcake myself. I
didn't want to show up empty-handed."

Magee set the cake in the fridge, then rushed to find
Tiger. "I love how your mother invited the strawberry
woman to a family birthday party. As if Bitsy and Helen
aren't enough."

Tiger said, "She's not just the strawberry woman,
sweetie. That's Lorraine Crimmins." He pauses. "Bill's
daughter. Pick's mother."

It took Magee a minute, but then the puzzle piece
snapped into place. "Ohhh," Magee said. This, then, was
the woman who'd had an affair with Wilder Foley. This
was the embodiment of the skeleton in the Foley family
closet. It was *this* story that made Magee so intent on
having a nice, normal family: Mom, Dad, four boys, no
drama greater than a stomach bug or a misplaced hockey
stick. "Why did Kate invite her? I thought she *hated* her."

Tiger shrugs. "No idea," he says. "But I'm going over to say hello."

When Mouth reaches for his third lobster, Genevieve turns to her brother and says, "Want to go for a walk before we do cake?"

"Hell yes," George says. He removes his plastic bib and stands to pull out Genevieve's chair. They both look around the table to see if they need to excuse themselves, but everyone is busy chatting—Jessie with Helen, Kate and Bitsy with the strawberry woman from Main Street (George can't believe that woman was telling the truth, that she did know his grandmother and she used to be his mother's babysitter), and Kirby with Tiger and Magee. Mouth is busy wrangling with his lobster—Genevieve showed him how to use his cracker and pick—and the boys are playing tag in the sand.

Genevieve and George walk toward the water, then head east.

"What's up with Sallie?" Genevieve asks. All George said when he arrived solo was that Sallie didn't feel up to coming. Everyone had seemed relieved, maybe even happy—except for Kirby, who announced that she adored Sallie and found nothing wrong with a May-December relationship. "Hollywood is built on them," she said.

"She broke up with me," George says. He tells his sister the whole story: the blind date with Cousin Dana where he bumped into Sallie, then his break-in at All's Fair, cutting his hand, going to the ER, where he saw . . . Cousin Dana, the phone number on his hand, lunch at the pharmacy.

"Are you upset?" Genevieve asks.

"Not really," he says. "There were times when Sallie acted . . . like my mother. She spoke to me like I was a child. It was, I don't know, weird."

"So will you call Cousin Dana?"

"Yeah," George says. "I will. She works for Dukakis."

"Ha!" Genevieve says. "Brilliant. A Democrat."

"What about you?" George says. "Are things serious with Andrew? I heard him telling Kirby that you two are moving in together."

Genevieve's stomach lurches and she emits a lobster-y burp. Gross. "I'm breaking up with him," she says. "But I'm waiting until tomorrow so it doesn't happen *on* my birthday."

"You always were smarter than me," George says. He sighs. "We should probably turn around."

They should, Genevieve thinks. Though she doesn't want to.

"Do you think there's something wrong with us?" George asks. "I always thought we were special. Or maybe not *special,* but not regular either. I mean, even the story of our birth is unique. We're the first grandchildren, we're boy-girl twins, Mom went into labor on Main Street, and Grammy drove in reverse down Fair Street. Dad was in Houston, sending man to the moon."

He pauses. "Though I do think it's screwed up that neither Mom nor Dad called us today."

In the distance, Genevieve sees the candles glowing on the long table and the lights of their grandmother's house across the road. The sand is cool beneath her feet, and water swirls around her ankles. "They're the ones who are messed up," she says, patting her twin brother on the back. "You and me? We're fine."

The impossible happens and Magee agrees to go back to All's Fair with Tiger and the boys instead of staying to oversee cleanup.

"The caterers did most of it anyway," Jessie says. "Just go."

"We're on the first ferry tomorrow," Magee says, extending her arms for a hug. "So this is goodbye."

Goodbye, goodbye, goodbye—everyone says, *Goodbye, thank you, what a memorable evening, all that butter, my arteries.*

Helen Dunscombe says to Jessie, "Call me when you get back to the city. We'll go to Dorrian's and get dinner."

"I don't know," Jessie says, grinning. "That's pretty far uptown."

As Jessie is carrying a stack of dessert plates smeared with whipped cream to the kitchen, she's confronted by her mother and Rain, who are standing shoulder to shoulder in Jessie's path.

Kate says, "Rain and I have mended fences. And we both agree that you and Pick should get married."

Jessie opens her mouth but no sound comes out. She has spent the evening in a state of suspended disbelief. Kate has forgiven Rain, and Rain forgiven Kate—just like that?

The "just like that" Jessie is referring to, she realizes, is a matter of thirty-five years, longer than she's been alive.

"We'll think about it," Jessie says.

The ladies don't budge and Jessie has to laugh. "I'll talk to Pick when he gets home from Germany. We'll discuss it. Now, if you don't mind, these plates are getting heavy."

Her mother and Rain step aside, and Jessie heads for the kitchen, thinking, *How nice of you to give us permission to marry.* If she and Pick wanted to get married, they would have eloped; they'd nearly done it half a dozen times. There was a Thursday afternoon this past spring when Pick called Jessie at the office and said, "Meet me at city hall in an hour. We'll get hitched, then I'll take you to Union Square Café for dinner."

Jessie said, "I'm in the middle of discovery here, darling. How about a week from Sunday?"

"City hall is closed on Sunday," Pick said.

"Oh, well!" Jessie said, and Pick sang a few bars of Tiffany's "You Just Keep Me Hanging On."

It was a running joke, them together but not

married, and yet there was something hard and unyielding underneath their lightheartedness, and that something was that their mothers hated each other.

No longer! Jessie thinks. She's suddenly seized by such a heady elation that she leaves the dishes in the sink and runs for the phone on the sunporch. She's going to call Pick overseas and tell him about this, phone bill and time difference be damned.

But when she gets to the sunporch, she finds someone already on the phone. And that someone is Kirby.

Reading is a great place to find your next movie — but so, as it turns out, is a family reunion.

After Kirby sobered up — this took four glasses of ice water, a strong cup of coffee, and a three-hour beach nap — she found herself alone under the umbrella with Magee. Everyone else had gone up to the house to shower and get ready, but Magee said her only responsibility was to melt ten pounds of butter (ten pounds!), which she could do "in her sleep," and she was determined to now enjoy the golden hour in relative peace and quiet.

"I'm sure you see me as just a homemaker," she said. "But raising those boys and keeping things just so for your brother is a lot of work."

Kirby nodded. "I can barely take care of myself."

Magee said, "Has anyone filled you in on the twins?"

"What about the twins?"

Magee leaned forward in her chair. "I hardly know where to start."

She took the kind of breath Kirby imagined a person about to swim the hundred-meter freestyle in the Olympics might take and then she told Kirby about Genevieve dating the punk-rock drummer, Andrew, who went by the moniker "Mouth" and who had a tattoo *across his skull*. (Kirby didn't get to see the tattoo in person until dinner, when Andrew removed his baseball hat.) Andrew had recently left his wife and was apparently planning on moving in with Genevieve.

"At Brown?" Kirby said.

"That's not even the scandalous news," Magee said.

The scandalous news was George dating Sallie Forrester, Blair's best friend.

"Stop it," Kirby said.

"It's true," Magee said. "I found Sallie *naked* up in *Nonny's bed* at All's Fair. Isn't that disgusting?"

Naturally, Magee found it disgusting, but Kirby found it…something else. A seed of an idea took root in her imagination. What about a coming-of-age movie about boy-girl twins, set on Nantucket in the summer? One has gone punk with a full-on punk-rock drummer boyfriend and one is a young Republican, a devotee of George Will, who starts dating his mother's best friend. And then—then!—their cool aunt shows up from LA because their mother is in Paris and these kids needs guidance. Plot twist: The aunt is just as screwed up as they are, if not more so.

Kirby waited through dinner, collecting details like she would shells off the beach: Genevieve's hot-pink flattop and safety-pin earrings, George's bow tie, Sallie's conspicuous absence at the family dinner. She'll add in the aunt's failed attempts at recovery (maybe she'll even work in the scene with Blowman somehow).

The instant the party broke up, Kirby dashed to her room and scribbled down a pitch; it was still only dinnertime in LA. She used the phone on the sunporch because it afforded the most privacy, and she called Tyesha.

"I know you don't want to talk to me," Kirby said. "But listen." And Kirby pitched her.

When she finished, there was silence and Kirby thought for a second that Tyesha had hung up. But then Tyesha said, "You know, that isn't bad. It's got elements of a John Hughes movie but it's college instead of high school, which I like. And East Coast instead of West. No one has really done Nantucket in the movies or television yet—"

"Not correctly," Kirby said. In her opinion, *One Crazy Summer* didn't count.

"And we haven't seen boy-girl twins like this before," Tyesha said. "I think you might have something. So you flew out *east,* then?"

"I did," Kirby said. "Last night."

"Let's set up a lunch when you get back," Tyesha said. She paused. "I'm proud of you, Kirb. This could be good."

Kirby hangs up, thinking, *I guess I'm going back to LA? I guess I'm not the screwup aunt after all?* But no sooner does she set the receiver down in the cradle than her sister walks in.

I'm still the screwup aunt, she thinks.

Ugh! Jessie thinks. She has done an outstanding job of avoiding Kirby all day...but now here she is. Jessie's excitement about calling Pick is quashed. She turns to leave the sunporch, and Kirby says, "Jessie, wait. Please. We need to talk."

Fine, Jessie thinks. She pivots and shuts the glass doors firmly behind her, closes the curtains. Kirby wants to do this now, they'll do this now. Jessie kept an eye on Kirby throughout dinner; she drank only water and seemed, at least from three seats away, sort of like her old self.

Jessie pushes a pile of clothing and Andrew's backpack out of the way and takes a seat on the sofa. The sunporch is serving as Andrew's bedroom.

"Talk," she says.

"Why are you so angry with me?" Kirby says.

These words rip a scab off a wound that has only just started to heal. "If you don't know, then there's no point even having this conversation." Jessie stands up. "Are you *that* self-absorbed?"

"Wait," Kirby says. "I do know why. It's because I didn't come to Dad's funeral."

"You didn't come to the funeral," Jessie says. "You didn't send flowers, you didn't call, you didn't write a letter or a card, you did *nothing*. I'm your *sister*. David was my father, but he was your father too. From the time you were six years old, he was a father to you in every way but biology. And yet you couldn't be distracted from your fabulous Hollywood life to even acknowledge his passing. The man who raised you. Who loved you every bit as much as he loved me."

"I have an excuse," Kirby says.

"You always have an excuse," Jessie says. "Your life is one long excuse."

"I was in rehab when Dad died," Kirby says. "At a place called Clarity Farms, where we were allowed zero contact with the outside world. I didn't find out about Dad until I got home and heard the messages on my machine. I called Mom right away. We cried on the phone together. I was hysterical, as I'm sure she told you—"

"She *didn't* tell me," Jessie says. But then she recalls that, yes, a few weeks after David died, Kate called Jessie and said, "I finally heard from your sister."

Jessie had responded, "I don't want to hear about my so-called sister. Don't say another word."

Kate hadn't.

"Why didn't you call *me?*" Jessie says. "You must have known how badly I was hurting."

"I was ashamed," Kirby says. "I missed my father's funeral because I was in *rehab?* I didn't want you to know I was a screwup. I didn't want anyone to know, Blair and Tiger included. It was better if you thought I was just too busy or indifferent or whatever. So yes, you're right. I am self-absorbed."

Jessie closes her eyes; suddenly, she's exhausted. "You know I look up to you, Kirby. I always have."

"That makes no sense!" Kirby says. "I look up to *you*. You're smart, you're an attorney, you have a man who loves you, who applauds as you soar as high as you want to go." She stops to wipe tears away. "And yes, I do know you look up to me, which is why you were the one person I wanted to hide from. I'm supposed to be setting an example. I'm the big sister."

Jessie feels the anger evaporate off her skin. She thinks about her mother, setting aside a vendetta she has nourished for thirty-five years. What catharsis it must have been to sit next to Lorraine Crimmins, dip lobster into melted butter, and laugh.

"When I walked in just now, who were you on the phone with?" Jessie asks.

"My ex-girlfriend, Tyesha," Kirby says. "She's a producer and I was pitching her a movie idea—about our family, actually. The stuff going on with the twins—"

Jessie should have known that Kirby would cannibalize their family drama. "Was I in it?"

"No, but we can add you in as a character," Kirby says. "How would you like to be portrayed?"

"Set the movie here at the house next summer," Jessie says. "I'll be the aunt who's getting married."

"What?" Kirby shouts. She rushes over to Jessie, pulls

her to her feet, and gives her a crushing hug. "You and Pick are actually going to do it?"

"Yes," Jessie says. "Mom and Lorraine are all buddy-buddy now and they gave me their blessing, so . . . yeah. I was just about to call Pick and propose."

"Don't let me stand in your way," Kirby says. "I should get to bed. This day has been a hundred hours long."

Just then the phone rings and Jessie and Kirby look at each other. It's a quarter to eleven — any phone call at this hour is bound to be bad news.

Please let it be nothing, Jessie thinks. Let it be benign — Tyesha calling back or Pick calling because he somehow intuited what had happened with the mothers.

Jessie picks up the receiver. "Hello?"

There's a pause, then a voice that sounds like it's coming from the other end of a long tunnel. "Jessie? It's me."

"Blair?" Jessie says.

"I tried calling earlier but nobody answered," Blair says. "So I'm standing in a phone booth at five in the morning and I charged this to my credit card, which is already maxed out. Are the twins there?"

"No," Jessie says. "They're . . . out."

"Oh, shoot," Blair says. "How are the kids? Did they have a nice birthday? Did anything interesting happen?"

Anything interesting like all of them seeing a skull tattoo up close and personal for the first time, like George sleeping with Blair's best friend, like Kate and Bitsy's geriatric antics, like Helen Dunscombe venturing out in public for the first time since her husband died of AIDS, like Kirby showing up at the front door drunk and high delivered by a person nicknamed Blowman, like Magee outdoing Martha Stewart with her hors d'oeuvres aesthetic and that rum punch, like Lorraine Crimmins showing up with the best strawberry short-cake any of them had ever tasted?

"It's been kind of dull, actually," Jessie says. She gives Kirby an exaggerated wink and Kirby doubles over in silent laughter.

"Even so, I wish I were there," Blair says. "I've been beating myself up all day. I shouldn't be in Paris, I should be there, in Nantucket."

Jessie feels a rush of sympathy for her sister. *Attitude adjustment complete,* she thinks. Despite everything, Jessie realizes she wouldn't have missed this weekend for all the world.

Acknowledgments

There are two unsung heroes in my publishing life that I would like to acknowledge here. The first is the man to whom this collection is dedicated: Timothy Ehrenberg. Tim and I started working together several years ago when he took over as the marketing director for Nantucket Book Partners. He has, pretty much single-handedly, taken my career to its present height. With every new book of mine that's released, Tim brainstorms inventive ways to get signed and personalized copies into the hands of both longtime and brand-new readers. Could people buy the book from a big-box store or the biggest retailer in the world? Sure. But Tim has created an elevated book-buying experience in what is the backbone of our civilization: the independent bookstore. He also came up with the ideas for all of my merchandise, including the wildly popular Elin Hilderbrand Christmas ornament. No detail escapes his notice. He is a strict taskmaster and before each novel's release, I spend hours and hours in the dim, scary basement of Mitchell's Book Corner, signing books. It has never felt like anything but a joy because Tim sits with me and I like him so much as a person that the time flies.

We have some belly laughs; occasionally, we drink wine; and always, always, we talk about what we're reading. Tim is the magic behind the Bookstagram @timtalksbooks—it's where I get most of my recommendations. I call Tim my "work husband" because we spend so much time together. He's the secret to my success, and above and beyond that, he's my treasured friend.

The other gentleman I would like to thank is the great Terry Adams, the digital and paperback publisher at Little, Brown. Back in 2013, Terry asked if I would consider writing an e-short for my novel *Beautiful Day*. He wanted something that was a companion piece, not necessarily a sequel. Because I had attended the Iowa Writers' Workshop, I had a lot of experience writing short fiction and I loved the idea of exploring a story that wasn't included in the novel. I wrote "The Surfing Lesson," which takes place a few years before *Beautiful Day* and delves into Margot and Drum's marriage, something there wasn't time or space for in the book. I loved this idea so much that I did it again for my novel *The Matchmaker*. Terry has been a smart, incredibly kind, wonderfully supportive member of my publishing team from the beginning and I am so lucky to know him and benefit from his wise sensibility. It's thanks to his keen editorial eye and his belief in my characters that I felt inspired to write all these pieces.

As always, I want to thank my brilliant editor, Judy Clain, and my agents Michael Carlisle and David Forrer.

Acknowledgments

Thank you to my beloved inner circle on Nantucket—you know who you are—and my children.

Finally, thanks to all of you who read my novels and love my characters, flawed though they are, and are willing to read about what happens to them before and after. I send a heart emoji to each and every one of you, the best readers in all of publishing.